C0-DKL-352

Of Dragon Rage

— Part I —

Duskfell

D. W. Pettifor

Duskfell
ISBN: 9781729141724
Copyright ©2018 by David William Pettifor
All rights reserved

To my children, Lilah and Lucas.

Contents

THE PROPHECIES OF KING VALDÓR

As told during his final moments
24th of Wheathall, 75 E2
High Haven Castle, Furskarth

King Valdór lied on his bed, the cool autumn breeze blowing in through the window. Outside, the Gyllentides had completed their unveiling of their golden waves across the skirts of the mountains. The King took a long, weary breath.

"I can feel his presence linger. He has spread to the hearts of men of this land. But it will not be enough. I can see his approach coming."

Winged beasts of red and black. The Ashblood are reborn.
A sea of pale from a land forgotten, in flown a tide to tip the balance of war.
Night rests upon the sun's ascent, the new King is found.
Hold fast the city of Rhim, for during the days of light they rest,
but upon the falling of dusk awake.
For *One* the darkness is prepared for, ceasing to lay his claim
Ere the lands of green birth ceases to remain.

The King took his final breath, shutting his eyes on the world. On this day, the world lost a man of purest heart. Son of King Odin, grandson of King Valdemar, father of Nýland and King of the Gronndelon, was henceforth known as The Good King for never falling into the corruption in which he slayed during the Great Battle, ending the Dökkári War.

He was 135 years old when he took his final breath.

Book I

As Days Darken

CHAPTER I

LAKE VANALTA

— 25th of Gyllden, 1866 —

The sun glowed a strong yellow on the late summer lake. It was nearing evening, and the tops of the western pines touched the base of the setting sun. A warm breeze carried the sweet water's scent across the lake and onto the shore. Reflections of the sun danced on the lake's top, which was gradually changing from a deep orange to dark blue the further the sun drifted from the far shore-lines. Crickets creaked in the tall waving grass on the lake's edge and the local birds were chirping their evening songs, apparently they had much to discuss before settling down for the night.

Sploop! "Did you see that Gracie? That was that big one again!" Edlen said as he pointed out to the direction from where the sound came. Gracie caught only the ripples and missed the big fish that quickly returned to the deeper shadows.

"Can I have another?" Gracie asked her big brother. Edlen handed her a crumble of stale bread. She tossed it with an umph off the end of the dock, their legs swaying back and forth above the water as they sat next to each other. It sailed to the surface, small ripples echoing away. *Bloop!* Another fish grabbed the morsel.

Edlen took a deep breath, his blonde hair slowly waving in the breeze. It was long enough to catch the wind, but did not fall much further down his face than his green eyes. And although he was already fourteen years of age, his skin still held onto the darkest of childhood freckles across his nose and cheeks.

He loved the feel of cooling air, especially on the lake. He watched pink clouds floating by towards the coming dusk. The tall pines on the western shore stood all in shadow save the tips, which were still lit with the yellow-orange light of an aging day. It was going to begin to chill soon.

"Do you think the lake will ever run out of fish?" asked Gracie. Six-year-olds tend to ask a lot of questions.

"No," replied Edlen, "Pa says the fish that live in this lake, they will always be around. And do not worry about that! This is a big lake!" He tossed another piece into the water, trying to test his distance in some proof of the lake's size.

"What about other animals? The deer or rabbits? They'll always be around too, right?"

Edlen looked down at his sister, "Boy, someone's hungry! Don't worry, sis, Pa is a great hunter and fisherman." He put his arm around her and grinned. "Besides, Pa said I'm nearly old enough to start learning the bow. Soon I'll be bringing home the trophies!"

Gracie smiled and responded "Not if you hunt like you fish!" Edlen tackled and pinned her to the dock. Gracie was laughing uncontrollably at the reminder of a recent fishing accident Edlen had while on the fishing boat with his father. In between laughs, Gracie was able to get in "You forgot to tie down the net!"

"Did not! I just wasn't expecting the rope to be so slippery!" he came back with more light jabs to her sides. "Besides," he continued, "Pa found it the next day in the shallows, so it wasn't all that bad! Either way though, I didn't see *you* out there with us!"

This kind of argument was common between Edlen and Gracie, as is with most siblings. Back and forth they tried to trump each others comments that usually were not of bringing themselves up, but rather an attempt of making the other seem less important. Edlen usually won these arguments, especially since Gracie was less than half his age. But once in a while, as Gracie has quickly learned what really sets him off, she pulls out a comment (or sarcastic question) that really gets his blood boiling. When this happens, Edlen usually resorts to some sort of physical dominance to quickly end the matter. Still though, it makes Gracie feel good to be able to out-wit her older brother.

Edlen continued to torment Gracie with tickles in the neck and sides for that embarrassing reminder. They were the two children of their home. Their father Eldor had married Hellen, a childhood friend from a neighboring town, both in the Gronndelon. He grew up as a trapper, and sold pelts to the traveling caravans who would in turn take them to the larger holds. The larger towns, and the numerous exporters of Port Brisrun were the usual good buyers. Wolf and bear pelts seemed to have brought in the most coin, and many of the bear pelts were sent north to the borders of the Boreal Forest.

Over the years, Eldor saved up enough to purchase a lot of land on the shores of Lake Vanalta from the Jarl of the nearby town of Riverwood. There he built a house of three bedrooms in hopes to fill two of them with little ones some day. It had a large common room that served as both a kitchen and where the dinner table sat. The cellar was cold and damp and lined with stone from the lake. The construction took a couple of years, but which he found surprisingly easy after the fortunate discovery of a bountiful clay deposit that happened to be on the lot he chose.

The wooded land surrounding the lake provided more than enough material for his project. When Edlen was on his way, he started working on a pier and soon after, a small fishing boat to go with it. The waters on the lake were rarely violent. No sails or ships were needed to handle her. While he went off on his hunts and fishing rounds, Hellen watched Edlen and looked after the garden and chickens. The garden was on the south side of the house in full sunlight. It was a beautiful place to keep it, and often produced a bountiful harvest. Surrounding the garden stood tall a well-built wooden fence in which honeysuckle climbed all around, inviting thirsty butterflies and bees. A horse they had also, and kept it with the chickens in a small stable across the front yard. Soon enough, Gracie made her appearance and the last bedroom of the house was filled.

Lake Vanalta was a large lake just to the south-west of the center of the Gronndelon. The Gronndelon itself was a wide area surrounded by three mountain ranges to the West, South, and East, and bordered to the North was the Great Northern Sea. Because of its walls of mountain ranges and easy access to the sea, it was naturally dotted with lakes, ponds, streams and rivers. Lush with great pines and redwoods in the center, the foothills of the mountains were carpeted in a lighter fabric of wood. In the fall, the foothills to the south turned bright gold from their Aspen skirts, giving them their name: The Gold Forest (sometimes referred to as Gyllentides in folk-lore, as this was the original name in the ancient tongue).

The culture of the Gronndelon was of unity and pride. Neighboring towns and villages often competed in friendly games and competitions. Most were centered around the life styles of the townsfolk, which meant trapping, hunting, and fishing were the dominant competitions. Each year the people of their town's realm would come together in the capital city, Furskarth. There, they would hold a yearly festival show casing each town's champion for final judgment. Upon selecting, the winner for that year would receive a bronze trophy with an emblem of the category he had won. It was a festival for every age, and street vendors found it to be their most profitable event of the year.

The city sat on the southern borders of the Gronndelon near the edge of the Gold Forest. It was surrounded with thick, tall stone walls and was partially protected by the Misty River that curved around the Western side of the city to act as a natural moat. The river emerged out from the city where, at the city's rear, falls from a cliff face far above the city's highest towers. It crashes at the rocky bottom and provides the capital city with fresh water year around. At its base, the roaring falls give off a mist that clings to every surface, giving the city its main center courtyard, known to any in the hold as The Falls.

"Edlen! Gracie! Time for dinner!" their mother shouted. The house sat nearly seventy yards from the dock and large redwood trees and pines grew tall in between. Her shouts echoed, but were enough for Edlen to hear over his sister's laughter.

"Last one there's a raven egg!" he shouted as he leaped off of her, getting a rather unfair head start. He kicked the remaining piece of bread off the edge of the dock then leaped from the wood to the dirt path leading to the house. The bread splashed into the water, bobbing up and down. Gracie stumbled to her feet, already out of breath. Seeing Edlen so far ahead, she decided it would be pointless to try. As she walked up the dock, she looked to her right and saw a small school of fishlings encircled around the bread. Each one trying to summon the courage to be the first to take a bite.

Gracie continued up the path, wiping her hands on the redwoods she passed. The breeze off the lake flowed around her from her back and the lose strands of blonde hair waved around in some dance. It was starting to cool as the sun was now only peeking through the tops of the western trees. To the east, in glimpses through the redwood leaves, speckled starlight of the brightest stars began to emerge, waking up and showing themselves. She approached the house and entered through the front door. It shut with a *thump*, and the lake was left to sleep for the night.

"There's that raven egg!" Edlen shouted. He was already seated in his usual spot at the table. Gracie glared at him as she walked to the water basin to wash up. Their father was also seated. He was a broad man, tall with wavy dark-blond hair that flowed to his shoulders. He usually kept a single strand braided down his left face, past his emerald-green eyes. He had a full beard also, and a well-worn face. No gray could be found on his head though, and his voice was deep and could be heard clearly without much effort. He turned with a glance at Gracie, grinning.

"Better a clean egg than a dirty hare," he said as he turned and looked at Edlen. Edlen's smile was wiped from his face as he looked back at his father. "Come now, go wash as your sister has done." Gracie stuck her tongue out at Edlen. Edlen, feeling less like the winner of it all, got back up and headed to the basin.

"That stew is filling the house with a smell that has woken my appetite!" Eldor said, giving credit to the hard work Hellen had put into it.

"And the bread! I *love* your bread mama!" Gracie said smiling at her father.

Their mother was a fine cook, but as any house-wife could tell you, it helps having fresh meats to cook with. The family had a rather usual routine of meal rotation. It would start with stew and fresh bread, which the bread would usually last for the week. When the stew ran out (after a day or two), the bread went fine with seasoned fish or roasted rabbit. Pheasant was another common meal, and once in a while when Eldor had success at big game, deer steaks were the treat for the night. The rest of the trophy, including the pelts, were usually sold or traded in town on their weekly trips to the market. Only Eldor would go to the market in Riverwood, but lately Edlen had been tagging along to learn how to make honest trades. It was difficult for Edlen to figure out the dishonest traders, but over time Eldor had become familiar, even friends with his usual trading group. Introductions of Edlen had been made, and he was excited but a bit shy to meet so many new faces.

It was during these trips that Eldor would bring back goods and treats for the children. Cheese was something he would often return with, as it kept well in the cellar, unless a barrel was chewed through by a particularly hungry rat. Other goods were brought back as well. Flour, seasonings, and various materials needed around the house. Their garden produced enough vegetables for their family nearly year-round, and Eldor's skills kept fresh meat coming in regularly.

"See anything exciting out there?" Eldor asked his children as they were returning to the table.

"'Saw that big 'ol fish when we tossed the old bread out!" Edlen explained. "Must be five feet long now!"

"Well! Sounds like we need to do something about him!" Eldor replied. "Tomorrow we'll go out on the boat and see if we can't find this floater you keep fattening up!"

Edlen smiled with excitement. "Better get the big net for him, Pa! He's huge!"

"I didn't see anything..." Gracie commented.

"You weren't lookin' neither!" Edlen replied.

"Well now, if we're planning on fish tomorrow, we better eat up this stew tonight." their mother explained. "Can't be spoiling my hard work just because you boys want to run after some big fish." Their mother was right, as this stew took a long time to cook. She had a wonderful way of seasoning it, having her own recipes that adjusted to the ingredients within. Beef was the children's favorites, of course. But tonight it was pheasant stew with rosemary. The potatoes and carrots were cooked to perfection, and the meat tender and juicy. Even though it wasn't beef, there were no complaints or hesitations that night. To top it all off, sweet honey wheat bread and fresh butter from the market.

The family sat down and Hellen served everyone. She was also tall, nearly as tall as Eldor. She was fair-skinned with long light-blond hair that ran straight down her back. Her eyes were a light-blue, almost frost-like. She had a caring voice and hands that were warm and shared the love she had for her husband and children. She was thin and kind-hearted, but watched over her children like a tiger to her cubs.

Their faces were lit up by the candle center piece in the middle of the table. It was made of three hollowed out mountain goat horns. They made perfect mounts for the candles, and it was light enough to read at the table. The fireplace behind Eldor lit most of the rest of the room with a soft red glow. It crackled quietly and kept the evening chill from creeping in through the cracks.

"Word in town is there have been sightings of men from the Empire, from west of the mountains." Eldor began to tell.

"Who told you that?" Hellen asked.

"Radholf, when I was trading some meats for some of his honey yesterday. He told how he was talking to a fellow who claimed to be from the East Nýland. Rode a strong white horse and had two other men with him. All three were dressed in heavy armor and were armed fair, wearing the emblem of the Empire. Radholf described him as a strange man that seemed to be urgently wanting to find the Jarl of Riverwood. So Radholf pointed him in the direction of the Jarl's quarters and that was it. It has been four days ago he saw him and has not seen him since.

"Although I do not wish to meddle with them, I was still concerned of their intentions. I asked around about what they could be here for. No one is sure, but we haven't seen visitors from the Empire in ages. I do not know if I have ever met a single one. Hopefully, though, they stay where they belong." He tore a large bite of bread from his piece to let this news spark some feedback.

"Imperials? They better not be trying to push some new tax on *our* lands!" Hellen replied.

"I certainly hope not! We have made it clear long ago that the Gronndelon belongs to us, and us alone. We have our own way of life and it has worked well for us for centuries. I will die to protect it too, if it ever comes to it."

"Dressed in armor? I would have wanted to see that!" Gracie exclaimed.

"I do not think you would, my dear. Imperials are never good news. But that is not all. I have also heard rumor that over a week ago a similar group of men claiming to be from the East Nýland, traveled to Elwood with the same request. They never got to the Jarl though, as he was in Furskarth on business. They say these Imperials tried waiting but some brawl broke out in the hold's inn, the Fallen Timber. Whoever it was chased the Imperials out, and they haven't returned since."

"They'll never make it here, will they Pa?" Gracie was visually concerned about this conversation and these visitors they had been discussing.

"Of course not, dear. Even if they would, there is no real need to fear them. I'll always be here to protect you, your brother, and your mother." he replied. This settled Gracie's concerns, but Edlen wasn't as easily convinced. He knew Radholf, and knew he was an honest man that didn't share news unless he thought it be important. He also knew that Riverwood wasn't too far from their home. If the Imperials had made it to Riverwood all the way from East Nýland, there would not be much more of a journey to where they live. The inquiry to talk to the Jarl particularly held Edlen's thoughts. Just from hearing stories and news from the men his father traded with gave him enough sense to know that requests to speak to the Jarl was for no light matter. Something serious was trying to start, and it was not likely to be the last of this kind of news.

"Should be any day now that our new chicks will be breaking out of their shells!" their mother said, breaking the silence in effort to leave the worrisome news behind. Gracie smiled at this. "I'll even let you name them, Gracie!"

"Can I keep one in the house, Pa? Please! I promise to clean up after it!"

"You know the rules, Gracie. Chickens belong outside with the rest of the chickens. You would not want to take the poor baby chick away from its mother and siblings, would you?"

"I guess not." she replied with a saddened face.

"We should be getting seven or eight before too long! Better start thinking of names before they get here!" Hellen reminded Gracie in hopes to lift her back up. Gracie looked up with a smile. She continued to finish her soup, pausing between spoonfuls when a new name popped in her head. Her smile slowly grew full again.

After dinner, Hellen began to pick up the dishes, taking them to be cleaned at the basin.

"Edlen, come with me. I need your help in the fishing shed," Eldor said as he and Edlen headed behind the house to prep the fishing nets for their quest in the morning. Gracie stayed inside and played with her doll. It was a gift for her sixth birthday earlier that year in the spring. Her father had brought it back from the market the week prior to her birthday. It was made of hardwood from the trees near town and had horse's tail for hair, a light blond in color. It came with a single dress of a similar pattern as one of Gracie's outfits. It would have looked exactly like Gracie, if it only had her freckles and her mother's eyes.

She loved the doll and played with it regularly. Even with only having it for several months, it was already smooth from being handled so often. She sat quietly by the fire humming songs, dancing her doll back and forth on the stone floor. It cast a shadow long across the common room from the fireplace, and you could hear the clash of wooden dishes being cleaned with the crackle of the fire. It was a quiet night.

"What do you make of the news?" Eldor asked Edlen back in the shed.

"Of the Imperials?" Edlen responded. His father nodded. "They must have something serious to talk about, if they wanted to see the Jarl." Eldor breathed deep as he continued to fold his net.

"They certainly are here for business. But what is concerning is their visit to both towns in the west. If it was only Riverwood or only Elwood they were visiting, that might lead to other suggestions. They may have been after some thief or wanted criminal that chanced to cross the western mountains, but to search the western two holds that are on opposite ends of the Gronndelon, I have doubts that their quest was for something so simple."

Edlen stared at the net his father was folding. His mind wandered from thought to thought about what the visitors meant, what their mission was. What this would mean for him. Then he started to think about the future. He understood already that the future would not hold the same life and comforts as what he had grown up with. Change is never comfortable, and he hoped he had enough courage to face these changes, whatever they were. But he had no idea how much his courage would be tested.

"I will not always be around, you know," his father said. "There is a reason why you have been going with me to town on my trades, why you have helped me fish, and why you are nearly old enough now to learn the bow." He knelt to Edlen's level, dropping the net. He put his hands on Edlen's shoulders and warned him.

"I am not immortal, Edlen. I won't be around forever. You will have to watch over your little sister, and even your mother, if I should be taken away." Edlen nodded his head. His test of courage had just begun.

As they continued to prepare for the day ahead, Eldor shared further words of wisdom. Such words that are meant to be shared between a father and his son. Words that did not seem to find their place in Edlen's heart just yet, as they were of things he had not yet seen. But Eldor knew that they were the necessary tools Edlen needed to hear, so his heart would be ready for what the world could offer.

"Well, that should just about do it." Eldor replied, folding the last fold in the net and placing it in the cedar chest at the back of the shed.

"We should get an early rest so to meet our wet friend bright and early! Come, let us go see what our girls are up to." He put his arm around Edlen as they walked out of the shed. Eldor locked it up, and the sudden *clink* of the lock startled the crickets into a silence for a brief moment. The stars were out strong in most of the skies above them, and the tops of the western pines cut star-less black shapes on the horizon.

Back inside, Edlen and Gracie were getting ready for bed. They had changed into their night gowns, and Edlen said good night as he carried his candle stick to his bedroom. He got into bed, sitting upright, while thinking about his conversation with his father just moments ago. His father turned into his doorway.

"What we talked about, Edlen, that stays between us. Understood?"

"Yes, Pa. I understand," Edlen replied.

"You will grow up to be a good man, son. That I trust." Edlen gently smiled as his father shut his bedroom door, leaving it cracked open enough for the fireplace to spread its warmth to that far corner of the house. Edlen remained sitting in his bed, staring at his fur blanket. It was deer, and the pattern of tan and white had become so familiar to him. It was a real comfort to hold on to. It brought him warmth and memories of his childhood. Good memories, and it smelled like home. He lifted it close to his chest, then leaned over and blew out his candle.

Edlen's back was against a shared wall between his room and Gracie's. He could hear his father saying goodnight to her, but she wasn't quite ready to go down yet.

"Please, Pa, can I have a story?"

Apparently the talk from earlier still rattled her thoughts enough to make her want to forget them all together.

"Fine, dear. I will tell you the story my father sung to me as a lad."

Eldor paused for a moment. The crackle of the fire from the hearth could be heard in the background, and the cold night breeze pushed the tall trunks outside Gracie's room into a sway. He breathed heavily so to remember how the song began. Then in a low and calm voice, he began to tell the story:

> Many moons ago, before our long ancestors reached this place, it was *wild*. Filled wide with rolling hills of grasses, there was not a tree in sight! Then the tree shepherds were sent out in great numbers, planting acorns and walnuts, seeds and saplings! And the god of growing all things green saw what was happening and smiled.

> But there was one acorn whom did not believe he could become a mighty tree. He told the tree shepherd: "Do not plant me! I am not worth the dirt you would put me in..." and he wept. But the tree shepherd said to him: "You will grow mighty, and your little acorns will sprout a mighty forest!" And he placed that little acorn deep into the rich, dark soil.

> Years went by, and the little acorn sprouted and grew! Oh, how he grew! Yet, he could never grow taller than those trees around him. At this, he wept again. And even though he was shorter than all the other trees around him, still he worked hard at pushing little acorns on the ends of his thin branches.

Then, a mighty fire-storm came. A dragon! Swooped down from the mountains and burned every tree, every bush! Everything that was green! Except the short little tree. For he had been hidden in the fallen around him.

Once the dragon had gone, he shook his branches in the wind. And his little acorns scattered! They rolled down hills, swept away on rivers, and spread across the lands around him.

From those acorns grew a mighty forest. Dense and deep, and gave home to many creatures. This mighty forest, we now call *the Wild*. And even today, it is said that deep in the darkest, most hidden corner of the mighty forest, still grows the now mighty oak tree, from that little acorn that did not think he was worth being planted.

Gracie's eyes were already shut, and a smile was on her face as she had begun to drift off into sleep.

Edlen listened through the wall to his father's song. He knew little of the stories that had been passed from father to son for centuries. Through the ages and tellings, facts had been lost. Rumors added. And what may have been true had been rendered a legend, though what of the story that was left was true, no one really knew. As legend passed to myth, myth to story, and now the only preservation upheld in a bedtime song, the ideas still sparked wonder in the young-lings that heard it. Edlen shut his eyes. With his mind wandering on the *Fire-storms* of old, he had completely forgotten of the talks he earlier had with his father, and so did Gracie.

Edlen jolted awake. A loud *bang!* had startled him, and he could hear his father shouting. His room was dark and the glow from the fireplace through the crack of his opened door was too dim to see. A candle light was moving frantically throwing shadow castings back and forth. He leaped from his bed and darted into the common room.

"What's going on?!" he shouted as he realized his mother was holding a candle at the far side of the room. As she turned towards him, he caught a glimpse of his father, with his bow and a single arrow in one hand, reach up above the front door and pull down a weapon that was apparently mounted. Edlen never noticed it before, but it was clearly, now, some sort of blade.

As the front door opened, the sounds of the family horse could be heard in great distress. Below the neighs and cries, a deep and raspy growl could be heard.

"A bear is attacking the stable!" his mother replied.

Edlen raced towards the door, grabbing his rusty dagger off the mantel on his way. If his father needed help, he would surely be there.

"No, Edlen! Don't you go near that thing!" she shouted at him as she attempted to restrain him back.

"Let me go, mother! I can help!" he replied, with the thought of finding a chance to prove his courage. As he jerked free and stumbled out the front door, he missed the step off the ledge and fell flat on his stomach.

He looked up to see his father standing just feet in front of him, bow fully drawn. *Twang!* The bow sung, sending off the arrow and hitting its mark true as any.

The great beast roared. The arrow had pierced just under the right shoulder blade, puncturing a lung. Nothing but the quiver and a bit of staff was sticking out. The bear turned around and stood on its hind legs. The beast towered over ten feet, and cast a shadow twice as long across the gravel walkway in the moonlight. It let lose a growl that sent a shocking chill through Edlen's limbs. He lay there paralyzed by fear, looking past his standing father at the open jaws of the great bear. Eldor certainly had the bear's attention now, and for the time being, the horse was no longer in the bear's mind.

"Edlen, quick! Get inside!" his father demanded as he drew the blade from its sheath. The blade looked cold as black steel, and had engravings that swirled up and down its body. A few shapes or characters could be noticed, as the engravings shimmered in the moonlight. The bear charged.

Edlen stumbled to his feet and fell backwards towards the door ledge. His father held his blade back, ready to thrust. The bear lunged at him, tackling him to the ground.

"Pa!" Edlen shouted, reaching out to his father buried under the deadly beast. Out the back of the bear, outlined in a crystal blue shine from the moon, was his father's blade. Nothing of the pile of fur was moving.

Edlen raced over, dagger ready, just a few steps when he could hear the grunts again. But this time it was Eldor. Muffled under a thousand pounds of fur and power, Edlen heard, "Help get this beast off me!". Together, they rolled the dead animal to the side and Eldor sat up.

"Pa!" Edlen cried as he hugged his father.

"I'm alright, son. Too close for my own comfort, but unharmed for the most part," he said as he inspected his arms for scratches. "Especially compared to him," he said, glancing over at the lifeless creature.

Edlen was still in shock, and could feel the excitement rushing through his system. He didn't know what to say.

"Eldor! Edlen! Thank the Gods!" Hellen shouted from the door. At her side was Gracie, who clamped on to her mother's legs, eyeing the dead bear. She obviously didn't trust that this wasn't some trick the bear was playing, and would rather not take any chances to get any closer to it.

"Not the first time I've had such an encounter with a bear, but..." Eldor said, then looked over. "But not one so big."

He continued to look at the bear in thought for a moment, then stood to his feet. Edlen sat looking up at his father, and it seemed to him that his father looked stronger than ever. He felt a real sense of safety now, and released a deep sigh of relief.

Eldor leaned down towards the bear and grabbed the hilt of the blade. He slowly pulled it out, and the red blood dripped black off the blade in the dim moonlight. He wiped it on the fur of the animal, and laid to the side for a more thorough cleaning later.

The blade had Edlen's attention. He gazed at it, and thoughts raced his mind as he had never noticed such a beautiful weapon in their home before.

"Dragonsbane," Eldor said, noticing where his son's focus was at. Edlen looked up at him.

"That's its name. Dragonsbane. It was given to me by my grandfather, and to him by his father."

"But why have you never mentioned it before? I didn't even know it was there!" Edlen said with great curiosity.

"We don't usually get attacks at the home. This is the first since I can remember. We have never needed to use it before, but are you not relieved of its hiding place now?" his father replied. "It was good to have had it ready there, and there is where it shall remain, if we should ever need it again." Eldor walked to his wife and Gracie, and hugged them both.

"I will be needing my dressing knife. We should clean it before morning. A pelt that size will almost be worth the trouble," he said. Edlen continued to gaze at the blade in wonder.

"If you are that interested in it," Eldor said, then turned and looked at his son, "then you can clean it."

"Yes, Pa," he replied.

"But wait until morning. I could use some help getting this meat separated."

Gracie and Hellen went back inside. Hellen put Gracie back to bed, and after several hours of skinning and dressing in candle light, Edlen washed up. By now the night was cold and he could see his breath. The dried blood had made his hands almost numb by the time they were finished, and it was a relief to finally wash them. After so much time, the excitement had worn off, and Edlen headed to bed exhausted. Though his mind still raced of the events, replaying them over and over and imagining alternative outcomes, it did not take long for sleep to find him.

A week had passed since the incident with the bear. The horse was found unharmed, and the events were nothing more now than a memory save the pelt that was now ready for market. Gracie was glad to know it would no longer be there to remind her of the nightmare that happened, and until it was taken to be sold, she found it hard to sleep at night. Eldor and Edlen readied the cart and headed into town for trading.

When they arrived, Eldor and Edlen opened the back hatch and put on display their items up for trade or sell. Eldor instructed Edlen to stay at the cart, and if anyone wishes to buy, to make good decisions. Edlen was old enough and had been to the market enough to know what was a fair trade by now, and prices for coin were to be final as previously agreed upon. In the meantime, Eldor was going to go find his fur buyer, as he too was anxious to sell his large pelt, along with a couple other smaller ones he had hunted earlier.

Edlen stood by the cart. Eventually, Radholf approached.

"Good afternoon, Edlen!" Radholf greeted. "How is Eldor's son on such a day?"

"Greetings, Radholf," Edlen replied. "Fine, but a bit bored." Radholf was an older gentleman. Well built, a tad short for a man, and with long flowing silver hair. His face was tan and started to show signs of wrinkle and wear, though some of that hidden by the scruff that covered his cheeks and chin. Still young enough to hold up in a brawl, no doubt. He and Eldor had known each other for years, as Radholf had for many years lived in Riverwood. Where he was actually from, Edlen didn't know. Through various stories, Edlen knew Radholf to have once been in some militia or army, and knew he was a skilled swordsman, or at least was at one point. But ever since Edlen had known, Radholf had settled down just outside of town. He mostly went to and fro, gathering news from across the Gronndelon and beyond, and making local trades at the markets.

He was more of a barter, as far as Edlen could tell, but always seemed to be well adverse with the natural elements. Often times talking of mushrooms, various roots and plants, and even had some tales of odd creatures he had encountered. "Protectors of the forest," he described them, and would refer to them as *Arborians*.

"Is your father around? I wanted to see if he might be interested in joining me in a small trip I am thinking of taking to the south. Just a day or two. Got news of a mine where we might find some interesting ingredients!" he asked.

"He is out looking for Peregrine to talk about the pelts again," he replied.

"Ah! Very well then. I shall catch him in a bit. Thank you, Edlen! I will be seeing you later!" Radholf said as he waved and headed towards the center of the market.

The market was fairly quiet then. A few shoppers paused and looked now and then, and one did buy some of their produce. It was slow, though, for the most part. On a good day, the market would be bustling with traders, news-carriers, and craftsman of all sorts. Orcs were not uncommon to see, and usually had some well-smithed weapons and tools for trade. Although they tended to be hard to drive a good bargain with, and thought themselves to be tougher and stronger than the common man (which in many cases were true). And proper manners seemed scarce among them, but was not all entirely lost. Most Orcs lived south of the Southern Mountains, in the desert. Their homeland being dry, arid, and hot is usually credited to their tough nature.

Different races of Elves were very rare in the Gronndelon. Edlen had met some, and they carried a sense of superior intelligence with them. They did not care for Men or the Gronndelon culture, so Eldor's interactions with them were brief, if any. Most were very earthy, and had a respect for natural things. Therefore hunters, trappers, and fishermen were not particularly favored in their eyes.

The day grew gray and cloudy, and the birds sang loud in the unusually humid air for late summer. There was not much of a breeze, and Edlen found himself hard to keep awake.

"Edlen!" shouted Taryn, one of the sons of another trader that often would visit the market. Taryn was a year older than Edlen, and over the trips Edlen and his father had made to Riverwood, Taryn and him had become friends.

"Hey, Taryn! Glad you are here today!" Edlen responded as Taryn ran up to him. Taryn's father was a woodsman, and they brought works of wood, in both raw lumber and various furniture to the market. The work of the woodsman was very time consuming, and often left Taryn to explore on his own. Sometimes leading him to trouble.

"Edlen! You have got to come see this!" Taryn exclaimed as he was trying to catch his breath.

"What? What is it Taryn?"

"A hidden door! I found a hatch under some hanging moss on the back side of the Jarl's house! It's behind some rocks, small but big enough for us to fit through!" he explained.

"A door? But isn't it locked?" asked Edlen.

"It was! But the lock has rusted through, and I was able to knock it clean off with a stone! We *have* to check this out!"

"I don't know, Taryn. If it's locked..."

"Was! Was locked!" Taryn interrupted.

"...was locked, it probably was meant to keep people out. Besides, I can't leave the cart! My Pa would have my backside if I —"

"Edlen!" his father called. "Edlen! We do still have the pelts, yes?" His father approached with Peregrine, who was very interested in seeing the bear pelt.

"Yes, Pa. We still have them."

"Hello, Taryn, how is your father?" Eldor greeted Taryn.

"Fine, thank you! Sir, may Edlen and I go out explorin' for a bit?" Taryn asked before Edlen could say a word.

"Fine by me, Taryn. Edlen, be back before the church bells ring."

Edlen sighed. "Yes, Pa, I will."

The bells rang at six o'clock each evening. It was the traditional way the town of Riverwood would signal the end of the working day. Traders, woodsman, even training soldiers would stop at this time and head for the nearest inn for some mead and song. This, of course, marked the busy time for the local bartenders. By then, Eldor liked to be heading home.

"Come on, this way! It's over here..." Taryn said as he led Edlen across the market and down a walk path.

"So where is Valp? You usually bring him to the market..." Edlen asked, as he enjoyed playing with the small puppy.

"Oh he stayed behind at home. Got into something that turned his stomach the wrong way. Made a mess all over Asta's nice dress! It was hilarious!" Taryn laughed.

"That doesn't sound so nice! Is Valp going to be okay?"

"Oh, yeah. He's fine. Pa didn't think he'd be up for a ride to town though. That is why we left him at home."

They rounded a couple of buildings and found themselves at the back of the Jarl's house. It was a shaded part of the town, damp and the base of the house were lined with rocks. Taryn and Edlen climbed over one of the larger stones and cleared some hanging moss off the backside of the rock. At the rock's base was the door. It was wooden with an iron framing. There were scratch marks all over the latch from where the lock had been tampered with, and eventually smashed. Pieces of rusty lock were scattered around the door.

"Well, here it is." Taryn said. The boys both looked at the door, then at each other.

"Well?" Edlen said. "You gonna open it?"

At this point, curiosity overthrew any sense of danger or moral in Edlen's mind. What laid behind the hatch was too tempting to leave alone.

Taryn looked down and grabbed onto the latch. Edlen scooted to the side to make room, and with both hands, Taryn pulled hard on the door. It cracked open, and a cloud of dust shot from the edges. Creaking open, the boys found themselves peering down a dark stone-lined corridor.

"You first," Taryn said. Edlen stuck his head in the hole and found the wooden ladder leading down. It was only a few steps, and the wood was heavily aged. The hall was dusty and dark. The floor was made of dirt and sounds of dirt crumbling from the low ceiling echoed into the darkness. It smelled musty, and the dust burned his eyes. He took a few steps forward.

Thunk! Edlen hit face-first into a wooden surface. As their eyes adjusted, they found an old wooden door, and discovered the corridor was no more than about ten feet in length. On the door was a cast-iron handle, and it was clearly unlocked. In the center of the door was mounted an iron emblem in the shape of a Redwood with stars lit up around it: the Riverwood symbol.

"Should we?" he asked as he looked back at Taryn.

"Why stop now? Not much interesting in this dark place..." Taryn replied.

Without second-thinking, Edlen pulled open the door. The door gave way to a pile of barrels, stacked on their sides three high that had been placed against the door. Beyond the barrels was a storage room, dimly lit. It was stone-lined on the walls and floor, and the ceiling was the wood of the floor boards of the above story.

Between the floor boards, Edlen could see the shadows of boots and several chairs sitting around a table. Voices talked back and forth, and it became clear the one in command was the Jarl.

"The Jarl's storage room!" Taryn whispered excitedly. The danger of being caught breaking into the Jarl's house suddenly became real again to Edlen. He had a brief moment of panic, and his face suddenly become hot as if blushing, and he was a bit embarrassed to find himself conducting such an offensive deed.

"We should get out of here," he said. "Now!" But Taryn wouldn't budge.

"Let's grab something! They'll never notice! We can't do all this explorin' without taking home a prize for all our hard work!" he responded. Taryn then climbed over the lowest barrel and into the storage room. No one was in sight, and the candles on the sides were burning low.

"Taryn!" Edlen shouted in a whisper. "We could get in so much trouble!" he warned as he reluctantly followed. Taryn headed straight for a chest that sat on the far side of the room. It was a large chest, and trusting in the storage room's security, was unlocked.

"Bet there's gold in there!" Taryn said as he sat down on his knees. He pried it open and found not gold, but an assortment of single-handed weapons. Daggers, short swords, and a variety of sheaths. Edlen paid no attention to what was in the chest. His eyes were fixed on the door at the top of the steps. Light shown through its cracks, and he could hear the muffled conversations just past it. It seems that at any moment, the door could open and they'd be caught.

The conversations from above, though muttered, were clear enough to be understood.

"You can tell the colonel he has one month to conduct his business, but that is IT!" the Jarl commanded.

"But your honor," said another voice, "he has a decree signed by Jarl Sigurbjorn to allow him to come and go freely, as he wishes."

"I do not care what Sigurbjorn allows him to do in the rest of the realm, but here in *my* hold, he has one month!"

"Yes, sir," replied the second man, taking a few steps across the room.

"Oh," he added as he stopped. "What should I tell him of his personal request?"

"*Tch!* I will not aid him in his chase of fairy-tale cities. Tell him to head east towards the mountains...maybe that will get him off our backs," the Jarl answered.

"As you wish," replied the man as he finally took his leave.

"Taryn! Hurry it up! We must leave this place!!" Edlen whispered loudly, breaking his concentration of the above conversation, remembering what danger they were in.

"Just a minute!" he said as he dug through the chest. "Ah!" he shouted. He reached down deep past a few blades and pulled up a small sapphire. It was magnificent. A deep blue and although small, shown bright even with the little light they had. It was obvious to have belonged to some hilt or blade and had fallen off in the chest.

Just then, the upstairs door swung open.

"Hide!" shouted Edlen in a whisper, grabbing Taryn by the shirt and pulling him off to the side. They crouched down behind a stack of crates in the corner next to the chest, which was left wide open.

Thump. Thud. Thunk. Thump. A short fat man was walking down the steps humming a song often heard at the local inns. He had a bit of cheese left in his hand, and his mouth was savoring the last bites. Edlen's heart raced and he swore he could hear it *thump-thumping* out of his chest. He struggled to contain his labored breathing, and at that moment felt like crying in fear of getting caught. Every step the man took felt like a moment closer to being marked a criminal. He knew how serious the Jarl was, and what kind of punishment would come of stealing from his house. Imprisonment, indentured servitude, or even death didn't seem that much of a stretch to imagine as possibilities.

The man reached the bottom of the steps and strolled right past the open chest. His eyes were on the shelf across the room to the right of their present place behind the crates. He stood in front of the shelf, scanning the various cheeses, and popped the last bit in his hand into his mouth. Then without skipping a beat, grabbed the next wheel slice of goat cheese. He turned around and headed back toward the stairway.

Edlen was breathless. He tried his best to be quieter than a mouse, and it looked like it was going to pay off. The man took his first step up the stairs, then paused. He looked down to his left right at the open chest. Edlen's heart dropped to his stomach.

"Huh...that's odd. What possessed you to open?" he said. He took a step back down and studied it for a moment. Glancing around the room, he found nothing out of place.

"Oh, well," he exclaimed as he kicked the base of the chest to knock the lid down. He then went back up the stairs, humming the same song, with a fresh bit of cheese to snack on. *Ka-chunk!* The door shut.

"That was a close one!" Taryn said.

"We need to leave. *Now*," Edlen demanded. Quietly, the two boys climbed out from behind the crates and crossed the room. The barrels did an excellent job of concealing the door behind them, which had been wide open the entire time. They climbed over those and back into the corridor. Slowly, Edlen shut the door and they climbed out back into daylight, which despite being gray suddenly seemed bright again.

"We never should have been in there!" Edlen yelled. "They could have taken our heads, if not our hands, for being down there!"

"Relax, Edlen! We've made it! I wasn't worried a bit. I knew what I was doing!" Taryn said in defense, hoping to calm Edlen down and bring him back to what he believed was reality.

"But I will need you to take this," he said as he held out the small sapphire.

"My mother finds anything I bring home, and there's no way I could explain this one."

"What do you want me to do with it?" replied Edlen. "I can't take it home either!"

"Then hide it! Maybe some day it'll be worth something. I'll tell ya what, we can split it, if we ever get it to someone who will buy it." Taryn said in hopes for a fair compromise for holding onto it.

"No, I can't take it. I didn't want to go down there in the first place!"

"Here just hold onto it for a bit!" Taryn said as he pushed it onto Edlen. Edlen quickly stuffed it into his pocket. As the sapphire left his fingers, the church bells rang and Edlen jumped.

"Oh! I have to get going! I'll talk to you about this later, Taryn!" Edlen said as he ran off towards the market. As he ran, he felt as though his one pocket weighed ten pounds heavier. His mind was scrambled, trying to think of what would happen, and how to avoid letting his secret slip. It ate away at his conscience. Every step he felt heavier and heavier, as though he was losing strength in his legs to run. Eventually, he got back to the cart.

"Edlen! Cutting it a bit close, are we?" his father said as he approached, out of breath. "Find anything interesting?"

"No," he replied, catching a breath. "Just some old grave stones with funny names,". It wasn't the best excuse he could think of, but his mind was running hard, and his story would be hard to disprove.

"Grave stones, eh? Isn't the graveyard back to the west? You came from the east just now." His father looked curiously at him. Edlen just stared back, breathless and tired. His face revealed the feeling of giving up. He didn't want to carry that burden, and wanted to rid the nagging weight from his side. He looked down.

"Father," he began. This caught Eldor's attention, as his son only used that word for serious matters.

"We did something bad," he said facing the ground. He reached into his pocket and pulled out the sapphire, and held it under his weeping face, shameful of being its possessor.

"From where did you come by this?" his father asked sternly.

Edlen then told the story in whole from beginning to end. He didn't skip any details, as he knew his father would make all the right decisions. In his heart, he was relieved to release such a secret, and hoped his father would come up with some solution that avoided any trouble. At the end of his confession, his father sighed deeply. The look of disappointment on his face drew more pain in Edlen's heart than he thought possible.

Eldor opened out his hand. Edlen dropped the small sapphire into his hand and the amount of relief he felt was much less than he had hoped. Eldor closed his hand.

"Come with me, son." He led Edlen across the market to the Jarl's house. The guard outside questioned their reasons for visit, and his father simply stated that they had something of the Jarl's that needed to be returned to its rightful owner.

They entered the house and the door shut behind them. Edlen felt as though this was the last he would see a free day. They approached the Jarl. As Edlen glanced around the room, he noticed a set of guards at the door, and one to the right of the Jarl. They were all clad in armor with their swords sheathed.

The Jarl sat in a large wooden chair covered in deer skins. He was slouching a bit, which was the natural pose in a chair with such high arm rests. The chair sat upon a raised stone platform, wide enough for his guard to stand on with him. Above the Jarl and his guard, was a giant set of antlers, twenty points easily. The fat man from the storage room was nowhere to be seen.

"My guards tell me you have something of mine. Well, speak! What does a hunter possess that belongs to me?" the Jarl demanded. Edlen's head hung low. He could not gather the courage to look the Jarl in the eyes.

"A sapphire," Eldor said as he held out his hand. Edlen lifted his head a bit, curious as to the response. He then noticed one of the Jarl's rings, which had a vacant spot for a gem on the outer edge. The guard to the right of the Jarl approached Eldor, picked the sapphire from his hand and presented it to the Jarl. The Jarl inspected it closely, then placed it into the vacant spot on his ring. A precise fit. Although loose, it was clearly the missing gem.

"By which means did you come by this sapphire? Did you take what did not belong to you? Did you steal from the Jarl's house, off my own hand?!" the Jarl asked and was clearly outraged. At this, the guards at the door drew their swords and stood directly in front of it, blocking any hope of escape.

"Your pardon, I beg of you," Eldor said. He then quickly explained what had happened in vague detail, and seemingly left out any part of Taryn at all. Although this seemed unfair to Edlen, he had not the slightest bit of courage to try to correct the story. Instead, he simply stood there looking at the wooden floor. It was well worn and the cracks were filled with dirt and dust. He certainly felt like a criminal, and knew his punishment would soon arrive.

"I see," replied the Jarl to the story. "This sapphire has been missing from my ring for nearly a month and a half! And you claim to have found it at the bottom of my arms chest?" He directed his question to Edlen.

"Yes, sir," Edlen squeaked out. At this he briefly glanced at the Jarl.

The Jarl of Riverwood was quite young, yet his tone carried with it the sense of spoils and power. His name was Audun, the son of the former Jarl of River-wood, Jarl Sivert, from which Eldor has purchased his land from. A few years prior, Sivert fell ill after a failed campaign in the mountains to help aid Elwood of a bear problem. He passed on, leaving his barely-of-age son as the new Jarl. Although novice, he was taught well at an early age. But there still remains an important gap between being taught and exercising it. And Jarl Audun demonstrated this all too often.

"Hmmm," thought the Jarl out loud. "You are familiar with the punishment of thievery in the strong hold of the Gronndelon, are you not?" he directed back towards Eldor.

"By your mercy and grace, my Jarl, I beg of you a fair judgment for just a lad," he replied.

"Just a lad, yes. But I do not need to remind you that stealing from the Jarl is punishable by death!" Edlen tried not to weep. He clamped his eyes shut, but the tears rolled down his cheeks, as he knew the most common practice was beheading. Beheadings and hangings were an event for the whole town to attend, throwing rotten vegetables and name calling. Such events his father never encouraged to participate in, but to imagine that this was what his end would become was almost too unbearable for him to handle.

"But I am a just Jarl. I will spare the boy's life, as it seems his misdeeds are softened by the finding and returning of my missing sapphire."

"Thank you, my Jarl!" Eldor exclaimed. Edlen could swallow again, and took a deep breath.

"But," continued the Jarl. "A theft is still an offense, and cannot go unpunished. As his father, I hold you responsible for his actions." Edlen felt shock waves pulse through his body, and an extreme nausea set in his stomach. He didn't want to take the punishment, but even worse was to make his father suffer for his actions. He felt like crying out, but was too upset to do so.

"You are Eldor, hunter and trader from the Lake Vanalta, are you not?"

"Yes, my Jarl. We trade nearly once a week at the markets," Eldor answered, knowing where the Jarl was going.

"You provide us with good meats, and I bet you can make a shiny bit of coin while doing so. As punishment for the deeds that took place on this day, I demand a tax be applied to your sales and trading. Six gold for every ten you make. Any trades will also be taxed as they can be. You must conduct all business with the aid of one of our guards, who will ensure the taxing is completed," he concluded. The Jarl looked at Edlen, who was still in tears. "For both of your lifetimes."

With that, the Jarl dismissed Eldor and Edlen, and sent them on their way. Their walk back to the cart was quiet. Eldor packed up the cart, while Edlen sat in front with his head hung low. He knew the tax would be difficult on his father, and felt so much regret for what had happened. He wished so hard to be able to go back to just hours ago, and change his decisions to have avoided the entire thing. His father climbed up front and set the cart in motion.

The clouds had given way to the sunset in the west. It was beginning to hide behind the western peaks and the horizon above turned a bright orange. The high level clouds had moved out to the east, and their western most fingers were stretching towards the sun. Their tips lit up bright pink, but cast a pale indigo and gray blue across the central sky, and the eastern-most a dark gray. Edlen didn't know what to say, and the first part of their trip home was entirely quiet save the sound of the horse's hooves *clop-cloping* on the stone path.

"What is done is done," his father said. "We cannot change the past; we can only make better decisions in the present and onward."

"Did we really need to go to the Jarl, though?" Edlen replied. The way he saw it, none of this would have happened if they had just forgotten about the whole thing.

"We did what needed to be done, Edlen. We were honest, not cowardice thieves. If we would have kept the gem, we *would* be thieves. If we had thrown it away, there would have been no difference to the Jarl. It would have still been a theft. We are not thieves. We are honorable and honest traders."

Edlen sat quiet for a moment. He didn't like the answer, but the more he thought about it, the more he realized this was the only way to purely rid of the guilt he had carried that afternoon.

"I will need help making up the tax difference, Edlen. What we now bring to the market, we will need to bring half as much more if we want to keep our returns. Tomorrow, we will begin your bow training."

Edlen perked up at this. He had long wanted to hunt like his father, and for several years he was told he wasn't old enough to handle the responsibility.

But the reason behind the start of his training seemed to have robbed him of the joy he expected to come with it. Although excited, he knew that he would now be partly responsible for feeding his family, and this also likely meant he would be hunting on his own soon, which frightened him a bit.

The rest of the ride home, the discussion was of hunting and bowing. It was a relief to Edlen to talk about something else, although it was much more serious than he had imagined. His father explained the dangers and safety of bowing, and talked of confidence and bravery when out alone in the wild. Edlen was far from either at this moment, and knew his road ahead would not be so easy. But he really did not know how challenging his road was about to become.

CHAPTER II

RAVEN FALL

— 23rd of Wheathall, 1866 —

Ominous gray clouds blew low just above the tree tops. The cooling wind racing through the aging underbrush gave the first glimpse of an oncoming winter just weeks ahead. The rain holding back, no sun to give warmth, the single deer felt isolated and alone. It bent down to take another bite of the fading grass.

The stretch of the bow's string quietly *creeeked*, concealed down-wind from the target. The deer, checking once more, lifted its head into view. Without pausing its chewing, its cupped ears twirled around, back and forth, listening for any twig snap or rustle. But none came from the pupil or his father during this hunt.

Twang! The arrow released and cut through the wind. Thrown off by the hard blowing across, it met the deer inches off from the shooter's aim. Missing the gap behind the shoulder, it pierced across the front chest of the deer just below its throat. The deer took off in a sudden rush of panic, kicking and bucking as it struggled to shake what was grabbing it so painfully out of its sight.

"For how harsh the wind is, that was not a bad shot!" Eldor said. Edlen stood, smiling at his father, then watched and listened to the distancing rustles through the bushes.

"Come, let us find where it rests," Eldor said.

As Edlen led, he followed the drips of blood hanging from the bushes and grass. Moving bent branches here and there, he followed his prey to where it had taken its last breath. Lying motionless, the arrow still hanging from its grip. Edlen's hunt was successful that evening.

Three weeks had passed since the events with the Jarl and his sapphire. Edlen's training had gone well. He had gone on a couple of hunts with his father for practice, successfully bringing home a buck on the first trip. The second trip would have been fruitless, if it were not for Eldor stepping in and saving the shot on the wild boar. A few more practice trips, and Edlen would be ready to venture out on his own.

On the far shore of the lake, hidden Aspen trees that dotted between the evergreens started to reveal their golden faces. The air was dry, and the smell of Autumn was on the breeze. Inside, Hellen was working on a savory pork stew with the seasonal wild mountain cranberry and a fresh harvest of home-grown carrots and onion. Above the mantel, hung a large fish on a finely selected center cut of redwood trunk put on display as a trophy. It would reach four feet in length, if stretched tight enough. Nevertheless, it had been the talk of the household for several nights after the catch day. It had won the first place in Riverwood's competition for fishing, which meant it was selected to represent their town's trophy in the festival at Furskarth. Edlen was bursting with excitement, and the family was all ready for the trip.

Edlen had never actually been to the festival, nor to Furskarth. It was a long day's trip, if you didn't have the luxury of stopping at some half way point. Since the family had never won a competition before, they had no real reason to ever go. But seeing as Edlen and Eldor had an entry, and Gracie was now old enough, it seemed the perfect time for such a trip.

"Gracie! Time to get up!" Hellen announced as she stuck her head into Gracie's room. Gracie got out of bed and walked out into the common room. The early morning sun was shining a glaring yellow through the windows and lit up the room nice and warm. Right outside the window, the morning birds were singing their songs louder than usual as they appeared quite happy of the coming day. It certainly was going to be a beautiful day.

"There is my morning bird!" Hellen said, as Gracie rubbed her eyes. The bright sun, however beautiful, was a bit much to take in at the moment. Eldor and Edlen sat at the table finishing up their breakfast of eggs and bacon with leftover biscuits. Eldor sipped on his spearmint tea, fresh from the garden, with a drop of honey. Edlen seemed to be scarfing down his breakfast like a starving dog in pure excitement. He was clearly anxious to get going.

"Hurry up, Gracie! We don't want to be late!" Edlen instructed his sister. She sat down at the table as her mother placed a bowl of dried berries in front of her. Gracie was a bit of a picky eater, and didn't care for eggs nor bacon.

"Take all the time you need, dearest," Hellen said in response. "The festival will be there whether we leave now or as the sun summits."

"Summits?! We better be on the road by then!" Edlen said, sounding a bit frustrated. He left the table and darted to his room to ready himself. If they were going to be delayed in their departure, he wanted to make sure it wasn't on his account.

After everyone had finished their breakfast, Hellen cleaned up and Eldor readied himself. He loaded the packed bags and satchels into the cart and readied the horse. The cart had two bails of straw for Hellen and Gracie to ride on for comfort, and Edlen would ride in front with Eldor. As Hellen made sure Gracie was all set, Edlen sat at the cart waiting impatiently, and feeling more frustrated as each moment passed. The sun was warming the land and began to burn away the morning dew on the grass around. Birds chirped loudly and the breeze felt like a mix of cooled and warmed air as it swirled around. The sky was a pale light blue, completely cloudless. A perfect day for traveling.

"Up you go!" Eldor said, as he hoisted Gracie to the back of the cart. He lent Hellen a hand as she climbed in behind her, and Edlen sat feeling relieved that they were leaving. Eldor locked the house doors, climbed up front, and shook the reigns as the horse started forward with a snort.

Much of the ride that morning was enjoyable. The cool breeze kept the sun's touch welcoming. Eldor kept the pace moderate, not enough to upset the cart in an uncomfortable jog, but enough to make it to Furskarth before dusk.

The morning route was a small road, lightly traveled on. Stones laid in the dirt that made the path, and the hooves of the horse *clomp-clomped* at a steady pace. The stillness around, them mixed with the rocking of the cart, made for a drowsy ride at times. With little going on around them, the quietness was only occasionally broken with talk of the festival. Both Gracie and Edlen were very much looking forward to the events that would take place the next day, and their imaginations ran wild with images and thoughts of the answers they would get back from their parents.

Before long, they arrived at the main road. It was a much wider road than the one they had been on, and the stone way was much more worn and smooth. The fork was marked with two short piles of stones on either side of the road they came from. One had a flag sticking out the top, red with the Riverwood emblem sewn in it. Around the left side pile, was a nice clearing under a tall maple tree. This made for a perfect place for a quick rest and a bite to eat.

After they were done, Edlen laid under the tree and looked up through its long branches. They were filled with large wide leaves, that were half way turned from a deep green to oranges and reds. The wind swayed the branches lightly, and a few leaves decided their early timing was now, and fell gracefully to the grass below. Edlen heard a rustle in the tall grass behind the tree. He stood up and saw in the distance, an old woman wearing a well-worn gray cloak walking down a small path. His curiosity was too much to bear, and thought the walk would be good prior to the last long leg of their trip for the day.

He looked back, watching Hellen and Gracie still finishing their lunch, and his father tending the pony. Content in his absence going unnoticed, he began making his way through the tall grass. He found the path in which the old woman was taking, and followed quietly behind her.

The path wound back and forth like a snake through the tall grass. It was much taller than he was used to, blocking his view save a couple tree tops nearby. There were no side paths that forked off, so he was not worried about finding his return.

The old woman turned a corner, and as Edlen followed, he found himself on the edge of a large opening. The ground was lined with tombstones. Some looked very old, others not so much. None of them looked fresh, as they all had a worn and weathered appearance. In the center of the graveyard was a tall oak tree, dead and brittle. Its limbs bent crooked in all directions, and the top broken off. It looked horrible and menacing, and filled with foul memories and sadness.

The old woman was stopped, kneeling at one particular gravestone. The grass was dead under her knees in an odd circle that formed perfectly around her. Edlen didn't dare approach, but kept watch. He was ready to take off at a moment's notice. This place felt dark and restless. Even the graves seemed unsettled.

"You are leaving the comfort of your grave," the old woman said out loud. Edlen startled at the sudden sound of her raspy voice.

"Do you feel the fall? Will you see the blame at all, Edlen?" she hissed his name as she turned her head slowly towards him. Her long nose peeked out from her cloak. Edlen stared hard at her, feeling vulnerable now knowing his presence was known.

The old woman stood up and ran towards him with a hissing cry. Edlen fell backwards as he scurried to his feet, but she was already at his feet. He sat on the ground, staring at the old woman. Her eyes were frosted over a pale blue, and skin was white and wrinkled with touches of gray. Her breath smelled horrible of decay. A necklace of old worn out back bones clanked and knocked as it hung down. In between every other bone, a black feather was tied in.

"Dead flowers I place at your grave, broken and gray. In the days of sun you stand tall, but when the rains of pain sweep down, you will drown in your own sorrow. The shadow will consume you," she hissed at him, as she pointed her long black finger nail over him.

"The shadow will consume you!" At this Edlen took a swing at her out of fear, but his fist met nothing but air as she vanished into a dark cloud of dust. It rode the wind in a swirling rage, finding its way to a sick looking willow tree which seemed to absorb it entirely. A moment later, a black raven left the tree crackling.

"Edlen!" he could hear his father's call echoing above the tall grasses. He looked around, and the dead oak tree remained still over the countless graves. It felt now that the graves, and their occupants, were back to resting. Even the grave, in which the old woman had recently knelt at, was back to its lively green color.

"Edlen! It is time to leave!" he could hear faintly. He took off back down the path and met his family at the maple tree. His father was helping Gracie back into the cart.

"There you are, my boy! We were just about to leave you behind!"

"Just taking a quick walk before we set off again," Edlen replied. He didn't bother to tell of what he found, or his encounter. It would likely bring more trouble than he cared for from his Pa. Already it seemed to be a memory in the far distance, almost as though to have not happened all together. As soon as his mind was ready to let go of the memory, the black raven called out again in the distance. It was faint though, faint enough to almost think it was nothing but the wind making some movement against the trees, but he knew the bird was watching.

The more he tried to forget the whole ordeal, the more her words echoed in his mind, and the raven's occasional cry served a terrible reminder. As the afternoon matured, he found it difficult to ignore them, and it felt as though his mind had been stung by some dark poison, and it was beginning to spread. The cries of the raven continued to echo in the distance as they made their way south.

The afternoon matured, evening approached. As they came upon the sight of Furskarth, the road became busier and more new faces greeted them with smiles and waves. Everyone around the city loved the festival, especially the merchants.

Their road wound through trees and ahead it seemed to dip down out of sight. At this, a wide open space appeared, and far to the south stood tall the southern mountain range and at their feet, fingering around the edges of the city, the Gyllentides. The road wound down a steep hill, sloping smoothly at the bottom, leading the way to the city of Furksarth. Surrounded by the tall stone walls that protect it, Edlen saw for the first time the Misty River. It sparkled orange, reflecting the setting sun's last light in the evening sky above. Far on the other side, up the slopes of the mountains, small high up clouds slowly crawled across the sky, tainted orange on their western face fading to a deep pale blue. The city itself seemed to glow with its own light.

The sight of something so magnificent cleared Edlen's thoughts, and the joy and excitement of the festivities to come erupted once more. As they led down the long winding road into the valley, Edlen suddenly realized it had been some time since he had heard the raven's cry, giving a relief of weight off his mind.

"I'm glad that raven has left us," Eldor said. Edlen was shocked at his father's sudden words and realization of his knowings about it. Eldor looked down at him.

"It had been following us since we stopped for lunch at the fork. I do not know where you visited, Edlen, but a raven is an unlucky thing to have follow." Edlen stared off into the distance, not saying anything.

"Do not worry yourself now, Edlen. It has taken its leave, as it seems. But be wary as you lead off the main path. Not all that dwell off the main roads are friendly, even here in the Gronndelon."

"Yes, Pa. I will be more careful," Edlen replied. He was relieved to hear that his problem, however small it may have seemed, had left without much incident. And his focus now was on the nicer, safer things that lay straight ahead.

As they approached the front of the city, they came to the Furskarth Stables just before the main stone bridge that crossed the Misty River. There, they stopped and Eldor paid for a spot at the stables for their horse and cart. The stable owner was a nice man, and seemed quite passionate about taking care of his horse-guests. As he owned and operated the stables, his wife ran the inn paired with it. This made for a profitable business as many visitors found it quite convenient.

"Here for the festival, eh?" the stable owner asked Eldor.

"Yes, traveled here from Riverwood. It is the first time my children have been," he replied handing the owner the necessary coin for their horse's two-night stay.

"Ah! First time goers! Well, welcome to Furksarth, young lad and my young lady!" he said, making sure to acknowledge Gracie. "Much to do in a single day! Oh, but you'll be having a grand time in the city walls. Best be getting your rest though," he said as he stepped aside, revealing the main entrance to the inn.

"My wife Sigrid is the inn keeper, and she'll take good care of you. Her beds are mighty cozy," he said as he leaned in close to Edlen. "And if you ask her for the bedtime snack, she'll be sure to leave one of her fresh sweet breads at your bedside," he said with a wink.

"My name's Regnar," he said holding his hand at his chest. "And don't you worry about your fine horse. He'll be well taken care of as you enjoy your stay!"

"You are very kind," Hellen said with a nod.

As they headed into the inn, they were greeted by Sigrid.

"Welcome to the Haystack Inn!" she said with a smile. "We offer comfortable rooms, two beds each, and our kitchen is open late. I should take a guess as your need might include two rooms?" she asked Eldor.

"Please," he said with a friendly nod.

"Next to each other, if possible," Hellen added, holding Gracie.

"Oh, of course," Sigrid responded. "We have two lovely rooms just down the hall here. Follow me!"

The room they stood in was a tall room, but not very long. It was even in width and depth, and the back half of the room was lined with counter space for drinks and places to eat. Above the counters, ran thick beams that had various herbs and cheeses hanging down from thick wooden pegs. On the walls, were lined shallow shelves of mugs, ales, and various fruits. Between the shelves on the support boards were goat-horned candles, giving the room plenty of warm light. In the middle of the far wall was a pair of swinging doors that led to a well-lit kitchen. The smell coming from it was delicious and rich of cooked meats and vegetables.

Down the hall that they were being led, they passed several doors to already occupied rooms. Each door had a unique carving on the front of it. Most were a representation of some sort of forest creature, but some were a distinct tree or plant that was easy to identify. In between the doors were mounted various trophies and horns. It was decorated, and well taken care of.

Sigrid stopped and opened the first door on the left of the hall.

"Here we are! This and the room next are yours for your stay," she said. "I hope you find everything to your comfort, and if you need anything, I will be at the dining counter."

"Thank you very much," Eldor said.

"Oh! And one more thing," Sigrid said before taking her leave. She walked into the first room and pulled out a small brass key from her pocket. On the wall to the right as she entered the room, was a thin door that led to the next room. She inserted the key and *click!*

"There you go! These two rooms were built for such parties as yours! Now you can stay as a family, as a family should."

"Very kind of you," Hellen said, and Gracie felt relieved knowing they were all going to stay together. Sigrid nodded and took her leave to the hallway.

The first room had a rabbit shape carved on the door. It was well decorated with small rabbit furs and throw-rug which bore a white rabbit shape in its center. There were two beds and a single dresser between them. On either side of the dresser top was a candle in a bronze candle-holder to match the beds. In the center, a plate with two slices of sweet bread. Next to it was a note with a message from the inn keeper:

Thank you for staying at the Haystack! We hope you find everything to meet your satisfactions. Any complaints can be raised immediately to the head-staff on duty in the main hall.
∼Sigrid

On the far wall was a small hearth and fire pit. It was already filled with small kindling and on the hearth a small stack of thicker logs to last the night. On the mantle, small trinkets and decorations sat atop, including several small wooden rabbits that caught Gracie's attention. Above the mantle, a beautiful white rabbit skin hung on the wall.

"Well, this place is quite charming!" Hellen said looking around.

Edlen wandered into the next room through the slim door. He found the room to be decorated in a more earthy theme. Carved into the far wall was a tall tree with swirling branches. Leaf symbols were dotted along the thinner branches and their tips. The beds were made of a more rustic wood. Cedar by the reddish color of it. There also were two beds covered in fur blankets, and a dresser with matching candles to go with them. The same plate and hand written letter lay on the dresser.

The room was also given a similar hearth and stack of wood. The mantle had its own decorations of ceramic leaf-shaped plates and a decorative owl on the far edge. Above this mantle on the wall hung an intricate dream catcher, decorated with the feathers of eagles and small turquoise stones found from the bottom of the Misty River. It was a beautiful piece, and brought peace upon looking at it.

"I want to sleep in the bunny room!" Gracie exclaimed.

"Very well! Gracie and I will stay as the bunnies," Hellen said with a smile.

"Edlen, go and fetch our luggage from the cart," Eldor instructed. "Let us settle in first. Then, we will find our way to the dining room for some supper."

"Yes, Pa!" Edlen said, as he left back through the first room. Edlen followed back the way he came, enjoying the fine decorations of the halls and into the main room. The smells from the kitchen grew his hunger, and he was filled with warmth and excitement to be in such a wonderfully, comfortable place. He opened the door to the stables, and found his way to the main stable hall.

"Good evening, young lad! Looking for your cart?" Regnar greeted him.

"Yes, sir. I need to fetch our luggage," he replied.

"Oh, of course! Let me lend you a hand. This way!" Regnar led him down the main hall to a stable where he found his cart parked on the side, and their horse enjoying a trough filled with sweet hay. His tail flicking in satisfaction. It was comforting to Edlen to see that even their horse was enjoying their stay.

Regnar and Edlen picked up what luggage the family needed, and brought it back to the rooms. Regnar bade them good night and returned to the stables to finish up readying things, before the stable-boys started their watch. After the family was settled and had their things put away proper in the dressers, they found their way to the dining counters.

They were served well and found the food to be warm and delicious. The meats were salted and juicy, the cheese strong (the ale stronger, as Eldor was happy to find), and a shared plate of roasted vegetables left the children full and sleepy.

Hellen carried a very drowsy Gracie back to the room, and even Edlen found it hard to keep his heavy eyes opened enough to make it down the hall. The beds were soft and warm. Only was the fire in the *Rabbit* room lit, as there was no need to light both fires if the warmth could be shared between the two rooms.

It did not take long for Gracie and Edlen to find sleep despite the excitement of the fun activities planned the next day. The days leading up to their trip left them with flying thoughts and anticipation, and it was a relief to have finally arrived. The next day was going to be one to cherish for a long time.

After a heavy night of sleep, Edlen and Gracie were more than ready to start their adventurous day. Much to their aggravation, their parents were not in such a rush to ready themselves. After dressing and preparing some spending coin in a tightly-bound coin purse, Eldor and Hellen made sure to go over some common-sense rules with their children.

With such a big city to explore, it was important that no one end up lost. With nods of agreement from Edlen and Gracie (mostly to expedite the lesson, in which they would agree to absolutely anything their parents would say), the day could finally begin. They passed through the main hall of the inn, bidding a good morning to Sigrid, who was already prepared with breakfast, and opened the door of the inn to a brisk and cool morning.

Past the stables, they approached the main stone bridge. It had once been a draw-bridge as two towering pillars on either side of the river gave way, but with generations of peace within the Gronndelon, it had long been made permanent in stone. The festivities had begun the night before, as it had seemed, and the gates to the city were propped open for any visitor or guest to be welcomed. As they passed through the large wooden gates, a long wide stone road led them straight into the heart of the city. On either side of the road, were well-groomed trees in long rows, and behind them were the shops and merchants. Banners and flags were hung on rope between the trees, and every merchant had their best on display in front of their stores. The town was already in a bustle and hum, even so being just after breakfast time.

Edlen and Gracie had their eyes open wide, trying to take in everything they could see. Some shops had small attractions and puppet shows going on to attract customers. A music shop had a live entertainment showcasing the finest crafted instruments available, and many crafters were giving live demonstrations of how they do their craft. Canoe carving, ale brewing, woodworking, and especially candy making (with their free samples) were all entertaining to watch as they passed by.

Straight ahead, the stone-paved road led deep into the city. Shops, taverns, and homes rose high in the middle, covered in wooden shingles and decorated with small towers and flags. Behind them, in the distance, The Falls fell from a great height, at the rear of the city. Its mist glistened and glittered in the morning sun, and small clouds birthed from its base rising high into the pale blue morning sky.

"What should we do first, Pa?!" Edlen said in excitement. There was so much to see and do, so much to explore. He could hardly contain himself and wanted to dart here and there to take it all in.

"The first thing we do is find the registration table so we can submit your catch!" Eldor replied. "I have been told we may find these tables in the city's main square, of which this road will lead us to!"

Edlen and Gracie didn't like taking care of business first, and it seemed to be something that could have waited. But since it was a good idea to get it out of the way, and the road would lead them to more interesting happenings, neither of them argued about it.

As they continued down the road, they passed through the Moss District. This was a small part of the city that was constantly over-shadowed by the taller buildings and the cliffs to their south. It was mostly occupied by taverns and inns, of which the fronts were decorated with flowers and mosses that do well with little to no sun light.

The woodwork on the porches and entryways were in pristine condition, having not the sun's harshness to deal with. It was cool and comfortable, and the shops were close together. It smelled rich of earth and water, and despite being shadowed, was well-lit thanks to numerous lanterns that spotted the overhangs and porch-roofs. Herbs, bulbs, and other various greenery also gave the outsides of these buildings a welcoming warmth.

The end of the Moss District was marked with a bend in the Misty River that flowed directly from The Falls. Starting at their base, the river flowed straight north towards the entrance of the city, but takes a western bend just before reaching the Moss District. The river flowed strong and fast through a stone channel that was guarded with a low stone wall to prevent accidental fall-ins.

To the west of the bend, naturally nestled behind the river as a moat, sat High Haven Castle, the quarters of the Jarl of Furskarth. Within the same boundaries were its soldier's barracks, and the castle courtyard where ceremonies and private parties were held. The castle was tall with a main hall that branched off into north and south wings. It was the most well-defended castle in all The Gronndelon, and has long been considered the safe-haven of its people.

Their road wrapped to the east around the bend and continued south towards the main square. As they followed the opposing river on their right, they passed by the Sunrise District. This was largely consisting of homes. Towards the center of town, the homes tended to be stacked on top of each other, giving depth to the shadow that passes over the Moss District to the north. But as they spread further to the outer limits of the city, they tended to spread out more to stand-alone huts. A few shops of specific expertise were dotted here and there.

The district was very well taken care of and decorated as this was the living place of most in the city. The natural moisture in the air made the faces of buildings and flower boxes very green and lively. Vines climbed tall on the sunny walls, and there was an abundance of flowering plants and fragrance, even at this time in the season.

As they approached the end of the road, they met the main town square. It wasn't so much in the shape of a square as it was a half circle that hugged the south side cliff face. In the middle of the giant circle came down the roaring falls. They crashed at the bottom into a deep circular pool and bubbled and turned in place. The atmosphere was vibrant and cheerful, full of energy and refreshing. The large pool flowed under the town square and emerged on the far north side as the river, which started somewhere under their very feet.

As they entered the square, they passed under a large arbor with thick-grown ivy. At either side, there were two guards standing, watching. Their eyes followed anyone that passed by, and they were quite heavily armed. Edlen watched his father studying these men, switching his focus between their faces and the Grizzly bear emblem they wore on their armor, of the Empire. As they passed the apparent soldiers, Eldor stared deep into the eye slots of their helms, and the solders stared straight back. Not a word was exchanged between them, and Eldor passed by without a flinch. To Edlen, his father gave a presence of an mountain unmovable, a stronghold intended to stay. Eldor made sure it was clear that they were not welcomed.

Along the edge of the outer circle were the various categories of competitions, each with their own registration tables. In between the tables stood tall stone pillars, which looked ancient in their weathered appearance. Above each table was a small banner displaying the symbol of the competition. On the right pole of each was a set of rules, guidelines, and requirements pertaining to that specific competition.

Edlen and Eldor led the way around the square looking for the fishing competition table as Hellen and Gracie followed. They passed all sorts of competitions, even ones that their local town of Riverwood didn't have. Log cutting, sword-fighting, and even field dressing were all new to Edlen. Then he spotted one that sparked a great deal of interest.

"Archery! Oh, please, Pa! Let me join that one!" Edlen asked in great excitement.

"Archery, you say? Well, you have done well on our hunts..." his father thought for a moment. "You do realize, though, that you will not be using your hunting bow, but one that they provide," Eldor continued.

"But I know I can do it!" Edlen continued to come up with reasons as he felt this would be a way to prove not only to himself, but to his father that his skills as a hunter had improved. This was a way to show it other than the meats they brought home, and he wanted to test his new skills against others in the realm.

"Perhaps after we find what we came here for, then we can talk about other activities. Besides, we haven't seen them all yet! And you don't want to over-commit yourself!" Eldor replied. Keeping his eye on that table, they continued walking until they found the Fishing Competition. They walked up and noticed the list of rules:

"Good morning," Eldor said to the attendant sitting behind the table. The attendant sat low on a stool, seemingly nodding off. He stood at once when Eldor spoke.

"Ahhhh," he said with a stretch and a yawn. "Good morning, sir! Have an entry do we?" The man was young with short blonde hair and barely enough rough on his face to not be considered smooth.

"Indeed we do," Eldor replied. He set his pack on the table and pulled out the beautifully mounted fish on the table.

"My son Edlen is submitting this as champions of Riverwood," he said lifting his pack off the table again and strapping it back to his shoulders.

"Whoa!" the attendant said in delightful surprise. "What a catch! Looks like a wonderful spotted lake bass! We have had a few entries for this species already, but this one will certainly give them a run!" Edlen smiled at this, and felt a sense of pride as the attendant wrote out his name and town on a label, and attached it to his entry.

"Here is your entry slip," he said handing a folded piece of paper to Eldor. "Keep that safe! You won't be able to collect any prizes or your trophy back without it!"

"Thank you," Eldor said in return, slipping the paper into his satchel.

"At midday, the town bell will chime. This is when submission competitions will be judged. The judging takes a few hours. You can stay and watch if you would like, but I find it rather boring and tedious. In the center of the main square there," he explained as he pointed towards a large monument, a statue of some noble man, knelt on one knee with his sword pointed at the sky.

"When the sun is hitting only the top point of there —" he paused for a second and smiled at Edlen and Gracie. "Well, you will not want to be missing that!"

"What is it?" Edlen asked in great curiosity.

"Why, the start of the ceremony of course!"

"And this will be some time near dusk?" Eldor asked.

"As the sun approaches the horizon, close to dinner time in my home. I imagine it is similar to most as it seems most people around here bring their food with them. 'Tis why most food vendors still refer to it as *the golden hour*, ha!"

"Thank you," Eldor replied. "Come now, let's go see what other activities we can find." He led the family through the rest of the registration tables. Already there were trophies of other sorts on display, and the square was bustling with people getting their entries registered.

After having seen all that there was, it was decided that Edlen would register for the Archery Competition.

"We only have time for one event, so if you are sure archery is it, we best get registered before noon." Eldor explained. The rules were as expected. Edlen was to compete in a class of similar age group. Skill competitions, unlike trophy-centered competitions, had no overall champion. The reward was similar — a small memento signifying placement, usually a large coin of some sort of precious metal.

As Edlen wrote his name on the registration list, he noticed a familiar name also on the list.

"Pa! Look who else is competing!" he said pointing down at the entries.

"Well, if it isn't your friend Taryn!" Eldor replied.

"What a coincidence!" Hellen said looking over at the list. "Nice to have a friend here!"

Edlen smiled and was happy to have someone else he knew at such a big place. He looked around the square hoping to spot his friend nearby, but the crowd was growing dense, and it was quite a large place. As he scanned the crowd, Edlen couldn't help but to also notice the presence of armed men. Their bright red bands made obvious their presence, and he knew that this was a bit odd. But he wasn't going to let a few outsiders ruin his day. He was in a wonderful place, with wonderful people and a fun afternoon planned.

"Archery competition takes place in the Jarl's barracks across the river. Here is your registration papers. You will need them to get past the guards." The attendant behind the table handed the papers to Edlen. He looked at them with pride. It had the official seal of Furskarth in large red ink at the top, and the words *Archery* in large fancy letters. Below were instructions on how to prepare, simple rules, and the classification process.

The second page was a rough map on where to find the barracks. Edlen was full of excitement, and was already going over what his father had taught him about archery. He wanted to do his absolute best.

They walked around a bit more as the sun began to approach the center of the sky. It was a perfect day for such a festival, and everyone seemed friendly and in good spirits.

"Best we feed our champ-to-be before he shows us his best!" Eldor said smiling at Edlen. "Let us find something hearty to eat!"

Eldor had wanted to try the infamous tavern of Furskarth: The Bighorn Tavern. It was well-known in the nearby towns as the best place to eat, and even in the far reaches of the Gronndelon, most people had heard of it. He led his family there for lunch, and it fell by no means short of its reputation. It was tastefully decorated to place its customers on the side of a mountain, filled with still-action critters and mountain dwellers. The door handles were made of two large bighorn sheep horns, the inside walls of sheer rock, and it held an environment that pleased everyone from traveler to local, child to elder. And the food met the reputation in full, the same way its customers always left.

The family spent the next hour eating and talking about all that they've seen, and much about Edlen's chances of winning the two competitions. Thoughts and wonders of how the archery would go, and other places they wanted to visit before they had to leave the next day. Before long, they could hear the town bells chime.

"Midday!" Edlen said. "We better get to the barracks!"

"Yes, indeed!" Eldor replied. He left his payment on the table, and the family set off to High Haven Castle.

Upon approaching the main gates, they met a pair of guards. These were not the Imperial guards that they had seen throughout the festival, but guards of Furskarth, fitted in their traditional green and brown uniforms. This made Edlen feel more comfortable, and they certainly seemed more friendly.

Edlen handed his papers to the guards and they directed them down a long hall. The hall was very tall, and made completely of stacked stone blocks that towered to large wooden arches which supported the ceiling. High up were hung banners and shields of the different towns in the Gronndelon. He passed many he recognized, and some he didn't. After passing through much of the hall, he found the banner bearing the symbol of Riverwood, and their matching shield colors. He felt proud to be walking under it, and knew he wouldn't let his town down.

At the far end of the hall was a rounded wooden door. As they opened it, they found themselves facing the main courtyard. The door led to a wide patio made of stones and a cast-iron rail. The patio was lined with flower beds and places for watchers to sit and enjoy the events. A short set of stone steps led them to the ground level, and on the far side of the courtyard the archery range was set up. There was a small crowd gathered around the official's table, and that's where Edlen headed.

As he approached, he could see the targets and their ranges. Some looked a good distance, a bit further than he was used to. He began to have some doubts, and felt a little nervous about competing in front of everyone. He approached the table, and handed his papers to the assistant.

"Ah! You'll be with the small group of young lads over at range number seven," he said after glancing at the first page. He pointed down to the other end of the ranges, and Edlen could see three young boys standing in a small group, one of which he recognized.

Edlen walked up with a smirk to the group behind Taryn.

"Imagine meeting you here, huh, Taryn?" he said smiling.

"Edlen! What are the odds?! So glad to see you here!" Taryn said as he threw an arm around him. "So you are trying out archery as well?"

"Of course! Wouldn't pass up a chance to show you how a *real* bowman shoots!" Edlen replied grinning.

"Ha! *Bowman*. More like bow-*boy*!"

Before Edlen could respond, the boy standing next to Taryn introduced himself. He was from Kaltáin, a river-town far in the northwest corner of the Gronndelon, near the Great Sea. The third boy was a local from Furskarth, or at least lived just outside of its walls. They were all quite friendly, and this helped Edlen feel a bit more at ease.

"Greetings and welcome!" the assistant shouted as he walked towards the center of the ranges, holding up his hands. "Welcome to the Archery Contest of the Furskarth Festival! The rules apply to all groups competing, and are as follows. Each archer will have three attempts to place his mark on the target. The closest to being on target will be his entry. If all three attempts fail to land on the target at all, you will be disqualified! Order of archers will be as registered. Bows and arrows will be provided to use to ensure fairness. No outside bows nor arrows are allowed in the competition!

"After your final arrow has landed, you will remove yourself from the range to allow the next archer to proceed. A judge will attend each range to monitor and ensure complete fairness." He paused and looked over at the castle door where the Furskarth guards emerged, carrying bows and quivers of arrows. They proceeded to hand each archer a bow and three arrows. Edlen grabbed on to his and inspected it.

"These are Gronndelon guard bows!" Taryn said in excitement.

Edlen's doubts returned. He was used to his hunting bow, not a guard bow. His hunting bow was shorter and more curved. It provided a good deal of throw with little draw, but the string on these bows felt loose. He could already tell he would need to pull back further to make his mark, but how much, he was unsure of. He began to plan out his attempts, and knew his first arrow would be wasted on feeling out these bows and their arrows.

"Alvaldr, of Kaltáin. You are first," an elder man said, as he walked up to the group looking at an unrolled piece of paper. The other boys stepped back as Alvaldr approached the standing mark.

"Whenever you are ready, lad," said the elder man. The boy picked up an arrow from the three that laid on the dirt ground next to his feet. He drew the bow back, and held it steady for a moment. Then with a *twang!* the arrow sailed down the range and landed on the very top edge of the target.

"Not bad, but not the best," Taryn said to Edlen under his breath. Edlen wasn't so sure, but he studied carefully. The boy drew again and released. This time the arrow stuck to the left leg of the mount for the target, which counts as a miss. Edlen noticed his stance. His legs at shoulder width, and his arm was sharply bent backwards. The bow looked fully drawn, and *twang!* Another arrow made its mark, but again on the bottom-left edge of the target. The judge approached the target and inspected carefully the two arrows that had made their mark.

"Fourth ring!" he said out loud.

"Well done," Taryn said to Kaltáin as he returned. He nodded and smiled.

"Good job," Edlen said, still a bit nervous.

"Taryn of Riverwood," the elder man called. "You may proceed when ready."

Taryn shot his three arrows, and all three made their mark. After his third arrow, the judge approached.

"First ring," he said out loud. The closest was just outside of the center, which meant he was in the lead.

"Beat that!" he said to Edlen as he came back. "It is not as easy as it seems!" he added as he returned his bow to the judge.

The boy from Furskarth had his turn, but he failed to land any arrows closer to Taryn's. They mostly hit, except one, which stuck into the ground just before the target mount. If Edlen was going to win this, he would have to hit in the center circle.

"Our final archer, Edlen of Riverwood. Whenever you are ready, lad," the elder man said.

Edlen picked up his bow and walked to the standing spot. He gazed down range at the target, and the world around him seemed to vanish. The sounds dampened, his vision focused, and now it seemed that his target wasn't so far away after all.

He bent down to pick up his first arrow, and he drew the string. His hands and fingers were unfamiliar with the bow they held, and he first found himself drawing too short. So he pulled back further, and he could feel his shoulder stretching. He held for a moment, adjusting his aim. He aimed high, in anticipation of an arch and the possibility of a weaker throw. He took in a deep breath, and as he exhaled slowly, he let his aim fall just where he wanted it. *Twang!* The arrow let loose and flew clear over the target, missing it completely, and finding itself deep in the wooden wall of the barracks.

Snickering came from the group behind him, and he felt crushed. His cheeks and eyes felt hot, but he had nothing else to do but try again. He picked up the second arrow, and pulled back. He pulled the same distance, but this time left his mark directed exactly at the center. The sounds of the busy bodies around him began to grow, and the evening breeze blew chilly around him. *Twang!* The second arrow flew down the range, dead center. He glanced hard as his eyes followed it with high hopes, but it never made it to the target. It fell short, kicking up a trail of dust as it scraped its way to the base of the target mount. The snickers grew louder.

"One more," he said to himself. "I can do this," he encouraged himself.

"Come on Edlen! You can do this!" he heard his father shouting from the patio. This made him feel courage again. And he really felt that he had it this time. He bent down and picked up the last arrow. He drew again, perhaps a bit more than the last draw. He held for a moment, steadying his aim. The court-yard seemed to have grown very quiet, and he knew everyone was watching. But this didn't seem to bother him. And as he stood there, the world began to draw away again. He saw nothing but the target. The space between seemed somehow obtainable, like he could reach out and hold it within his hands. The target, too, seemed within reach, and he had a sense of ownership of the entire situation. His goal was suddenly simple. Place the arrow at the center, and that's exactly what he was about to do.

Twang! The final arrow flew down the range at great speed, creating a perfect arch, then *THUNK!* Landing on the target with great force, the arrow ended half-way into the target itself. The judge approached the target for inspection, but Edlen already knew the outcome.

"Second ring!" the judge said.

"Yes!!" Taryn shouted jumping up and down. "I knew you couldn't beat me!" he said at Edlen with a wide grin.

"Well done, Taryn," Edlen said in good spirit and a polite smile. Edlen walked up to the patio where his family had been watching with a slight grin, knowing he had tried his best.

"Good job, Edlen! That was great!" Gracie said, as she had never seen an archery contest before.

"Those long-bows are a bit different to work with," Eldor said putting his arm around Edlen. "Not as strong nor tight as the bows we use for hunting."

"Certainly not, Pa. That's why it took me a couple of tries to make the target," Edlen replied.

"But made it you did, a task that is not easy when getting used to a new tool."

"We are very proud of you," Hellen said. This made Edlen smile, knowing his father was proud of him, and the rest of his family. And it seemed that he placed second, which was not at all bad for not planning on such a competition even as of that morning. The judges called out for the participants to collect their prizes at the main table. When he approached, they handed him a large medallion made of silver. On it was stamped the Furskarth emblem, along with an arrow at an angle across. It had a small hole at the top, if the receiver should want to hang it or mount it in some way with a chain. The late afternoon sun showed a rich yellow on its dull surface, and it felt heavy for its size.

"You two represented Riverwood well today!" Taryn's father said as he approached with Taryn to pick up his medallion.

"Yes sir, I'm happy that we both won," Edlen replied. Taryn smiled, and the two talked of the contest, their strategies, and the challenges they each faced.

"Edlen! Come boy! We don't want to miss the ceremony!" his father shouted out. Edlen said his goodbyes to Taryn and his father, and ran off to meet with his family once more. As they left the courtyard and through the castle, Edlen admired the medallion he had won. It wasn't first place, but the longer he held it, the stronger his pride grew of himself.

The family entered the town center, and the monument sat still and lifeless in the center. It seemed everyone was circled around it, watching and waiting. The sword of the monument reached high into the sky, above any other building or wall in all Furskarth. It appeared to be made of a metallic substance, steel perhaps, but it shimmered more like glass. At the base, the man's cloak spread out far and wide, branching out like roots of a tree that dove straight into the stone floor. At its very peak, a large gem was encased with exposed faces to the east and west. It was the size of a full-grown man's fist, but appeared small and hardly noticeable from the ground. The bottom half of the monument was now in shadow, and the top half glowed orange in the setting sun's light.

"What's going to happen, Mama? Why is everyone looking at the monument?" Gracie asked Hellen.

"Patience, my darling, and keep watch. Something magical is about to happen," she said pointing at the top of the monument.

The shadow line was clearly moving at a rate that you could see before your eyes. It climbed higher and higher as the sun sank further down behind the western mountains. Then something caught Edlen's attention. The gem at the top began to glow orange. The higher the shadow reached, the brighter the gem glowed. Murmurs began to rise and people in the crowd were pointing at the same. Brighter and brighter it glowed, until the shadow met the base of the gem, and then consumed it.

At that moment, when the last sun light left the top of the gem, it burst to a bright white. Swirls of silver-white shot down the center of the monument and spread through the draped cloak, shooting straight into the ground. From there, the light spread out into silver lines engraved into the stone itself, swirling around like vines on a fence. The crowd gasped as these veins under their feet erupted in white light, sparkling in some magic. Off the main veins, the smaller lines swirled to thin endings. But the larger trails extended all the way to the outer edge of the center where they climbed up the stone pillars, forming a beautiful silver tree on each. As they approached the top of each pillar, a large fire erupted on top. There were eighteen in all, and together with the glowing stone veins, the entire center was lit up beautifully for the evening activities.

The crowd cheered and clapped in amazement. Edlen had never seen anything like that before, and he found himself quite speechless and a bit overcome in the beauty and magic he had just witnessed. He gazed at the pillar closest to him, when he noticed at the base of each pillar was a name carved into the stone, and they were all quite faded. He was able to make out the letters, though, and spoke it out loud to himself.

"*Dalmann*," he said.

"Yes, Dalmann was one of The Good King's sons," his father responded. "Eighteen sons in all, a pillar for each. And the center monument is for The Good King himself, King Valdór, founder of the realm of The Gronndelon and of Furskarth, slayer of the Draugrthrall, purest of heart. It was on this day that he died, in some ancient time long ago." He looked down at Edlen with a smile. "And it is only on this day in the autumn that the sun hits the gem just right enough. That is what this day is celebrating. That is what the festival is really for."

Edlen wanted to hear more of these tales, and the history of Furskarth (of The Gronndelon as a whole) was quite interesting to him. But the festivities had begun, and the crowd was eager to hear the winners and placements so they could continue on with their late-night celebrations. And late into the night did the celebrations and party-going last.

With tired children, and the emotional excitement of the contests, Eldor and Hellen carried their children back to the inn. They left the city to continue the celebrations as it proved too much for the younger family members. With Gracie fast asleep and Edlen fighting his heavy eyes, the two were laid down in the quiet rooms outside the city walls. The fire grew warm, pleasant dreams were dreamt, and much needed rest was obtained. Tomorrow would be a relaxing trip home.

It had been a week since the festival, and Edlen returned only with his archery medallion. The family kept the fish, of course, and returned it to above the mantle place. It was an excellent catch either way, and brought joyful memories of the time they had spent in Furskarth.

"Here you are, Strawberry, a nice clover flower for you!" Gracie said as she held out her hand in front of the horse's soft lips.

She was very fond of the family's horse, who didn't bother naming him at first. But when Gracie found him nameless, she didn't hesitate to name the poor beast after her favorite little red fruit. In her defense, the horse was brown with a reddish tint in the bright sun, and speckled with black splotches, almost resembling the fruit. She continued to feed the horse more wild flowers she had found from behind the stable.

The sun soared high in the sky, showing signs of its sinking descent. Eldor and Edlen were on the lake, casting their nets once more. The fishing had been exceptionally well, and they were trying to make the most of the unusual loads they were bringing in.

Gracie held out her hand again, this time with some pedals of black-eyed susans in her palm.

"These are sweet, Strawberry! They smell really pretty!" she offered. The horses ears turned backward, and he snorted, scattering the pedals to the ground.

"What is the matter? You love the yellow ones..." she said as she picked them off the straw-laced dirt and offered again. The horse stomped and dipped his head, snorting again. Something was disturbing poor Strawberry.

Off in the distance, Gracie could begin to hear the soft rumble accompanied by multiple hoofs. Galloping horses, many of them, were breaking over the hill towards the house. Mounted soldiers, fully clad in armor and carrying the flag of the Empire were approaching. Gracie dropped the pedals and she darted towards the house, calling for her mother.

"Whoa, this is a heavy one, Pa!" Edlen shouted as they began dragging in their nets. Struggling to hold on, Eldor and Edlen managed to get the large load onto the boat. It was indeed one of the larger loads of the day, and even had some mud crab with it. Eldor paused as he gazed at shore.

"Fold up the net, son, it looks like we have company," he said. On the shore were six horsemen in armor, and a horse-drawn carriage driven by a seventh man in lesser apparel. In front of them was Hellen, with Gracie in her arms. Hellen was waving at them, signaling them to return. One of the horsemen carried a banner with a giant Grizzly bear sewn into it.

Edlen guided the boat to the dock and Eldor stepped off, studying the horsemen. As he approached, Edlen tied the boat down. Their catch would have to wait in the boat for now.

"To what do I owe this visit?" Eldor asked the front-most horseman, who was obviously some sort of colonel. He had his helmet removed, but he was the only one wearing a bright red cape that was stuffed in the back of his armor. It draped down over the back of his saddle, and even his horse had a helm with a single steel spike, polished to a mirror.

"I am Colonel Remus. You are Eldor, master of this manor?" the colonel asked.

"Yes, I am master here," Eldor replied.

Remus unrolled a piece of parchment paper.

"Our records show that you indicated to be of Nordic descent. Is this correct?"

Edlen had caught up to his father at this point, and stood beside him. All were quiet as Eldor paused in answer.

"We are proud of our family's origins. Just like you, we have history. Only our history belongs on this land, our home. You see, Colonel, I am where I belong. I am not sure the same could be said of you and your men at this time." Eldor replied. The other horsemen glanced at each other. A few of them chuckling at the attempted offensive comment. Remus wrapped up the parchment and placed it in his satchel. From another satchel, he removed a scroll, much more official in appearance as it was cased in ivory and capped with bronze at the ends. He pulled it open.

"Official of 1866 E2, the High King Gunvald, King of the Freemen Empire, wishes to welcome you and your family into the Imperial protection. Upon agreement signed by Jarl Sigurbjorn, Jarl of Furskarth, capital of the Gronndelon, all men within the Gronndelon realm fall under protection of the Empire." He looked at Eldor, then to Hellen, and gave her a grin. Eldor sternly looked at the Remus, trying to keep his scowling at a minimum. The colonel glanced back at Eldor and the grin fell from his face as he returned to his scroll.

"As a token of your loyalty to the High King Gunvald, we ask that you provide a one-time offering of gold pieces in the amounts as follows: 50 pieces for each man of age, 30 for each woman of age, and 20 for each child. If such amounts are not available at this time, sources of other offerings may be provided as substitute." He put down the scroll and looked at Eldor.

A strong breeze picked up from the west and blew Eldor's hair to the side. His braid hung heavy, and he turned and looked at Hellen.

"Well, Nord? Do you have the required offering?"

Eldor did not agree with what was unfolding before him. Taxation for a "service," he didn't even want to be part of. He knew well that this was not just a "one-time offering,", and as soon as they saw weakness, they would take advantage of it. But what choice did he have? He walked towards the house and entered.

Moments later, he returned with a coin purse. The contents although meeting the requirements, was all but a few coins the family possessed. He threw the purse at the colonel with some force, throwing him off balance enough to cause the horse to snort.

"Well," Remus said, "the Empire is happy to be of service." Eldor turned his back to return to Hellen, hoping that their business was over. He signaled Hellen and Gracie to return to the house.

"Oh, one more thing, Nord," Eldor heard from behind him. He turned, looking at Remus, knowing the found weakness was being tested.

"The High King has also tasked us to find individuals that might better serve him and the Empire in day-to-day tasks. The High King would sure enjoy the company of some, fairer maidens for his household," he said with his grin returning as he glanced over at Hellen, who was nearly to their front door. His brown teeth showed dull from behind the cracked lips that curved up. Hellen heard the request, stopped, and turned towards Eldor. A wave of fear sank her heart and flowed to her toes. Fire erupted in Eldor. Edlen, who had been watching, was not fully aware of the request of the colonel, nor prepared for what was about to happen. Eldor looked at Remus, taking a step towards Hellen.

"Her service is here with her family. I am sure you can respect that," Eldor replied, trying to keep the situation from exploding. The other soldiers drew their swords. Gracie was clearly frightened as she tucked her face into her mother's neck. Hellen stared at Eldor, knowing what was going to happen. No tears fell, as she was a strong woman and true to her bloodline. Edlen stood beside his father, staring directly at the colonel.

"You cannot have her, Nýlander," he replied. At this, the horsemen unmounted with their swords at hand. Edlen took off towards the house.

"Edlen, no!" Hellen shouted.

"Take the woman and the girl-child too!" Remus ordered. Two soldiers headed towards the house, and Eldor went after them.

"Do not do anything stupid, Nord!" Remus demanded as he drew his own sword. Edlen had beaten the soldiers inside with Hellen and Gracie, and after shutting the doors, darted into his bedroom. The soldiers forced the doors open as Eldor approached.

"Keep back! This is not your house! You have no right to enter here!" Eldor shouted. Hellen was screaming at them to leave, and Gracie began to cry from fear.

In the main room, Eldor kept trying to convince the soldiers to leave, standing in their way and doing his best to remain non-violent.

"Remove yourself, Nord! This is Imperial business! Don't make me skewer you!" one of the soldiers shouted as he held the tip of his sword at Eldor's throat. Eldor remained still. *Twang!* The sound of a bow from behind sent an arrow flying across the room and found a separation in the soldiers side armor, piercing his stomach. The soldier spat blood before collapsing, spraying Eldor's face with red.

The second soldier lunged at Eldor who pulled the sword from the falling soldier's hands and thrust it forward, blocking the attack. With a quick thrust upward, Eldor severed the soldier's blade arm off, and one more quick swing removed the soldier's head. It fell hard with a *thud* as the helmet hit against the floor. The body collapsed like a rag doll, pouring blood out the top and arm into two pools that expanded to one.

"Edlen! Why?! You should not have done that!" his father shouted. Edlen remained in shock as to how quick his actions exploded the following events. He was only trying to protect his family.

"I could not let that man kill you father! I would not stand it!" Edlen cried as he began shaking.

"Run, Edlen! They will kill you if they find you! Take the back window. Go!" his father demanded. Edlen shed tears and found it hard to see as he stumbled across his own home. Hellen and Gracie were hidden in the back master bedroom with the door shut.

Edlen ran into his room, grabbed his dagger, and retreated to the rear window where he crawled out. He threw his back against the outside wall and shut his eyes, trying to gather his thoughts, and his breath. He was in a panic and fully crying. He knew he had to get out of there. He could hear shouts from the other side of the house, his mother screaming and Gracie's cries. He didn't want to go on, but he didn't want to let his father down.

He looked up, and perched on a low branch of a redwood tree was a black raven. In its beak, it held a dead flower, wilted and gray. Staring straight at Edlen, it let out a loud cry, releasing the flower. It fell hard and steady. Its pale gray pedals, which had lost all memory of their color, flaked off as it made its way to the ground. The raven *caw! caw!* over and over. In Edlen's mind, its cries echoed the same words he had heard, haunting him now in realization, *fall! fall!* Louder and louder it sounded. Until the last jolted him back to reality. He had to get out of there.

As he climbed to his feet, a soldier, sword drawn, came around the corner.

"There you are! Come here!" Edlen took off in the other direction, heading for the thick underbrush of the woods. Around the opposite corner came a second soldier and they collided. Edlen collapsed to the ground, as he was no match for a full grown man in armor. They grabbed his arms and removed his dagger. Binding his wrists in rope, they led him to the carriage. He looked across the front of the house, and saw his mother and Gracie being dragged out.

Stumbling to the ground, Hellen struggled to hold onto Gracie, who was yanked violently from her arms. The soldiers struggled with Hellen, and after some time bound her in rope. As Edlen was thrown into the back of the cart, his head was covered with a burlap sack. It stunk of old vegetables and soil. He could not see much save a few rays of golden sunlight through the small holes. He could hear his mother crying out, and Gracie too.

"Bring him out!" he heard the colonel shout. Metal clanking was heard nearly fifteen feet towards the house as the soldiers carried out the heavy prisoner, and *ka-thunk*, his heavy body hitting the earth. He could hear his father coughing in the dust. Edlen struggled, and tried to shake the sack off his head. He then heard Gracie's crying come towards him, as she too was tossed into the carriage. Edlen managed to get to his knees.

"Ya!" shouted the driver, and the carriage took off. Edlen lost his balance and struck his head against the side. A splinter from the wood caught the sack and ripped it off as he fell face first, and it left a nasty scratch against his left cheek. He looked up, back towards the house, to see his father on his knees and Colonel Remus in front of him, bow fully drawn.

His mother, still fighting in the background, was screaming in a raging fit, fighting for her husband's life. High above, the crow flew and it unleashed a horrible wail. At this, Colonel Remus released the arrow, and Eldor fell backwards with the staff and quiver sticking out of his chest at an angle towards the house.

"No!" Gracie cried in a raspy shriek that pierced the ears of the soldiers nearby. A flock of birds burst out of the trees in a panic clatter above and swirled around towards the lake, then turned sharp towards the west. Edlen was motionless, never blinking, seemingly deaf and paralyzed, as he stared at the body of his father until they passed the crescent of the hill. His mother crying out, pain echoed off the trees around them, and Gracie cried without breath.

Thunk! Gracie's cries suddenly stopped. And with the helm of his sword, the soldier also struck Edlen in the back of the head. *Thunk*. Everything went black.

Edlen awoke to an arousal of commotion. Yelling he heard from every direction, and the sack had been placed back over his head. It was dark, not even the sunlight was peeking through the sack. He heard the horse cry out and more shouts. He could hear a brief *clanking* of sword fights before the carriage was overturned. Edlen rolled out across the gravel, and hit his head against a large rock. It all went black again.

CHAPTER III

INTO THE WILD

— 2nd of Kalddager, 1866 —

The screams of Gracie echoed in Edlen's mind. He felt as though he was falling, as he endlessly sunk further and further away from his father lying on the ground. Drawing back, he felt carried away by a force he couldn't control. No amount of struggle made a difference, and the piercing cries around him haunted like night creeping through the tall trees. The darkness swallowed him as the last echoed screams faded.

His head felt swollen and painful. He didn't want to open his eyes from the pain, but he peeked one open to see a tall wooden ceiling and square-cut beams holding it up. It was the corner of a room, and he was lying in a straw bed.

The room was dark, save the low glow of a dimly lit candle that flickered in the small drafty room. Fine dust settled heavy, giving the room its own slight fog. A green wool blanket was covering him, and his forehead felt odd. He reached up to touch it, and found it wrapped in linens. His left arm, too, was wrapped in a sling. Moving it just a little shot an achy pain through his shoulder.

After looking around, he noticed a chair in the corner sat empty, and a dresser on the other side of a small oval floor mat. On the dresser, there laid a sheathed sword. It caught his attention as it looked familiar, but he could not place where he had seen it before as his head was still fogged. Next to it, a small wooden bowl with a couple of red apples in it paired with a slice of goat cheese. He was starving.

He managed to sit up and rest against the side wall on his left. Outside of his room he heard the sounds of conversation and laughter, and someone was playing a flute (to his despise). The sharp notes that managed to sneak under the door pierced his ears and seemed to make his headache worse.

Through the bottom of the door, a bright orange-yellow glow came off the wooden floorboards. This place was all new to him, and he had no idea how he got there, and who bandaged him up. More importantly, he wondered if Gracie was out there, or at least near. And although it seemed too high to hope, perhaps even his mother.

As he pondered this, the recent memories returned more life-like than when they occurred. Eldor was really dead, his own father. It all exploded so quickly, and what was a beautiful day on the lake with his Pa turned so dark in only moments. So much regret filled his heart and mind, he burst into tears, weeping quietly. He was so afraid. Afraid of those men, afraid of living a life without his Pa. Afraid of what lied just beyond the door in front of him. He sat there in his window-less room, feeling like a prisoner in a cell of fear, and his mind fogged of foul thoughts and suffering.

After several moments of letting his heart grieve, he looked around his room, which spoke to him a different story. A *prisoner*, with a sheathed sword on the dresser? He was bandaged up, at least attempted with some level of care, and it appeared that his captors wanted to make sure he was fed.

His thoughts began to turn around, and his hunger started to return. He managed to reach across, half way out of bed, to grab the slice of goat cheese. It smelled like the cheese his father would bring home, and the sorrow returned. He held it for a minute with a lump in his throat, and tears returning to his cheeks. Eating would be difficult, no matter how hungry he was.

A voice quickly grew louder outside the door as a man approached. The voice carried some familiarity with it, then the door opened.

"Edlen, my lad! Glad to see you awake!"

"Radholf!!" Edlen immediately felt a wave of relief at the sight of his father's friend. "How? Where are we?" his mind was flooded with questions, but he knew that Radholf was friendly and that he was himself, for the most part, safe.

"Calm yourself a bit, Edlen. I'll give you a full account of what happened, to the best of my knowledge."

"Where is Gracie? My mom? Are they here?" he asked anxiously.

"I'm afraid not. Let me start from the beginning," Radholf replied in hopes to keep Edlen's focus as he took a seat in the chair.

"I received word that a campaign of men from the Empire were harassing the neighboring towns. They had just made their way through Riverwood and continued east towards Lake Vanalta. I knew they would not settle well with your father, so I hurried as fast as I could to send warning. Unfortunately, it was too late. When I arrived at your home, I found your father lying on the ground with an Imperial arrow in his chest. There were many prints in the dirt, of hoof and foot, and no one else was in sight. Edlen, I am deeply sorry for what happened."

Edlen lowered his head and shut his eyes, tears dripping down and falling onto the blanket that covered his lap. They soaked in as he struggled to contain his pain.

Under his breath, he continued to ask questions that also weighed heavy on his heart.

"How did you find me? How did I get here?"

"You see, Edlen, there is much you can hear if you listen. A flock of sparrow had followed you, and I learned of your headings on the cart from one such a bird. I jumped on my horse and headed towards the fort Stonehaven. They have a base camp there, as the town itself has fallen under complete control of the Empire. This is where they were taking you. Your sister and your mother, I cannot say. I can only assume they were taken there too. Night had fallen while I continued to chase down your captors, and from a far distance, I heard a great commotion.

"Your captors were attacked by a group of local rebels, quite a large group. By the time I approached, I found bodies all over the road. Dozens of dead men, soldiers and rebels. There were broken crates scattered and wasted supplies from what I assume was their cart. Dead horses, blood pools all over the road. In the far distance I could hear hooves moving frantically into the night, at least two from what I could make of it. None of the bodies were of the Colonel, so I knew he had escaped the fight.

"I dug through the rubble and waste to see if I could find any traces or clues of you and your family. Under one of the crates, lying against a large rock, I found a very broken and beaten up son of Eldor. I picked you up and brought you here."

"You let them take my mother and sister?!" Edlen was furious. His regret and pain of his recent loss had made the smallest of pains seem unbearable, and he began to lash out in anger at everything that piled up against him.

"I would have been no match for a colonel plus one, both on horses, Edlen. It would have done nobody any good to walk into such a wish for death." Edlen sat staring at Radholf, upset and disappointed, but knowing he was right.

"And where is *here*?" Edlen asked, short on patience now knowing the fate of his remaining family.

"An old friend of mine, someone we can trust. This is her inn, the Grassy Knot. You are in Leafenfell, young Edlen. Safe enough from the Empire for the time being, as they have not made it this far east yet. Dargmara is her name, and she has agreed to let us stay until you are well rested and recovered."

"We have to get my mother and sister back! You said they were heading to Stonehaven. That is just north of here, right? We cannot just leave them to those monsters!" Edlen was clearly over estimating his strength, and Radholf's, as his love for his family pushed him into nonsensical thinking. He desperately wanted to have something positive to hold on to, some form of hope, some feeling of control again as his life had now spiraled so far out and his loss so great.

"And what? Take on the strongly fortified stone walls of Stonehaven, just the two of us? We would both have our heads on spears at the main gates before a moment was over, if we approached the walls with aggression. There is a reason it is called a *fort*, young Edlen. Their fates are outside of our hands. I am sorry."

Edlen turned away and threw himself back down on the bed, covering most of his head with the covers. He did not want to agree with his recent care giver, and despite the luck and kindness of his hostess, was quite upset and angry at the whole situation. His aches and bandages only frustrated him further.

"Be grateful, Edlen," Radholf said as he stood from the chair. "You still have control over your fate, and that is more than many can say with this turn of events." Radholf walked out of the room and shut the door to leave Edlen with his thoughts. Rest is what he needed. Rest from the head and arm injury, rest from his emotions. Edlen laid there for several hours trying to process his situation, letting his emotions out and clearing the fogs from his thoughts.

There was a knock on the door, and Edlen woke up after falling asleep exhausted. He didn't know what time it was, nor what day for that matter. His headache faded, and he sat up with a remaining dull ache in his arm. His throat was sore from weeping.

"Come in," he answered. The door opened slowly and in peered a tall, thin woman with braided blond hair pulled back tight. She had sharp blue eyes and pale lips, and wore a low-cut dress with a tight leather center.

"Good evening, master Edlen. I am Dargmara, keeper of this inn. I..." she paused a moment and stepped further in, shutting the door slightly behind her.

"I am sorry for your losses. I cannot mend painful memories, but I can offer my inn and services to you as long as you should need them. Radholf is a friend of mine, and I would love to help any friends of his."

"Thank you, ma'am." Edlen responded, remembering his manners and turn of good fortunes thanks to their mutual friend.

"I shall be readying for bed soon," she continued. "The night watchers will be in the common room if you should need anything. Oaván will be available, and do not hesitate to request my assistance if anything else comes up. Good night, Edlen."

Edlen smiled a bit at the last of her kind expressions. As she left the room, Radholf entered and shut the door.

"Beautiful *and* kind. Humph! They don't come like that too often by what I have seen," he remarked as he sat in the chair. "She is a good friend, as I have said." He sat there staring at Edlen, who remained silent, pondering further on the inn and his new hostess.

"How is your head feeling, lad? Let us take a look." He removed Edlen's head wrappings. The creamy-white linens quickly turned dark red as more layers were removed. His head suddenly felt chilled from being exposed for the first time in days, and his skin felt raw.

"A bit of a washing should do it now. You will be right enough in the morning, I should expect."

"Right enough for what? Where will I go?" Edlen asked, knowing he couldn't stay in Leafenfell forever, especially being so close to Stonehaven.

"Ey, you cannot be staying here, and neither can I. The Imperials will be looking for anyone who opposes their new *'laws'*, and now we know what they're willing to do to enforce it. We must not stay in the west, Edlen. It is not safe. We will travel north and east, far from the reaches of the Empire, to the only place I know that could be safe from the outstretched fingers of the Empire's recent conquest."

"Where, Radholf?"

"To Arboran, Edlen. The Valley of the Elves! The lush forest south of the Boreal Mountains, Kingdom of the Woodlen Elves, masters of all things natural. Not even the *High* King Gunvald himself would be foolish enough to take on the Woodlen Elves. I know their Master, as I had once served at his side many ages ago. He would greet us with the most welcome acceptance."

"Arboran! But that's so far away!"

"Exactly! It'll be a journey, no doubt. Weeks by foot if we take the straight roads."

Edlen didn't like the sound of this. He would be walking for weeks on end, further and further from his home. The only place he knew, the only comfort he had ever felt. Now turned bitter, and it seemed for the first time that he had no home. Emptiness filled his heart, and he suddenly felt as if he had nothing more to give, and nothing more to lose.

"But I do not plan on getting there entirely by foot, young Edlen! We will, however, need to walk to Brisrun first. A week's journey at a slower pace, what with your injury and all, but we should manage just fine. Simple, really! The Vanalta River that runs right out of Leafenfell, it will lead us there."

"Brisrun? I've heard so much about it, but never been," he thought out loud. "I have not been to Leafenfell for that matter. Save once when I was a baby by my father's tales. But what of your horse? Can't we ride him to Brisrun?"

"Riding to Brisrun from Leafenfell on the back of a horse, with *me* as the driver would not be comfortable at all! No, we will walk and my horse shall carry our supplies. It will be a fine trip. And Brisrun; a trader's paradise! A beautiful city with more vendors, traders, and goods than you can imagine! Being one of the largest ports on the coast of the Great Sea, it has its advantages! We will resupply there and take the next available ship to the borders of Arboran."

"And then we will meet the Elves?" Edlen asked in anticipation. He was nervous about the plan as he had never traveled before. New places, new faces. It made him feel uneasy, but what choice did he have? He couldn't go back; he couldn't return. And it appeared that this was the road his only friend now was about to take.

"Patience, lad. One step at a time! But yes, before long, you will be resting safe deep in the borders of the Elven Valley. But first, a good night's rest is in order! I will have Oaván bring you something to fill your belly, nice and warm. We have a bright and early start waiting for us in the 'morrow!" he said as he got back out of his chair and headed towards the door.

"Oh!" he said, stopping as he passed the dresser. "This sword. It belonged to your father, being passed down from his father. It being a sort of heirloom, should be passed to you. I remembered your father had held on to it in hopes that it might aid you, should you ever find a proper use for it." Radholf placed his hand on the sheathed sword, staring at it as though digging deep into memory. His pause told of his thoughts.

"Dragonsbane," he said in a whisper. He turned and looked at Edlen with no smile on his face. "It is named Dragonsbane, and it is yours to keep." Edlen sat still, staring at Radholf then shifting his attention to the sword.

"Rest now, lad! Our adventures begin soon!" he said as he left the room.

Moments later, Oaván came in to deliver some roasted rabbit with potatoes and butter on the side. Paired with it, a nice pint of ale, as was usual with meal requests (and Oaván thought it to be a nice gesture, on the house of course), not realizing Edlen's younger age. The rabbit smelled wonderful, and aroused his appetite back again. The ale sat on the dresser while he scarfed down his meal. It did indeed warm him, and brought some level of satisfaction with it. He then decided to try the ale, realizing no one was there to stop him and the curiosity now seemed guiltless.

"This is for you, father..." he said, holding onto his mug, then taking several deep gulps. Having nearly half of it down, he began to weep again. The reality of his father's loss was settling in deep now, and he gave his emotions completely to the mourning that was needed. Setting the half-finished mug on the floor next to the bed, he fell asleep with tear-soaked cheeks and a swollen throat.

The next morning, Radholf woke Edlen bright and early, as he had promised. Edlen's arm was still sore, but his forehead had cleaned nicely and could go without bandages. The blade on the dresser sat waiting for its new master to take hold, and fortune was with him as it wasn't his right arm that was injured. As he picked it up, he noticed something familiar about it. The dark metal and silver lettering told of what sword it really was. Dragonsbane, the sword from his house. The familiarity of the sword brought a flood of emotions back. This was his father's sword, a gift of protection, and Edlen felt a connection again to its previous owner. He struggled to keep his mixture of sorrow and gratitude contained, but he certainly was thankful to have this token of his father now always by his side.

"Come, Edlen! Dargmara wished to see us off. Best not keep our kind hostess waiting!" Radholf said peeking into Edlen's room as he was tightening his new blade to his waist.

Edlen stepped out of his room into the common room. It was the first time he saw the room. It had a vaulted ceiling made of wood, and a large rectangle fire place in the center where wood could be piled up to keep the inn as a whole warm. There were multiple doors leading to small individual rooms coming off the common room, and across the way was a larger door, the exit.

To his right was the main counter, and behind it stood Oaván, wiping it down. Behind him, a set of stairs that led to the basement where the kitchen and storage room rested quietly. The common room was dark and windowless, lit only by the center fire and some mounted candles on the beams that stood between each of the rooms.

"Edlen. Glad to see you are feeling better," Dargmara said as she came from her own private room near the back counter.

"Thank you, ma'am. And thank you for your hospitality!" he answered. Dargmara nodded and smiled in return.

"Radholf, are you fully supplied? If you need anything more, please help yourself to anything in the kitchen or armory," she offered.

"Thank you, Dar! We are fine enough as is. And I appreciate your help during this time," he replied.

Dargmara looked back at Edlen.

"I hope to see you again, Edlen. Stay safe out there. The road can be a dangerous place. You are in good hands, though."

"Thank you again, Dargmara," Radholf said. "We best be going now, Edlen! I will send message when we reach Brisrun. May the gods be with you, my friend!" he said as he gave her a hug.

"And also with you," she replied, then looked at Edlen. "And with you as well, young Edlen." Edlen smiled and bowed, and the two headed out the door.

The morning was in silence. It settled heavy and humid as a thin fog settled just above the roof tops. A soft white glow filled every corner of the small town as the sun struggled to pierce the mist. Everything was laden with dew, robbing every surface of any warmth.

As they walked out, Edlen took in his first view of Leafenfell. He stood on the wooden porch which was long as it spanned the entire length of the inn. Its cover was supported by whole tree trunks, and had a waist-high railing running along the front. A hen clucked nervously next to the front door, as it seemed that their sudden appearance had broken her concentration in egg laying as she sat on a pile of straw.

In front of them was the blacksmith's forge. It appeared cold, save a thin trail of smoke slowly rising from its center, carrying memories of yesterday's work. The town was quiet as it was still early for most. The air smelled of saw dust and wood-working, and no birds were chirping. The entire town felt heavy and dreary.

"Beautiful morning for a journey," Edlen said sarcastically as he looked up at Radholf.

"Ha-ha! The sun may not be bright, but at least it came up! This way, young Edlen!" Radholf said as he turned to the left and headed towards the end of the porch. Radholf's high energy and optimism so early in the morning was a bit much for Edlen at the time.

Edlen followed down the three steps leading off the porch. The ground was soggy as if a heavy rain storm had recently passed. Radholf's horse was tied up at the end of the porch, already prepared with supplies. Next to the horse stood tall a large man. He had braided long black hair and dark gray skin. As he turned, Edlen noticed his facial features that gave away his race. An Orc, with a wide flat nose and sharp pointed teeth. Two of his bottom teeth curved up out of his mouth, with the left one pierced and a black ring run through it. His brow stretched across in a flat line, and his eyes were wide and very dark.

"Morning, lad." he said to Edlen, "It's a pleasure to meet you." His voice was very deep and a bit dry.

"Edlen, this is my long-time friend Oatikki. He will be joining us on the road to Brisun. And do not let his appearance fool you! He is softer than a rabbit's tail!" Radholf said with a grin and a wink. Oatikki grumbled at this with a look most displeasing, but he didn't argue it. Edlen smiled.

"Though he gets a bit grumpy in the morning..." Radholf added.

"Nice to meet you, Oatikki."

"Could have chosen a better morning, Radholf. This weather is for the worms!" Oatikki said.

"I completely agree..." Edlen added.

"When the day comes that we can choose our own weather, I will rub Oati's big ugly gray foot here until he falls fast asleep." Radholf said as he untied his horse. Oatikki grumbled at this, as it too was a bit early to handle Radholf's jokes. Already Edlen felt as though the trip was going to be a bit more light-hearted than he had anticipated. With Radholf leading the horse, the small group headed towards the center of town.

A single road led through town. It was poorly maintained with no stones. Tall grasses grew on the edges and it was a bit soggy. They passed the forge, then a mill. On the other side of the mill flowed the Vanalta River. It roared and sprayed a fine mist into the air. The smell of saw dust started to pass as they made their way beyond the mill, and the smell of the sweet river rapids began to take over.

"The mill," Radholf said, "is Leafenfell's primary exporter. They saw up logs and send them down the river to Brisrun. There, they are exported to all over the coast. 'Tis how Leafenfell got its name."

It was strange for Edlen to see the river so far down stream. It was fed by Lake Vanalta, and being where he grew up, he only saw glimpses of the birth place of the river, at the far eastern shore where the lake narrowed down and eventually fell over a twenty-foot drop, feeding into the river. He looked back west up the river, knowing that was the direction of home. He began to feel terribly home-sick, and miss his family and quiet life he lived too recently. The sight of the river brought back pain and sorrow every time he looked back. He continued to follow his new guides with his head hung low, tears rolling down his cheeks.

As they approached the edge of the town, the path soon led to a stone bridge that crossed the Vanalta River. The entrance of the bridge had tall grasses and some different shades of violet and blue mountain flowers growing at its sides. It was well worn and smooth to walk on, and had raised edges that kept a full grown man from leaning too far over. It crossed the river in one long arch, with two smaller arches allowing the river to pass under.

Edlen stopped in the center of it, looking over the raised walls. The Vanalta River, with crystal clear water rushed under them and almost immediately over sharp facing rocks. The rapids and slight drop-off sprayed a fine mist into the air, and the bridge smelled of fresh water, clean and pure. It revitalized Edlen in both body and mind, and lifted his spirits up a bit. Maybe traveling wouldn't be so bad after all.

"Try to keep up, Edlen! Brisrun awaits!" Radholf shouted at the other end of the bridge, without looking back. Oatikki continued next to the horse, not losing focus of the road ahead.

They continued down the path that wound along the side of the Vanalta River. Most times, it was up high above a cliff face that fell straight down to the river, but occasionally would dip down almost to the river's level. The surrounding area was thick with dense trees and underbrush. Their path was laid out in stone, for the time being, which made it easy for travel.

"This road to Brisrun is not heavily used." Radholf said to cut the long silence. "Most roads eventually join the Ravenrun, as it cuts through the heart of the Gronndelon. Its birth is at Furskarth and end at Brisrun, but this road runs more eastward. It may be a bit longer, but my hopes is that we'll go unnoticed for the most part."

As the day aged, the fog lifted. Wispy white clouds formed and flew quickly on the breeze, revealing the light blue sky above. The song birds enjoyed the warmth and found various insects on the path around them. Often times they would find wild berry bushes of early fall on the sides, and the tall grasses that fenced in the dark forest concealed chirping crickets.

Most of the day went on without much event and little conversation. The sun seemed to warm Edlen's thoughts, and he always enjoyed being outdoors. Although he had never taken this path before, it strangely felt comforting. Much of the Gronndelon was similar. Thick forested areas with rivers running through. It was difficult for anyone who grew up in the hold to feel out of place anywhere else within its borders. Soon, they broke for lunch, a meal of bread and dried meats topped off with an apple for each, including the horse.

"We are traveling well, Edlen! And with such beautiful weather! I knew that fog wouldn't last long," Radholf said, finishing up the last of his apple.

"Let us hope it continues!" Oatikki added. "It is the cold that gets to me the worst. How are you doing, Edlen? You've kept up with us well."

Edlen's legs were already tiring. It would take a while before he grew used to traveling. But the scenery helped, and the quietness of the road set peace upon his mind.

"I am not used to traveling, but the pace seems fair. I will get used to it soon, though," he responded.

"Yes indeed," Radholf replied.

"Those little legs of yours will be nice and strong before we end our journey!" Oatikki said with a half-grin and a bit of apple spraying out from between his words.

Before long, they were back on the road again. Soon, the afternoon began to age.

"Here it is!" Radholf said, stopping suddenly. In front of him stood tall a menacing tree, old and sparse with leaves. It was a type of tree Edlen did not recognize, as it had no bark, and was white as dried bones. Its leaves were like spears and had jagged sawed edges. In the trunk of the tree was carved the face of a bear. Not like that of the symbol of the Empire, but a bear giving a deep and long growl.

"This is the border of *the wild*. Here, we enter Bjornwood Forest. This land has been untamed since before the road was built, and even then, men have only stayed on the road. Do not lead off the path, for opportunities of misfortune will be waiting."

Their path led straight under the tree's large branches. At the top, Edlen saw a raven perched. Not moving, only watching. As to wait for them to pass underneath. And pass under they did. As they entered the forest and continued to follow the river, Edlen looked back at the large tree. The raven had flown off silently, content in their decision. This made Edlen feel uneasy.

The rest of the day was largely similar to the morning. The trees around them were quite a bit older than he was used to seeing. The underbrush thicker, but the river seemed to take no notice of any such border. Once in a while, Edlen thought he heard rustling in the woods around him. Strangely enough, the horse would tilt its ears back at the same time. But most of these events ended with a sparrow or chickadee revealing itself in a thorn bush just before taking off across the river.

There seemed to be quite a bit of back-and-forth with the little birds, as though they themselves as a group had business to take care of, or messages to be passed. Either way, as Edlen watched, their busy little lives and matters seemed to further bring peace to his mind. As the sun began to sink, the warmth of the day also started to lose its life. The sky was turning a beautiful pink to the east, and the birds began their evening discussions again.

"Best be finding a good camping site soon." Oatikki said as he gazed up at the colorful sky.

"Yes, I believe I have had my share of walking for the day," Edlen replied.

"Ha-ha! Indeed we traveled well! I am sure you will be sleeping well tonight!" Radholf said.

They came to another dip in the road that came close to the river's surface. It was a lip on the shore that spread along the edge of the river. There, the ground became more sandy and proved to be a perfect place to sleep. Oatikki gathered stones to make a fire pit, while Radholf collected wood from across the path. The horse was tied down to a boulder near the entrance where the shore met the path where a small maple tree had sprouted. At its base grew a large bunch of wild asters. The horse flicked its tail in joy as it snacked away on the purple flowers.

Radholf got the fire going, and they roasted some potatoes and carrots he had in his sack. One carrot he gave to his horse as compensation for their travels that day. The fire was warm and resting on the soft sand helped to heal Edlen's aches and sore legs.

After supper, Radholf boiled some river water with some wild spearmint he had collected earlier that day. It made for a refreshing and relaxing tea that he shared with Edlen. Oatikki was not fond of tea, as he so clearly stated in refusal and pulled out a bottle of strong spirits from his sack. As they sat at the fire, the sun sank beyond the horizon and the stars began their show.

The entire sky was lit up with thousands of sparkling stars, brighter than any other night Edlen could remember. He looked across the fire at Radholf, who sat very still, staring at the fire. His face was lit up with a flickering orange, and he held his cup close to his mouth, letting the steam warm his face.

Concealed in the crackling of the fire, Edlen thought he had noticed the sound of rustling from across the river. At first, it hardly seemed noticeable. But it continued, and he eventually glanced over. The edge of the river dimly sparkled in the weak fire light, and the water looked cold and black. He couldn't find the center of the river, as it was concealed in darkness.

The far shore also was in shadow, and only the tops of the mountains could be made out as they cut starless shapes against the sky. The meaning behind the name of the Rhims became clear now, as the mountains before him cut a long black rim on the horizon of the sky. But somewhere in the void, the rustling continued.

Edlen glanced over at Radholf, who continued to stare into the fire. He looked at Oatikki, who was also aware of the sounds.

"Must be the trees waving their branches..." Edlen said in hopes to calm himself down.

"On a windless night?" Oatikki stated.

"Nay, not the wind. And not the trees themselves," Radholf said as the steam from his tea spiraled up in a swirling dance. It flowed high above Radholf's head, disappearing into the night sky. There certainly was no wind that night.

"We are not alone out here," he said.

"What do you mean? What is out there?" Edlen asked feeling a bit vulnerable.

"Do not worry, they mean no harm."

"They? How many? Who are they??"

"Arborians. Three of them, from what I can count. Two on this side of the river, one over there," he said, nodding to the other side of the river.

"They have been following us since we had stopped at noon."

"Arborians? You mean the tree-people?" Edlen was shocked as he had only ever heard of them from old folklore and bedtime stories.

"Aye,"

"Protectors of the forest," Oatikki added.

"I have only ever met one in person, many years ago. And it was in the realm of the Woodlen Elves. It has been centuries since they have been seen in the Gronndelon, but they once inhabited this realm as natives, in another time." Radholf continued.

"What do they want? Are we in danger?" Edlen grew more concerned.

"Oh no, most certainly not. They try to avoid men all together. But what their interest in our little party is, I cannot say. I only know they are keeping quite a close eye on us."

Edlen peered over the river, suddenly feeling watched. His eyes did their best to pierce the black shores but they saw nothing. He then looked back up the path at the horse, who seemed quite content and resting. Radholf realized Edlen's concerns, and so continued telling the story, although knowing it wasn't the best story to tell to help ease his mind.

"They are peaceful beings. Said to have been created by the gods themselves to command and master all things earthy and green. Although they resemble a man in figure, their skin is like bark and they have no mouth. Their fingers are twigs and have feet like roots that grasp onto the ground with each step. They have hearts of bee hives, and as long as the hive stays intact, they cannot perish.

They watch over the forest, protecting it when in need, and do not concern themselves with outsiders. They are old, as old as the forests, and many of them planted the ancient ancestors of the very trees we see today.

"They are also the blood ancestors of the Woodlen Elves, of whom are more like you and me. But even the Elves rarely come into meeting with any Arborian as they are quite scarce and timid."

"What happened to them?" Edlen asked in curiosity.

"It was not long before the Men of Ancient Gronndelon discovered the value of their hearts."

"Their bee hives," Oatikki added.

Radholf nodded and continued.

"It is the honey from these hives which hold great healing powers. Further more, the consumer would feel revitalized and seem to have an edge in battle. The effects wear off, of course, after a period of time. And so the honey from their hives became a very sought after, and expensive material.

"The problem was, though, in harvesting. You cannot simply open up the hive and take the honey, as you would any other hive. This would kill the hive and the creature with it. But it did not take long before, after some gruesome experiments and failed attempts, a process by which the honey could be extracted while keeping the creature alive was found. This meant that a method was discovered where they had a reliable source of this rare honey."

Oatikki interrupted, "But this method was terrible, and involved capturing these creatures in an ill-manner. Keeping them as prisoners in cells, and the extraction process was torturous and painful. Even though the process didn't kill the hive, it slowly killed the spirits of the creatures that housed them."

Silence suddenly fell over their camp. The crickets seemed to quiet their chirps for the moment, and even the waters of the river hushed for a short time. The fire continued to crackle at the wood, giving no notice of the storytellers or their story.

Radholf continued.

"Arborian after Arborian went missing, as the Men of Ancient Gronndelon continued to capture and imprison them in secrecy, gaining wealth and power in the process. Before long, word got out of their doings, and the Arborians declared war against these Men. Of course, being of the earth, they were weak to fire, and the war began in terrible slaughters of hundreds of Arborians.

"The forests in which they found and grew, their homes, were burned and leveled to the ground. Special weapons were made to target their hives and take them out swiftly. In the Arborian's eyes, it was a massacre."

"They were annihilated," Oatikki added. "Only those that lost enough body but kept the hive intact were kept. After all, the ultimate goal was to harvest."

There was a long moment of silence as the thought sank in deep to their minds. Then Radholf spoke again.

"The news of this war reached the ears of the Woodlen Elves to the east. The Elves are known to be distant descendants of the Arborians. To the Elves, the Arborians are known as "mothers," or *Aiti* in their native tongue. The Elves then swore that they would drive out all Men of the Gronndelon, and return this land back to the Arborians. Partly to undo all that the Men had done, but mostly to give their mothers a long-lasting home. And so it was that the Elves joined the war, and their swift fighters and superior skills proved no match for those of Men. This is how the Gronndelon was then lost from the grasps of Men.

"Most died in the war, but those that were spared were given chance to flee to the Western Mountains, and to find refuge in East Nýland, thus ending the time of Men in the Gronndelon over fifteen-hundred years ago, until a long decedent of the Good King returned from the home land."

Edlen sat, listening to Radholf. Knowing that they were timid and peaceful helped ease his mind, but it was still concerning knowing such a creature was watching over them, especially with such a violent past. He only hoped that they were aware that they meant no harm, and were simply passing by. Still, though, he felt a sense of danger and malicious eyes upon him. He looked over at Oatikki, who had laid down on the bank and was already headed towards sleep.

In the quiet of the night, Radholf began to recite a song of old, a song of reflection of a battle long ago.

Sing now Mother, find calm in your blame,
Call your children home bathed in golden flame.
I pray thee, seek us now, take us home,
Take us now, O' Mother, bring us home.
Hear our cries, catch our tears that they may never fall
Meet your earth below our feet, O' Mother, save us all.
We call thee Mother, bring us home, save us from our pain
Of fearful years, a thousand tears, bathed in golden flame.

Edlen continued to watch the fire, listening to Radholf sing quietly in the night. The sound of the fire crackling relaxed him. The two blended soothingly with the rushing sounds of the river behind him. Shallow waves rocked against the shore, and he started to give into his heavy eyes. Eventually, the lull of the water, the cool sand he laid on, and the warmth of the fire proved too much for Edlen's tired body, and he quickly drifted off to sleep.

The breeze turned cold, and the sky a dull gray. Edlen brushed his hands against the very same redwood trees that surrounded his home. The woods were silent, and even his footsteps muted. He felt numb, and his breathing was slow and heavy. The trees seemed to go on forever in every direction, and he couldn't tell which way was which.

He continued to wander aimlessly, hoping to find someone or something, but it was all more of the same. Tree after cold tree. Then he heard an echo. A faint cry that bounced off the trees all around him. The cry turned to a crackle as a black raven circled him from afar. As Edlen continued to walk, the raven tightened its circle, *caw*ing as it got closer and closer. Edlen watched it with hatred and annoyance.

The sky began to spit red. Chilled blood dripped from the gray fog high above the trees. It was cold, and familiar. In a strange way, he knew who it bled out from. And it was soaking him. His hair dripped red, his clothes, his fingers. He looked up at the sky and it splattered across his face. He was chilled to the bone. The raven's cry calling out *cre-caw!* Its call changed, as if it were trying to call his name. The chills ran deeper.

"Edlen!" He jolted awake and sat straight up. "Edlen boy! Come here and get out of the rain!" Radholf invited him. Oatikki was placing the last of the logs of a lean-to against the side of the small cliff that formed at the edge of their dip near the river. The fire had also been moved to just in front of the main entrance, but the old fire was still burning. It was still very dark, and a sudden rain shower had apparently decided it was the perfect time to wash the land. Edlen gathered his wet bedding and pack, and joined his companions in the makeshift shelter. He curled up next to the rock, of which he found just as cold, albeit dry, and shut his eyes. The warmth of the new fire spread quickly in their new shelter, and he fell fast asleep for the rest of the night.

They awoke the next morning to a soggy land and drizzling sky. They had a wet breakfast that was quite uncomfortable, and packed up to get on the road again. As the morning aged, it became clear that their pace was slowed by the drizzling rain. It dripped a *pitter-patter* cold on their hoods, which were soaked and began to smell of wet leather and cloth. Edlen felt miserable, and chilled to the bone. It made his muscles ache, and his arm hurt even more. His clothes were heavier and the road sloppy. He had a hard time keeping up with with his two guides.

The day went on quite uneventful. No birds made their presence known as most wanted to stay dry and warm. The soothing sounds of the rain left the travelers feeling sleepy, and masked any noises that may have come from the surrounding forests. Even the river seemed to be muted at times under the blanket of rain drops.

The group continued their travels along the road for the next several days. It wound back and forth, following the snaking river, and only leaving its route temporarily. At times, the road seemed much less a road and more an animal trail. Wild, thick underbrush had long taken over the wide clearings of the ancient road. The road passed under thick trees with dense leaves, leaving the road in dark shadow. It was here that Edlen spotted many types of mushrooms and moss, some of which he had never seen before. Radholf ignored most of them.

The nights were cold and miserable. Huddled around the campfire, Edlen tried to stay warm and dry. Makeshift shelters were thrown together. Perfection was not given, as they were only a single night solution. Taking their rest, the three travelers sipped their drinks of choice, what ever they needed to bring the most comfort. The *pit-pat* rain surrounded them in a cloak of sound, and Edlen felt isolated from the world.

"Why would a man do something so terrible?" Edlen said out loud, breaking what silence fell over the fire itself. He glanced up at Radholf.

"What would drive a man to ruin my life? A man whom I had never met; a complete stranger! What sort of man would do such a thing?"

Radholf gazed into the fire for a moment.

"When men who drive the forces of the world make decisions based only on logic," he began, "then a world filled with suffering they create." He took another sip of his tea. "It is when we begin to forget to look from the other side, to see what our actions can do for others, that we lose the faith in ourselves as men. It is this downfall, the narrow vision of doing only what benefits yourself that destroys trust among friends. And when you lose trust, love fades. The love that is meant to exist among all of us. A unity that collects the goodness in our hearts for a common purpose. The purpose to grow, and live, and to better our world."

The rain continued to *pit-pit-pat-pit* around the small camp. The world, filled with corruption yet holding on to the hope of goodness, now seemed to be sitting idle. As though resting on a balanced point in that the smallest action could determine the fate of so many. Yet now, all around them seemed empty and restful.

Radholf's words gave Edlen his answer, and he had much to ponder on as his eyes grew heavy. Though the fire's warmth seemed weak, it was enough to allow Edlen to find sleep and ready for the next day's travels.

The majority of those days were wet and soaked. It rained often, but a few breaks would come and go. The sky teased of relief, but as soon as hopes ran high, it taunted the travelers and opened its rain gates once more. It was a miserable way to travel in the rain, and rarely did they stop in a place that allowed them to rest and dry out. The musky smell of his clothes bothered Edlen almost as much as the chill. His spirits hung low.

"Sons of Vlaten!" Oatikki shouted as the next round of rain showers began. "Give us a break! Let us be. We are all washed out now..." he said under his breath while looking up at the sky.

Despite Oatikii's request, the rain continued steady into the afternoon and evening of that third day. Every inch of their clothes, every corner of their bodies were soaked. Their clothes hung heavy on them, and Edlen found it cumbersome to take each step.

"We are deep in the Bjornwood Forest now, my friends. Keep a weary eye as this place can be a bit more wild than the rest of the Gronndelon," Radholf said. They continued up a dirt path that began to stray away from the river to the top of a hill. It was not an easy climb as the rain had formed with the road, and gave birth to thick, slick mud. At the top of the hill, a small path continued up a second tier to the east that led to a tall set of stone steps. The steps curved around a short cliff face, but beyond the trees on the side of the hill stood tall a stone tower.

"Ah! Eastern Watch Tower. An ancient tower built in the first era, to watch the Rhim mountains. At the top, you can see for miles and miles in every direction!" Radholf explained.

"Yeah? Not in *this* weather," Oatikki added.

"Either way, this will be our shelter for the night. It will be dry and safe enough to build a fire. Follow me!"

Edlen liked the sound of this. A real shelter, and who knew what they would find! Radholf tied his horse to a tree at the base of the steps.

"He will be well enough here as there is no room in the tower. Better he be here sheltered than up high and exposed." Edlen followed Radholf, and Oatikki behind him, as they made their way to the steps.

The stone was covered in a fine moss on the edges. The rain had added a coat of slime on their surface, making them difficult to keep a solid footing. They wound back and forth as they climbed the steep rock face, and hanging moss and vines hung along the edges of the rock faces surrounding them. They approached the top of the cliff, and found the tall tower looming into the cloudy sky.

At the base of the tower was a wooden door that was broken and decayed. Vines hung all around the entrance, keeping it concealed and not easy to find.

The base of the tower was nothing but quiet. It was filled with a solid silence, a void with no signs of life. Dust had settled in every nook, filling the cracks of the stone floor.

BOOM! A sudden appearance of Oatikki's battle-ax burst through the rotten remainders of the door, clearing the way for the three weary travelers. The tower, whether it wanted or not, suddenly had company.

Inside they found themselves in a circular room with a set of steps that led up in a spiral around the outer edge of the tower, and to their left, a set of straight steps that led down.

"Each tower had its own small dungeon for when any enemies were caught trying to sneak across the borders. It would be wise to stay out of such a place." Radholf said as he glanced at Edlen.

"Why? What is down there?" he asked.

"Foul memories mostly. But this tower might have other secrets it hasn't revealed yet. We need to stay together."

They looked around the room they stood in. A few wooden crates dotted the far edge, all were empty save a little straw here and there. There was an old rotted table and a brass lantern that had long been empty of any oil or light.

At the base of the steps were a pile of crumbled stone. Oatikki broke up the crates in to smaller pieces for a fire, and Edlen and Radholf gathered what straw they could find for some softer bedding. The room smelled old and the dust was light enough to make Edlen's nose itch. There seemed to be a sickening stench coming from the stairs that led down. But before long, the fire burned away the strong odors and gave warmth to the small circular room.

The wind blew in from the door and was a bit chilly. It fed the fire though, and kept it burning bright and warm all evening. The fire's smoke rose up the tower, swirling around to follow the stairs going up, up high. It eventually found its way through some top level of the tower. Their clothes were hung to dry next to the fire, and their bellies were filled with warm food and heavy biscuits Radholf had saved. Edlen quickly dozed off on his soft bed of straw, in the dark dusty tower high on the hill in the depths of the Bjornwood Forest. Now, the tower that has seemingly been vacant for centuries had new visitors to enjoy its shelter. It did its best to protect its guests from the wind, and the only sound Edlen could hear as his eyes closed was the crackling fire just a few feet away.

Edlen slowly opened his eyes as his ears perked up to a sound near by. It sounded like a call echoing off the stone walls of the tower. He slowly sat up and looked around. The fire was dull but still flickering, and the light in the room had shrunk significantly. Both Radholf and Oatikki laid asleep near by.

Oatikki was snoring loudly, but this was something they were all starting to get used to. But over the snoring, the call continued. It was faint, though Edlen could make it out. *"Hello?"* it called out. A few moments passed and he heard it again. *"Hello? Is anyone up there?"* It sounded small, like a little girl calling for help. Edlen got up quietly and took a few steps. It was difficult to make out the direction of the sound in the stony round room. *"Please help! Anyone?"*

This time it was obvious, as Edlen took a few more steps towards the dungeon stairs. The stairs led down into a dark shadow of which Edlen could not see the bottom. He took the first couple of steps down, kicking small grains of crushed stone crumbling down the stairs. The stench from what laid before him was far fouler than he recalled. Not of green or fresh, not of anything living. This smell was reek of death.

"Edlen!" Radholf said, suddenly standing behind him at the top of the steps. "What are you doing, lad? What did I tell you?"

"But, Radholf, I heard a voice! Someone is down there!" Radholf's face turned grim. Oatikki came up behind them, also looking quite concerned at this news. He turned quickly and grabbed a piece of wood, wrapping some spare linen around and lighting it on fire.

"A voice, as a voice of a child?" Radholf asked.

"Yes! A little girl..."

"Calling for help, no doubt..."

Edlen nodded. Oatikki approached the top of the stairs and handed the torch to Radholf, who drew his sword with his other hand. He took a few steps down and the torch suddenly lit up the bottom of the steps. A small landing led to an opened iron gate. They approached the gate and tried to peer in. *"Somebody help me!"* the cries echoed. Edlen looked up at Radholf. His pale eyes gazed hard to try to pierce the darkness. The flames of the torch flickered light against his rough, silver beard.

"What is it?" Edlen said breaking the silence, now realizing it wasn't a little girl. The situation didn't make any sense, and Edlen's senses told him danger was around the corner. Radholf took a step back, eyes wide.

The flame of the torch weakened, and Edlen saw the dense darkness of the dungeon advance towards him. It was as if he was staring into a void, and it approached his being.

"Edlen! Get back!" Radholf yelled. "Do not let its darkness touch you!" he said yanking Edlen back towards the steps.

"What? What is it?" Edlen shouted as he stumbled against the stairs.

"Shadow Wraith!" Radholf said as he stared hard into the darkness. He closed his eyes, and began to chant in a deep voice in the language of the ancient Men.

"Mother of light, let us not fall into the void of night. Send back the shadow before us, let us show this darkness the might of your light!"

The flames returned to full strength on Radholf's torch, and the darkness crept back into the corners of the dungeon that laid in front of them.

"What cursed place have we come across?" Oatikki asked, grabbing two more makeshift torches.

Radholf looked up at the arch over the iron gate. There was writing on it, scratched into the rock. The first set were familiar to Radholf, in the language of the ancient Men of the Gronndelon. But below it, were markings that were not of any language men spoke, nor were they made by any tool crafted by men. No, these markings were made by the sharp edge of tooth and claw, in a language too ancient for most men to recognize. The writing above the door looked as follows:

ᛗᚠᛋᛏᛗᚱᚾᛈᚠᛏᛉᚺᚾᛏᛈᚹᛗᚱ

᛫⠂᛫ᚩ ¹

Radholf stepped back, and a wave of fear fell over his face.

"We have made a grave mistake." He looked down at Edlen, then up at Oatikki. "We must go, now!" He shouted as he took off up the steps.

"What?! What is it, Radholf?" Edlen shouted as he suddenly felt as though the darkness was reaching out to him from beyond the iron doors of the dungeon. He followed up the steps after Radholf, who stopped in his tracks in the middle of the circular room. From outside the broken door in the deep darkness of the wild woods, a deep *hooooowl* echoed into the tower.

"Wolves," Oatikki said, pulling out two battle-axes from their secure leather bindings on his back.

"Not just wolves..." Radholf said. High-pitched barks and yips could be heard echoing in the distance.

"Should I put out the fire?" Oatikki asked.

"No. He already knows we are here."

The pack grew louder and more clear as they approached. Cries of distress could be heard from Radholf's horse, and barks and growls accompanied it. Through torturous calls and terrible sounds, the panicked wails of the horse gave way to the sounds of a pack tearing into its midnight meal. Edlen's face drew pale in horror. Radholf grew angry. His grip tightened around the hilt of his sword and knuckles grew white. He shut his eyes tight as the sounds of his dying horse echoed through the halls. He took a long, deep breath and slowly loosened his grip again, regaining control of his anger. The barks and howls continued. Closer and closer, and the echoes changed to tell their presence upon the stairwell in front of the tower. Then all at once they stopped. Edlen drew his sword quietly.

"Who knows we are here?" Edlen asked in a whisper under his breath. Then in a jolting thunder, a deep and horrible *howl!* rattled the tower. Dust was shaken loose and fell from the tops of the room. Edlen dropped his sword, startled, and covered his ears from the loud howl that pierced his body. It was horrible, and it sent a paralyzing fear through him, who found himself helpless to do anything, but coward and close his eyes tight. He peeked out and Radholf stood there strong, not moving, not flinching. Oatikki began rolling his shoulders in preparation, as his axes were large and heavy, but very sharp. They glistened in the dim firelight. Edlen bent down and picked up his sword again. The rumbling howl had shaken him, but seeing his fellow fighters beside him gave him some amount of courage.

There was silence, and nothing but blackness at the door. No rain, no moon. Even the wind seemed to bow in respect to the great beast that stood just beyond the rotted, broken door. It seemed as though moments passed in silence.

No movement or sounds came from outside. Edlen was beginning to wonder if anything was out there at all, or if by some magic or spell, they had all imagined the sounds.

Then from the dark void, a voice rumbled deep.

"What sweet little rabbits have wandered into the home of the wolves? Do these rabbits wish to join us for supper?" The voice was nasty and greedy. Yips and laughs could be heard all around the tower. Edlen glanced over at Radholf, who took a step forward towards the door.

"And what would a large pack of wolves want two little rabbits for? We would merely arouse your appetite without settling her back down again!" Radholf said in hopes of fooling the beast as to their true count.

BARK! "I thought you said two! I clearly smell three rabbits from even out here! A lying rabbit makes me only hungrier!"

"Forgive us, your worthiness, greatest of the Wolven, hunter of hunters." Radholf replied in hopes of settling down the beast. "We simply want to pass along without incident. No need to split *hares* on such matters." At this, the wolf pack erupted in barks, yips, and laughter. But the giant beast *bark*ed suddenly with great volume, and all ceased to make any sound.

"You seem to know who I am, rabbit the fast-talker. But I do not have your name, if rabbits are still given names," he replied.

"I am Radholf, and I only ask for your pardon, Amarok the Wolfking."

"Radholf? Radholf the Verndari? My, what luck has brought such a rabbit to my home indeed!" A few yips echoed at this. "It has been a long time since you last slipped from my jaws. I will not let that happen again!" the deep voice commanded.

"Listen, your furriness," Oatikki interrupted. He clearly was running out of patience.

"We've given you your only option. Let us pass, or we will make our own way."

The crowds of wolves outside erupted in barks, howls, and growls. The Wolfking *grrrowl*ed in furious anger. Then in a deep, aggressive voice, spoke his final threats.

"You rabbits came into *my* home, threaten me with your tiny little teeth. You insult *me*, the Wolfking! My brothers will feast upon your flesh tonight, gnaw your bones for nights to come, and there will be *nothing* left for anyone to find of you.

"Your memories will be lost for the rest of time, O'Radholf the clever-less—you and your two rabbit friends. Oh, how you have given us your only option, little rabbits. Death awaits you, and here we come." At this the pack surged towards the tower, barking and howling, teeth gnashing and claws grasping.

"Run! Up the stairs!" Radholf yelled. Edlen headed up first, then Radholf and Oatikki behind them. As they ran up the stairs, the wolves burst in the doorway like a flood of black and gray fur. They swirled around the fire and rushed towards the stairwell. Running up, higher and higher, they passed a few small windows on the outer wall. Radholf counted them out loud, which seemed odd considering the horrible danger they were in at the time. But as they rounded the fourth window, Edlen suddenly realized the real trouble they were in. He looked up at the path ahead, and found that the top of the tower had collapsed in, and their stairs ended at a blockage. They seemingly were trapped.

"Radholf! The stairs!" Edlen shouted in terror, pointing upward. The reaches of the fire were at their limits already, and they had a hard time making out the faintest of shapes. But the wolves were gaining quickly.

"Nevermind the stairs! Five! Edlen, the window!" On the outside of the wall, just under the line of collapsed stone was the fifth window. Outside, Edlen saw nothing but darkness, but he knew they were quite high up.

"Through the window, Edlen! Jump now!" Radholf yelled as he pushed the poor boy out the window. Radholf followed, and just as the first wave of snapping white teeth reached out, Oatikki leaped last, and the sound of *clasp-clasp!* could be heard behind him.

Edlen fell through the black night, tumbling in every direction, waving his arms out in hopes of finding something to grasp on to. The barks and yelps began to fade as he continued to fall further down. The further he fell, the more he anticipated the hard ending, and the more he realized this was going to be the end. And in the moment, he thought to himself that perhaps finding death in this way was less tragic than being torn apart by savage wolves. And perhaps Radholf was sparing him of that torture by pushing him out the window. A little bit of Edlen was ready for the landing, ready to be over with all that had happened. Ready to end the struggle and pain.

His mind flashed in thoughts, as he desperately wanted his last moments to be with his family, the lake, his home. He could hear its waters now in the breeze. They grew louder. He suddenly realized Radholf's plan the very moment he hit the surface of the river.

Splash! Edlen sunk deep into the roaring river. Its cold waters rushed all around him, and he frantically tried to get back up to the surface. The river pushed him in every direction, spinning him around and hitting rock after rock. He gasped for air, reaching for anything to keep him afloat. Then one final blow to his head on a large boulder knocked him out cold, and he continued to float down the Vanalta River for miles on end.

Cough! Edlen choked up river water and spat it out, grasping for air. He rolled to his side, coughing and wheezing. He found himself on the shores of the river, and the grass felt cool to the touch. The morning sun shined a bright yellow on the bank.

"Boy! You are alive! We all thought you had died in some terrible accident!" a friendly voice said. Edlen looked up, and all around him were a group of men in clad armor. Their arms had tied around bands of red with a black Grizzly bear mark. There were six of them, and he frantically looked around for Radholf and Oatikki.

"Looking for your friend? He's over there, hasn't come to yet though." The soldier pointed to another group of men, four of them, standing in a circle a couple dozen yards away. Edlen jumped to his feet, which was far too soon as he nearly tumbled over immediately.

"Whoa, boy! Take it easy!" a soldier said helping him back up. Edlen ran over to the men and there laid Radholf on the ground, unconscious.

"Radholf!" Edlen cried as he shook the man. But there was no response. Radholf was cold as the river, and lost all of his color. Furthermore, he was limp as a dead crow. One of the men standing there looked at Edlen and Radholf with an intrigue expression on his face.

"Radholf, you say?" the man asked Edlen.

"Is this the Radholf of Riverwood?" The man asked more sternly. Edlen stared back at him, now realizing the possible danger of what he just said, hesitated. Another soldier leaned in and whispered in the man's ear. In an inaudible tone, Edlen could make out the words off the man's lips, "...and I bet this is the boy."

Edlen then knew they were aware of his story, and felt completely helpless. He looked around and found no sight of Oatikki. Thoughts of the river swallowing him up came and went as he began to lose all hope.

"Come with us, boy. I know a certain colonel that would be very interested in seeing you again," the man said grabbing Edlen by the arm. His arm was almost healed by this point, but it was still quite sore when he was grabbed.

"Radholf!" Edlen yelled in his last attempts of awakening his lifeless friend on the ground.

The Imperial soldiers led Edlen to one of the many carts they had in their caravan and bound him in rope.

"The man, too!" the soldier called out. Two other men picked up Radholf by his arms and legs, and carried him over to the cart. They tossed him up, and bound his arms and feet.

"Wouldn't want him waking up, if he really is not all the way dead yet!" one of the men said with a nasty grin that showed his black teeth, giving Edlen a wink.

"We're still a long way from Brisrun. But the trip will be worth it, certainly for us anyway! Ha-ha!"

CHAPTER IV

DRUNKARD'S BANE

— 13th of Kalddager, 1866 —

Edlen had his head slumped down. The road was still bumpy as they were heading out of the wild. His captors were rude, and took little care of him. They had traveled all day in the bright sun, and the rope around his wrists and ankles were burning, digging into his raw skin. Radholf laid on the floor of the cart, wobbling back and forth with the rhythm of the cart on the road, like some sort of bloated body filled with water.

Occasionally, he thought he would hear rustling in the underbrush around them. The path was narrow, and the overhanging branches of bush and tree often reached into the cart. The flies were terrible at this time of the day, and he found it difficult to fight them off. They bit hard and relentlessly, having so little to feed on during this time of the season. As the day grew, so did Edlen's aggravation. He tried to ask questions and make conversation, but he was largely ignored. Only if he was persistent did they recognize his existence, and it was through a whip or lash that they did so.

The day aged to evening, and the group made camp. Edlen was to stay in the cart next to the lifeless body of his recent friend in front of him. Foul thoughts and sorrow settled deep into his heart. Having lost his father, his family, and now his only friend, tears began rolled down his cheeks. But fear didn't seem to bother someone so low to the ground.

"Cough-cough!" Radholf spit water out of his mouth as he rolled over, grasping for air.

"Radholf! You're alive!!" Edlen shouted, as he crawled towards his friend. Slowly, Radholf's color came back to him as he took a few deep breaths.

"But how? You have been motionless all day! You should be dead!"

"Patience," he said, still trying to catch his breath. "Let me breath first!" He took the next several moments to collect himself. Then he sat up, as best he could.

The night air was chilled, and the cart they sat in was far from any warmth of a fire. Two guards sat near by, finishing their evening meals and starting their bottles of ale. Crickets chirped all around in the clearing they had found, and a large fire pit trailed smoke up into the leaves and branches of the nearby trees. Their under leaves lit up and dancing in the rising heat, giving a sense of shelter underneath.

"How can you be alive? We all thought you had drowned!" Edlen said breaking the silence.

"Ha, yes," he paused, collecting his thoughts. "My how I hate those wolves! Seems like every time I come across them, they find a new way to inconvenience me!" he said in reply. He looked around, and then noticed the rope around his wrists and ankles.

"Seems that we have found ourselves in quite a tight spot!" Then he noticed the guards and others in the camp.

"Hmmm," he said glaring at the group. "So we've escaped the den of wolves only to run right into the bear cave! Our luck certainly hasn't been with us, eh boy?"

"We are on our way to Brisrun," Edlen said, then leaned in close to Radholf. "To see the Colonel."

"I see." Radholf looked around to analyze the situation. "Then the Colonel we shall speak with! No sense in trying to do anything about it now. Our destination was Brisrun to begin with, and well, at least we have a ride there as it seems!"

"But what of the Colonel? They know who you are, and they know me!"

"Oh, do they! They may know my name, young Edlen, but they do not know *who* I am."

Edlen wasn't sure what he meant by this, and he wasn't so confident in his answer. But he did manage to avoid being eaten by the wolves, however, their situation wasn't much improved either. But they had no other choice. There was no way they could escape, not now with so many eyes and opposing blades. It seemed for the time being, they would simply have to wait until they arrived at Brisrun.

Rustling came from beyond the borders of the clearing, deep in the woods. Edlen thought he could almost hear a voice accompanied by it, but it was too faint and far away. The guards looked over in the direction of the noise, but the forest floor was concealed in shadow and darkness.

"Argh, must be a wild critter stumbling in the dark," one guard said.

"Ey. Get any closer and it'll be in some real danger!" said the second, chuckling.

Edlen gazed out in the darkness and heard only silence once more. He looked at Radholf, who had a look of content on his face.

"Arborians?" Edlen whispered.

"Nay, no Arborian would stumble so clumsily in the dark, nor would they curse any tree root in which tripped them," he replied with a grin.

"Then what? Not a wolf again, right?"

"Ha-ha, no, not wolves. I do believe our friend Oati is trying to quietly approach us. Though he is not doing it so well, and he won't make it in here. As soon as he sees the size of the campaign, if he hasn't already, he'll know to keep his distance."

Edlen smiled at the thought of big Oatikki stumbling and cursing his way through the dark, and was relieved to hear they had a friend watching over them. This gave him some sense of safety, both now and for their future.

As the night chilled, Edlen found it hard to sleep. He was certainly tired and his body ached, yearning for sleep. But his mind was too full of questions and doubts, uncertainty and fears. He couldn't get his mind off of the previous day's events as they replayed over and over in his head.

"Radholf?" he said in a small voice, keeping his volume just between him and his friend. Radholf stirred and groaned.

"Yes, young Edlen?" he said in a sleepy voice.

"What was that thing in the dungeon? The thing that sounded like a child?"

"Are you sure you're up for *ghost* stories now?"

"I cannot stop thinking about it...so curious, isn't it? Still, it does haunt me..."

"*Sigh...*, I suppose it wouldn't hurt to uncover their truths," Radholf replied, realizing he wasn't going to be returning to his slumber soon.

"They're called *shadow wraiths*, or sometimes referred to as *spøkelse-tyv* in the ancient texts. They're hollow beings whom have lost their souls. Because they have no soul, they crave those of others, yet any that they consume does not satisfy their hunger, as no soul could ever truly replace one you are given. So they wander for ages, never being able to satisfy the hunger.

"They live in the darkest corners of the world, for they fear the light. They cannot stand it, and are weak against it. But do not trust the weaker lights such as that of torches or lanterns, for they are able to extinguish the weakest of these.

"It only takes a single touch from their void for them to absorb your soul. This is what makes them so dangerous. Never ever allow even a small part of your body to fall into the shadow they cast. Upon a single touch, the skin turns pale white. Before nightfall, you too will begin your wandering about, looking for the unobtainable fill of the void. You become one of them. This is what was waiting for us in the depths of that dungeon. This is what was so dangerous down there."

"How did it sound like a child though? I was entirely convinced!" Edlen asked.

"When a shadow wraith absorbs a soul, it gains parts of the person it came from. Memories, personality, even how they sound."

A brief moment of silence settled upon them, broken only by the soft *crick-creek* of the crickets all around them.

"How could such evil exist in the world?" Edlen said in deep thought. Up until recently, his life had been a comforting blanket of balanced joys and happiness, with any struggle of driving away sorrow being at minimum. Until recently, he had not become so familiar with grief. Although it was relative, and if asked any days prior, he could tell you the hardest part of his life, but they all seemed so dwarfed now in comparison.

"The evil in this world exists because of the dark forces against our creation. The evil things of this world are the servants and weapons of the on-going battle. Yet, it was many years ago that this evil took the next step by corrupting the hearts of men, twisting things that were good into bad. It is this corruption that makes it the most dangerous kind of evil, and it has lurked deep in the hearts of men for ages."

Edlen laid there, listening to the warnings of his friend and fellow prisoner. It gave him much to think about, to ponder on. And so he did for several moments, before his thoughts turned once again to the obvious evil that lurked in the dungeon.

"What was it doing in a wolf den?" Edlen asked, fishing for a continuation of the story despite the horrors and warnings it had led to.

"Well," said Radholf, "the best I can piece it together, the shadow wraith and the wolves had struck up a kind of deal. You see, the wolves let the wraith stay in the dungeon where it could lure in humans. In exchange, the remains of the humans would be trapped, and find themselves cornered by a pack of hungry wolves. If the body is destroyed, or consumed in this case, it never gets the chance to transform into its own wraith. Quite a sweet deal for the both of them, really."

Edlen was shocked as to the cooperation between two such horrors. But it was the only sense he could make of the situation.

"You knew it was a trap, then?" he asked.

"I was quite suspicious of a shadow wraith when you said you heard the voice. But it was the markings above the door that gave away the trap. Above it was the name of the tower: Eastern Watch Tower. But below that was another kind of marking. The name of the Wolfking."

"Amarok." Edlen whispered.

"Yes, Amarok. He has long wandered the wild, hunting those that hunt his brethren. He is the only one of his kind that speaks the common language. He is far larger than even alpha wolves, and far more intelligent. Though he uses his projected fear to control his hunts, and is far too eager to attack. This was the weakness in his plan. He does not *think* through his attacks, as he really does not need to most of the time."

"He said he knew you, that you had narrowly escaped once before. What happened then?"

"Haha! That was quite some time ago! Perhaps a story for another time..." he said as he turned over to his side, trying to get comfortable. Edlen sat in the dark, with his wrists bound, thinking about how fortunate he was to have escaped such danger. He thought about where he was at, as it seemed his captors at least wanted to keep him alive. And the fact that Radholf had come to again to keep him some friendly company. He laid down on the hard wooden cart floor, and shut his eyes.

Feathers cutting through the wind could be heard right above him, and as they stopped, a raven landed on the branch. *Craaack!* It crowed as it looked down at Edlen. Edlen felt a wave of frustration and fear, and refused to open his eyes. The bird gazed down at him. *Craw!* It shouted at him, trying to get his attention.

Then two more swiftly perched on nearby branches. *Craw! Caw-caw!* They began to make quite a racket. He kept his eyes sealed tight with intense control. He couldn't cover his ears, only lay still in hopes they would leave, but he felt too vulnerable. Louder and louder they cried, and Edlen began to groan.

"Stop it!" he shouted with sudden force. Radholf jolted up and the two soldiers looked over. The ravens continued their cries and torment.

"Shut up, boy!" shouted one of the soldiers, but Edlen paid no attention. More birds flew in, and soon the tree was heavy with black feathered bodies and shining eyes staring down at him in the night sky. The tree had become a blackened cloud that hung above Edlen's head, and the noise began to hurt his ears. He couldn't take it anymore.

"Stop it! Leave me alone!" he kept shouting. Radholf sat, staring at Edlen.

"Edlen! What is attacking you?" he asked with a sense of urgency.

"Those ravens! They are so loud! They mean to harm me!"

Radholf looked around but saw nothing. Yet, Edlen heard their storm of cries as clear as a river against rocks.

"If you don't shut up, I'll shut you up!" came a booming voice of a soldier now standing next to the cart.

"Edlen. Relax your mind. Know where you are." Radholf advised to Edlen.

"But I *don't* know where we are, Radholf." Edlen said with tears beginning to stream down his face from fear and exhaustion. The crows kept echoing in Edlen's head, and the cloud of them in the tree above grew dense.

"Release it," Radholf said. "Let it go."

Edlen focused his mind, shut his eyes, and slowly exhaled. The cries of the ravens echoed off his mind, and faded away. He looked up to find the tree empty and still in the night sky.

"Not another peep!" said the soldier, who stormed off back to his resting place and ale.

Radholf looked at Edlen with concern.

"Your mind is poisoned, young Edlen. You have someone following you, do you not? Some evil has kept its eyes on you." Edlen gazed over to the sight of a black feather falling quietly to the edge of the cart, and landed without a sound.

"Someone is after you. You have some importance that is yet to be seen, young Edlen. Something I cannot see, or you have kept from me."

"I know nothing! I do not know what it could be!" he replied in a whisper.

"Hmm. And yet you are continued to be tormented. It may become clear yet, but at this time, we must take this as a sign of your importance. Wherever you go, I will offer my protection as best I can."

Edlen sat in the cart, staring into the night. Radholf leaned over and blew the raven's feather off the edge of the cart and into the grass below.

"Get some sleep boy. The raven has left for now."

Edlen laid down, eyes open, waiting for the worry to leave his mind and restlessness his body. As he laid there, he felt as though the hours crawled by. His thoughts he kept empty, yet sleep never found him. The soldiers had been long snoring through the dry air, and the fires dim and barely holding their glow. The night chilled, and the grasses gave off their dew. He would glance at the horizon, expecting to see some hint or sign of the sun's return, but it never seemed to come. Black shapes floated in the night sky, cutting black emptiness far above. They all moved slowly as if sailing ships across the horizon.

But one seemed to move quickly, and it appeared to be a trick in Edlen's eyes. Almost a very low cloud, black and starless. But it moved much faster than the others, and was much smaller, yet far too large to be a bird. The darkness made it impossible for Edlen to focus. Quiet and swift it moved, and before he could think too far on it, it had made its way beyond the tree tops and out of his sight. Edlen took a deep breath, and continued to lay in the cart, thoughtless, for what remained of the night.

It took a few more days of travel in the rough and bumpy cart before they started to see signs of civilization again. During this time, very little was seen. No signs or sounds were heard of possible tails or followers. No howls at night, and it seemed strange, but even the birds appeared to be avoiding the noisy campaign as it made its way through the dense underbrush of the edges of the wild.

The flies continued their relentless biting. Edlen was being covered in sores, and they buzzed loudly in his ears. Nestling into his hair, holding onto his body heat, he itched in great pain. The cold winds only made his sores worse, and the dusty smell of aging underbrush they were traversing made it uncomfortable to breath. The road was exhausting, and traveling like this went on for the next three days. Days of bug bites, of cold winds, of hard breathing. It wore him down physically and mentally.

In the early afternoon of the fourth day, they emerged from the outer edges of Bjornwood Forest, passing under another large tree of similar appearance. It also bore the same carving in its trunk facing outward, but it hosted no raven. The thought of leaving the wild was bittersweet for Edlen. He was now safe from the dangers of that in which found the wild a home and was returning back to the safety of civilization. Yet he knew what dangers civilization had in store for him.

On the eve of that night, they arrived at Brookstone, a small town on the edge of the now mighty Vanalta River. Since its birth, it had picked up flows from various streams and smaller rivers that came running down from the Rhims, each one adding to its strength and life. The town hosted a large tavern, a building greater in size than any other in the town. This is where the campaign stopped for the night.

The prisoners were kept in the cart in the outdoors, as no coin would be wasted on their comforts. Only did the selected soldiers gripe about who drew the shortest straw in taking watches during the night while the others stayed in the warm tavern, and enjoyed pints of ale and shared in song before passing out drunk.

"How far are we until Brisrun, Radholf?" Edlen asked. The sky was covered in a dull gray blanket of clouds that absorbed all color from the land and surrounding buildings. The night was still, no wind blew, and was very quiet. The sun was mostly set, and it was only the torches and passing Brookstone guards with their lanterns that gave any shapes away throughout the town.

"Hush up!" a soldier groaned. Edlen's voice carried far in such a still setting.

Radholf scoffed quietly at the guard, and turned his attention to Edlen and his question.

"No more than a day's journey on cart. By this time tomorrow, I anticipate our fates will have been decided."

"Why can we not run? Why have we not tried to escape? It is dark enough now..." Edlen said in a very quiet whisper.

"Patience, lad. Does a cornered snake lash out or run at every moment that passes? No, it stays curled up in the corner and waits."

"Wait for what? To be struck down?"

Radholf looked at Edlen with the slightest hint of grin.

"It waits for the out-stretched hand to get just close enough before making its strike." Radholf sat back and tried to get comfortable again, as best he could on the hard cart floor.

"Remain patient, Edlen," he said in a continued whisper. "Sooner or later, the out-stretched hand will get too close. Then the snake will bite." He closed his eyes and was silent for the rest of the night.

Edlen laid in the cart, looking up at the gray night sky. His homesickness settled in heavy that night. He wished so much he could go back to the life he had. He missed his home, his comforts, his bed. He desperately missed his family, and the bitterness of their loss sparked rage in his heart. The hope of seeing his sister and mother again had begun to forsaken him, leaving him with an overwhelming feeling of doubt. He felt broken, as though his mind had fallen apart, and he was left to lay in the pieces of his own sorrow. It was a very bitter night for Edlen. As his tears pooled and dampened the boards he rested his head on, he drifted on the edge of sleep until dawn brought the day he had been in fear of.

It was midmorning when the group started off again. After leaving Brookstone, they were only on the road for a few hours before finding themselves at the gates of Brisrun. It was surrounded by a large stone wall, topped with a wooden walkway and roofed with wooden shingles. The walls were all covered in ivy and running flowers. The road had left the roar of the Vanalta River some time back. The entrance to the city was far inland from where the river was released into the Great Sea.

Brisrun was a wide city with its northern border as shores and beaches. Many of these were stone walls built on top of rock faces that towered out of the surface of the crashing waves. There were three major ports along the cliffs where the city opened up to the sea. Many piers stretched their fingers out into these bays, the largest of which was the main port for large ships to come and go. The other two were primarily used for fishermen and small vessels for travelers.

The city was in no way crowded or packed, not like Furskarth was. The market was a wide open place with cloth tents and stone walkways. The smell of fresh fish filled the air, and the sea danced on the winds. There were hundreds of merchants, selling their spices, tools, pottery, furs, and many other goods. There was quite enough of anything one might think to buy, and everything one could need could be found here.

As the cart passed through the city gates, Edlen felt the looks and glares of the city-folk staring hard at him. It was strange to feel like a criminal, even to his own brothers and sisters of the Gronndelon. Some looked at him with disgust, yet others showed more of a worried feeling, almost compassionate and pity, for there was much controversy in the presence of the Empire. And it had become clear to many: that prisoners of the Empire did not necessarily mean criminal acts against the folk of the Gronndelon. But no one would challenge such a large campaign riding through the gates.

Through twists and turns, down main streets and past stone buildings, they made their way to the Castle Graywater. It was the largest structure in all of Brisrun, and was the only one visible from outside the city walls. The outside was covered in clay, giving the castle a gray color, which was flaked in certain corners and edges revealing the stone blocks underneath.

The front of the castle began with a very wide set of stairs that began in a curve, and slightly narrowed at the top. On either side, every several steps, stood guards equipped with spears and swords. The edges of the stone steps stood tall walls and large bowls of fire to light the way, day or night. At the top of the steps was the entrance to the castle, six tall stone pillars that held an overhang forty feet high. Globes hung down between the pillars, also lit with fire.

The Imperial soldiers pulled Radholf and Edlen out of the cart, and marched them up the steps. The guards on the stairs didn't flinch, staring only directly in front of them, almost statue-like and lifeless. They approached the double-wooden doors fortified with iron brackets and trim. The soldiers pushed the doors open, revealing a vast hall, as tall as it was wide, and twice as long. The floor was a beautiful mosaic, telling the story of Valmundur's return from Gamli-heim as he crossed the Great Sea, battling sea monsters and giant water wisps, and finding the place that is now Brisrun.

Surrounding the giant mosaic was a natural stone border. The sides of the hall were double-storied walkways, the second of which kept a beautifully trimmed stone rail. High above these walkways were stained glass windows, most of which were colored various tones of the sea. The sunlight shown bright through these windows, and gave strong columns of light gleaming into the center of the hall, lighting up the mosaic floor in bright twinkling colors. The castle was to serve as a testimony to Brisrun's wealth as the central trading port of all the known lands of the west, and it certainly did it justice.

At the far end of the hall was a tall platform with half a dozen steps leading up to the Jarl's chair, in which the Jarl of Brisrun was occupying. The sound of the doors opening echoed in the large stone hall. The soldiers led Radholf and Edlen across the hall and to the front of the Jarl's seat.

"Jarl Halvar of Brisrun," the first soldier said in a bow.

"What crimes have these two committed in which require them to be bound and dragged to my feet?" he said looking quite concerned. He was an older man with a long beard that was braided into two strands, silver white. He was built, though, and seemed wise and kind-hearted.

"They are wanted criminals by my Colonel. May we take them to see him so he may decide their fates?"

"Humph! Letting an outsider decide the fates of my own kin, within *my* walls!? Tell me, Imperial. What crimes *did* they commit to be so wanted by your ...Colonel?"

"We believe this boy escaped previous imprisonment after killing a soldier of the Empire in cold blood. And this man to have helped him escape."

"That is not at all accurate!" Edlen piped up.

"Hush up, you!" the soldier yelled, kicking his legs and forcing him to kneel on the ground.

The Jarl looked painfully at Edlen, then at the soldier with a glare.

"Hmm," he said in response. "You may take them to your leader, but I will not hear of any such harsh punishment as death to my own people. Report back to me what he says, and I will decide if it shall be allowed."

"Yes, sir, Jarl Halvar," the soldier said with a hint of sarcasm, and they turned to lead Edlen and Radholf away.

"You Imperials keep pushing the lines..." the Jarl added. "Push any further, and I *will* push back." The soldier stared at the Jarl over his shoulder for a moment, then nodded with a sly grin and continued to lead the prisoners to the hallway on the right.

They walked down a hall and turned to climb a set of spiral stone stairs. At the top, they entered the first room on the left. The room was low and had a long wooden table with a large desk in the far back. At the head of the table was a face that had haunted Edlen's thoughts since the day he lost his father.

A sudden wave of fear and anger erupted in Edlen's heart. He wanted to lunge at him and steal the breath from his lungs, taking any life a cruel man like that might still possess. Yet, at the same time, he felt timid and fearful. Helpless and vulnerable. He felt paralyzed, and he stared down in a tunnel at the man sitting at the end of the table.

"Here is the map of the Rhims you asked for, Colonel," said a man, handing Colonel Remus a large roll of paper.

"Thank you," he said, laying it down to his right on the desk.

Remus looked up, and for a moment, didn't recognize who was being brought to him.

Then his face lit up.

"Well! Look at the little rat which has wandered into the lions' den!" His focus changed from Edlen to Radholf.

"And look, you brought a friend. Radholf of Riverwood?"

"Colonel." Radholf replied, keeping his proper manners.

One of the soldiers approached Colonel Remus and spoke quietly into his ear. Remus didn't act entirely pleased, but nodded and dismissed the soldier before he had finished his whispers.

"Well, son of Eldor," he said with a snide attitude, "it seems as though the Jarl of Brisrun will keep you alive for a bit longer. Seeing as this is not my realm to judge, but you *are* my prisoner now. I will take you to Nýland and let the family of the soldier you killed decide your fate." He grinned at Edlen. "And I cannot imagine they would just simply forgive and forget."

"Forgive and forget?" Edlen said with the erupting fire growing strong within him. "No, I would not expect the family of a man who had been killed in cold blood to simply *forget*. And I would fully expect a burning desire of revenge to have taken them over completely. A fire that would not die down until the scum that took a life of the innocent suffers beyond imagination." Edlen's face was burning and his heart pumping hard.

Colonel Remus sat in his chair, grinning wide. He leaned forward, focusing his attention to Edlen.

"You were nothing more than a splinter in my thumb. Then you showed yourself, and here you are. I will cast you into the ocean, and you will not hold a single memory in my mind as I live the rest of my days, ridding the world of other splinters like you." Then he leaned back into his chair.

"A splinter, in the wrong place, can lead to a very painful death," Radholf spoke in support of his friend. Remus gave notice to Radholf.

"Radholf. The wise? What would an old man have such interest with a brat like this?" Radholf held his tongue and kept his face without expression.

"Very well, you shall join him and fall under the same judgment." Colonel Remus waved them off in dismissal. As they began their leave, he spoke up again.

"Oh! Speaking of splinters," he continued, "your mother *was* quite a sharp one! But as all annoyances I have come across, they eventually can be broken. I will say she gave my soldiers quite a run! Ha-ha! Many of them went to bed quite worn out before she broke, but broke she is now. Almost a waste of the leather whips they wore out." Edlen stood still, feeling the flames of fury burning through his veins, tears rolling from his cheeks.

"Your sister was quite a bit easier, of course. Too bad you had not arrived a few days sooner. Could have sent you on the same ship to Nýland. No matter though, as you won't *ever* see them again," he finished as he returned to his work.

Edlen couldn't breathe, he was so stunned in rage. With his face boiling, heart broken, yet another burlap sack was pulled over his face.

He was thrown into the cell hard as the guard held onto the bag, whipping his head backward as he fell to his knees and bound hands. The cell floor, walls, and ceiling were of stone blocks, and the floor was covered in dirt, moss, and other matters that smelled too horrible to imagine what they were. *Clank!* The guard locked the iron door, which had a small barred window, letting very little light in. He ran to the window and tried to look around at the most extreme angles possible.

There were multiple cells lining a long aisle, as the doors told, and hanging lanterns gave a grim lighting. The entire place was very humid and stunk rancid of filth and grime. He couldn't see much, but knew another prisoner was being tossed into the cell beside him. He assumed and could only hope it was Radholf. *Clan-clank!* The other door shut and locked, and the guards left. Moans of pain and agony could be heard echoing through the chambers.

"Radholf?" Edlen cried out.

"Yes lad! I'm right next to you! Move to the back of your cell!" he called out. Edlen went to the back and found a chipped away block of stone that had eroded enough to give a small gap between it and the outer wall. There, through the small gap, he could see Radholf's face waiting for him.

"Radholf! What are we to do?" he said with a great deal of panic and pain on his voice.

"Patience, lad! It is hard to see any light in such a dark place, but our opportunity is approaching! Fear not, young Edlen, as there is much that is at work around us! Try to keep composed, it will not be much longer."

Edlen sighed heavily.

"I do not see how things could possibly work out from *here*. We are prisoners of the Empire, who intend on *killing* us the moment we step foot in Nýland!"

"That moment will never come to us," Radholf replied. "Now try to get your rest, as you'll be needing it quite soon."

Edlen leaned back against the cold stone wall at the back of his cell. His thoughts stayed low, and he felt completely helpless against the desires of revenge. Hatred burned bright in his heart, and it was tormenting his mind and body. He stared at the cell door in front of him, locked tight. In the corner straight ahead, he noticed a black object. A raven feather rested in the dirt and dust. It was banged up, mangled in a mess. Yet it brought with it darker thoughts and hollowness to his heart.

"I hope I get my chance to take back what was taken from me..." Edlen said out loud, intending only for Radholf to hear it. He needed to get his hatred out, it burned too brightly to be contained.

"Take back?" Radholf replied. "You are owed nothing, young Edlen."

Edlen stared through the small hole between their cells.

"I want to be staring into his eyes as I take his life. So he knows what pain I have suffered. I want that monster to suffer as I have."

"Monster!" Radholf said shockingly. "That is no monster! He was neither crafted nor birthed behind any gates of fire and darkness! He is but man! The same as you, myself. The same as your father." Radholf knew Edlen would not take that easily.

"How could you say that?" Edlen shouted, his words echoing through the stone walls of the prison, "after what he has done? Only such evil could come from monsters!"

Radholf took a moment for Edlen to regain control of his feelings. Then he continued, hoping Edlen would understand fully the nature of man, as any boy his age struggles as they begin to comprehend.

"A darkened heart gives birth to darkened thoughts. These thoughts, as each of us struggles with, may slumber in some dark corner until eventually they are awoken through our actions. If willed strong enough, we *can* defeat them. But it is often too easy to let them slumber. This is the greatest lie we lead ourselves to believe, my boy. That we are not what our thoughts are filled with, and thus not what our hearts birth. To have a corrupted heart *is* the burden we carry. It is the fiercest battle we face. It is the battle we face within ourselves. A battle we fight every moment.

"Some men have stronger wills. Some men have darker hearts. The challenge is never equal, but a challenge we all do face. This is difficult, but crucial to understand. The sooner you grasp this, Edlen, the better your world will become."

Edlen sat deep in thought, trying to fully understand all that Radholf had explained. As his thoughts placed him between himself and the Colonel, echoing down the hall, a prisoner began to sing a song as his days were numbered:

Born in fire's breath, and you defy your sentenced death,
rise from the ashes, prepared for war.
Release me, fall my chains, seal my fate!
Take me with you when you go.

When death is drunk on my brother's blood,
And reaching out for a cup of my own
Bring me back to join your ranks.
Take me with you when you go.

Make rise the sun in our endless night,
bring an end to the darkness fight.
Make fall the halo of the dead.
Take me with you when you go.

Edlen sat in his cell, listening to the words their fellow prisoner sung. It was deep and powerful, full of passion. It brought to him a realization of something bigger than himself, something he didn't quite understand. Parts of it made him curious.

"Radholf, who is he talking to?" he asked through the small hole in his cell.

"Have you not heard the legends? The Good King, at the time of his death, spoke of a prophecy. He was the purest of heart, and in the final battle of the Dökkári War, was the only one resistant of the spread of corruption that infected all of those around him.

His heart remained untainted, and spoke of a great warrior who would rise from the ashes of the fallen. One who would declare the final war against all evil. All those who had pledged loyalty to the destruction of evil before their death would be brought back from the grave and made whole again, to join in the final battle. At the end, any who fight the good fight will be taken to live in the great halls above.

"This man who sings has already made his pledge, and he is about to be sent to rest until the great warrior comes. He sings now, in hopes that he will be given a chance to fight along side so he may one day join those in the great halls."

"I want to fight," Edlen said, "I want my chance to take back what was taken from me."

"A war with evil cannot be won with such hatred. Revenge is a weapon of the wicked, not its bane. This is the battle we fight today. And it is one that many do not realize, or struggle so greatly with."

"That man deserves to die. He took my father's life. He took the life my family lived. He deserves at least the same." Edlen said in a furious wrath as he did not want to hear what Radholf had been telling him. He threw his back hard against the stone wall and scoffed at their conversation. He was in no way ready to just walk away from the monster that had destroyed his life. There they sat, in silence, for the next several hours.

"Ha-ha-ha! I bet half of them will be dead by morning!" Edlen startled awake to the sound of a drunken guard's conversation with another drunken guard. They stumbled down the center hallway, peeking in at each cell.

"So...you wanted to see your friend at the end here?" one of the guards asked a third individual following them. "Yes, I wanted to bid him a final farewell before he is sent off tomorrow," said the familiar voice. It sounded dry and the low tone echoed off the stone walls, clear as day to understand. Edlen stood to his feet as he watched Oatikki pass his door, who glanced at him with a wink.

"Edlen!" Radholf whispered through the hole. "Sit down and pay no attention!"

"It is Oatikki! What is he doing here?" Edlen whispered back.

Radholf smiled.

"Giving us our opportunity." He then proceeded to the front of his cell, and pulled out some dried mushrooms he had hidden in a small pocket.

"There you are my friend!" Oatikki said to the poor man in the last cell. "I came to say my farewell wishes."

The man in the cell peeked out with a puzzled look.

"I do not know you!" he said in a nasty voice.

"It's me! Your old friend Grendlar!" Oatikki continued.

"Leave me be, fool! I don't want my final hours to be wasted on such stupidity," the man replied back.

"He has obviously lost his mind!" Oatikki said to the guards. "No sense in staying here then. Thank you for this chance," he said as he started back down the hall, heading to the exit door. As he passed Radholf's cell, he stopped suddenly. Glancing in, he could see Radholf stuffing mushrooms into his mouth.

"Hey!" Oatikki shouted. "This man's eating mushrooms! He's not supposed to have anything of the sort in here!" he shouted as he pointed at Radholf. The first guard quickly (as quickly as a drunk man could), unlocked the door and swung it open. There stood Radholf with a mouth full of mushrooms, stems sticking out of his lips, and two more fist fulls.

The guard quickly yanked the mushrooms out from his hands.

"Give those to me!" he shouted and took his leave of the cell. *Clank!* The guards locked the iron door.

"Thank you, friend," the guard said to Oatikki. "Here, have some! These look delicious..." the guard offered as he handed a few to his fellow guard.

"Very kind!" Oatikki said as he took a couple and tossed them back, swallowing them in a single gulp. The guards followed his lead and ate every last one

Radholf had. Without a moment gone by, both guards began coughing hard, gripping their stomachs.

Blood sprayed from their mouths, splattering on the door of Radholf's cell. Hunched over, they both took a couple of steps towards the exit door before collapsing entirely on the ground. Motionless, pools of blood slowly spread from their mouths, soaking into the stone floor. Oatikki stood over them, waiting to make sure they were really dead. He bent down and fished the cell doors' key from one of the guard's pockets. *Clan-clank!* He unlocked Radholf's door.

"Oati! My friend!" he said with a hug. "My, how I am glad to see you! What is this, the fourth time this has worked?"

"Drunk and eager, always..." Oatikki replied.

"Come! Let us get our other companion out!" Radholf said with a grin.

Oatikki opened Edlen's door next, and he stepped out to see the two guards lying dead on the ground, blood pools under them.

"But how? Both you and Radholf ate the same mushrooms!" Edlen asked Oatikki.

"Ah! The mushrooms, yes!" Radholf replied. "Drunker's Bane as most who are well-adverse with fungi know it. Toxic only if consumed with spirits or wine! The more consumed, the stronger the toxin. And based on their behaviors, even just a single cap would have meant their end."

"We had better get moving if we want to keep our absence a secret as long as possible," Oatikki interrupted.

"But where will you go?" a prisoner asked, his voice echoing down the hall.

"Never mind him," Oatikki said. "Let's get moving."

"You won't make it far!" the prisoner shouted. "You have nowhere to hide!" Radholf looked at Oatikki, who nodded in the direction of the door showing his impatience. Radholf stepped over one of the dead guards and approached the door at the end, and the opposite side of the aisle from his recent cell.

He looked in through the bars on the door and saw a scrawny man with wild, thin hair. His skin hugged close to his cheekbones, and his green eyes bulged out and dark-green tattoos swirled out from the edges of his eyes and into his temples and tops of his cheeks. He had a thin mustache and a thin braided beard. He was sitting in the middle of the stone floor, hands bound in cloth and chains. He was glancing up at the door with his eyes only, not lifting his head past what was necessary to make the view. Radholf studied him for a moment.

"And what would a wizard have to propose we do? What route of escape would such one know that I would not?" Radholf asked him. The wizard grinned slyly, then dropped the grin in sudden seriousness.

"Release me, and I shall show you," he said in reply.

"I do not trust this fool," Oatikki said sternly. "Let us leave him here to rot, we can make our way."

"Oh?" said the wizard in a thin, high voice. "Will you make it through the ranks of their men? All by your lonesome? I was unaware that the strength of an Orc surpasses that of fifty men."

"What is your plan, wizard?" Radholf asked.

"Trust," replied the wizard. "A wizard never cheats a favor! Release me, and I will get you and your friend to safety."

"Friends..." Radholf replied. "The three of us, plus yourself, if you are inclined to join us in your *safety*."

The wizard lifted his head far back, not breaking eye contact with Radholf, then lowered it again.

"Deal," he said abruptly, with the sly grin returning to his face.

Oatikki grumbled, but unlocked the door much to his disagreement. Radholf entered and released the wizard from his bound hands, the chains falling hard to the floor, making a rattling sound that echoed sharp against the stone walls, and the bunched up clothes floated off his hands, revealing the patterns of swirls tattooed along his hands and up his fingers.

"What is your name, wizard?" Radholf asked.

The wizard glanced at Oatikki, and then at Edlen who stood behind him cautiously.

"Luno," he answered, looking back at Radholf.

"Well, Luno," Radholf said holding out his hand towards the door. "Lead the way!"

Luno approached the door of his cell and stopped to look at Oatikki. Oatikki stared back at him, not saying a word. Luno snickered at him, and with his head low and eyes forward, walked past him to Edlen. Edlen stared at him, not knowing what to say. He had never met a wizard before, and knew very little of magic. He was afraid of him, and shared a bit of Oatikki's concerns of their new fellow escapee.

"I am Edlen," he said as the wizard walked by him, hoping to start things off on a good note. The wizard paused and looked over at him. He was much taller than Edlen, but just as skinny.

"Nice to meet you, Edlen," he said in a queer way, as though his intent was to be sarcastic without anyone noticing.

Luno walked down to the end of the hall and approached the door. Radholf followed, then Oatikki and finally Edlen. Luno slowly cracked the door open and peeked out, looking up and down the hall that the door led to.

"First, we must find where they have taken my things," Luno said in a whisper.

"It would not hurt for all of us to get our things back," Radholf added. Luno glanced back and smiled. "Indeed!" he said. "Follow me."

The four walked down the hallway to their left, as quiet as possible. Their footsteps echoed well in the stone hallway, so stealth was proving to be difficult. At the end of the hall, light began to flicker from around the corner and the sounds of armor clanked as shadows were thrown back and forth against the far wall. Luno quickly darted to the next door and creaked it open. The others followed, rounding the corner just in time to avoid being seen, and slowly shut the door in silence.

Luno was frantically sifting through chests and barrels. He was completely avoiding the obvious weapon treasury they had come across, looking past war axes, long swords, daggers, arrows, and many more quite useful weapons in such a bind.

"It must be here! Where is it!" he said out loud with panic.

Oatikki had his ear pressed against the door, listening to the armed men march by their room.

"What are you looking for?" Edlen asked. Luno ignored him and moved on to the next chest.

"His staff, if I am not mistaken," Radholf said, as he picked up one of the sheathed swords Luno had rejected. Radholf gave himself two blades of his choosing before digging again in the next barrel.

"Here you are, Edlen!" Radholf said, handing Edlen Dragonsbane. Edlen sighed a deep relief, and tied his father's sword to his waist.

"Ah! My satchel!" Luno shouted. "Excellent! My staff *must* be around here some place!" he said as he continued to dig through the chests.

"Hey!" Yelling could be heard from down the hallway. Oatikki took a step back from the door.

"So much for keeping our absence unknown!" he said, taking out his two war axes, one in each hand. "They'll find us in here for sure!"

"Ha! I found it!" Luno said, holding up quite an old and twisted wooden staff. At the top, a dragon carved into the twists of wood, and a foggy white gem mounted in its mouth.

"Oh, good! Magic-hands found his stick. So are you going to blow them away with fire, oh, dragon bearer?" Oatikki said sarcastically.

"Oh no! I'm not that kind of wizard!" Luno replied with a grin and giggle, finding Oatikki's comments humorous.

"Not that kind of wizard?!" Oatikki fired back. "What kind are you then? The kind that offers no help or aid?"

"What *is* your plan, wizard?" Radholf asked, feeling a bit nervous.

"Trust me," Luno replied, handing each of them a glass marble from a small pocket of his satchel. They were clear with a hint of pale blue, and seemed to shimmer white in what dim light they did have.

"Do not drop these!" he said, putting each one in everyone's hands. "They are very rare, and I will not be able to protect you if you do." He returned to the center of the room, holding his staff and looking at the door. His eyes squinted, revealing the black crow's feet at their corners.

"Prisoners are missing! Sound the bells!" a soldier shouted from the dungeon. He looked down at the two dead guards on the floor and drew his sword. The tower bells began to chime out, and dozens of armed soldiers stormed the halls of the castle. Soldiers scanned the doors of the hallways until reaching the room where the four escapees were hiding.

Boom! The door flew open and there stood three soldiers looking in. The room was empty save a lonely soldier, fully dressed in armor, holding onto Luno's staff.

"What are you doing in here?! We have escaped prisoners!" the soldier in the doorway shouted.

"They are not in here!" the soldier replied. "I've checked the chests and barrels; the room is empty."

"Come! Keep looking!" The three soldiers continued down the hall. The lone soldier walked up to the door and peeked up and down the hall, then slowly shut the door again. He slid his hand down the staff. As he did, a clear veil fell from his head down to his feet, uncovering the soldier disguise to show Luno's self. At the same time, Oatikki appeared again sitting on a chest, Radholf standing in the corner, and poor Edlen ducked behind a barrel in the corner. The glass marble in Edlen's hand had been glowing bright white, and it suddenly faded away.

"What are these?" Edlen asked, handing it back to Luno.

"Lunar gems, young one!" he replied. "They store the moon's light and use it as a veil under my spell to hide those who possess it! Although I fear we may have used up what moon light they possessed, and will need to gain their strength back before becoming useful once more."

"How did you change into a soldier? You were so convincing, my eyes must have really been cheated!" Edlen said.

"Illusion is his type of magic, is it not, Luno?" Radholf said. Luno smirked.

"Did you like the soldier? I crafted that one myself," he said looking back at Edlen.

"Black magic! Whose soul did you steal to get such a power?" Oatikki said angrily.

"No soul!" Luno replied in defense. "Only a drop of blood! No harm came from the gentleman I just portrayed. In fact, I know he is alive and well! Otherwise my crafted spell would not have worked! Here see! I keep the gem stained with his blood right here!" Luno pulled a small white crystal out from a mounting slot carved into his staff. It was stained dark red in its flakes and veins. He showed it only for a moment before dropping it back into his satchel.

"So what do we do now?" Radholf asked out loud.

"We wait!" Luno replied. "We wait for a few moments, then we return to the dungeon."

"What for?" Oatikki asked, with suspicions already high.

"For that is the way out, my big Orc friend," Luno answered.

Moments later, the door creaked open, and Luno peered around the corner. The hallway was quiet and empty, although it was certain the upper levels of the castle were still in a bustle looking for the escaped prisoners. They quickly made their way back to the prison doors, where two more guards stood watch just inside. The door was already pried open.

Luno lifted his finger to his lips, and slowly pulled out two daggers from hidden sheaths he had picked up in the recent room. One was gold in color, but made of a metal harder than steel. It was very sharp, and had a jag on the opposite side of the blade. The second was a double-bladed dagger, black, with crystal blue engravings on it. He turned into the room without making a sound.

Edlen sat crouched in the hallway, listening intently. Oatikki was fingering his axes, ready for action. Radholf waited patiently in silence. All at once, brief commotion was heard. *Slick! Thump. Slick!* Gurgling followed before a quiet *thump* ended the commotion. Luno stuck his head out, grinning.

"Come! The passage is safe now."

The four entered the dungeon where Luno had taken another cell key. He walked up to another occupied cell and opened the door.

"Go! You are free!" he said to the man sitting at the back of the cell. The man stood up, looked at Luno, and exited the cell.

"Thank you, kind stranger!" he said as he passed, then looked at Radholf and Oatikki.

"You have done me a great favor! Gods be with you!" he said as he ran past Edlen and into the hallway.

"What'd you do that for?!" Oatikki shouted at Luno.

"He is doing us a larger favor than what I did for him," Luno replied. He then walked to the end of the hall and opened the last door on the right. It looked like a cell from the outside, but inside was a hatch in the floor. The dungeon key unlocked it, and they found a long drop into a black abyss.

"The path awaits," he said holding his hands out toward the hole. Radholf approached, smiled at Luno, and slid in. Oatikki gave Edlen a nudge as he did not want to leave Edlen out of his sight. Edlen walked up to the hole and peered in. Nothing but blackness could be seen.

"Come, Edlen! The drop is not far!" He could hear Radholf's voice echoing from below, although it sounded quite far. Reluctantly, Edlen slid into the hole. Oatikki followed. Luno shut the cell door, slid into the hole, and pulled the latch shut as he followed down in.

On top of the outer walls of the castle, soldiers ran up and down with bows ready, eyes glued to the streets below. The sun had been long sunk past the horizon, and the night sky was clear and cold. Stars twinkled high above the city, which was dimly lit with lanterns that lined the streets, revealing the paths through the shops, homes, and businesses. The castle was lit up bright, and nearly every stone along the wall had some shred of light upon it. Shadows were many but none were completely dark. Escaping would be difficult for anyone.

"There!" one soldier shouted out. "A prisoner! Release!" Pointing down at the corner of the wall, just outside of the castle, a cloud of arrows rained down. Many missed their mark, but it didn't matter. Nearly half a dozen arrows stuck out of the back of the escaped prisoner as he collapsed to the ground.

Soldiers bearing sword and spear ran up to the man lying in a pool of his own blood. It soaked into the stone, winding down the paths between the laid blocks, expanding out. They approached, spears pointed. A group ran to the hatch he came from and peered in. An empty corridor remained quiet before them. They dropped in, one at a time, and continued to work their way back towards the castle.

On the far side of the castle, the Vanalta spread out wide as it opened into the Great Sea. On the western bank, a barred drainage pipe opened up, draining unused water into the mouth of the river. It trickled out, and echoing from deep within were the sounds of footsteps splashing in the shallow waters. From the dark, Luno peeked his head out into the night air, his breath a cloud that faded into the darkness.

CHAPTER V

SCURRY NOW

— 15th of Kalddager, 1866 —

Sounds of creaking crept out from the wooden corners. A beast of a ship rocked gently on the water, splashing against the thick wooden hull. Deep in the bowels of the ship, a low and damp cell sat empty, waiting for its next prisoner. Lined with old and musty straw, it stank of past decay and sorrow. Little light shed upon it. Its floor boards slippery and worn from the moisture; its bars cold and sharp with rust. It was a dark and cold place, with so little thought of comfort, it had sucked the will out of countless prisoners already.

A screaming cry broke the silence of the empty prisoner hold of the ship. A cry of a child, a little girl struggling to deal with the recent separation from her mother. A cry that told of a broken spirit, a world collapsing down around her. Broken slurs of words and syllables echoed through the empty cells as the two soldiers of the *Freeman* Empire wrestled the six-year-old girl to that waiting cell at the far end of the hull.

Clank-clink! One soldier unlocked the cell gate and with a grunt, threw Gracie with a harsh force into the cell. Being so light, she flew across the cell like some accident, and hit the back wall with a thud. A small splinter sound came from the impact, hard to tell if it was the ship or Gracie who suffered the damage, though the silence in her brief pause of her cries told more than any scream she could give. *Clank!* The rusty gate shut hard.

"Good to lock that *rat* in the cell!" one of the men shouted in anger.

"What, you cannot handle a little ship rat?" the other man said in mockery. "Ha-ha! She sure is a wild one! But save your strength, her *mother* is next..." he said, slapping the first man on the shoulder with a grin.

Gracie laid in the corner of her cell, her voice raspy and throat sore from her screams and crying. She was covered in sweat and tears, shaking violently from the trauma. All that she knew had been flipped upside down. Every man she had ever met before had been caring and polite, her world of comfort is all she understood the world to be. Her father, the one protector she could always trust and rely on, suddenly taken out from under her. How could these strange men from afar be so cruel? How could their hearts be so black?

Her mind floated between reality and nightmare, unsure of which it was in. Although it was all real, her heart tried to protect her from accepting it. Here she laid for moments, nothing but the sound of her raspy sobbing among a creaking ship.

Then the sound of the door opening broke again. Multiple footsteps came down the wooden steps with heavy shackles clanking against them. Gasps of air were trying to be caught from the next prisoner, her body exhausted from the crying, screaming, and beatings.

Into the dim candle light, a woman barely recognizable by her own daughter stepped down. Clothes torn and soaked red, she was led down the narrow walk-way towards the cell next to Gracie's. Giving no fight, for all the fight had been taken from her, she willingly followed to her assigned cell.

"Wait!" one soldier said. They yanked her chains hard, jerking the brace around her neck forcing her head to dip back suddenly. She found it hard to breath, and choked at the tightening against her throat.

"Not this cell..." the soldier said. "I do not want them next to each other. No, keep them separated by a full cell. This one!" he said, opening the door to a cell two away from Gracie. Separated by a single wall of rusty bars, no more than ten feet apart, Hellen looked up with blood-shot eyes at her little daughter. Tears rolled down her torn cheeks, the burn from their saltiness too familiar now. Between her wet and wrangled hair, Gracie's bright blue eyes met her mother's, filled with the same tears.

The men yanked hard on her chains to back her up, and shoved her into her cell. The chains were left on her, and the same *clank-clink!* locked her cell gate. Two of the men left without saying a word, the third spat at her in disgust, angry at what work it took to break her. With a few more steps up the stairs, the last man shut the wooden door at the top, leaving the broken family in silence.

The dull sound of the waves splashing against the other side of the hull filled the chamber. It took little time before Gracie reached out for some comfort.

"Mama?" she said in her broken voice, sniffling despite the stench of the ship's prison cells.

"I am here," Hellen replied in a very quiet voice, barely able to make it to Gracie's ears.

"Mama..." Gracie said again, this time breaking out into a heavy sob as the memories of their recent trials came back to haunt her. She began to shake again, fighting off the thought that this was not some terrible nightmare in which she could not wake from.

The sight of watching her daughter suffer was too much for Hellen to bear. She was a strong woman, but being out of reach to offer no comfort at all was by far a worse torture than anything physical any man could bring to her. To be chained down, locked in a dark cell, with just enough light to see her young daughter in such fear, this is what broke her spirit.

The moment was short-lived, as the door opened again and the next prisoner forced down the steps. They creaked and sighed heavy as a large Orc was led down in heavy chains. He also gave no fight, as the two soldiers who followed kept spears pointed at his back. He was led to the cell between Gracie and Hellen, and sat down with a hard *thud* as his large body rested against the back of the cell.

Gracie paid little attention to him after he sat down. He was a pale green, like most. He was completely bald, no hair on his head nor face. One tusk was broken off, only his left one remained and it had no rings on it. In fact, all of his rings were stripped of him as the multiple empty piercings across his ears and brow told. A single tattoo he had on his right bicep, a swirling pattern of twisted knots all the way around like a band. He sighed heavily and shut his eyes, knowing they would all be down there for some time.

The same sound, now becoming familiar, came from the opening door as the next prisoner was led down. This time, it was another girl, slightly older than Gracie. She was sobbing and scared, going where she was led. The two soldiers leading her took her to Hellen's cell, which seemed to be a cruel joke that she would share her cell with a girl not of her own. And this was more torture for Gracie than anyone else, seeing another girl able to find comfort in her own mother, and jealousy soon grew in her heart.

This girl looked similar to Gracie. Long blond hair that was once in a braid now fallen apart in a frayed mess. Light skin with light brown freckles, but green eyes rather than the frost-blue that Gracie shared with her mother.

The girl sat in the front corner of her new cell, eyeing Hellen through tears, afraid of the bloody mess Hellen had become. It made Hellen feel like a monster, to have a little girl look at her in such fright and shock. A monster born under the evilness of others, of those *men*. She was made into something she was never meant to be, and it made her hate herself for it. Hellen broke her stare at the girl and looked across her right to Gracie's cell.

Gracie had calmed herself to only tremors now, trying to catch a fresh breath of reality. Although grim and painful, they were both still alive. Hope seemed like a foolish thing to ponder on, but with the spirit of a woman such as Hellen's, though it may flicker, could never completely fade.

For the next few hours, more prisoners were gradually brought down and filled each cell. Each with their own story, each with their own reasons for being captured. Some may have deserved to be there for some were truly corrupt in their minds. Murderous monsters of hate, so sunken down in their ways that no mercy could be given from their own hearts, so they would receive none.

One such a man was tossed in with Gracie. His wrists shackled behind him, ankles only enough for him to take steps. As he sat up, he spat and swore at the soldiers as they locked the gates again. Like a wild animal suddenly caught in a trap, he thrashed about the cell. Hitting his head against the bars and shouting, he continued to slam himself against the gate. Gracie tried to hide in the corner, balled up, and trembling with fright.

"Will you calm yourself!?" the Orc shouted. He was quite irritated with the commotion.

"You have nowhere to go, your efforts are fruitless, fool."

The man suddenly threw his attention to the Orc. His eyes wide, still filled with rage, he pressed his face against the shared wall of bars, breathing heavily.

"And what is an *Orc* going to do about it?!" he shouted, showing his bottom teeth. They were rotting and he smelled horrible.

The Orc stood up and walked over to the same wall, his chains dragging along the floor. He was a good deal taller than the man, but lowered himself to meet eye to eye with the crazy on the other side. And there, they stared at each other for a few seconds before *BANG!* The Orc slammed his head against the bars hard, knocking the man flat on his back.

"Maybe *that* will shut you up," the Orc said as he returned to the back of his cell, sitting himself down. The man laid motionless on the floor, not making a sound. Gracie looked over at the Orc, who turned a glance at Gracie and gave her a small wink.

Ding-DING! Ding-DING! Ding-DING! The ship's bell rang loud and commotion could be heard on the deck some floors above. They were setting sail, starting their journey to Nýland. The boat slowly began to rock back and forth, making it uncomfortable in the hard cells. With no other light save the dim of the candles, it was difficult to keep track of time. Slowly, it seemed, the hours passed.

Questions raced through Gracie's mind as she began to come back to what was now her life, her reality. The heaviest of emotions had run their course, sorrow had exhausted her. So much uncertainty surrounded her, and what lied within the shadows of her fate crawled through her thoughts. The unknown was more frightening than where she found herself at the moment. As it grew on her mind, it soon became too much to contain in herself.

"Mama?" Her voice sounded like a little mouse stow away on the big ship, like it didn't fit in place. Having time to calm, the rasp had left her throat, returning her back to the sweet innocence that she was. No answer came.

"Mama?" she said louder. Silence fell over the cells, only the creaking and rocking of the ship could be heard.

"Mama..?" she said a third time, this time emotion returning to her voice as she held back more tears, afraid of the reason for the silence. Feeling very alone, Gracie's heart began to break.

"She is asleep," a voice came from her cell. The voice of the other little girl sounding not as childish as Gracie's, but still kind. Gracie blindly accepted this answer, as it was the best possible explanation for the silence, and one she could easily bear.

"I am Eira," the girl said. "She is your mother?"

"Yes," Gracie replied.

"What is your name?" Eira asked.

"Gracie."

"I am eight years old. How old are you Gracie?"

"Six," Gracie replied. It was good to have someone to talk with. Gracie had moved to the edge of her cell to get a better look at her new friend.

"Where are you from?" Eira asked.

"Riverwood," Gracie said, knowing that was probably the closest thing to home Eira might know.

"Oh!" Eira replied. "My Pa used to travel there on his longer trips! He would bring back warm furs. I live on the Lake Hámarki. Or did before..." she paused, not quite ready to talk about the events that led her to where she was now. There was an awkward silence between the two, not sure of what to ask next as it seemed to each that any question could bring back painful memories. And not wanting to relive any themselves, they were both at a loss of conversation.

"Huuuuuugh..." the man in Gracie's cell began to moan. Gracie quickly recovered back to her corner in the cell. The Orc opened an eye and watched what the man would try next.

He rolled to his side, moaning, sore and wishing his hands be free. Facing Gracie, he laid there for a moment before slowly opening his eyes. He stared at her for a few minutes, slowly coming to, not sure what he was staring at, and not entirely sure where he was. Once he realized a little girl was staring back at him (and with quite a frightful face), he managed to sit himself up.

His head hung low. His thin hair was long and draped over his face. His breathing was labored, and he had no shirt on. His belly bulged out, was greasy, and covered in dark hair. But it was his smell that was the most repulsive, and Gracie felt trapped to be in a cage with such a being.

"So..." the man began to speak, his words slurred in a half effort. "What has a little girl such as yourself done to find yourself in a cell with a killer like me?" He looked up enough to meet eyes with Gracie. His crooked brown teeth revealed behind a smile of gruff. Grace looked at his yellow-brown eyes, not speaking.

"Don't be shy, little ship mouse. I cannot do you much harm shackled like this..." he said, grinning as he twisted his back to show the chains and braces around his wrists and ankles. He shook his head from side to side, parting his long hair to the sides to reveal his worn and rough face. His nose was long, and he was covered in sweat.

"What is your name, little darling?"

Gracie did not answer, she only stared at the man. She was too afraid to say anything.

"Oh, come now! Did your mother not teach you to be polite? To answer an adult out of *respect*?" he said as his smile dropped from his face. Gracie looked to her left at her mother, still motionless in her own cell. Eira watched from behind her bars, scared for her new friend.

"Ha!" the man said. "Perhaps not! Either way then, Old Tom here was only looking for a little...conversation...to be had." His pause and emphasis on the word *conversation*, hinting fouler intentions.

But wanting to try to be brave, and certainly not wanting to be rude (although under the circumstances, it rarely seemed appropriate to worry about such a thing), Gracie answered.

"Gracie," she squeaked out. She would rather make friends than make those around her angry or offended, especially if she was sharing a cell with them.

"Ah! The mouse does squeak!" He said as he sat back down, relieving his position on his knees.

"So what are you doing *here*? Surely a sweet daisy like you does not belong in the dark of a ship like this..." he said as he began scooting across the floor to get closer. Gracie did not answer as his sudden approach made her nervous. Something told her he was as dangerous as he was strange.

"Huh little daisy?" he said with a quieter voice, inching closer. Gracie tried to make herself as small as possible, tucking herself as far into the corner of the cell as she could. Trembling in fright, tears began rolling down her cheeks again.

"Stay away from her!" Eira shouted. The sudden demand from the eight-year-old shook awake many of the prisoners.

"Old Tom just wants a smell of the sweet daisy..." he said as he leaned in, getting closer to Gracie's face. He was far too close for Gracie to feel safe.

"Gracie!" Hellen's voice shouted suddenly with fear and anger as she awoke to the horrific sight of such a foul man approaching her innocent daughter. Trapped in that cell, Hellen was useless to help. Yet the fires of hate and anger boiled up in her. The rage of that mother tiger wanting to protect her cub exploded in her.

Then a sudden jerk back on Old Tom's neck threw him against the bars. In a single moment, he was thrust away from Gracie's face, sweat and water flying off his long hair.

BAM! BAM! BAM! Multiple hits against the shared wall of bars between Gracie and the Orc's cell, and a heavy *THUD.* Old Tom was knocked out again.

"Stay close, little one." The Orc said, now standing at his feet. "Stay close in your corner and you need not to fear *him.*"

"Thank you!" Hellen shouted in relief. "Thank you for your kindness..." The Orc turned and looked at Hellen, giving her a slight nod of approval before sitting back down in his own cell. Gracie sat in her ball, crying from fear of what had just happened, of the sudden violence, and still feeling vulnerable.

"Gracie!" Hellen cried out to her. "Gracie listen to me..." Gracie gave no sign of response. Her body was beginning to slip into a shock and denial, her mind unable to handle what was going on.

"Gracie, stay strong! Do not give up hope yet!" This was the first time Hellen had the opportunity to speak to her daughter without soldiers or guards around to tell her otherwise, so she wanted to be direct with her words, of which she chose carefully.

"I know not what is to come. I can only tell you now to never lose who you are. Never forget what your father and I have always taught you. Keep your innocence, think with your mind, and trust in your heart. Be the light in the darkness of the world. In the trying times, Gracie, hold fast to love and never take what is not yours. Be the right when all in this world is wrong."

THUNK! The door at the top of the steps flew open hard as two soldiers came running down.

"Hey! What was all the noise down here?" one soldier demanded. He then looked around at each cell, and within each they received stares back from its inhabitants. All save Gracie's, where they found a knocked out murderer and a small child still in shock.

"Hey, look here!" one soldier said to the other. "Looks like he wore himself out!"

"Eh, but what of the girl? She looks like she has seen something terrible!" Gracie never broke her distant stare, never blinked.

"Oh, I'm sure she has!" said the first, laughing and elbowing the second. The second soldier did not find this as funny, and returned a serious look back.

"Oh, come on now! She is not bleeding or anything...she'll be alright! Besides, he's out cold!"

"Hmph!" he replied, walking back up the steps wanting nothing to do with what he may or may not have witnessed the ending of.

"Now not another word from any of you!" the remaining soldier demanded. "That thumpin' woke up most of the crew now! Any more of it and we'll be back down to *silence* all of you!" He concluded and returned up the steps. With a *thunk* the door returned shut.

Despite giving no reaction to any of what just happened, Hellen's words sank deep into Gracie's heart. Echoing through her mind, they became engraved into her being. They were words she would live by, words to define who she was, for in the darkest moment of her young life they had been the only beacon of light in her world. A light that would eventually become finely focused and ignite a burning fire within herself. For the rest of the night there was little sound that came from the prisoners.

The next morning woke the prisoners with the sounds of seagulls and footsteps walking across the floor above them. The wood creaked and sighed as soldiers and sailors went about their morning business.

Gracie opened her eyes. Before her, laid Old Tom still in the same place he had been knocked down onto the evening before. Although relieved, she remained in her corner, near the only thing that had proven to show any sense of care towards her. And for hours, she sat in her corner, staring at Old Tom.

Much of the remainder of the trip was the same. Soldiers would come down once a day to toss in food and water, and twice a day to do their routine checks. For days this went on, and from the events of that first night, any talking or noise making was prohibited.

One prisoner tested this. A nameless prisoner on the far side of the ship. He was determined to make his presence known, refusing to cease in his noise-making and complaining. It seemed his goal was to be released, to avoid finding what was at the end of this trip. As the soldiers opened his cell, it seemed he was to be given what he sought, though not the end he may have preferred. For he was led up the steps still in shackles and the door shut hard. Moments later, a loud splash came from the other side of Gracie's outer wall followed by the cheering of men high up on the deck.

After four days at sea, the soldiers finally decided to investigate further why Old Tom had still remained laying in the same spot. To horror, yet relief of Gracie, they found he had died days ago. His blood split and seeped into the cracks between the boards, giving no spill or pool, no signs of his demise. It took two men, but they too gave him to the same cold, deep grave as the noisy prisoner before him.

"Excuse me..." Hellen whispered from her cell towards the Orc next to hers, careful not to cause such a commotion as to bring attention to her from the guards. The Orc remained motionless with his eyes shut.

"Excuse me...sir?" she said again, hesitant to wake him, yet knowing she *must* talk with him.

"I am no *sir*" he replied with eyes remaining shut. But then he turned his head towards her and opened his eyes to give her little attention.

"My name is Dawoud."

Hellen looked around. No guards were present, and everyone else seemed to be asleep or paying no more attention than she wanted.

"Dawoud...I am going to need your help," she whispered in secret. Her frost blue eyes pierced through the dark red blood stains on her face. Surrounding them revealed her lack of sleep, her weariness of emotion and pain. But in them, the fierce determination of sacrifice for her child.

Her stare broke through questioning and doubt in the Orc's mind of her intentions.

"And why should I help you?" he said, resting his head back against the wall and shutting his eyes once more. Hellen scooted closer to the edge, nearly pressing her face against the cold, damp bars that separated them.

"Have you no children? Have you not eyes to see the innocence? I ask not to free myself, for my path is not to freedom. But I ask to give my daughter the chance to a life once taken from her. Help me set her free! I cannot do it alone."

Her voice was desperate yet firm, knowing this was the only way to save Gracie. It broke her heart to need to beg for the freedom of a six year old girl, and the unknown of what should become of her should this work gave her fear. Yet it was the knowing of what would happen if her freedom was not to be had that was certain, and any freedom would be a better life than that.

Dawoud returned his attention back to her, then stared at the floor boards of his cell. His thoughts dove deep as he remained motionless for several moments. Over time, his face turned to grief as what ever memories he had uncovered took their toll on his heart. He then looked over at Gracie, asleep in her cold corner.

"When the ship docks, we will have some time before they take us to shore. The slave master will divide us, each to where he sees fit. You will undoubtedly be taken to the castle and serve as a maid or in the kitchens. Your daughter...she will either be sold as a slave, or also taken to be trained as a king's servant. Neither are fit for a girl her age..." He moved closer to Hellen.

"Before they split us up, they will need to unchain our shackles. They would never remove our cuffs entirely, but this may give us the chance we need." He paused and stared hard at Hellen.

"We will need to cause a disturbance in the crowd. Such a disturbance that a *child* could easily become lost or misplaced."

"I am willing to do what I must," Hellen replied, knowing in her heart she would sacrifice everything without hesitation.

"I fear you alone will not be capable of such a disturbance as what is needed." The Orc replied. "You will certainly need help."

"You would help us?"

Dawoud sat back again, staring at the cell around him. The rocking of the ship swung the hanging lamps back and forth, their light casting shadows in a rhythm that matched the creaking sounds throughout the ship.

"I am to meet my end at this ship's docking. Perhaps one more good deed to spite my captors is a good enough ending for my name." At this thought, Dawoud gave a hint of a grin. Motivated to be as reckless as possible carried with it some joy in his mind.

"But if freedom is to be had by your daughter, she will need to reach out and take it for herself."

"She will. She must." Hellen replied, then took a deep breath knowing this was their only option now. She laid her head back in her cell and shut her eyes. As she began to drift, Eira laid on the far end of the cell. Her eyes opened wide, and mind full of what she had just heard. Perhaps there was hope for herself yet. Hope for her and her new friend Gracie.

DING-DING! DING-DING! The ship's bells chimed out above the sounds of seagulls as the ship approached the harbor. There was much more control over the ship's rocking and turning, and a halting grind cried out from the walls of the lower decks as the ship as a whole came to a halt.

There was much hustle and rapid foot steps heard above as the crew began to unload their cargo. Before long, the door to the prisoner's level burst open. Several guards came down with long chains. One by one, they opened the cell doors and ran the single line of chain through each loop of each prisoner's cuffs.

First was Hellen at the front of the line. Behind her, Eira stood in waiting. Hellen glanced down at her with a worried look.

"Do not worry," Eira whispered. "I will help Gracie too." The risk of a spoiled plan sent a shock through Hellen's mind. Without giving too much warning, she gave Eira a look of extreme caution, pursing her lips together in an inaudible hush. She slowly turned back to face the front of the line, making no eye contact with the guard just before her. The guard, paying no attention, fiddled with his spear against the wooden floor boards.

Behind Eira came Dawoud, then a prisoner from the other side of the aisle. Behind him was Gracie, followed by several remaining men.

"Alright you! Let's get movin'!" the guard in front commanded, as he tugged on the chain. The line followed up the steps and through the two levels of floors that had been above them before emerging into the bright sun of day. Above, the skies were a bright blue with swift, thin white clouds high above the earth. The sea breeze was strong and cool, and smelled of salt and fish.

Beyond the edge of the deck stood tall a great city, wide and deep. In the center and high upon a mound was the Gammal Keep. This was the state of Kathlon, the northern most state of Nýland, but where King Gunvald had made his home, for Gammal Keep was as large as any castle in the empire, and the city surrounding it was far richer than any other.

Another hard tug at the top deck caused Hellen to stumble over, as she fell to the wooden boards. Her wrists being bound by the chains jerked her hands up, taking them away from catching her fall. She hit with a hard *thud* and Eira stumbled with her.

"Get up, you!" the guard commanded. She brought herself to her feet and felt the eyes of everyone around her watching. She became incredibly nervous, as though any hint of a plan could spoil it all now, and would most certainly be caught.

They were led across the main deck of the ship and to a ramp with ropes strung as rails on either side. It led them down to the main level of the pier, all wooden, and all of it wet from the sea air.

As they made their way into the crowd, mutters and lull discussions surrounded them. Everyone was talking, pointing and conversing like customers discussing the best of a new crop for sale. Hellen's eyes darted from person to person, knowing they all could be bidding for ownership of her daughter. Fat men with long greasy beards. Old women with rotten teeth and skinny pointy fingers. In the distance, some well off men with well-groomed white beards eyeing the slaves passing by.

Hellen tried to look back, but could see nothing past the Orc, and only could trust Gracie was still back there. No shout or call could have reached her in the commotion that already was about them. And every time she tried to look back, she was tugged forward again.

After some distance, Hellen suddenly found herself at the base of a very short staircase leading up to a large stage. Being pulled upward, she emerged out of the crowd and led before a long table at the far end where several officials sat under a brightly colored awning. It was bright yellow and red, the colors of Kathlon, and surrounding them were several guards of Gammal Keep, and more were soldiers of the Imperial army.

The presence of such strength began to cast doubt in Hellen's mind. Questions ran through her carrying fear. What if this was all for nothing? What if her intentions were to be discovered, and the punishment set for both of them? The idea that this plan could outcome to be far worse than what they had now shook Hellen into hesitation. She suddenly wanted to avoid the whole thing.

After the entire line was on the stage, a soldier of Kathlon made his way down the line, releasing each set of cuffs from the single chain. As the chains ran out from Hellen's cuffs, she knew the time was about to come. Her heart raced and she forced herself to control her own breathing as sweat began to bead on her brow. She felt nervous, and hoped it would not all be in vein. She could not see Gracie, but knew she was behind her somewhere. As she looked back, she could see the top of Dawoud's head, and as his cuffs were released, he tilted to the side to make eye contact with Hellen.

Like a pause in time, in that moment, she knew it was about to become. They had to wait a few more seconds for the chain to run past Gracie's cuffs, or it would be too easy for the guards to retake control and her opportunity would be lost. Hellen never broke eye contact with the Orc in those moments before he gave a solid nod.

"First prisoner!" the commissioner at the center of the table shouted. Hellen suddenly looked over at the table. She was not ready to give up yet. She knew this was her last opportunity to give Gracie that chance.

As Hellen hesitated, the guard having unchained the last of the line was returning to the front, coiling the chain around his shoulder.

"Prisoner!" the man shouted. This time a soldier approached Hellen. She didn't know what to do. Taking a step back, she heard a commotion. Dawoud grabbed a hold of the chain from the passing soldier and knocked him off the stage and into the crowd. In one swift motion, he threw a loop of chain around Hellen's neck and thrust her back.

"I will not be taken again!" Dawoud shouted in defiance, using Hellen as a hostage now. He took several steps back as soldiers rushed towards him, spears out and swords drawn.

"Release her!" they commanded. He took a few more steps back before finding Gracie, who was in tears at the sudden betrayal.

"Mama!" she cried out. But Hellen could not give any hints, even to her. Not yet. Instead she continued to play her roll as she struggled to breath under the light pressure of the chain.

"Release her or die!" they shouted, advancing towards them. In a loud rumble of a cry out, the Orc leaped backwards, taking Hellen with him, and knocking poor Gracie down as all three of them fell off the stage and into the crowd.

A wave of soldiers followed in their attempts to regain control. Gracie, on the floor and under some parts of Orc and men, met eyes with her mother.

"Go! Now, Gracie! Now is your chance! Get lost in the crowd and find your way home!" Tears rolled out from Hellen's eyes. This was the moment that if Gracie were to have freedom, she would need to take it for herself. Hellen did not want this to be, she did not want to lose sight of her daughter. But where she was going, she would not be able to watch over her any more.

"Mama, I cannot leave you!" Gracie cried out.

"You must, my darling! You must go!"

Hearing the debate, and knowing her time was quickly closing, Dawoud turned his head downward to face Gracie.

"Scurry home, little mouse" he said to her.

In a sudden jolt, Hellen was thrown upward and swallowed into a group of soldiers cloaked in yellow and red.

"Scurry now," Dawoud said at final before a sword pierced his back and his breath was stolen from him.

With tears rolling down from her eyes and overcome with fright, Gracie slowly backed up on her hands and knees and disappeared into the crowd. It was an easy thing for her to do, as the sight of an Orc killing and such a commotion drew the crowd in closer. Such a sight was a delightful treat for much of the crowd. Cheers and hollers came loud as people pushed tighter for a quick glimpse of the gore. So much so, that no one took notice of a little girl pushing her way backwards, away from the mess.

Hellen was thrown back on stage where the officials took their seats again.

"Well! What a mess!" said the commissioner. "Back to our work! First prisoner, approach!" he shouted at Hellen.

She looked out over the crowd. No signs of Gracie could be seen as the crowd was dense and tight at the edge of the stage, and it was not until it met the markets and alleys some distance inland that it began to disperse and thin. It looked like, at the moment, she had gotten way.

A soldier suddenly pushed Hellen towards the table as her attention was demanded again.

"Name?" the commissioner asked as he looked at his papers.

"Hellen," she gave him.

"Hellen..." he said, following the tip of his quill down the sheet.

"Ah, yes!" he said, marking a point next to her name. "And your daughter, Gracie?" he looked up at her and at the rest of the prisoners on the stage.

She began to tremble with fear, finding it difficult to hide. She had not known they kept such track of their prisoners, or did not realize it. She had no answer to give, and suddenly felt as though the trouble she had feared with this plan would come with its vengeance.

"I am Gracie," a voice came up behind her. It startled Hellen as she was not expecting her daughter to speak up, and for a short moment felt her efforts, and the death of poor Dawoud, was wasted. But the voice that spoke was not as familiar as Gracie's.

Eira stepped forward, grabbing Hellen's hand. Hellen was lost in the sudden shift from fear to hope, and gave no response.

The commissioner looked at Eira, then down at his papers.

"Gracie..." he said, then returned back to Eira. "You are not six years old, or so you are the tallest six year old I have met!"

"Six? Oh no, sir. I am eight years old," Eira replied. She was quick for a child, but her confidence in her answer saved them all in that moment.

"Eight," he replied, then glanced at his papers. "I see," he said, as he rounded the end of the *six* into a full top loop, correcting it to an *eight*.

"As recent events have warranted a change in our board policy, family members of incoming help under the age of coming shall remain within the same bunking quarters as their parents," he said, looking up at Hellen and Eira. Hellen's face fell with her heart.

"What..?" she replied softly under her breath, filling with regret. She could feel the tears swelling up in her eyes.

"Although you will be given different roles to fulfill, you will still share a cot at the end of each night."

Her tears flowed from her eyes, down her cheeks and found their spots on the wooden boards at her feet. If she was to weep, she had to softly, for no mother would be weeping of sorrow to know she would remain with her own child. It was this moment in which Hellen found the most challenging to keep her strength about her.

"Hellen..." the commissioner said looking back down at his papers. "I have no doubt you are a good enough cook. You will be assigned in the kitchen to help prepare meals in the Gammal Keep." He made his mark on the papers in representation of this assignment.

"And Gracie!" he said, looking up at Eira. "You have taken care of smaller livestock? Chickens, goats..." he asked, being polite for the young girl.

"I have..." she replied, knowing the pain Hellen must be feeling, yet relieved to have someone so friendly to stay with.

"You will help take care then of such in the Keep's yards," he concluded, making his final mark for the family to stay together.

"Next prisoner!" he shouted as two guards led Hellen and Eira off the stage and to a cart waiting several yards away, ready to take them and several others to Gammal Keep.

Deep in the crowd, Gracie stumbled on her hands and knees to make her way through. She was lost, crying, and very afraid. Her mother told her to run, and the sight of Dawoud's death left yet another scarring memory.

The ground was filthy stone. Feces of cattle and horse were caked down between the cracks. Everywhere she turned, men and women yelled at her to *"get up!"* and *"watch what you are doing!"*. Her tears blinded her, and she had no way of knowing where to go, which way was which, or how to escape the closed in crowd around her.

In a panic she was in, she turned quickly and ran right into another stranger. Her head hit his shins hard as he fumbled to keep his footing.

"Hey!" he shouted, looking down at her. "What do we have here?" he asked as he knelt to get a closer look.

His face frightened her as it was well worn and strangely decorated. He had no hair, though it was trying to grow out however thin. A cloak he wore, with a wide hood and a long blond beard, also thin. But what frightened her the most was his eyes. They were a very pale blue, and lined with black around his lids. His nose was long and thin, and he had piercings in his ears.

As he looked at her, he noticed her cuffs. She gave no sense of wanting to flee, for she was completely lost and exhausted in emotion. He glanced back at her face, soaked in tears, and back up at the crowd around them. Looking back down, he quickly pieced together what she was, or where she had come from.

"Better stay close, little one," he said as he brought her to her feet and wrapped her in his cloak. It smelled strange of herbs and other things natural. Her face was the only thing given away in the concealment, apart from her bare feet under.

"What is your name?" he asked her quietly as they walked out of the crowd and into the market place. Gracie felt an extreme sense of caution about this man. Her entire world had been shaken, and she found no trust in places where she had expected it, yet had found it in places she did not expect. What intentions this man had for helping her, she did not know. But deep in her stomach she felt not to answer. Although it seemed he was aware of her situation, she did not want to give her real name, so she remained quiet.

"Very well, I will give you my name either way!" He stopped and looked down at her with his wide eyes, and without blinking told her, "Stelli is what you can call me." Gracie gave no response, only looked up at him.

"Hmmmm..." he said, tilting his head side to side while studying her face. "If a name you will not give me, then a name I shall give you!" He did not touch her, knowing her trust was kept close to her and not yet had for him. He smiled, though, with tight lips and bright eyes.

"I will call you Clara. Yes! Clara is quite fitting." He looked up at the sun shining high in the blue sky behind the white clouds floating by. He looked back down at her.

"It means *bright*, which indeed you are." Gracie revealed a small grin at Stelli's kindness, and began to feel not so much in danger. Stelli stood back up and continued to lead her.

"I will take care of you, little Clara. You need not to be afraid of me," he continued as they disappeared into the crowds of the market place of Kathlon.

CHAPTER VI

A CAGED BIRD

— 21ˢᵗ of Kaldagger, 1866 —

The cart bumped over uneven stone as it made its way towards Gammal Keep. The sound of hard wheels crackling over dirt and straw masked the *clop-clop* of the horse that drew it. A cart filled with fear, with regret. A sorrowful delivery of hatred was on its way to the king that declared himself just and forgiving. To the west, the sun was approaching the horizon and the breeze began to pick up off the ocean, carrying with it a harsh chill.

"The irony is sickening," Hellen thought out loud, staring at the bare wooden boards at their feet.

"The *Freeman* Empire! And where has that brought us!" she began to shout. Her fear had begun to settle too deep, returning as anger with her reality having been accepted.

"Pipe down, you!" a guard following the cart shouted, pointing his spear at her.

"Please, ma'am. I will not make it far without you!" Eira said, looking up at her.

"I did not choose to look after you," Hellen snapped back. Eira's face fell, and tears swelled. Hellen paused for a moment.

"I am sorry, child, my anger has bled into my heart and off my lips. I did not mean that." She placed her hand on Eira's and crouched down close.

"You have saved me in many ways, more than you may ever come to realize. I will look after you as my own daughter."

"Gracie will find a way home. I am sure of it," Eira replied. A tear fell from Hellen's eye as she grinned.

"I can only trust to hope so," she said.

Across from Hellen and Eira, a man sat bound in chains, staring at the pair and listening intently. Hellen took notice of this man, and lowered her voice to keep their conversation more private.

"If we are to remain together, and as safe as one could be in our circumstances, I will need to refer to you as *Gracie*. It is believed by all others that you are my daughter, so my daughter you must be."

"Understood, ma'am," Eira said.

"No, you must also refer to me as *mama*."

Eira nodded in agreement.

Hellen looked up and found the man across from her making eye contact, a slim grin across his face. He spoke something to her, making no noise but moving his lips in secrecy. What he was saying, Hellen could not make out. He had a thin mustache, dark in color, and smooth lips. A small dark patch on his chin was lined with silver as a badge of his age, and his hair was short and clean.

Hellen leaned back in to Eira.

"Let us not speak any further until we can find a place with fewer ears to listen." She sat back, tall and firm, maintaining eye contact with their fellow prisoner, who did not break his for some time. His grin he wore until they arrived at the Keep.

The horse snorted as it stopped at the tugging of reigns. Before them was Gammal Stables, the end of the line for the cart. The stables were at the base of the rocky cliff that held atop Gammal Keep. It was far higher, and significantly larger than its appearance would give from the market place. The cliff face was rough all the way up before meeting layers of stone that formed the northern wall of the castle. High up at the top of the nearest tower, dots of silver helmets could be seen keeping an eye over the land.

"Servants of trade!" one of the guards shouted out. "Follow along the path to my left to the road's end and find your assignments!" Several men rose from the cart and took their steps down to the road, following as instructed. The man across from Hellen did not move, and gave no acknowledgment of her presence.

"All others, follow me to the castle! We will show you your places at the top."

A woman at the back end of the cart stood first, and Hellen helped Eira to her feet as she also rose. It was not until Hellen had reached the rear that the man finally stood, being the last one off the cart.

"What a castle!" Eira said to Hellen. "I have never seen a place so large before!"

"Built on the blood of servants such as our own," said the man behind them as he looked up at the cliffs and stone above them. Hellen placed her arm around Eira as protection.

Scoff! "You need not to fear me, *ma'am*," he said to Hellen with a wink. "Nor do you, *Gracie*."

"We do not know you," Hellen spoke with a controlled intensity. "I do not care for your tone, and ask that you keep yourself quiet!" The man remained quiet for a few moments, carrying with him only his grin.

"My name is Edgar," he said after allowing for some time to pass.

"I care not of the names of eavesdroppers," Hellen returned to him, keeping her sight ahead.

"I beg your pardon for what my ears overhead in a small cart. And I meant not to frighten nor offend! I find your compassion refreshing, like a beam of sunlight during the storm that has hit all of us." Hellen stopped and turned towards Edgar.

"For you and your daughter," he said, looking at Eira, "I want only to help."

"We did not ask of it," Hellen replied, not giving him a hint of trust, and returned to the road upward. Edgar watched as they walked upward for a moment, a grin growing on his face before a guard approached him from behind.

"One that fancies the chase, lad?" the guard said, grinning at Edgar. "Come along though, cannot be falling behind the others." Edgar gave no reply, only continued to keep up with the guard.

As they reached the top of the winding road, they approached the massive stone wall. An arch supporting the weight of stone above it gave way to a long and dark hallway, lit only at first by the natural sunlight coming from the dusk to the east. On either side of the entrance stood a dozen guards on a raised stony platform, covered by an extending wooden cover, colorfully decorated by the same colors of the Empire. High above, two banners matching the height of several stories of the castle hung flat on the castle walls, each bearing the symbol of the Empire.

The breeze was strong high up on the cliff. Smaller banners hung from the tall ceilings inside the entrance, flapping heavily in the cool breeze as Hellen and Eira entered the castle.

"Have you ever seen anything so impressive?" Eira said in a whisper, each new sight an awe in her eyes.

"Stay close," Hellen said to her, keeping her eyes on the men clad in armor lining the halls.

"Look at the bear!" Eira said pointing to one of a dozen highly-prized trophies mounted in an attacking position being shown off to guests of the castle. Along the walls, higher up were large portraits of past kings and rulers.

"They are beginning to fade in color..." Hellen noticed as the hallway lengthened.

"Those are older kings," Edgar spoke up behind her, nearly startling her again. "As sons are born and kings retire, they shift the portraits down to make room for their new ruler. These..." he said pointing towards the end of the hallway, "are centuries old. Names nearly forgotten, but a tradition never lost, and remains as the authority of the Keep's history."

"Authority of history…" Hellen said, suspicious of the choice of words.

Edgar took a step closer to keep their conversation more private.

"There are some who claim the lineage is broken. That some time in the past, some ruler along these walls, *took* the claim to the throne and covered it up in a conspiracy that no one was able to prove. And even now, to make such a claim is punishable by death."

"How could such a tragedy be covered so well?" Hellen asked, not quite sure if she could believe this tale.

"It is easy to keep secrets behind such thick walls. And if whomever claims to possess evidence that contradicts your claim, how can that evidence come to light when the *king* sentences you to death?"

"Even so, with such hard walls to keep things in, whispers tend to echo and find ears to tell their tales." Edgar released his closeness to Hellen, feeling content in what he said, ready to end his storytelling. By this time, the group had reached the end of the hall where it forked to the left and right. Before them, a stone stage commanded attention, as well did the officials standing there.

"Welcome, guests! Welcome to your new home, the infamous Gammal Keep! We are happy to have you join our family, the Freeman Empire!"

"Hoorah!" the echoes sounded from the surrounding guards in a sudden chant that startled most of the *guests*.

"To your left," the announcer continued, "you will find a hallway that will lead you to the first spiraling stairs on the left side. Take these down to the absolute bottom level where you will find your sleeping quarters. That is right! You will be staying *inside* the castle!" he said enthusiastically, with a bright smile.

"What a privilege! The *safest* place in all the west is now your home," he boasted. "Come now! Go and find your bunks and get settled! Your assignments will begin shortly after!" He turned to his left and disappeared around a stony corner in the opposing hallway.

"Come, Gracie," Hellen spoke out loud, grabbing Eira's hand. "Let us go and find our little corner."

As the mother and daughter rounded the stairwell, they came to two other landings that led to other places. Each one with a shut wooden door and each door with its own small window that let light pass through.

"How deep does this place go?" Eira asked out loud. "I hope it is not much further! The air is getting heavier with every step!" It was clear that the castle was as deep as it was massive. That the builders had dug deep into the cliff, and they were heading it the bowels of the great Keep, for that is where new servants were placed.

"Oh, finally!" Eira said as they reached the third and final landing with no where else to go. Before them was an open door that led to a large room lined with cots along the stone walls. On the far end of the room was a fire pit, burning bright. No natural light shown so far down at these depths, and the air itself felt heavy and polluted.

"Over here, Gracie," Hellen said, leading Eira to an empty pair of cots in the corner of the room.

"How old?" A woman approached, directing her question towards Hellen. Hellen turned immediately being a bit startled as to the sudden boldness of such a stranger. The woman was dressed in heavily used clothes with an old dirty apron.

"I beg your pardon?" Hellen replied, inquiring again as to the question.

"No one yet of age gets their own cot! Your daughter sleeps with you until then!" she ended with a stern expression across her face. As though Hellen had not already struggled enough, she swallowed her sorrows to keep the act up, for she must live the lie to protect not only herself, but Eira too.

"It is okay, Mama. I do not mind sharing a cot," Eira said.

"Despite still being young, my girl..." Hellen said with a smile, "you are making this as easy as you possibly can. And I admire that." Eira grinned back at her.

"That's Madam," a young male voice spoke up, breaking the moment between Hellen and her little girl. "She gives the orders around here, sort of runs this place." The young man was no older than fifteen, and carried a little extra weight around his cheeks and waist.

"My name's Bard," he said as an introduction. "I see you are new here, and..." he stumbled over his words, realizing it might be awkward to be greeted by someone of his age and figure.

"And well, I know it can be a bit confusing getting used to things around here; I see it a lot with newcomers. But not all of us are like Madam! We're all sort of trying to make it day to day, and well, some of us just take it better than others." He looked down in a bit of shyness, not wanting to overwhelm his new acquaintances.

"Thank you for your kind greeting," Hellen said. "My name is Hellen, and this is my daughter Gracie."

"Nice to meet you!" Eira said offering her hand for a good shake.

"And nice to meet the both of you," Bard said in a bow, knowing his proper manners. "This is a fine spot you have picked out if it is privacy you are after, but it is also the coldest corner in the bunks," he glanced over at the fire on the far side of the room.

"It will serve us fine, especially with the two of us to keep each other warm." Bard smiled in agreement.

"Well..." he continued, hinting at the need to end his conversation. "I best get back to my cot. Wouldn't want Madam finding it in the mess I have left it!" He gave each a nod and returned to the center of the room. Hellen watched as he turned a corner where more room expanded beyond the center archway, where the men slept on the other side.

It was then that Hellen noticed Edgar, standing next to the fire, studying the crowd. Within moments she felt his stare upon her, piercing through the haze and light smoke, through the bustle of the new settlers, finding her precise attention in the dark corner she tried to hide in. It gave her an uneasy feeling, but she could not break her stare in return, until he eventually gave way, turned to his right, and disappeared through the same archway Bard had so recently done.

"I do not trust that man," she said out loud.

"Which? Bard??" Eira replied. "I found him quite pleasant!"

"No, Bard is kind. Edgar, that man that walked with us from the cart. I do not trust *him*."

"Yes, he does seem a bit queer. I would rather not talk with him again," Eira added.

"Let us hope he keeps his distance," Hellen said, continuing to stare at Edgar's exit. She then looked down at Eira and concluded, "And try your best to avoid him." Eira nodded in agreement.

After some time of settlement and chatter among the tenants of the lowest hall, two men in matching uniform walked into the women's side with Madam tagging along. She was to help guide the two men to each of the newcomers so they may officially set their assignments. With Hellen and Eira at the back, they were to be the last to receive their duties.

Hellen studied them as they went from woman to woman, some old, many young. Each one nodding in obedience to their assignments as they were given their instructions on what to do, and when. Swiftly they came through, before finally approaching the pair in the dark corner.

"These are the last two," Madam said in a crude introduction.

"The last two..." said one of the men holding the same scroll from the market place. "There must be some sort of mistake," he said, showing the scroll to his fellow official.

"There should be three more! A mother, her daughter, and a lone girl. I see only the mother and her daughter!"

Hellen's heart began to race again. She felt the sudden wild fear of their secret being discovered claw up from her gut once more. But she knew they had already established their story, and it would be far more difficult to disprove it. She found it easier to control, at the moment.

"Where is she?" the official asked Madam, looking for someone to blame.

"Huh!" Madam replied back, feeling absolutely no threat from the two men. "I can only answer for what exactly you and your buddies send down here! And this here is all that has been sent!" she snapped back at them, feeling rather offended at their possible accusation, and giving just as much offense back to them.

"Well, our records show —"

"Psh! *Your records.* A parchment and ink do not put a human body right before us, now does it!" she interrupted.

"I know who she is," a man spoke up behind them. Edgar approached from the musk that settled in the room. Hellen's heart skipped a beat if not several, and her legs began to feel weak.

"You know where the stray girl is at?" the first man asked.

"Oh, yes, I do," Edgar answered. "And so does Hellen here," he said, staring right at her. Hellen couldn't speak, she only swallowed hard. Her eyes felt as though they were swelling, and her breathing became labored. All attention was on her at this moment, and it quickly became obvious she was distraught.

"Ma'am?" the man said to her, looking for an answer. Then the second man spoke up: "Ma'am, are you alright?"

Eira watched Hellen begin to fall apart. Her mind raced backwards, recalling the events of the past several days. Further and further back she remembered. To the market, to the ship. Remembering Dawoud and Old Tom. Then she spoke out at that last thought.

"She fell!" Eria shouted.

"Fell?" the man asked in suspicion. "Fell where?"

"O-off the boat," Eira stumbled, feeling suddenly nervous.

"Ah," he replied back. The second man asked Hellen, "Is this true?"

"Yes," Hellen spoke. "She is no longer with us."

"Leave it to the loving heart of a mother, without any doubt, to mourn for any life so innocent," the second man said compassionately, establishing a link between what was said and the feelings Hellen was displaying.

"Well..." said the first man. "Let us continue then. You-" he paused for a moment, then slowly turned to his right and glared at Edgar.

"May I help you?" he said.

"Just here to help!" Edgar replied.

"*Scoff!* Some help you are! Now go back to your cot, sir, or we shall put you there ourselves," he ordered. Hellen was suddenly filled with joy to see Edgar put in his place and removed from their presence.

"Now then, to your assignments," he said as Edgar slowly walked back and through the archway. "Hellen, is it?" he said referring to his scroll.

"Yes, sir," she answered.

"Each morning, you will report to the kitchen's dressings upstairs. You are young enough..." he said inspecting her up and down, looking around her sides as if he was judging her figure. "...yet, to be a server, and I assume plenty strong to serve dishes to guests and royalty. You will be dressed and made up to please the eyes, as are all servers, and await for dishes to be served. Most meals are served in the common dining hall, so there you will take them unless instructed otherwise." Hellen nodded, though she did not appreciate the judgment of a stranger. Still, though, it made her feel proud to still hold her youth enough to be recognized as a strength.

"And Gracie," he said, checking off the last of his records. "Like your mother, each morning you wake, you will find your way to the stables outside. There you will find Mr. Torbjorn. He is in charge there and will give you your list of chores for the day."

"Yes, sir," she said, following the manners Hellen had demonstrated.

The man rolled up his scroll and folded his hands behind his back.

"Each morning the bell will ring. This is your signal to report to your stations. At the end of each day, you will be released by your masters. Then, your time is your own and you may do as you wish within the boundaries of the servant's quarters." He took a deep breath as he continued to recite the ground rules he had already gone over a dozen times that day.

"Under no circumstances are you allowed to leave the castle grounds, nor are you permitted to wander the castle outside the servant's quarters. Doing so is punishable to a degree matching the offense determined by The King's chief commander." He lowered his voice in seriousness. "And *he* is quite just." He turned towards Madam.

"Thank you for your time, Madam. You have a good group of newcomers!" The second man nodded at Hellen as a polite farewell, and the three of them disappeared into the back of the room.

Hellen sat on their cot, deep in thought. The hum of those surrounding her fell silent as her heart could not help but to feel defeated. The walls she built up were beginning to crumble, her strength beginning to flee. She placed her face in her palms and wept silently.

"Are you ok?" Eira asked, placing her hand on Hellen's back. Hellen gave no answer. Eira knew little to say that would comfort her, so she too sat silently next to her.

"Got everything figured out-" a voice said then stopping suddenly. It was Bard, returning to see how their assignments went.

"Oh..." he said, breaking his question. "I, um..." he struggled to find words of encouragement. "It is not all terrible here," he said, trying to find light in a dark time. "We are always fed well, and kept dry and warm in the winter! Well..." he looked back at the fire. "As warm as we *can* be down here..." Hellen struggled to calm herself and find the strength to continue her politeness.

"So, where are you assigned?" he asked, hoping to start a new subject and find something worth talking about.

"I am in the stables!" Eira said, excited to have the chance to work with more animals.

"Oh, the stables! Well, that should be fun for you! You are still little enough to not be given the *hard* work, and I am sure the ponies will enjoy your company!" he said with a wink.

"And your mother?" he continued as an attempt to get Hellen involved in the conversation.

"She is a servant! Serves plates and food and such, that is." Eira answered.

"Wonderful! I will likely see you in the kitchens then!" At this, Hellen looked up at him. Her eyes swimming in tears, but it was good for her to hear news that was not all terrible.

"I bake!" Bard added. "Or rather, help bake...mostly breads and sweet rolls and such. I do not plate them, though. That takes a *special* talent. One that I have yet to master," he said hanging his head low. "But!" he perked up again. "When the morning bell chimes, I can show you the way to the kitchens! It is not a far walk, and one that is easy to remember."

"I would like that," Hellen said behind a sorrowful voice. Bard smiled in kindness.

"Well...I will leave you two to get your rest. It is difficult to tell when night approaches down here, but it is beginning to feel that way now! I will see you ladies in the morn. Good night!" he said with a bow and took his leave.

"He is quite nice!" Eira said, crawling into the corner of the cot. "It is good to know that kind people are still out there."

"It *is* nice to find a friend," Hellen said. She too laid in the cot as the ambience had settled down around them. It was difficult for Hellen to lie next to a little girl whom was not her own daughter, to have to share a bed with her.

As her thoughts continued, grief began to take over her mind. A barrier of hatred formed between her and the sleeping girl next to her. Hatred undeserving to Eira, but born in the heart of the sufferer.

For hours Hellen laid there without sleep. Her wrath boiling up, growing, ready to lash out. More and more she continued down this painful trail in her head. Tears fell, hours came and went. Each moment wearing her down further until her body could not take another. That night she fell asleep with an anger filled heart and ill-intentions in her mind.

Ding-ding! Ding-ding! The chiming bell echoed loud through the stone walls. Grunts soon followed, and Hellen and Eira rose with them.

"Whoa, I did not sleep well..." Eira said rubbing her eyes. "These beds are terribly uncomfortable! I felt like I was hugging the stone wall all night!"

"It is something we will have to get used to," Hellen replied, still lingering in her dark thoughts. Eira picked up on this.

"It is not all that bleak," she said. She scooted over close and began to whisper.

"Remember what you told Gracie on the boat?" Hellen looked over at Eira, her face sour with pain. "'Be the light in the darkness of the world...be the right when all in this world is wrong.'" Hellen's face fell, her pain giving way to something else, something she wanted to keep hidden. A mask was being pulled over her face, and Eira had not the connection with Hellen to recognize it.

"Come, Gracie," she said out loud. "Let us get ready for our day." Hellen stood and began to head for the back of the room. Eira waited a moment, watching in concern, but had nothing else she could say or do. So she followed as they reached the archway on their left.

Here they found a central room, as tall as it was wide. It was the joining circular room with three exits. One on the opposing side led to a similar bunking room for men. A second, to their right, led to a lit flight of stairs. Through this doorway people were busily walking through on their way to their duties. The last door, leading to the woman's quarters, Hellen and Eira walked through.

Throughout the central room there were tables, benches, and chairs filling the floor space. At the back of the room, opposite of the stairway exit, was a roaring fire pit and large mantle. The rounded walls were lined with shelves, book cases, and cabinets. Higher on the walls were hung flags of the different states and villages of the surrounding country side, with a large flag of Gammal Keep hanging from the ceiling in the center of the room. At the tables were several occupants, finishing up their breakfast before starting their day. One of these was taking his last bites of biscuits before finding Hellen and Eira in the archway.

"Oh!" Bard shouted. "You missed breakfast!" he said as he left his plate of crumbs and walked over to greet the two.

"Missed breakfast?!" Eira said throwing her arms down in disappointment.

"I am sorry but I am not allowed into your wing during sleep hours...I figured the smells of everyone else's would have woken you! But I understand a deep sleep may have been needed on your first night..."

Eira gazed over at the plates left as people emptied the room. Seeing what was left, she raced to the nearest plate and scarfed down the left-over biscuits and sausage, not caring who had left it.

"Come, Gracie!" Bard said to Eira, who stuffed as much into her mouth as she possibly could without choking.

"Mm commnn!" she mumbled with crumbs spraying out, sausages in both hands.

"I will show you the way to the stables, at least the first bit. It is on our way to the kitchens." He looked at Hellen. "I hope you slept decent enough..."

"Not quite enough," Hellen replied. "Actually quite little..."

"It must be hard..." Bard continued. "To have to leave behind what life you had before for...for *this*."

Hellen paused for a moment, and trying hard to avoid thinking about the recent events, changed the subject to her new friend as they headed through the exit and up the stairs.

"You must have had a hard time too, but you seem to have adjusted well," she said to him.

"Oh, I remember very little of the time before. In fact, the castle life is all the life I have known! I know nothing of my mother and father. Every time I get a chance to ask, it seems no one knows. No one can find any record of me."

"That's terrible..." Hellen replied.

"Oh, not so much. I have heard much worse stories of those that come and go through here. So much taken from them. The suffering and sorrow..." he found himself in deep thought, but snapped out of it and smiled.

"I have not had to experience that! I have had little to be sorrowful for, and have made a lot of friends here!"

"Well, you are easy to befriend!" Hellen replied as a compliment.

"Is that a crack of a smile I see?" Bard said with a grin. Hellen broke into a full smile at that remark.

"You are very light-hearted, dear boy," she said. "It helps..."

"Glad to do so."

By this time they had reached the top of the stairs and had begun walking down a straight hallway. Here, they reached the third branch-off that led to a set of wooden doors.

"Here, Gracie! Now, if you go through those doors at the end of the hall, you will find yourself in the castle's barnyard. To the left and out a ways are the stables." Bard instructed.

"Head into the stables and find a large man with a thick black beard. That would be Mr. Torbjorn. Tell him who you are, and he will tell you what to do from there."

"Thank you, Bard!" Eira said as she headed down the hall.

"And Gracie!" Bard shouted as she turned back, but continued down the hall backwards.

"He likes a good sense of humor! Do not be shy or fearful of him. He may look like a bear but he is far from it!" Eira smiled and waved as she headed towards the wooden doors.

"She will do fine!" Bard said, hoping to settle any worries Hellen may be having.

"Come now! The kitchens are not much further!" They continued to walk down the hall before finding it turned to the right at a hard corner. There, another set of stairs began at an archway opening to their left, and in front of them were two more wooden doors.

"Here we are!" he said as he opened one of the doors, allowing Hellen to be the first through. As she entered, the aromas of breads and meats surrounded around her. The kitchen was well-lit with multiple fires and stoves. On the far wall was a window with natural light shining through. The window had no cover on it, and the breeze swirled in, mixing with smoke and steam, quickly losing any chill it may have brought with it.

Everyone there was already deep in their work. Preparations were being made as chefs grabbed dried herbs off the stone walls, dashing bottles of oils and dried seasonings to and fro. The sound of sizzling and bubbling were only masked by that of dishes clanking. Very little talk was happening as each cook knew their work, knew their place, and worked hard to make the best they could make.

"This is incredible," Hellen said under her breath.

"Yes!" Bard replied. "This is, after all, the kitchen that feeds Gammal Keep!" Hellen took another moment to watch the show that was before her, as she had never seen anything like it.

"Ahem," Bard cleared his throat to get her attention. "You will need to go through those doors to prepare for your service."

"Thank you, Bard. You have been more than helpful."

"Of course, ma'am! If you happen to peek through that window there," he said pointing to an opening with a large flat counter joining the kitchen with the room on the other side, "you might be able to see me in the back! That is where I will be all day! Throwing rolls of dough into the oven and pulling them out again!" He smiled as he headed towards the back, grabbing an apron off a cast-iron hook on the side wall.

Hellen approached the door and walked through to a long room that followed the shared wall with the kitchen. There were several doorways on the opposing wall, each leading to a small dressing room, and a set of stairs at the far end of the room. Lanterns were lit along the wall to provide good light, and other servants were getting their matching dresses fitted and worn.

"Oh! A new hand!" a woman said approaching her. "My name is Dahlia. You should get dressed! You cannot go up there looking like that!" As Hellen looked around, she noticed all the servants were young women, most of them in their late teens, none of them much older than she was. And all of them skinny and fit.

"I beg your pardon..." Hellen said, not sure where to go from there.

"In here!" Dahlia said, leading Hellen to one of the small rooms on the side. Hanging on the wall was already a uniform for her to wear. A dress of light blue to match the other girls, slightly faded though, and a small hole torn at the bottom of the skirt. With it, a pale-yellow apron just around the waist.

"They all are meant to fit anyone they send up here..." Dahlia said. She looked Hellen up and down.

"You should not have much trouble I should guess! Hurry now and come out when you are ready!"

Dahlia left Hellen to get dressed, but with no door to provide privacy, she felt extremely vulnerable. Hesitant and quickly she disrobed, and slipped on the used clothing. They were far tighter than her liking. The top of the dress was cut extremely low, and she felt far too uncomfortable with it. She knew, though, this was not done without purpose, as though her dignity was being robbed of her, and she had no choice but to accept that.

As she emerged, she carried with her the clothes she had worn. Just a few steps out she wondered how she would be able to climb steps with so little room to move her legs, for the skirt was restricting beyond anything she had worn before.

"What do I do with these?" she asked Dahlia, holding up her clothes.

"In the dresser!" she said without turning her back, knowing that would be the first question Hellen would ask. Hellen looked around and found a single dresser to the right of the door she had come through. As she found a space in a drawer, her heart began to fall apart again. She found it hard to keep back her tears.

"What life is this to be worth living?" she thought to herself as she placed the last things that defined her as she would want them, stuffed into a cramped space in a dresser.

"Our job is simple enough!" Dahlia said as Hellen returned to the counter, plates being shuffled across into their room. Simply take a tray of plates up into the dining area. Most meal times are served there, and you can expect to head there unless otherwise instructed. Find a seat that doesn't have what you are carrying and place it in front of them.

"They may reject it with a wave of the hand, and that means no offense, though they could not care less if it did..." Dahlia continued. "So just move on to the next seat! Once you've served all you can, come back down and get more until everything has been served. Then return to the room and wait quietly along the wall until you are called upon, or they are finished. It is also our job to take plates back down once they are finished!"

"What about the time between meals?" Hellen asked, trying to work through all that was expected of her.

"Each morning we are given a room in the castle to be in, between meals. Really, you stand there unless you are called upon. Then do what ever it is they tell you. It is not usually difficult, most of the men that come here are too lazy to do the simplest tasks, and I expect most of them do it to feel important, or like they are in charge, rather. And I should not need to warn you about the foul thoughts most of them carry about in doing so...but do not hesitate! The punishment is far, far worse!"

"What sort of punishment...?" Hellen asked, feeling very vulnerable.

"Why do you think that dress you are now wearing was available?" Dahlia answered, putting several plates of fried bacon onto a tray before heading up the stairs.

"Hurry now! Lateness is also not tolerated!" she called back.

Hellen took a deep breath. Her strength had been tested heavily to this point, and nearly failed her several times. But this would be the worst test to get through yet.

She grabbed a tray and placed several large bowls of fried potatoes on it, along with smaller serving plates to pair with them. She lifted the tray without difficulty and followed the other servants up the stairs.

The walls were close together up the stairwell, enough to force the tray in front of her, for there was too little room to her side. As they rounded up several flights of stone, they emerged into a grand hall, beautifully lit with the morning sun shining through tall, thin stained glass windows on either side. The sight of the room was enough to take away the breath of anyone who had not seen it before.

Large, complex chandeliers made of glass and precious gems hung low from the tall wooden arches, giving support to the ceiling high above. Five of them in total as they spanned the length of the room. The walls were covered in tasteful art work, of life-size portrait paintings, sculpted figures of some important rulers of the past, and scenic memories of different places throughout Nýland.

In the center of the room laid a long carpet with a beautiful pattern, and was nearly as wide as the room, giving about ten feet of a stony border on all sides. On top of the carpet sat the dining table, fitting the room's length, capable of seating dozens upon dozens of guests. And at the end of that table sat the king himself, cheerfully laughing at whatever conversation was being had among his closest guests, comfortable in the golden throne that seemed overly large for the table he sat at.

He had a trimmed beard, silver and white with just a hint of its original dark brown color. His hair was of matching color, neatly groomed and thick. Even from the opposing end of the table, Hellen could see his dark brown eyes, and very dark eyebrows to match it. His skin was slightly wrinkled, but fair as though it had not seen the sun in some time.

"Not every seat is taken..." Hellen whispered at another servant. The other servant opened her eyes wide, looking down at Hellen's feet, then seriously up to meet her eyes. Hellen understood then, there was to be no words to come from *her kind.*

She followed the line around, watching how the others placed their plates and bowls down. It seemed simple enough, to find an open spot and how to interact with the guests. She followed their patterns and etiquette, gently placing her two bowls of fried potatoes within reach of everyone. Then quietly placing the serving plates at each guest.

Their conversations were not kept secret, but were loud and obnoxious. Though they were difficult to understand behind the laughing and full mouths, food spilling out and spraying everywhere. Hellen did her best to keep the look of disgust from being too obvious.

"Well, look here!" the king shouted, leaning away from Hellen as she placed the last of her plates on the table, giving his full attention towards her.

"I do not believe we have met!" he said, holding out his hand, showing the oversized rings on each of his hands.

Hellen's mask fell over her face, and she greeted him with the best smile she could come up with. As she took a step towards him, she bowed down to kiss the rings on his fingers. Looking down, she found his hands to be covered in grease and bits of the king's breakfast. Still though, her strength did not fail her, and each ring received a kiss from her lips. The hardest thing she had done up to this moment.

"You are quite the delight!" the king complimented as he lowered his arm to its rest.

"Thank you, Your Highness," she answered, bowing her head slightly, and hoping deep in her heart this would end.

"What would a wonderful sight as yourself carry as a name?" he said, leaning in and quieting his voice as to show intimacy.

"Hellen. My King." Her answer came stern, despite her efforts of being careful in her tone.

"Hellen..." he said with a smirk, then wiping his lips with a golden embroidered cloth napkin. "Why have I not seen you before?"

"I have only arrived last night, Your Highness..." Hellen answered.

"Oh! Well let us get to know each other a little better! Come to my quarters after breakfast. There we may talk with more privacy." He finished with a smile, a few of the other men chuckling quietly at the ending of their conversation.

"Yes, My King..." Hellen regretfully agreed, bowing a bit, and taking her leave back to the kitchens.

Hellen kept herself composed until she was safe at the bottom of the stairs and in the server's room. Like a flood, her emotions threw her into a panic. She became breathless, the tight dress giving no room, and collapsed to the ground.

"Hellen!" Dahlia shouted as she and a few others brought Hellen back to her feet, leading her to sit on a bench in the first dressing room.

"I....I cannot do this," Hellen said, out of breath. "I cannot go up there. I will not!"

"You *must!*" Dahlia replied. "You cannot disobey the *King's* orders! You will do as all other woman has in such a situation..."

"But what if..." Hellen's head was spinning with the horrific unknowns soon to come.

"You *will* do as he asks," Dahlia said sternly. "Or death will be your fate!"

Hellen's breath began to return to her.

"Death would be welcomed over *that* man..."

"Yes, a swift death, perhaps..." Dahlia continued. "But if you believe you have suffered thus far, you will be sorrowful to realize what suffering his men would bestow upon you. They can push you to the edge of life, and bring you back. It is never ceasing, and they are quite good at it."

Hellen stared into Dahlia's eyes, resuming her normal breathing and gaining composure once more.

"Must I go alone?" Hellen asked. Dahlia nodded.

"But I will lead you to his doors. There, what you decide will determine your fate. At least you still have that..." Dahlia pulled her up to her feet.

"Now, come with me. He will be upset if he has to wait on you."

As they began up the same set of stairs, Hellen had begun to accept her fate, but wanted to know more about what could come.

"Has he ever called you to his room?" Hellen asked as they climbed the stairs.

"Yes, like you, when I first began. This was several years ago though...and only once."

"Only once? What happened?"

"Nothing much, really. He talked and flirted, but..." she stopped at the turn of the stairs and looked at Hellen. She looked up and down the flight with no one else around.

"I'll tell you what I was told by my head servant, something that will probably save your life. The king..." she lowered her voice and moved closer to Hellen to make sure no one would hear.

"He is intimidated quite easily, if you know what kind of talk to give. He *does* enjoy conversation, but if you can outwit him in your conversations, he will become distracted and try to keep the upper hand. Continue with this, and he will lose interest in you. You see...he has no interest in what we have up here," she said, tapping on the side of her head.

"And if that is how you leave your mark with him, he will leave you alone."

Hellen smiled.

"I think I can do that," she said feeling more confident about what she was about to head into.

As the two of them continued up the steps and around the next bend, a soft footstep sounded around the lower bend of the steps. A lonesome individual peered around the corner, and listened for Dahlia and Hellen make their way further up. It was as he had said just the day prior: *whispers tend to echo and find ears to tell their tales.* Edgar then returned to his own responsibilities.

Dahlia and Hellen approached the king's doors. They were large, wooden doors with stained glass windows cut in two beautiful arching towers. The doors had two golden handles, one on each, opening from the center. Outside were two guards fully armed and keeping watch.

"This is Hellen," Dahlia told the guards as they shifted into a defensive stance, suggesting an inquiry as to their business there.

"She is requested by the king for an after-breakfast conversation."

"Very well!" one of the guards said, taking his hand off of his sword and reaching into his pocket for a brass key. The other guard returned to his post. *Click!* The sound of the door unlocking was smooth and light, and opened with ease and without any creaks.

"Remember what I told you," Dahlia said. "It may be a while before he comes up here, which will give you some time to think."

"Thank you, Dahlia," Hellen said. Dahlia gave Hellen a hug before moving to the side to allow Hellen through.

As she walked into the room, she was awed by the size and luxury before her. The floor was made of beautiful stone and tastefully dressed with intricate rugs of wool. The first and most obvious thing that caught her attention was the king's bed. With a canopy that met the ceiling, nearly twenty feet high, it was draped with royal red curtains that gave away light from behind them. The bed was large enough for an entire family to sleep in without bumping into each other during the night, and had more pillows than she could count in a single glance.

A large fireplace roared to her left, where she found a giant mantle and the head of the most impressive bear trophy mounted on the stone wall above it, frozen in some angry attack. Above it, the king's family crest engraved on a golden shield with a great sword and a battle ax crossing just under it.

To the right of the hearth, facing the south were doors to the balcony. They were clear glass encased in bronze, and through them the view was spectacular. Giving a sight that you were approaching the clouds, the king's room was on one of the highest points of the castle. And with the castle built on the tallest cliff in the region, it allowed the king to truly watch over his entire kingdom.

Hellen found a chair to sit in while she waited. The doors were left open as the guards kept a loosely watching eye on her. As she sat, she began to tremble with anxiety. She felt weak, but kept talking encouragement to herself. But after some time, she began to wonder if the king was going to return at all. Yet she knew not to give herself such false hopes. By now, the fire had dulled to quiet crackles and hot ash.

A mumbled, echoing voice eventually came through the stone halls and made their way into the room. Hellen's heart began to pound harder and harder. This was it, this was the most dreadful time she had to face herself. The cause of all the pain and turmoil coming to greet her. As the footsteps grew closer, Hellen stood to her feet.

"Hellen!" the king greeted with a smile, pressing the palms of his hands together in satisfaction. "I am happy to see you here waiting so patiently for me," he continued as he walked to a side table and poured a bottle of red wine into a silver goblet. The guards closed the doors to the king's room.

"It was as you had wished, My King," Hellen answered politely back.

"Yes..." he smiled as he glanced at her, then back at his wine as he set it back down and picked up his drink.

"Yes, I find it to be...joyous to get to know the new staff and hands in my castle. Tell me, my dear, what do you think of it?" he said holding his hands out, boastful of what he called his own.

"It is magnificent," she said honestly, "and beautiful." These were no lies in her heart, and were easy to share as they related only to the appearance of the nightmare she had been placed in.

"Magnificent! Yes!" the king proclaimed with a laugh. "And tell me, where does such a beautiful bird find her origins from? You are no local bird, am I correct?"

Hellen did not care at all for his attempts to flatter, but not wanting to upset the king, answered in what ever way she could while removing any negative emotion or accusations.

"I am from east of the mountains..." she answered.

"Oh, the Gronndelon!" the king said. "It seems more and more of your kind are flocking to My Kingdom! I suppose you are realizing what a better life we live here in Nýland, yes?" he said with a smile.

This ignited a dangerous fire within Hellen's heart. A fire whose heat burned her insides, whose wrath exploded with such a force that her eyes began to water. But it was in this moment that the echoes of Dahlia's advice came back around in her mind. She needed to regain control of the conversation, for the king, at the moment, was winning.

Hellen choked back her tears and swallowed her anger. She knew now was not the time to unleash it. So she bottled it up and hid it deep inside.

"Oh, yes," she answered. "Your ships are massive, and the city's market larger than any I have ever seen. But none compared to the sight of your Gammal Keep towering in command on this cliff!" The king smiled, and Hellen regained her strength over her rage.

"Now you cannot tell me such a pretty bird as yourself does not know any song? Come! Sing me a beautiful song!" the king commanded as he spread the drapes across his bed and laid himself against the far wall, still holding his goblet.

This caught Hellen off guard, and she stumbled for a moment trying to think of a song, any song, that she could sing. There was only one that came to mind, a common song about sailors that was well known over the lands of the west. And without hesitation, she began to sing her part in the song.

"No! No, no!" the king said, waving his free hand around and sitting up more. Hellen ceased, choking back the middle of the first verse with an abrupt halt.

"I do not ask the bluebird to sing the song of the seagull! Now sing me something from your land, from the Gronndelon! Enlighten me with a song of your people," he said, leaning back once more.

Hellen cleared her throat as she dove deep into thought. She could think of no song, and was afraid to the offense she might give off, for many of the songs sung in Riverwood were of freedom from such a ruler, or were clearly insulting of their neighbors to the west.

There was one, however, that Hellen had grown very fond with the melody of. The words she could not recall, but the melody was slow and beautiful, and she was certain the king had never heard it before. So she began to sing it, humming the sound quietly and growing slowly. She had her eyes shut so as to recall it, and her heart began to sink deep into what her voice was giving. And from this, she began to birth a new song. Her words chosen in memory of her fallen husband, of her children, and the horrible memories on that first day when this was all started. As she began to repeat the melody, she sang:

> In every moment I fail to find,
> The will to reclaim what was once mine.
> I cannot seem to walk this path,
> That has been laid before me with an angry wrath.
>
> This hollow place I must now call home,
> Is robbing my spirit of any hope known.
> So in this darkness should the smallest light come,
> Too late to save me, my days of hope are done.

Her heart was broken at this moment, in which the king caught her vulnerability. "Come, my dear," he said to her, standing out of his bed and pouring another goblet of wine. She stood only still until he approached her and handed her the wine. She took it and he led her to his bed side where she sat with him. She was too exhausted to fight, too tired to keep up any games. She was ready to give it all up.

Knock-knock-knock! The banging on the doors disrupted what deceiving spell the king could put on her, and she suddenly grew aware of the dangers she was about to enter.

"What *is it?!*" the king shouted angry at the interruption.

"Urgency, My King..." a voice came from the other side.

"Do you not know to avoid interrupting me when I am entertaining?!" he shouted back as he rose to his feet and swung the doors open. "What is so urgent that it could not wait?"

As the doors opened wide, Hellen watched the reveal of a short, balding man wearing a long robe. Behind him, a familiar face that brought a sudden wave of fear over her.

"This man claims to have knowledge of a treasonous action," the short man proclaimed.

"And this could not wait?" the king asked annoyingly.

"It concerns your present company..." he said, looking at Hellen. Hellen stood and placed the wine on the table next to the bed. She did not know what Edgar had to say, nor how she would defend herself. But she was very afraid, feeling surrounded by danger.

"Well, out with it! What claims of treason would be thrown against such a pretty new bird?" the king said in Hellen's defense. It was clear he was growing fond of her, which now Hellen was finding relief over grief.

"I overheard her talking with another servant, Dahlia, in the stairwell on their way up here, My King," Edgar explained. Hellen's eyes narrowed at him, now knowing what secrets he was about to reveal, she quickly became defensive.

"Go on..." the king said, suspicious of these claims.

"They...they discussed how to avoid sparking an interest from you. How to outwit you in conversation, and keep you from asking them up here again."

"Is that so..." the king said, turning to Hellen. Hellen began to tremble with fear, a soreness forming in the back of her throat, and she could not look the king in the eyes.

"Is this true?" he asked her. Hellen did not want to give an answer, but she nodded with tears rolling down her face.

"Ha!" the king laughed. "Of course you would be nervous to talk to me! But have we not enjoyed our time together thus far?" The king was giving her a chance to save herself, and without hesitation, she took it.

"Yes, My King," she answered.

"There now," he said, turning back towards the two men in the doorway. "Now if you will let me be, I would much rather not be bothered with such petty inquiries! Besides, the lack of desire to converse is no act of treason! Mere shyness! Be gone!" he said as he began to close the doors.

"But My King!" Edgar shouted as the doors began to swing shut. "There is something more serious I know! Hellen is not who you think she is!" The king held onto the door before closing, leaving a crack open.

"And who do you claim she is? A spy? An assassin? Such a gentle bird could be neither."

"Her daughter!" Edgar began. Hellen knew he was going to give up all of her secrets now, and there was no stopping it.

"She escaped into the markets! The girl that is with her is not her own!"

"Bah!" the king shouted. "I've heard enough of your storytelling. Guards! Escort this man back to the tower to resume his cleaning," the king commanded before shutting the doors completely. He then returned to Hellen, hoping to pick up where they had left off.

Hellen felt completely relieved of what had just transpired. Her secret had come out, yet was dismissed by the most powerful man in the country as a mere story.

"Now then, without further interruptions, let us drink!" he said, taking a deep gulp of wine. Hellen picked up her goblet once more and took a small sip. The wine was wonderfully delicious, even for so early in the morning. But she wanted to be careful not to lose her judgment in such a dangerous place.

"So tell me, little bird..."

Hellen began to grow quite annoyed at this name he had given her.

"Seeing as you *have* enjoyed our talks thus far, you would then *want* to have more of them, yes?"

"Yes My King," Hellen replied, careful of her answers.

"And you would not, for sake of our discussions, warn others to avoid talking to me?" he said with a sudden shift in his tone, becoming much more serious. The smile on his face fell, and his eyes grew vengeful.

"No of course not...My King," Hellen answered suddenly filled with fear again.

"Good..." the king replied. "But still, I cannot tolerate even the smallest menace of talk as you had heard from this...Dahlia is it?" Hellen nodded.

"A servant like yourself?"

"Yes, in the kitchens..." Hellen said, now aware of the king's ill-intentions.

"Guards!" the king suddenly shouted, startling Hellen. The doors swung open, two guards ready with their hands on the swords.

"Bring Dahlia to me immediately," he commanded.

"Yes, king!" they both answered, turning around and headed down the hall.

"You see, I know what you servants go through. I am not dim-witted like some of you may believe..." he continued as he poured himself more wine. Taking a sip, he walked across the room to the balcony doors and stared out.

"I know, little bird, that you are merely in a cage here. This is not your *home*. And if the doors were to open..." he said as he opened the balcony doors. A cool breeze blew into the room as three birds previously perched on the edge flew into the sky at the sudden opening.

"I know that any bird would fly home and never return. But where would that leave me?" he asked, turning back towards Hellen. "My cage would be empty! I would have no birds of whom to sing to me..." he said as he approached her, dragging his index finger down the side of her cheek. Hellen was petrified with fear.

"So tell me, Hellen," he said putting his goblet down. "Tell me what I should do with a bird who begins telling other birds not to sing?" Hellen gave no answer.

"Should I let the bird go? No...I think not. That would only result in flocks of birds fleeing from my lands and out of my grasp." He returned to the balcony, stepping out and approaching the ledge. He placed his hands on the stone ledge as he looked out far across his lands.

"Sire!" the guards called out as they entered the room, Dahlia bound in steel cuffs, her left eye swollen and bruising.

The king returned from the balcony. Hellen, still trembling, watched Dahlia with tear-filled eyes. Dahlia glanced back at her with fear, barely able to keep on her knees.

"Do I keep the bird locked up? Stored away in some separate part of the cage so her foul songs could not be heard by any other?" Dahlia looked at the king and back at Hellen, panic falling over her. She knew he was talking about her, but knew not why. The king studied Dahlia for a moment.

"You know, I remember not your name from any time prior, nor your face," he said softly to her, leaning down to get close to her face. "You are but a stranger to me, and yet you felt you could intimidate me? Imagine..." he said with all seriousness. "Imagine if a lion were afraid of a song bird..."

He stood back up.

"To death," he said to the guards. "Whenever you may find it most convenient," he concluded as he returned to his table and picked up his goblet.

Dahlia screamed in anger as the guards grabbed her by the arms and began dragging her out of the room.

"What a cowardly lion to have a bird sent to her death!" Dahlia shouted.

"Wait!" the king commanded, the guards halting. Without looking back, he gave his final orders.

"I think I will keep this little bird in her own cage. Let her sing her foul songs as long as she has breath." He turned his head towards Hellen, who was finding difficulty in controlling her weeping.

"Foul and not, I *do* enjoy any song of my little birds," he ended.

The guards drug a screaming Dahlia down the hall until the echos faded away.

"As for you, my Hellen," he said, ready to continue his day. "You will find my judgment fair, will you not?"

"Yes, My King," Hellen answered, as it was the only thing to say to such a monster.

"Of course you will," he said, placing the palm of his hand on her cheek, then giving her a very light pat on the side of her head.

"You may return to your duties," he said as he headed back to his balcony. "But I shall be seeing you again!"

"Thank you, My King," she answered behind falling tears as she swiftly left his room.

As she followed back down the way she had been led by her recent friend, she cried out in terror and anger. She hated so much the things Edgar had done, but worse, the way the *King* had treated them. Completely stripped of dignity, of identity. They were nothing to him. And her fear had suddenly shifted into pure hatred.

The rest of that day had gone on without any further incident. The king was absent from the other meals that day, yet his memory haunted her thoughts every moment. Recalling the words he said, the tone he carried, it began to consume her, and she grew very quiet.

As the servant quarters began to settle down for the night, Eira had made multiple attempts at conversing with Hellen. Eira had an exciting first day, feeling very little like a servant at all. Mr. Torbjorn had been just as kind as Bard had told her, and she rather enjoyed her work with the livestock. But having no responses from Hellen, Eira became concerned.

As they laid in their cot, the room grew quieter. But Eira could not sleep without knowing what had happened.

"Are you okay, Mama?" Eira asked, remembering to cover their story. Hellen gave no answer.

"I am sorry if you had a bad day..." Eira continued. "I do hope tomorrow is better."

"It will not be," Hellen answered.

"Why not?" Eira asked, growing in concern but relieved to finally hear Hellen speak.

"It will become dangerous for you, for all of us. But it will be for the better." Hellen said sternly, yet quietly.

"Why? What is going to happen?" Eira asked, now fully aware of something very wrong had happened.

Hellen turned to her side and stared intently at Eira in the dim light of their corner.

"Tomorrow..." Hellen began to answer, "I am going to kill the king."

CHAPTER VII

A LIGHT IN THE DARKNESS

— 10th of Frostbreath, 1866 —

The sun shined bright through the tops of the trees into a small meadow opening on the forest floor. Here, through a window of the canopy, rays of golden yellow grew tall grass, which was now beginning to fade from lively green to an aging brown. The tops of the reeds had their emptied seed pods balancing in the light breeze. Flies buzzed to and fro, and the surrounding area was all quiet save the sound of a rustling wild boar sifting through the matted bottoms, looking for grubs.

The pig stopped, and its cone shaped ears swung back and forth, listening for the faintest of sounds. After a moment, content in the loneliness of being so deep in the wild, it continued its pursuit of snacks.

Twang! An arrow came sailing through the grass tops from the shadows surrounding the opening. A trail of dust and clouds shot out from the tops it brushed against, and before the boar had a chance to react to the sound, it was struck on the side of the neck, collapsing into the bed of overgrown vegetation, hidden and motionless.

Edlen emerged from the shadows and approached the boar. It was a clean kill, and did not appear to have ended the boar's life in unnecessary pain, of which Edlen preferred. He pulled out his dagger, and began to slice into the pig's belly. The blood was warm, and it took some work pulling all the organs out and to the side. Cutting here and there, making sure to clean it as best he could.

Finished and content in his trophy, Edlen hoisted it over his shoulder and headed back into the shadows of the dark woods, leaving behind only a trail in the grass where the hog had been searching, and a fresh pile of soil burying the end of the hog's journey.

"There he is!" Radholf called out standing under a small overhang on the front of the tiny shed.

"And look at that! He actually caught something!"

Edlen smirked as he took the hog inside and laid it on the cleaning table against one of the four walls of the shed. It was extremely small, and couldn't sleep all four of them at once. It was barely held together, and the boards of the walls were rotting and gaping between themselves. The roof overhead was low, and had been patched up over the years with various barks, limbs, and grasses. The floor was dirt, and there was a single cot.

Under the cot was a chest, where the four stumbled across various hunting weapons and tools. Edlen found his bow and arrows, along with a cleaning dagger.

It had been several weeks since their escape from Castle Graywater in Brisrun. Following the Vanalta River back south, they made their way into the wild. But instead of following the river on the ancient roads, they kept their path on the eastern side, concealed in the thick forest, hidden from any eyes of the Empire.

But when the Vanalta River turned westward again, there they left its roaring waters and diverged south-east, deeper into the Bjornwood. Following animal trails and clearings where they could, they found themselves stumbling across a hunter's shed whose owner had long forgotten it, or which had an owner in a previous lifetime.

"Boar!" Oatikki said as he stepped inside. "Nothing like a good frying pan of sizzling wild hog!" he said smiling. He proceeded to inspect the kill and pulled out his ax. Holding the ax at the top of the handle, he began cutting the boar into its proper pieces for cooking. Much of it would be dried for later meals, but they certainly were not going to pass up a feast of wild boar for that night's supper.

The fire burned strong, and cracked the wood it was digesting in dryness and heat. It kept the night chills away, and what biting bugs had thus far survived the cold nights, also stayed away from the intense heat and choking smoke above. The forest was dense and dark, and the canopy so thick, only a blink of starlight could be seen between the waving branches above. The underside of the lowest branches glowed in the fire light, and the surrounding thicket gave a sense of protection, closing them in from the world around them.

"So, how long are we staying?" Edlen pipped up, while Radholf sipped on hot chamomile tea.

"This has been quite an enjoyment and fortunate rest, indeed!" Radholf replied. "But I do believe we should continue with our journey if we do not want to lose our way all together."

"We won't lose our way," Luno replied. "I know *exactly* where we are."

"Yeah, so do I," Oatikki said sarcastically. "We're at *the hunter's shed*." Edlen smirked.

Luno stared back at Oatikki with disapproval, then continued.

"We can leave tomorrow, if it makes you feel any better."

"And which way shall we be going?" Radholf asked, taking another sip.

Luno pointed with his small pocket knife, in which he had used to slice a wild apple, to the east.

"That way," he finished.

"Further east?" Oatikki asked. "But that would lead us deeper into —"

"The Old Forest," Luno interrupted grinning. After a stare at Oatikki for just a few seconds, he returned to his apple.

"Where exactly *are* you leading us, wizard?" Oatikki asked with directness in his voice.

"Oh! I am sorry, for you are mistaken, my big Orc friend! I am not *leading* you anywhere!" Luno replied. "I am simply going home. But you are welcome to join me as long as you see the need."

"You said you would guide us to safety," Edlen chimed in, taking a side of concern along with Oatikki.

"And I have!" Luno replied, opening his arms to the woods surrounding them.

"Hardly what I would consider *safe*," Oatikki commented.

"But safe enough from those that hunt you, for no hunter would follow a game such as yours *this* deep into the wild," Luno said. He paused for a moment, and the sound of the fire became the center of the conversation. The crackling seemed more troubling now than it had recently felt. Then Luno asked the next question.

"Just to settle my own curiosities, where did you plan on going? Before you were captured, that is."

"Our destination was, and still is, Arboran," Radholf said.

"The Elves?!" Luno said, giggling to himself. "You do realize that there is a *mountain range* between you and the Green Valley, yes?" he said, barely able to keep himself composed.

"Our plan was to board a ship in Brisrun and sail around them to the north, across the Great Sea. But the Empire has gotten in the way, and we apparently find ourselves far to the south, now that sailing from Brisrun is no longer an option.

"So we need to find a way through the mountains, preferably with a path that avoids the Old Forest. I know of a path whose head rests on the borders of the Old Forest, in the foothills of the mountains," Radholf explained.

"You cannot fly over the mountains, nor can you pass under them. No trail exists that runs through them, no path that cuts through the backbone of this land," Luno explained.

"The path you speak of no longer exists. The only route to your beloved Elves, my friend, is the path I am taking. The path that takes you first, to Skydale," Luno said, revealing his homeland.

"That path does exist," Radholf replied with concern.

"Nay!" Luno answered back. "It has been destroyed! Filled in by some terrible force between the mountains! No foot has made travel through it for generations."

Radholf sat in thought for a moment. He did not appear at all pleased by this news, and hoped to doubt. But he knew to be doubtful in a decision of such importance could end in disaster. At last, he spoke up with his answer.

"We shall follow you, Luno. Through Skydale if we must."

"What about the Old Forest makes it such a bad place?" Edlen asked, worried now and wanting to know what they were about to head into.

"There is nothing about the Old Forest that you need to fear, young Edlen," Luno said immediately, grinning. "At least, not if you know where the paths are, and are familiar enough with the routes," he said, turning his eyes towards Radholf.

Radholf sat in silence for a moment, then spoke up.

"The Old Forest is not well-known, and has never been tamed. Its age surpasses that of Men, of Elves even. The roots of its trees dive deeper than the Rhims themselves, with trunks larger than castles. Whose shade is never broken, keeping the forest floor in constant night."

"But that is not where the danger lies." Oatikki added. Edlen glanced at Oatikki, then to Luno, who was sitting, staring at Oatikki, with no expressions on his face. The four sat around the fire, its flames continuing to crackle and warm their faces as it danced in the night air. Then Radholf spoke up.

"Being never tamed, much of the forest has gone unchallenged. Things have been free to grow and live, to thrive with no restriction. Nasty things. Creatures which have grown in great size and strength, which would see us as nothing more than a morsel to snack upon. Things that our weapons would have less sting than a bee."

"But you need to fear not of such rumors," Luno said interrupting. "Not with such a guide as myself. I know the paths of safety, as I have safely passed through them many times."

"How long would we be traveling through before reaching the safety of your valley?" Oatikki asked.

Luno took the last bite of his apple and tossed the core into the fire. Chewing obnoxiously, smacking his lips in the juice of the apple, he leaned back.

"A week, with good speed," he finally answered.

Oatikki looked at Radholf, quite annoyed.

"And what lies at the end of the week's path?" Oatikki continued.

Luno leaned forward again towards the fire, and stared at Oatikki.

"At the end of that trail lies a cave entrance. Just inside is the guardian. Do *not* enter the cave without me, for he will kill and consume you entirely, bones and all, if he does not recognize you. He's a bit of a dumb brute, to be blunt, but can be easily calmed by a familiar face.

"Beyond his presence is a series of caves all linked together, one leading to another. Without having traversed them before, you would surely be lost. Dead ends really do end in death, and only one way can lead you to the valley."

"Is there no other way?" Radholf asked. "There must be an end to the backbone."

"There is, far to the east. But beyond the trail I will be taking, I know not of any other that reaches that deep into the Old Forest. If there was, if you could find your way, though, I would expect the next three seasons to pass before you would emerge from the far borders of the Old Forest, if you would emerge alive."

"Then we have no choice, at it seems. We will leave with you, Luno, at dawn's first light," Radholf said in resolution of the matter.

"It will be the last dawn we see for some time," Oatikki said, directed towards Edlen. Edlen had worry on his face, and did not feel the need to express it verbally. He wished very much that their path had not had the need to take them into such a dark place.

Night had long fallen. Insects were singing their sounds of harmony all around the camp. The fire flickered low, but kept its warmth strong. The trees overhead were too dark to see, and they gently rustled in the quiet chilly breeze of the night air.

Edlen had woken just on the other side of sleep. A small sound of annoyance had brought him this far out of his dreams, like the sound of a small paw scratching at a hard surface. He slowly opened his eyes and saw a tiny mouse not even a foot from his face. It was nibbling on some grass seed it had found in the dark, and it was staring straight at him.

Edlen smiled.

"Hello, little friend," he said in a whisper. Pausing for a second or two, the mouse continued his gnawing at the seed. After a moment, he finished it and began sniffing around the ground, looking for something else to nibble on. Such simplicity gave joy to Edlen. A small mouse, living his life in the forest, filling his belly with seeds before settling down for the winter. Oh, the troubles this little critter would never have to see. How simple a life he lives.

Edlen continued to think about his new little friend. How he must have a warm and cozy burrow someplace near - perhaps even a small mouse family. To the mouse, this was just another stroll in the woods, looking for a snack. Edlen took a deep breath and exhaled slowly. The mouse, in sudden realization of the size of the creature that was Edlen, took off running in an alarmed caution.

"Be careful out there, my friend." Edlen thought to himself. He shut his eyes and returned back to sleep.

"Radholf!" Luno whispered loudly, waking the group. "Radholf, come!" Radholf got up, a bit groggy and annoyed at their wizard friend for waking him in such a deep sleep. Luno led him to the side of the shed and pointed into the underbrush.

"A light in the distance. Soft and warm."

"A camp fire?" Radholf thought outloud.

"I heard rustling in the night, too loud for any creature that lives out here, too clumsy," Luno explained. Oatikki approached, curious, and Edlen following close behind. Radholf looked at Luno and back at Edlen.

"Stay here. I shall go and see what is making this mysterious light in the night," Radholf said as he quietly slipped into the a wall of leaves and branches. Edlen heard no sounds from Radholf, as the calm breeze made more sound than he did walking through the vegetation surrounding them.

Radholf moved tall grasses to the side gently, careful not to make a break in them. His feet planted exactly where they needed to avoid all sound, and his breathing slowed to silence. As he made his way through, under small trees and around shrubs, he realized the fire was a bit further than he anticipated. Yet as he continued, it grew closer and closer, and more details of the things around it became clear.

He sat crouched on the edge of an opening, using the tall grass in front of him as a shield against the fire light that shown strong. It was a large camp of nearly fifteen people. They appeared to be lightly armed, and many carrying bags and some crates. There were a few horses and two carts. There were women, and children too. They appeared to be worn out, and some were still settling in for the night. They were refugees.

Radholf stepped out into the opening and a man spotted him.

"Hey!" he shouted, drawing his sword. "Hold it! Don't take another step!" Several other men stumbled to their feet and drew what weapons they had. Some short swords, a couple of bows, and one man had an overweight war-hammer.

"I mean no harm, fellow travelers," Radholf said, holding his hands at his shoulders. "I saw your fire light from a distance, where my small party is resting.

I came to investigate..." he said as he looked around. The mothers of the children held them close and dear, in what small beds they had on the ground.

"You look as though you have come a long way," he continued.

"And who are you to be wandering so deep in Bjornwood?" the man asked, pointing his long sword towards Radholf.

Radholf put his hand on the tip of the sword and slowly lowered it, answering him.

"I am Radholf the Verndari, and you need not to fear me. I know what you run from, for we are prey of the same hunter."

"And your *small party*?" the man said, not entirely convinced of their safety nor of Radholf's intentions.

"They are the same. We escaped from the Empire and fled to the wild for safety. Where, by chance, are you headed?" he asked the man.

The man dropped his sword entirely and sheathed it.

"*Sigh*. We don't know. We headed out here running from the Empire as well, looking for a place outside of the reaches of danger."

"They tried taking our land, all we have worked for," said another man as he approached. "I am Adelmar, and this is my brother, Brandr. We fled from Furskarth over a month ago, and have picked up many on our way. We swept across the southern lands of the Gronndelon, intending to head to Brisrun. But we only made it as far as Stonehaven, when we saw the Grizzly flags flying on the walls."

"It was then that we knew we had to turn to the south-east, to the wild," said Brandr. "But we don't know where we are, nor where we're going. Our hopes were to find others, or to find our way in some passage into the mountains before winter in search of escape. But our hopes are fading swiftly. We have little food, and such traveling is harsh on the little ones." Brandr had sadness in his voice, and much doubt. His face showed how little hope was left in his heart, and his thoughts were of the women and children, knowing the struggles they faced in which a full grown man, such as himself, could more easily bear.

Radholf looked at the two men standing before him. The rest of the people were slowly gathering at a distance. He turned back towards the black wall of night from where he came, and whistled.

"Come! Bring the boar!" he shouted into the night, his voice echoing through the trees and fading deep into the distance. He turned back at Adelmar and Brandr.

"What all we have, we will share with you. We have three skilled hunters in my group, and one..." he paused with a grin. "He-he, one fine wizard," he concluded.

"A wizard?" Brandr asked.

"Is he trustworthy?" asked Adelmar.

"He has saved us from imprisonment, and seems to have a good sense about him," Radholf answered. Rustling could be heard in the distance as the other three approached the opening. Luno was the first to make his appearance.

"Besides," Radholf continued. "He is the only one who knows where we are at! May I introduce Luno."

Luno, holding several packages of wrapped dried meats, stepped into the light and looked around in shock as to the sudden attention. His eyes were wide with surprise and mouth dropped down a bit.

"Move over!" Oatikki said as he stumbled out from the grass, carrying all of their weapons.

"And our big Orc friend, Oatikki," Radholf said with a smile. The two men looked at Radholf with concern as to the insult of someone they had a slight fear of, half expecting the Orc to start a fight or burst in some outrage. Then Edlen stepped into the clearing, holding only his own possessions.

"And the fourth member of our party, Edlen son of Eldor." Edlen saw the men and the people behind, and nodded politely in introduction.

"Gentlemen, this is Adelmar and Brandr. Behind them is their traveling party." He took the meat packages from Luno, who hesitated a bit, and handed them to the two men.

"Please, make sure everyone gets a little something. It is most fresh and quite good! Edlen's catch for today!"

"Thank you very much," Adelmar said, smiling at Radholf and Edlen. Adelmar split the dried meats with his brother, and began handing it out to the people with them. They were sure to feed those most in need first, the children, women, and one ill man who looked old in age.

"We should introduce ourselves, get to know these people. They may be in further need, and it would be good to befriend them," Radholf said to the other three. Socializing was not something Edlen had practice with, and it made him a bit uncomfortable. He stuck close to Radholf's side, and figured he would follow closely behind.

Luno scoffed at this, knowing he was the most experienced and familiar with the lands surrounding them. He saw no need for such tedious and outgoing actions. Instead, he walked into a corner of the clearing, in shadow, and sat with his own thoughts. This did nothing more than solidify the reputation of a wizard. To be solitude, concerning yourself with only what could benefit one's self, this was the wizard's way. And it seemed to Luno that nothing of these lost travelers could do any good for him.

Radholf and Edlen walked around and greeted the people, being as friendly as possible. Most were quite welcoming of the new faces, until Oatikki was lastly introduced. He was sure, though, to remain friendly. Still, the stares of children and concerned adults gave away their thoughts, although this was nothing Oatikki was not already used to.

As they made their way through the camp, one girl caught Edlen's eye. She was older than he, sitting on the ground wrapped in a thick cloak. She had straight black hair that ran down her back, the end he could not see. Two braids were strung along the sides to keep her hair out of her face. She looked of age, but barely, and she stared into the small fire centered in the group she was sitting with.

He found it hard to continue to give the other people he was being introduced to their rightful attention, and found that any moment he did not need to meet eyes with those near him, he would stare in her direction, studying her. A spell had fallen on his mind, and he wanted it to flourish. He could not see her eyes, for she kept facing the fire. The people around were in small conversation, and Brandr approached with a share of the meats they had provided. She refused in some declaration of not being in need.

Before long, Radholf led them to that same group, the last of introductions to be made. As he introduced himself and Edlen, the people resting around the fire were friendly enough to meet the greeting, including the young lady Edlen had been a bit nervous about meeting. She spent most of her attention towards Radholf, who breezed by her with no special thought. After initial introductions were made, he gave a brief introduction to their other two companions, as he had done with all the others.

"Edlen and I have been fortunate enough have been traveling with a long time friend of mine, Oatikki. Though he be of Orcish descendants, you need not to fear him! He is now your friend too," Radholf said with a smile. Despite Oatikki's efforts of setting a friendly start with the people, most still found him threatening, and tried to avoid eye contact and conversation with him all together.

"Along our journey, we have had the great privilege to be joined by the masterful Luno! A fine wizard, if there ever has been!"

At this mention, a few heads turned to glance at the lanky wizard sitting on the edge of the clearing, near where they had originally come from. He sat in a grumble, holding on to his disapproval of the sharing of their goods. But one head caught Radholf's attention. The young lady, after a moment of study of Luno, had the slightest hint of worry, but was kept concealed well. She quietly raised her hood over her head and pulled up a thin black scarf over the bottom part of her face. Nothing but her eyes showed. A deep green with spikes of hazel, now apparent up close.

Radholf studied her, and she suddenly realized the attention she had drawn to herself. She stared intently at the fire.

"Something bothering you, my lady?" Radholf asked. She lowered the scarf again to reveal her lips.

"Just keeping the night chill away, sir," She replied and lifted the covering back in place. Radholf grinned slightly and paused for only a moment.

"No," he replied. This caught her attention as she looked straight up to meet his eyes.

"I am no sir," he continued. "Please, call me Radholf."

With that, he bid the last group a good night and left their presence so they may rest, for they were all weary.

The night breeze blew gently. It had grown quiet outside the small tent Adelmar and Brandr had set up for themselves. Only the occasional wave of a tree branch broke the what silence there was, and a lone cricket chirped, taking small breaks to rest his legs. The dotted fires flickered low, still being stirred by those that enjoyed their warmth, by those that were not yet asleep.

"So, as you can see, most of us in our group are but simple local farmers and hunters. Now my brother Adelmar and I, we were guards at Furskarth. But as the Imperials began to show up, we fled, knowing the fight would have taken us both," Brandr explained.

"Not of cowards or to flee our deaths," Adelmar added. "But to seek out those in harm, as is part of our oath as guards of the Gronndelon. We gave our word to protect our kin. Our fathers and mothers, sons and daughters," Adelmar continued.

"There is no safety to be had there," Brandr added. "They quietly infect our cities, an invasion disguised in a political hand-shake. Like a grizzly acting only curious to your camp before cornering you after it has gotten close enough."

Adelmar nodded in agreement, then returned his attention to Radholf.

"You have followed your oath well," Radholf said. Both brothers sipped on ale they had poured in small cups. The tent they sat in was low, forcing the occupants to sit on the ground in a sort of circle to include everyone in the conversation. Edlen had joined them, and so did Oatikki. Luno refused, and sat outside guarding the rest of his belongings. Most in the Gronndelon were raised to not trust those born into the life of Magic, and although he had no intentions of harm, he did not feel the same from them.

"And what of the girl?" Radholf asked. "The one of a different descent. She clearly is not of the Gronndelon, for her hair and eyes tell a different story." Edlen perked up and listened intently, relieved to know he was about to find out a little more about his recent infatuation.

Brandr looked at his brother Adelmar, who returned the same look in the face.

"We've inquired her about her origins, but have not gotten much out," Brandr replied. "She was roaming the roads outside the Wild, just to the north of the Misty River. She was weak and in need of food and healing. Her name is Livia, from what she had told us."

"And you doubt her?" Radholf asked, picking up on their subtle hints.

Brandr was silent for a moment.

"She seems...very quiet," Adelmar answered. "She was reluctant to travel east with us, but she was in such poor health, she had not much choice to fight us. We picked her up, healed her as best we could, and she has stayed with us since."

"And where is she from? Where was she going?" Radholf asked. Edlen began to grow concerned as Radholf seemed to be asking for quite a few details despite not having asked the same of any other in the party. And although curious to the answers, he also felt a sense of defense for her.

"She won't say," Brandr answered. "Though her language seems to still be young, as it can at times be broken, she tries to hide it by remaining quiet and not giving answers. Best we can figure, she was fleeing from something in the east as she appeared to be traveling west. I'm sorry to say that it's all quite possible she is a refugee from another land, perhaps her homeland, and has gotten caught in our own civil war, if that is what you can call it," Brandr answered.

"It is and I do," Radholf replied. "Quite unfortunate for someone to flee from one trouble only to find another like-" Radholf's words were interrupted by the horrible scream of a woman in fear from outside the tent. The scream echoed through the night, off the trees and leaf tops, and startled every soul in the camp to their feet.

Radholf ran outside, Edlen followed shortly behind Adelmar and Brandr. They frantically looked around to see what was causing the commotion. A lone woman stood in the center of the clearing, shrieking in fear. Radholf ran to her, yelling, "What is it?!" The woman gazed into the night sky, pointing up.

"It's up there! Above the trees! It has come for us! It has come for us all!" she yelled. Brandr drew his sword and looked around. Adelmar readied his bow. The commotion had caught Luno's attention as well, who stood just outside the tent with his staff. Slowly, Oatikki emerged from the tent, with his weapons still sheathed.

"What did you see, ma'am?" Radholf asked as he approached her. "What terrors have your eyes witnessed?"

With tears running down her pale cheeks, her eyes darted back and forth, struggling to pierce the darkness above before meeting Radholf.

"I saw it. A dragon as black as shadow! He is here!"

The others around the camp started to murmur and frighten. Mothers held tight their children, and looks of puzzling confusion spread across as the word *dragon* leaped from person to person.

"You must be mistaken!" one man said, half-approaching the woman, and feeling rather annoyed. "Dragons don't exist, they are of fairy tales! Your eyes have tricked you in some horrid mistake from lack of rest. Go back to your bed, and quit worrying the rest of those that share the same night around us."

Radholf watched as the woman's fearful expression heightened realizing her warning might go without heed. She glanced at Radholf, who looked puzzled.

"Perhaps you saw a bat fluttering through the branches. They do get large out here, but I assure you: they mean no harm." Radholf said in hopes to ease the burdens of the woman.

Here eyes full of tears and open wide, and her face pale as a corpse, she whispered, "I know what I saw. I know what is hunting us."

Screeeech! A sudden echo of terrifying sound pierced through the night air and bounced off all directions around them. It was very highly pitched, and was impossible to know what direction it came from. *Scraaaw! Screeeeet!* Two more were heard, distinct in their own way but none less terrifying and horrible.

"Everybody, down!" Adelmar shouted, drawing his bow. He seemed to be aiming into the pitch darkness of the night. The group as a whole dropped to the ground and hid, cowering under blankets and brush. Radholf drew his sword, and Oatikki his axes. The fires had all grown dim now, the shadows between pits had thickened. The bottoms of the lowest tree branches above could hardly be seen in the dim orange light. Nothing but blackness. Nothing but an emptiness could be seen above. Every armed eye was intensely focused on trying to spy the source of the cries.

Twang! Adelmar's bow released an arrow far above the trees, making it's mark. The horrible beast cried out in pain, screeching with a wrath more intense than before.

"It's above the trees!" Radholf shouted. "Adelmar! Hit it again!" Adelmar drew his bow again but failed to follow the target. Rustling came from behind him, in the tree tops far above the tent. *Twang!* He sent another arrow up, but heard only the arrow hitting branches and leaves.

"Aaaaeee!" A shrilling scream came from behind them, towards the far edge of the campsite. As they turned around, they caught only the last glimpses of the same woman being swallowed up by the night above the fire light's edge, carried by some black-winged creature with large claws clinging around her shoulders. Her cries echoed only shortly after disappearing from sight, then ending abruptly with no other sounds.

"There's more than one!" Oatikki shouted.

"Quick! Everyone to the center! Build the fires hot and bright! We need to see them coming!" Radholf commanded. Everyone scrambled, trembling in fright, trying to make it to the center of the campsite. Logs and brush were thrown into the main fire as it grew hot, but no sounds could be heard from the terrors above.

The armed men of the group, eyes wide and focused, were scanning the surroundings for any movement above. The four children of the group cried as their mothers held them tight, desperately trying to silence them. A shift in the trees far in the distance could be heard. Dozens of tree tops rustled as a cold dark wind wound through the forest. It engulfed the campsite, blowing debris swirling around. The fire lost its strength, as though some magic had robbed it of its light. The wind was relentless. Never ceasing, never showing signs of weakening, until the last ember of the fire flickered out in loss of life. Then silence once more.

Cries and screeches echoed through the night as they grew closer and louder. The trembling from fear was audible, people's breaths laboured in a controlled whimper, and Edlen stood in the dark with his hand on his hilt. The sounds of the beasts drew close, then ended in a deep, long breath.

Breaking the silence in a deep voice, loud and resonating through the earth, Luno cried out a powerful spell.

"Mother of light, show us the fury of Thinni!"

In a startling blaze, the entire forest floor exploded in a white light as pure as the stars, and as bright as the sun. At the center where the fire had so recently been ablaze, stood Luno with his staff high in the air. At its tip, the carved dragon's mouth held the white gem that was shedding the intense brightness.

As the light hit, a screech came from just under the tree tops near Edlen. He stood there, face to face with a black beast, winged and claws out. The sudden light terrorized it, and it halted its advances towards him. Trying desperately to shield its eyes from Luno's spell, it collapsed to the ground.

"Dragon!" Randolf shouted as he leaped towards the beast with his sword high above his head. *Twang!* Adelmar's bow sang as it sailed an arrow into the side of the creature. It leaped backwards and expanded its wings. Edlen stood in amazement to see such a thing. To see the wings spread side to side in a vast sail, each one nearly twice as wide as he was tall. Scales covered its body in armor, and held a wet shine in the intense white light. As it struggled to retreat, Radholf's blade met its throat, and the black scales were drowned in a red river. The beast collapsed to the ground with faint struggles of cries ending in gurgle.

The other two beasts cried out in terror and fear just above the tree tops, and fled the bright light. Their cries and calls carried urgency, having not the intent of harm, but to avoid it. They echoed into the night, slowly fading to silence.

Radholf stood in front of the fallen creature. His sword, clothes, and skin covered in the massive amount of blood. He only stood, staring at what lied in front of him.

"Rahdolf?" Edlen squeaked out as he approached behind. Adelmar and Brandr also stepped forward with their jaws dropped.

"That is no bat," Brandr said out loud.

"No," replied Oatikki as he joined the forming circle. "This is not a creature most men have seen."

"A dragon," whispered Adelmar under his breath.

"Not quite," Radholf spoke up, breaking his long stare and turning towards the forming crowd. "This is only a dragonling. Too young to have hardened its scales. Its fire too weak to be spat. And fortunate for us too."

"Fortunate! Fortune indeed!" yelled Brandr. "Fortune of an ill kind to have brought such a wretched creature to our camp!"

"Brother," Adelmar stated in hopes of calming him down, reminding him of the eyes that were watching his responses.

"Yes, fortune of some sort," Oatikki added. "If this were fully mature, not only would it have been impossible to slay with any weapons we here possess, we would have been cooked alive before knowing what hunted us!" This silenced Brandr for the moment.

"And what of the other two?" Luno spoke up, carrying his glowing staff now at a dimmed intensity, "Where would this one's *kin* be in such a hurry off to?"

Radholf stared at Luno with a dreadful and serious look. He glanced at Adelmar and Brandr, and briefly to Oatikki. He couldn't make eye contact with Edlen. Perhaps in an attempt to hide the truth. Perhaps to hide his fear. But he knew what real danger they were all in now. Radholf looked back at Adelmar.

"We must find shelter. It is not safe here," Radholf said as he began walking to their tent.

"Where will we go?" Adelmar asked.

"Luno, how far are we from the entrance to your valley?"

"Not close enough to avoid another encounter with *those* things," he replied. Radholf stopped and turned around.

"We make for the collapsed road. The entrance is not far from here, and we may find shelter. Or better yet, some ancient unremembered path. Two days north of here, if I am close to knowing where we are, and walking with little to no rest. We must pack now. We leave as soon as everyone is ready."

"I would not trust to your hopes, Radholf," Luno said in disapproval. Radholf glanced over at him. "But we certainly cannot stay here. I will follow," Luno concluded.

Radholf continued towards the tent. Just before entering, he shouted back.

"Oati!" Radfholf called without looking back.

"Will do!" Oatikki replied. He approached the fallen dragonling's head. It lay in the tall grass, eyes clamped shut and mouth open wide. He pulled out his ax and swung it hard down upon the dead creature's jaw, breaking its teeth off and into the matted grass. He picked one up, wiped it down, and slid it into his pocket.

"Oatikki...why do we need to leave in such a hurry?" Edlen asked in a dull whisper. "Are those things coming back?"

"Those two? Certainly not."

"Then why the urgency?"

Oatikki looked down at Edlen. Luno's soft-white light outlining the wrinkles and features of his face, shining bright off his tusk. He took a deep breath.

"When a bear cub is frightened, where does it run?" Edlen stood motionless for a moment, then dread fell across his face. Fear erupted in his heart, greater than he had felt at any time before.

"They run to mother bear," Edlen answered. Oatikki nodded slowly and headed to gather his things.

Edlen looked down at the head of the beast, and noticed a black feather sticking out from under his own foot. He looked around and found more of them, at least a dozen, scattered across the campsite. He had not noticed them before the great winds came along and blew the fires cold. In his mind now, he felt he knew where the winds had come from. Though he was too afraid to admit it out loud.

CHAPTER VIII

THE BATTLE OF REYNIR PASS

— 11th of Frostbreath, 1866 —

The forest laid quiet in a deep slumber that had not been broken in years, save that of an occasional feathered visitor or small guest. Foot paths that had been, now overgrown and swallowed back up by that which grew around them, could no longer be found. Aged vegetation stood tall, no longer growing so late in the season. In the deepest parts of the forest, deep in the Old Forest, winter's cold fingers could never penetrate. Trees slowed their growth, and only shed leaves for a brief few weeks, sometimes overlapping with other buds and young leaves.

But on the outskirts, where the feet of the mountains begin rising up the earth, the forest lost its grip. Trees thinned out, grasses grew weaker, and the icy cold fingers of winter crept down from the tops of the mountains and brought drastic seasonal changes. And at night, it got very cold.

As the night air chilled the tall grasses and underbrush on these outskirts of the forest, the silence broke to the sound of footsteps. Crickets paused their slow symphonies as the single line of men, women, and children struggled to carry themselves through the night.

Leading the campaign was Radholf accompanied by Luno and Edlen. Scattered through the line were the other men, lightly armed and with torches. At the back was Oatikki, keeping a close eye and ear out for anything that might catch scent of their trail.

Luno's staff had long lost its lust, leaving the group leaders with torches of their own. Radholf and Luno continued to talk about the details of their earlier encounter.

"I have meant to thank you, Luno, for your help stopping the attack. I know not what else we could have done that would halt a dragonling in its path."

"Not much I can imagine," Luno replied. "But I do not think even the magic I possess would be anything more than an annoyance to a larger creature of the same kind."

"Rather, a beacon to attract more likely," Radholf answered back. Luno nodded with a serious look of realization on his face. Edlen listened closely as he followed behind.

Luno continued to stare ahead at their pathless route. Edlen's worry grew, hearing that there might have been something else out there, other than a giant mother-dragon and her (now) two dragonlings. That seemed terrifying enough to be wandering out in the dark forest in the wild at night. He felt suddenly vulnerable. Like a small mouse being played with by a cat. He felt his end would be inevitably facing the dragon that hunted him, and he shuttered at this thought.

"What if we're not alone out here?" Radholf said to Luno.

"By what do you mean?"

"I have suspicions that not all in our little party are who they say they are," Radholf answered. Luno looked at Radholf, and knowing his accusations be not towards him, he looked back at the line that followed them.

"Whom do you speak of?" Luno asked in curiosity.

"The young woman, the foreign girl. When I first talked to her she seemed quiet and reserved. But when I mentioned your name, Luno, she shifted."

Luno's interest peaked.

"Shifted? In what ways?"

"She covered her face, and looked a bit afraid. I believe she knows you, or knows of you. And I mean not to pass judgment on others, but I do not believe her intentions would be friendly towards you, if you ever question her."

Luno stared back with eyes in a glare. Only a few people behind were visible as the group snaked through the underbrush.

"What does she look like?" Luno asked, now fully concerned.

"Her appearance reminds me of someone of far eastern origins, beyond the land of the Giants. Young, in appearance."

Luno's concerned remained unchanged.

"Eyes of green, I would guess?" he asked.

"Deep green, yes." Radholf replied.

Luno stopped momentarily. The people behind paused with him, as his sudden change had created a brief halt that rippled down the line. Under his breath he spoke quietly the name of the girl.

"Sabrina," he said to himself. Then realizing what awkwardness he had brought upon himself (as those halted with him stared at him with worry), he continued up the current hill they were traversing.

"You know of this girl?" Radholf asked. Luno remained silent.

"Never mind your silence, wizard. If you have history with her that you intend to keep, I respect it to be none of my concern. But if she were to pose any threat to myself or these people..."

"She would pose no threat," Luno ended.

"Very well, I will trust your answer. But do keep an eye on her. I know not what her intentions are."

"She will not stay with us for much longer," Luno answered in final. This was the last he wanted to discuss of the topic. Edlen had been listening to the entire conversation, and his interests in her increased greatly. He began to think of situations where she knew Luno. Had she known him this side of the mountains? Is she from the valley of the wizards? What magic does she possess? The more he wondered about her, the more obsessed he became. He began to desperately want to talk to her, and played out scenarios where they would meet on the trail. He would ask her those friendly questions and make her giggle (although he had a difficult time imagining what her laughter would sound like). The more he thought, the more he realized it might be difficult to approach her, and that it may be best to leave her be.

But no! He couldn't. He couldn't leave the thought of her alone. He continued to daydream, fantasize, and play out conversations in his head. The simple thoughts of just *being* with her made his heart flutter like the butterflies back home. It excited him and gave him hope of a possible happiness in these dark times. It was refreshing, and it was a hope he held on to desperately. These thoughts continued to run through his head as the night marched on.

As the dawn rose and the eastern sky revealed itself, the party had found themselves beginning to traverse the southern sides of the foothills of the vast mountain range. They had taken a few short breaks during the night and pushed hard throughout the following day. Little was heard outside of their own chatter and baby cries, and even less was seen. The walk became more difficult as the hills were more prominent the closer they came to the mountains, but this also meant the vegetation began to thin. It was easier to find a walking path now as mostly tall trees covered the grounds and less underbrush, and the insects did not bite as relentless as down deep in the forest below.

Radholf, Adelmar, and Brandr all felt that it would be best to gather rest during daylight as it would be easier to see fowl things approaching. So just after the sun had crossed the center of the sky, they halted for a meal and extended rest. Edlen thought this to be a perfect time to approach *Sabrina* and try to get to know her.

Everyone had eaten as there were several fires that were made on the forest floor. They had gained enough altitude that the trees had thinned out, and they found themselves in what felt like a completely changed world. There was little that was green anymore, as most leaves had changed to their fall-time colors of reds, oranges, and golds. Maple trees dotted the landscape and there were large groups of golden Aspen trees with bright white bark here and there. Brown rabbits darted across the openings, trying to gather what was left in the cooling wild before winter settled in. The breeze was gentle, and the sun warming and welcoming.

Edlen sat with his back against an aspen tree finishing up his apple. He could see Sabrina sitting by herself a ways under her own aspen. She was beautiful to him — almost elusive and mature, and perhaps misunderstood. He felt that he could offer her a fair understanding, and would be willing to listen to anything she would tell him, for anything she had done or could say would hold no fault in his mind. As she sat there under the aspen tree, the breeze blowing the ends of her dark bangs, Edlen began to summon the courage to go over and talk to her.

Thinking of what he would say, how would he start. Would it seem odd to her that he already knew her name? That he knows so much about her? It didn't matter. He knew that nothing would come from sitting and thinking. His heart began to pound hard, and he became far more nervous than he anticipated.

He stood up, and cleared his throat. Tossing the apple aside, he wiped his mouth on his sleeves and straightened out his shirt. His face felt hot and eyes began to swell. What was he doing? Could he go through with it?

"This isn't like me," he thought to himself. "I have never approached someone like *her* before. What will she say?" These thoughts caused him to stall for a moment, but only a brief moment. Swallowing his doubts, he took a couple steps and watched as she laid herself down under the tree to join everyone else in an afternoon rest.

He stopped and watched as his plans began to fall apart. He felt far too uncomfortable to bother her now, and it was easy for his mind to excuse his plans for a poor young woman who needed her rest. Perhaps it was best to wait for another day. And although his heart had ceased to pound hard out from his chest, it began to break in a lost hope of finding a thread of happiness that afternoon. He took a deep breath, and returned to his tree where the grass had been matted down from his lunch time sitting. This was probably for the best anyway, or so he thought. And although he didn't move for the next hour as he laid under the tree, he slept not, for his mind was too busy dealing with his own heart.

After a couple of hours of rest, the sun had begun to sink into the western sky. Brandr and Adelmar gathered everyone together to make best the last leg of their trip in the wild. Their route would continue in a north-eastern direction in hopes to find the entrance of the ancient road. The mouth of the road was tucked away in a very small valley, pinned between two cliff faces that proved to be difficult to find if one had not been there before. And although Luno had warned of the road being caved in long ago in some past, Radholf kept in hopes of finding some sort of shelter or alternate route nearby.

It was not long before the group was on their feet and heading in the right direction once more. All afternoon they walked, which proved tiresome and difficult for many, as many would tell you that a light sleep on tired eyes can often times be more harmful than helpful. But the encouragement of their leaders Adelmar and Brandr kept most motivated enough to keep up without falter, for they were a strong group.

The afternoon passed to evening, and the chilly winds of the mountains began to sweep down into the valleys and foothills. Extra layers and cloaks were handed out to keep people warm as the night approached, but the cool air kept all insects at bay, of which Edlen found to be a pleasant trade.

The moon peeked out from behind tall clouds and cast deep shadows of aspen trees in the blue-white light. The breeze had picked up, blowing the tops of the trees back and forth. The waving of branches and falling leaves left Edlen's nerves feeling overwhelmed. Movement and sounds came from every direction, and seemingly at random. But the light of their torches reached far with little to obstruct them, and the breeze seemed to help keep them glowing hot and bright.

As the march continued into the young night, Edlen found it to be a perfect moment to summon the courage and try to talk to Sabrina. He had been thinking of the questions and topics to talk about all afternoon and evening, and knew she was walking up ahead in the line. Picking up the pace, he passed women and men, and eventually found the beautiful young woman he had been so focused on. Slowly catching up to her, he eventually met her pace. An awkward silence settled between the two at first, as he tried to find the right comment to break it.

"It's getting quite chilly out here," he said at last, relying on one of the only things he was sure of they would have in common. She gave no response.

"I'm Edlen," he said in an attempt for a response.

"Livia," she finally answered. Edlen stumbled a bit in the falsity he was being told, but he couldn't correct her. He continued as though he knew nothing else.

"Nice to meet you, Livia," he replied. "So, you are traveling alone?" Again, she responded with silence, so he continued. "I'm with—"

"Radholf, I know," she said interrupting, and ending a bit abruptly.

"Oh, do you know him?" he asked.

"Not more than I know the rest of these people," she answered.

"Fair!" he said with a smile. "I also had been traveling with Oatikki, you may have noticed, the Orc. And an interesting fellow named Luno," he said as he looked at her, trying to find any clue of her knowledge of him. She only stared at the ground, watching her footing. He suddenly felt as though he may have put too much pressure on her, and was afraid of pushing her away. He began to panic in his head, and felt an incredible urge to make some proof of his abilities, and that he could be trusted. Without thinking much, he blurted out a promise of high confidence.

"Well, if you need anything, or find yourself to be in any trouble, I'll be around!" She grinned a bit and laughed a short laugh.

"If I need the help of a boy, I surely will be in trouble," she responded. He suddenly felt embarrassed, his face turning red. It was difficult to notice though with only the moonlight and spread out torches. Anger had boiled under his embarrassment, and he found himself without response. He only cleared his throat, and picked up his pace to head to the front of the line. Keeping in company of Radholf and Luno might help him forget what had just happened.

As he was catching up, a sudden sound of rapid, heavy footsteps was heard behind him. Oatikki ran past Edlen, almost not noticing him.

"Edlen! Come!" he said as he passed, sounding serious and urgent. Edlen ran hard to keep up with Oatikki, and they made it to the front where Radholf and Luno had been leading.

"Radholf!" Oatikki shouted. Radholf and Luno stopped, and Oatikki approached them as Radholf turned his torch to the Orc. Edlen quickly caught up.

"What is it, my friend?" Radholf asked. Luno's head was turned at an angle, appearing both slightly annoyed yet curious to the message he might be carrying.

"Radholf, we are being tracked," Oatikki said in a quiet voice so to not trouble any ears mistakenly listening. Radholf stood quiet for a moment, working out plans and thoughts.

"How many?" he asked. Luno began to look around, then back at Oatikki.

"Thirty, maybe forty," he answered.

"Have they started their encircling?"

"Not that I can tell. They're still in a single large group, southwest of us, and traveling fast." Radholf looked at Oatikki, then at Luno.

"We haven't much time. We must get these good people to the mouth of the valley. If we can keep from being surrounded and focus our efforts in front of us, we might stand a chance," Radholf instructed.

"We have maybe ten good men," Oatikki said.

"And a wizard!" Radholf said with a grin. Luno looked surprised at the inclusion of his skills as a positive thing against an attack.

"A wizard..." Oatikki said with disapproval. "Even then, we will be no match against such a large pack. Especially if *he* is with them, of which I do not give doubt." Oatikki argued.

"These people have no other choice," Radholf said, then lowered his voice to almost a whisper as he leaned into the two of them.

"If left out here exposed, they will not make it. Not a single one. We are their only hope, and our only safety is at the mouth." Oatikki nodded with determination and took off running to find Adelmar and Brandr.

"Edlen, you stay with me," Radholf said.

Within moments, the group was in a hurrying bustle and increased their pace. Men now carried the children. Oatikki and Adelmar brought up the back to ensure no one was left behind. They raced for what seemed to Edlen to be hours. His legs were sore as their incline steepened. They were making their way almost directly east now, rounding past mountain feet stretching out and into the wooded lands. The fear of being chased gave speed to those in the group, but exhaustion kept creeping up and taking individuals out for a rest. Not everyone could keep up.

Paces slowed despite constant encouragement and giving of motivation. After a long and tiresome journey, they rounded a long, large foothill.

"This is it!" Radholf shouted. "Come! We have made it!" Several hundred yards to the east, a second foothill stretched out, equal in height and length. On the insides of both, high above, stood two statues carved into the rock. They were of some noble rulers of the past.

Radholf took a deep breath of relief.

"King Reynir, my good friend. How I have longed to gaze upon your face again," he said putting his hand on his heart as he looked up at the statue on the eastern foothill.

"Who is he?" Edlen asked looking at the statue of a younger man on the western foothill.

"That is his son, King Rikk. This road was founded by the pair as it had taken nearly seventy years to complete," Radholf told.

Along the eastern foothill ran a small creek, leading out of the road entrance in the distance. It flowed swiftly and shallow, the waters ice cold and glistening in the moonlight.

"Come," Luno said, staring intently at Radholf. "Let us see what kind of trap we are walking into."

The foothills started wide and slowly merged to a point some couple of miles towards the mountains. The mountains were now straight ahead and were looming far above. Their white peaks glowed a soft blue in the moon light and ragged rock faces stuck out at sharp angles all up and down their bodies. At the convergence of the two tall foothills was a path that led up and left as it had been intended so many centuries ago.

The group rushed quickly to the path. At the base was at one point a well-constructed stone road, which now had lost its grip and given way to the natural world. Under the thin blades of grass that peeked up, thick stone could still be heard and felt under the foot. The road cut straight into the rock, with vertical rock faces that shot straight up hundreds of yards. The road was wide, though, giving plenty of space and a sense of awe. Along the right side at all times, the small creek flowed freely in its own private ravine no more than two feet deep.

The moon cast its blue-white light across openings in the road where the cliffs ended their shadows. It was a beautiful road, even in the night, and the faintest sounds of footsteps echoed endlessly around each corner. It wound back and forth, never breaking out of the cliff faces on either side, and always working its way higher and higher. After nearly a mile of winding back and forth, they found the place where the creek emerged. It fell down a shallow waterfall along the cliff side, right at a sharp bend in the road. The sounds of the water were healing in mind and body, as it trickled down the rock and flowed downhill. Edlen was saddened to leave such a peaceful thing behind.

They continued to travel up this road for what seemed to be another couple of miles, though perhaps not any further than a short distance as the eagle would fly. By the steepness of the road, it felt as though they were climbing ever higher. However, their view to the south was quite limited by the surrounding cliffs, so it was difficult to tell exactly how hight they had climbed.

As they rounded another corner, they were forced to come to a sudden stop. Much to Radholf's saddened heart, there before them stood tall a wall of crumbled rock. It was as tall as the cliffs on either side, and impossible to tell how thick. Fortune had not been with them that night, as Luno's tales and warnings proved to be accurate.

"Caved in," said Luno. "Blocked off and nowhere to go."

Radholf looked around in hopes of a secondary path, but found only disappointment. He took a deep sigh.

"Let us return to the entrance. We will have a better chance of surviving the night, if discovered and followed," Radholf said.

"If!" Luno replied. "You do not see where you have led us, Radholf? Cornered prey is precisely their intentions. It's how a wolf hunts!"

Oatikki approached the conversation and pulled out his two axes.

"Ha! And I cannot hunt unless *my* prey is within the reaches of my axe!" He held up one of the two axes and its edges showed bright in the moonlight, sharp enough to sever a wild boar's head from its body cleanly.

Radholf grinned as Luno scoffed at that reply. In a weak echo, a long howl came riding on the wind up through the carved rock. It sent chills through the people hiding at the end of the road, now feeling vulnerable and trapped despite the Orc's remarks. Oatikki turned and started heading down the road.

"Come, men! Our guests have arrived!"

Edlen's heart was pounding. His thoughts raced of their previous encounter with the wolves, and he knew not of any retreat or escape, despite the absence of such knowledge in their previous endeavors of a similar situation. He knew the beasts that had haunted his thoughts and nightmares since that night, the creatures he continuously checked for in the shadows over his shoulder, the fear of much of his travels in the wild, were waiting for him at the head of the road. He knew there would be no running. There would only be fighting, blood, and death.

Despite his fears, of the instinct to hide, he grabbed the hilt of his sword. He *hated* the feeling of cowardice, of feeling completely helpless. It had eaten away at his soul, and the fire that burned bright at its center burst through the shell of fear. He was no longer one who would flee from a battle. The path of flight was not what his heart desired, for it now desired revenge, fueled by rage. He drew his sword and joined Oatikki in the charge to the mouth.

Seeing such a boy and an Orc take the lead gave courage to the other men who were armed. Their leaders Aldemar and Brandr were the next to follow, shortly behind came Radholf and Luno. Six other men went with them, bringing their total to twelve.

Winding back and forth, traversing down the hill through the rock they went. Howls echoed all around them. They passed the emergence of the brook, and continued down to where the road opened up. There before them stood tall Amarok, Hunter of Hunters, and King of the Wolven creatures. Behind him were countless eyes glowing in the darkness. Growls and yips came echoing far back, further than the eye could pierce in the night.

Edlen stopped in his tracks at the sight of Amarok. The wolf was larger than any he had witnessed. He was silver grey and majestic in appearance, yet his yellow eyes pierced mind and body, giving command and fear. The creature was taller than Edlen was, meeting near in height to the Orc that stood next to him. The claws black, teeth white like a wet fire's smoke, and a look in his face of hunger. In the night air, the creature's tail blew in the wind, and his silhouette stood out in the dark, feeling menacing and large. Edlen's heart stopped, and for a brief moment he lost all courage upon such a sight. He felt the strength in his fingers flee, and his hilt beginning to slip.

"Amarok! My old friend!" Radholf shouted with a sarcastic tone. Edlen snapped out of the spell the creature had given off and regained his composure, grasping back his sword before it too had left him.

"I see you have brought your little pets with you! And my, how many you have!" Growling increased in the dark void behind the Wolf King.

"You have crossed great distances of *my* land, and swiftly! Yet the baggage you carry has been your ultimate folly, Radholf rabbit-runner." The Wolf King replied as the growls and barks continued. Although they carried far, Edlen's ears perked at the sound of small rocks crumbling. It had not sounded as though it came from behind, but to the east, as though from high above the cliff face. Though no sight revealed itself, he knew something was there. He focused his attention to the sides, as he quickly began to suspect an ambush.

"I have meant you no harm, O' Wolf King," Radholf continued. "And even now, you may pardon us and we will take our leave. There is no need for such a barbaric brawl to come of our meeting." Radholf was humbly offering a way out for the wolves, as an offering of peaceful intentions is traditional in most initial combat meetings among Men. Though expectations in Radholf's mind were none when talking to a Wolf.

"Pardon!" Amarok replied in a rage. "Too many times have you insulted our kin. Too many times have you managed to slip from my jaws. Not this time, Verndari. You will not walk away from this battle. And with so little to offer in a fight!" The wolf took a step forward and cocked his head.

"You disappoint me, human. I was hoping to have a little more *fun* with you and your friends before filling our bellies with your flesh," he said curving his lips and revealing his many teeth.

"I must apologize again, my Wolf King, of which I tire of," Radholf insulted back. "But I *will* be walking away from this battle, and quite unscathed." The Wolf King snorted at this in anger with a growl. "Walk away now, Wolf, or your fur I shall wear as a cloak before this is over," Radholf said sternly and with a sudden change in tone. Edlen's eyes widened at this remark. He looked at Oatikki who was grinning uncontrollably.

"Oati..." Edlen whispered, indicating movement of some creature above the cliff. Oatikki took a brief glance and returned his attention to Edlen with a wink.

Amarok growled fiercely, showing his long sharp teeth. His growl rumbled deep and shook Edlen in his very bones, as it was as terrifying as his appearance. "We will see who will be drinking whose blood!" he cried out, turning back quickly to return into the void night, littered with glowing eyes ever watchful.

"Ready yourself, lad," Oatikki said, taking a defensive stance. Barks and yips echoed along the walls of rock all around them. Edlen was frightfully nervous. Painful waves of fear echoed through his limbs, and he found it difficult to hold onto reality. He felt too afraid to run, and much too afraid to fight. His fears turned to sadness, as he felt deep in his heart that this would be his end.

But his sadness turned again to rage. The memories of his past life, of the life once had, returned to his mind, reminding him of all he had lost. The memories of running, of the terrors he had witnessed. Anger boiled up again in his soul. His face grew hot, and his grip tightened. He was ready to end this, regardless of the outcome.

Then a deafening howl, deeper and more piercing than heard at the tower came exploding from the darkness. A full wall of teeth, claws, and fur erupted towards them. Radholf pointed his long great sword out in front of him, yelling at the top of his lungs.

The first casualty came as the first of Adelmar's arrows soared through the darkness and pierced into the skull of a single wolf. It collapsed to the ground, and was quickly replaced by the wolf behind it. Another arrow shot out before the collision of fur and steel met, giving birth to showers of blood. Teeth clanked against sword, and wolf after wolf found their end.

But more came relentlessly in waves. Edlen found himself protected behind Oatikki, doing his best to take the blunt hits of the attackers. But even so, Edlen's blade made its own damage against the wolven numbers. He had learned much from Radholf and Oatikki, and held enough skill to keep his own against a wolf, one on one.

But how their numbers grew. More and more poured in, and it soon became clear that Oatikki's estimate fell far short. Oatikki's axes swung wide, smashing wolf skulls and slicing limbs on every swing. In the moonlight his axes glistened, flying through the night air and meeting fur and bone. The blunt force alone was enough to crack any wolf's skull, but the sharpened edge dug in deep, puncturing into the blood underneath. His destruction with the ax gave proof of his experience of many battles. Wolf after wolf stood no chance against him, but even Oatikki began to tire, and felt the oncoming need of some relief.

Radholf's sword swung in full complete circles, each one slicing through fur and bone. His wrath was far greater than even the Orc's. No beast could come within feet of Radholf without bleeding out. With a single stroke, the wolf's head was tossed into the air. The next lunged at him, finding only the tip of the steel blade thrust far into the back of its throat and out the other side. Radholf twisted and bent, blood-thirsty and ravaging through the waves of attacks.

Adelmar demonstrated his skills as a bowman as well. Arrows flew past friend and marking only foe. A few too close to comfort for some, but leaving no harm on them, for he knew exactly where to throw his arrows. They were swift and hard, each one taking its own kill.

Brandr kept the wolves from nearing Adelmar with his dual short-sword combat. Twisting around, getting very close to his enemy, he sliced through throat, lung, and heart. The two were a dreadful duo to match against. And behind them stood the others, taking care of the few beasts that had made it past the front line of men.

Another great howl emerged, this time followed by the mass army of the Amarok in full charge. Now that his prey had been weakened and tired, he was ready for the kill. The Wolf King led the charge, directed towards Radholf.

Radholf, seeing the coming danger, cried out behind him.

"Luno! Now! Give them light!" he cried.

Luno shouted aloud a great spell that shook the rock around them. His staff, once again with a beautiful gem in the mouth of the dragon, erupted in light that rivaled the living sun. This light was not white, but shinned with a yellowish tint. It was as though the sun had risen itself from the back of that little valley, at the mouth of the road.

The wolves halted their charge in sudden shock, squinting and blinded by the light, but only temporarily.

"Ah ha-ha!" The Wolf King's sinister laugh rumbled. "What foolish plans to think a *wizard* would provide any shelter from my storm! You do not frighten us, Verndari," he shouted at Radholf, "You only make the hunt so much easier, we can now see our prey so much clearer!"

"The light is not shed to blind you, Wolf. It sheds to give power to them." Radholf replied nodding behind the wolf pack. Three wolves at the back of the pack behind them were suddenly thrust high into the air. The attention of the entire pack was suddenly shifted to the rear. Cries and yelps came as the horde of wolves began to flee away the men. The assault continued on the front as the pack divided. Much of the efforts of the wolves shifted to attack the newly come allies from the south.

The Wolf King shouted in a commanding voice.

"Take out the Arborians! Bite their limbs, consume their hives!" The three Arborian creatures wreaked havoc among the wolves. One reached its arm out, as limbs like vines shot out and grasped a wolf by the snout, then squeezed tight until its skull collapsed on itself. The biting teeth of the wolves proved to be no match, as a second grew in height, high above the pack and began smashing wolf after wolf under its tree-trunk legs.

Furious, the Wolf King rushed south to meet the new challengers. He darted past his own kin, faster than any bird could fly. With a rumbling growl he leaped high in the air and tackled the third Arborian soldier to the ground, crushing the wooden cage that protected its hive. The then brittle Arborian fell to pieces and the hive went rolling along the forest floor.

Amarok took off towards it like a dog chasing a cat, snapping and biting when he came within reach. It slowed its roll and the Wolf King, filled with fury and rage, leaped to smash the hive against the ground. As he began to descend upon it, roots shot up from the earth and wrapped themselves around the hive like a wicker basket protecting something precious. As the great beast's teeth opened up, the ground swallowed the hive whole, leaving only dirt and rock left for the King of the Wolves to grasp down upon. He looked up furiously, trying to find where it would reappear again. Several yards to the east, the Arborian reformed, rising from the ground, and ready again.

Amarok was overcome with anger. He was tired of being tricked and played with. He looked back at the Men, back at Radholf. Then he looked to Radholf's right, and saw Edlen standing behind Oatikki, who was struggling to catch his breath.

"The boy!" Amarok shouted. "Kill the young-ling!" A full charge of every wolf in the pack began towards Edlen. Edlen's eyes opened wide in terror. The shift of attention gave Edlen little hope of surviving, and he became terribly afraid.

"Run boy!" Oatikki shouted.

"To the road, Edlen! Quick!" Radholf commanded, and began running in the same direction. Adelmar's bow sang as he shot arrow after arrow, trying to slow down the wolf charge. Oatikki stood his ground, waiting for the wolves to meet his axes. As they approached, he too began to run back to the north, towards the road's mouth. His axes swung left and right, severing heads and breaking backs.

The Arborians at the back did their best to keep up with the swift wolf pack, taking out any that they could catch up. It did not take but a moment for the Wolf King to make his way to the head of the charge, growling and barking. As the men made their way to the mouth of the road, Luno began to retreat as well. It was clear that the wolves were making too quick an advancement for Edlen to make it to the narrow road, where the wolf numbers might be easier to control. As Luno began to enter the road, a dark figure dashed quickly past him. He nearly ran into it, but recognized it not as it passed. He stood in his tracks and gazed back as the figure continued towards the oncoming pack, headed in the direction of the Hunter of Hunters.

Past Edlen, past Radholf, past Adelmar and Brandr, the figure uncloaked the hood it wore to reveal the dark-haired young woman. Edlen recognized her as she stood in the path of the Wolf King.

"Livia!" Edlen shouted. She stood down the giant beast, who took a leap at her, jaws open. She dropped to the ground and grabbed the Wolf King by the rear foot. He fell flat on his face and the pack around him halted. Her eyes were clamped shut with intense control. Her grip even tighter on the wolf's ankle. The Wolf King struggled to keep composure. He gave no growl, no command. His biting stopped as he struggled to keep her out of his mind.

Luno stepped forward.

"Sabrina! No! You cannot control him! His will is too great!"

She sat on the ground, never ceasing her spell. The wolves around her glanced at each other in confusion. The ones nearest to her began to feel dizzy and disoriented.

"What is she doing?" Radholf shouted at Luno.

"Giving us our chance..." Luno replied softly. The Arborians continued to make advances through the back of the wolf pack, crushing, flinging, and squeezing their innards out in a gruesome combat. Oatikki ran towards the girl, but the Wolf King began to shift the balance of his own mind back into his control. Sabrina struggled to keep her spell upon him, and his growls became longer and more defined. At once, the Wolf King's eyes opened, regaining complete control over his own mind, and threw Sabrina with a powerful kick. She collapsed on the ground in front of Oatikki as he stopped just short of her.

Grrrroooowl! "How dare you curse me, foolish she-man! Kill them all!" Amarok shouted. He leaped forward toward Sabrina, who remained unconscious on the ground. Oatikki leaped forward, tackling the Wolf King to the ground beside Sabrina. In an intense wrestle, Oatikki found himself pinned down under the fierce creature, whose teeth were inches from his face, and drool hanging just above his pierced tusk. His axes fallen from his hands, just feet from either one on both sides.

"I love the taste of Orc!" Amarok said. As he opened his jaws wide, ready to devour Oatikki's face, a great sound was heard far in the distance. It shook the rock all around them. Even the mountain itself seemed to tremble in the deep roar, despite it sounding as though it came from a great distance to the south.

Like thunder it rumbled, and its echoes bounced off the rock faces above them. Edlen could feel it in his chest, in his feet from the earth. Everyone in the small valley, the men, the wolves, the Arborians all stood still in horror from the sound they had just witnessed. Radholf stood next to Luno at the mouth of the road. His forehead dripping in sweat, and his wet long hair partially veiling his face, breathing heavily from exhaustion. He stared out into the darkness, southward into the Wild. He hoped against all else that he had not heard what had shaken the very earth. The battle had paused entirely as all waited to bear witness to what exactly had given off that thundering roar.

Once again it bellowed, much louder and intense. It had come much closer, as though leaping miles within the few seconds since the last cry. Radholf shut his eyes in sadness and pain. His heart ached to know what was coming, what he had thought for years would never return, but what he knew he was sent to do. The beast had finally come, though this was not the time to finish his task.

Upon the second roar, the Arborians cried out in terror and fled the rear flanks. The Wolf King looked up, at which point Oatikki shoved him off and escaped, grabbing his axes with him. Though Amarok fought not, letting his Orc prey escape. His will to fight seemed to have left him. Oatikki picked up the girl, and carried her to Radholf and Luno.

Smiling, Amarok glanced at Radholf.

"You see, my rabbit-friend! You will *not* be walking away from this after all! Haha!" He turned away and began heading back into the forest. "Let us see how you escape the wrath of the great flying fire serpent!" he shouted as he howled into the night air.

Radholf watched as the remainder of the wolf pack fled into the night.

"Luno…" he said. "You may dispel your staff now."

As Luno reached up to remove the gem from the mouth of the dragon, a third earth-rumbling roar came from the night that laid before them.

"What hunts us, Radholf? What comes for us at this hour?" Adelmar asked.

"From the depths of the fiery soul of the flame wraiths comes forth a birth of fire, wing, scale and claw. A terror that patrols the night sky in secrecy and stealth. Spitting flame and shattering rock, who roosts on the peaks of mountains. A fire drake whose rage cannot be matched, filled with hatred and greed. A serpent bathed in flame," Radholf explained, never breaking his stare into the night. A fourth loud bellow came echoing around the mountain side.

"Nothing compares to the fierce anger a dragon can possess. Her wrath can destroy entire villages, burn entire forests, and drive the men of the Gronndelon to near extinction," he concluded.

Oatikki reached into his pocket and pulled out the tooth of the fallen dragonling. He held it up in the moon light, twisting it around to show its black shape reflecting the dull moon's light.

"And we killed her offspring," he said raising an eyebrow at Radholf.

"Quickly! We must warn the others!" Radholf said as he took a turn into the road. Oatikki picked up the still unconscious Sabrina, and the surviving men began heading up the road. Before they could make it to the very first turn, a fell swoop rushed over their heads. A shadow, that spanned far beyond the opening above, flew over. With great intensity, the mother dragon released a deafening roar that shook the very soul of any in that little canyon.

The dragon took a turn and continued its hunt, looking for any that moved. Radholf continued the march up the road as the others followed.

"We must get to the others!" he kept shouting. The dragon continued to fly back and forth, as the men wound up the road.

They passed the emergence of the small creek and turned to the west. It was at this point that the dragon slowed its flight, and descended upon the next turn in the road to the west. It was far toop large to squeeze down into the road, as its wings, even when folded, clasped upon either side. She sat there, perched like a great raptor with her serpent neck bent crooked in a downward direction to better see her prey.

She was covered in dark grey scales that appeared dull in the moonlight. Two large horns shot back from behind her green serpent eyes. Shorter black spikes lined her spine, all the way down to the tip of her tail. A giant single claw shot out from the tip, and she whipped it back and forth in the night sky in an attempt to keep her balance on that rocky perch.

Her wings were like that of a bat, with a single giant claw emerging from the main joint. Webbed in thin skin that shown just the slightest moonlight through. Her arms and legs were a mass of muscle and strength, covered in thick scales like armor. But it was her face that was the most terrifying.

Scaly lips couldn't cover her long black teeth entirely. A fork tongue hid behind the dual-rows of teeth as long as a man's arm, and sharper than any spear. Her head was like a serpent, with two slots for her nose, resting at the end of a long winding neck. It was something of a nightmare to only gaze upon her.

Radholf stopped in his tracks. He stood still, as even his own courage was tested beyond any point he had been tried before. The entire group of survivors, who had recently felt victorious against the attacking wolf pack, were all frozen in fear.

"Who hath taken the life of which did not belong to?" the dragon spoke out. Her voice was deep and terrifying, and it echoed off the very mountain side in a thunderous boom.

"Who hath killed my child?!" she asked with orange flames licking out from the sides of her lips.

Everyone remained silent, with only the sounds of trembling coming from those whose spirit were about to break. The dragon studied the small group, looking for answers, looking for a target — any target, to invite her wrath. At this moment, Sabrina began to return as she lay in Oatikki's arms. She groaned, slowly opening her eyes. Upon realizing the horrifying creature that was before her, she shrieked in a frightful startle.

This brought the dragon's attention directly to her. The dragon's eyes opened wide and lips curled back.

"Was it you?! Little mouse! I shall burn you to dust!" she roared out as she reached down with her giant claws to snatch her up.

Edlen leaped out in front of Sabrina and Oatikki, trying to protect them, holding his sword out in front. The giant beast's claws wrapped around him and Sabrina, pulling her right out from Oatikki's arms. He gave every effort to hold on, but his arms became pinched between the dragon's fingers, and he fell.

Edlen's sword remained pointed into the palm of the dragon, and realizing the terrible place he had found himself, he pushed with his entire strength on the sword. It pierced the skin and sunk into the dragon's hand.

The dragon howled into the night in the sudden feel of pain, not realizing that the palms of her own hands were one of only a couple places that her scales were not as thick, not as hardened. She flung her hand out, tossing Edlen and Sabrina high into the night sky. They flew far to the east, over the crest of the hill in which the small creek flowed over. Their landing never sounded.

The dragon was furious. Flames pulsated out with every breath between her clenched teeth. Fury shone bright in her eyes. She frantically looked around to make sure every living thing before her would be engulfed in the wrath she was about to unleash.

Then the screams came. They came echoing down the road and over the tops of the cliffs. Those who had been left behind in safety from the battle, hiding at the end of the road, unleashed their fears in an audible echo upon seeing just the top of the dragon down below, and her whipping tail flying back and forth in the night.

The dragon looked over in sudden realization that there were more to this little party than she had recently found.

"No!" Radholf shouted as he ran towards the dragon. The dragon looked at Radholf, then with an angry face leaped into the air, beating her wings hard to quickly ascend up the side of the mountain. With little more than a few seconds, she perched once again upon where the road ended. Cries and screams poured out like a sudden dam breaking under a heavy lake. The dragon took in a deep breath, and unleashed her fury bathed in flame and heat upon the end of that road. The intense burning of fire sounded like the cracking of lightning and rolling of thunder, like white rapids crashing down at the base of a waterfall. It lit up that face of the mountain in a reddish orange light, and continued relentlessly until all had ceased. No screams remained. No wails of pain or terror. Only a burning end.

Brandr took off running up the road, passed Radholf, crying out in denial.

Radholf collapsed to his knees, tears rolling down his cheeks. His mind fogged and he felt nothing except sorrow and regret. Despite the countless battles he had been a part of, regardless of how many lives he had seen end in his days, nothing ever dulled the potent heartache of the death of the innocent. His intentions had failed him, for he had failed those whom he had sworn to protect.

"Brandr!" Adelmar called out, chasing after his brother. The dragon turned her attention back to the group, and seeing a lonely man charging with his swords drawn, she quickly struck down with her jaws open wide. Slamming down on the ground, Brandr became surrounded by teeth and tongue, and her jaws clamped down with a force greater than two clashing boulders. Tilting her head up, she swallowed Adelmar's brother whole.

Adelmar halted in horror.

"What cursed nightmare haunts us this night!" he shouted, not wanting to believe what he had witnessed, and desperate to wake up and leave everything in an unrealized memory.

"Radholf!" Oatikki shouted, grabbing him by the shoulder. "Adelmar! We have to go!" Although Radholf remained in a fog, Oatikki managed to get him to his feet. With tears still in his eyes, he stared at his Orc friend.

"Radholf," Oatikki said. "We must escape! We cannot be ended here!" Radholf's mind cleared and he looked around. Luno stood in the distance with his staff and behind him were two other men. Adelmar returned in a sluggish hurry, having difficulty letting what had just happened settle into reality. Behind Luno and the others, flowed the creek down the shallow declining hill. Radholf's eyes opened wide and clear.

"To the creek!" he shouted and the men took off. "Luno! What time can you give us from that horrible creature?" he shouted, knowing the dragon's fury was not settled. Luno reached into his satchel.

"I would hate to part with such a precious thing, Radholf!" he said as he pulled out a rough black sphere.

"Would you rather part from this world entirely?" Radholf replied. Luno sighed depressingly, but knew his sacrifice would be little compared to those who had recently left. He struck the sphere with his thumbnail, scratching it hard. Then cupping it in his two hands, he blew hard into it. It began to smoke and glow. Then he tossed it hard over the southern rock face and down to the mountain's feet. It glowed hot and upon settling in its resting place in some rocky corner, it exploded in a fiery ball.

This drew the attention of the dragon, who now thought her chase was attempting to flee into the forest. As they approached the creek, the dark silhouette of the dragon flew over head. She cried out again in anger, shaking the rock around them. They splashed into the creek, and followed up the wet rocks and stone. It proved difficult as the water was ice-cold and the footing treacherous.

As they approached the top, the dragon had begun circling, looking for the others she had left behind as her searching had begun to prove fruitless.

"Where are you, little mice?" she shouted, echoing through the night sky. "You can hide in the rock-corners or under the tree skirts, but I will smite you with flame and fury once you stick your little mouse noses out!"

Oatikki and Luno were the first to cross over the crest of the creek, followed by Adelmar and the other two men. Radholf remained high up on the crest as he gazed down through the small valley between the foothills, and watched as the dragon flew back and forth.

"This is not the end," he said in a whisper. "You will see me again."

Radholf continued up the stream where the others had found a way off to the side, leaving the stream to the west. They climbed over rock and boulder up and down cliff faces, and through ravines. This was their path for many hours. As the night continued on, they made their way over this side of the mountain and into the next. The roars and cries of the hunting beast began to fade.

After many hours, the sky began to shift, showing hints of a change in color and hue. Morning was approaching, and a pinkish red glow lit up the faces of the rock all around them. It was at this time, they stumbled upon the entrance to a cave. It looked empty, as though no foot had ever been placed upon this entrance, and was buried deep in a ravine in which the only way in or out was the path they had come.

"Is this one of your caves, Luno?" Radholf asked.

"Many carve through these mountains like veins," he replied. "It is impossible to tell which ones will lead to where."

Radholf sat down to rest. His body ached, but his heart ached even worse.

"I have failed you," he said out loud, wanting to get what was on his mind out to be free in the open. "I have failed all of you, and those whom we have lost." He began to shed tears again. Oatikki bowed his head in honor. Luno had a saddened look on his face, then began commenting.

"I had begun to grow fond of our little traveler," he said, knowing Radholf's heart ached the most for Edlen. "He had a good mind to guide him," he finished.

Radholf took a deep breath.

"A mind like his father's, I do not doubt." Radholf stood, and drew his sword. He knelt with his sword tip driven into the rocky landing they stood upon. With his head bowed, he said out loud, "Edlen, son of Eldor. We thank you for your service. Go now in the joy of your father's home, and wake not until the calling when our Great Warrior comes."

He paused for a moment, then continued with the same prayers for Brandr. To this, Adelmar bowed low and began to weep. The next several moments were sat in silence, in memory of all others who had been lost. Such times were difficult to keep going, and being surrounded by the tall rock faces of the mountains, created a cage that tormented the already heavy-laden mind.

Radholf stood up and sheathed his sword. He stood tall, facing the black emptiness that remained open in front of him that was the cave. The sun had nearly completed its unveiling from the eastern horizon, and cast yellow light upon the right side of the mountain above them, though it had not yet reached any of those that stood in the shadows of the ravine.

"Let us see what awaits us in the depths of the mountains," Radholf said as he took a step into the darkness.

CHAPTER IX

RESIDENTS OF JALL-DÖKK

— 12th of Frostbreath, 1866 —

Edlen awoke in a foggy haze. His body ached deep and his skin was painful. He felt such incredible pain, but he was able to move. It appeared as though he could move his arms and legs, though it hurt greatly to do so. He was lying on his stomach, and a little light shed from high above. It shown through like a column of white, breaking through a dark, tall ceiling at an angle and hitting some far edge of the room.

Through the opening, he could see white sky, and drips of water fell down from the ring above. Long hanging moss also hung down, yet it was far too high to be able to reach.

As he shifted around, he noticed the floor was peculiar. Hard to see at first, it felt as though it continued to shift as he did. After gaining his composure and sight, he suddenly realized, much to his horror, he was lying on a bed of bones. Skulls and ribs, arms and legs, all of different creatures. Deer, wolf, and human. He looked around frantically and found himself at the bottom of a large cave. He began to breathe frantically in a panic. Looking around for an escape, the only wall he could see was a far wall lit up by the indirect light shown from the white bones on the cave floor.

His heart was beating fast, and he felt trapped. He looked around again and again, then something caught his eye. Some darkened spot just outside the reaches of detailed sight in the shadows. The ground all around him was a bumpy texture of gray, a mass pile of skeletons and carcasses, save this one peculiar spot that rose out of it.

He stood to his feet, and as best he could, took a few steps towards it. Gazing hard, he realized it was jut another body. He looked saddened, and wondered who or what it had been. Then he noticed it had a braided strand of black hair. He rushed over to the body. It was Sabrina, and as he rolled her to her back, she jumped in a sudden startle and sat up, eyes open wide.

"What! Where are we?" she said out loud. Edlen sat down in front of her. She looked at him with worry, then looked around, trying to assess their situation.

"A cave?" she said looking back at him.

Edlen sat in thought for a moment, trying to recall what he remembered last. His head was pounding, making it painful to focus so intensely. Then he spoke up, recalling his last memories.

"We were thrown from the dragon's claws. You and I were trapped....Oatikki—" he stopped. Wondering where the rest of his group was presently, he feared the worst. A hard lump swelled in the back of his throat, then he swallowed hard.

"Oatikki was trying to hold on, but that *thing* snatched us up. I stabbed it in the hand, and that's when she threw us."

"It is just us?" she said to him with a fearful concern. Although Edlen did not care for her tone when she asked it, he answered her to his best knowledge.

"I only recently came to myself. I have not yet explored beyond..." he looked down at the bones they rested upon, then back up at her. She lifted a long bone that resembled a femur of some animal, and her eyes grew wide with fear. She focused to a distance as she looked around at the pile they sat upon.

"We need to leave," she said in a very quiet and forceful whisper.

"Why?" Edlen asked suddenly concerned. "What is this place?"

"Do you have a weapon?" she asked. He reached down to his sheath and found it empty. Sorrow suddenly swallowed him. The clasp of his hands at nothing where he expected to find the hilt of his father's sword left him feeling as though the last token of Eldor had now completely left him. With tears beginning to roll down his face, he choked out his answer.

"It..." he swallowed hard. "It must have been tossed elsewhere when we were thrown," he replied, then paused for a moment.

"I do have a dagger..." he said as he reached down by his ankle and pulled out a small steel dagger. It was something Radholf always told him to keep on him, as it would eventually prove itself useful.

"Let us find the edge of this...graveyard," Sabrina said, standing up. The two began to walk across the pile of bones and carcasses. Most of them were dried and long dead, but the stench of decay and rotten flesh still filled the cave. Edlen soon became anxious for a breeze of fresh air, but he knew it was not likely.

After a few moments, they managed to find the edge of the large cave room they were in. The bones had thinned out and dirt could now be found on the floor. The mound of bones was high, and it was difficult to see anything on the outer edges.

"If we want to find a way out of here, we will need some sort of torch," Sabrina told Edlen in hopes he had some item on himself that might provide useful. Edlen only stood, waiting for her next words, not understanding the inquiry she had just laid out. She rolled her eyes.

"Fine," she said in response, and she began feeling around the cave floor for some type of stone.

Grrraaaaaaaw! A cry echoed from far across the large room they were in. It echoed off all sides, taking a moment to fade to silence once more. Sabrina looked up from the ground, eyes wide open, frozen in her place. *Grawwwwol!* A second cry came out, different in pitch and tone.

"There's two of them..." she whispered to Edlen. Edlen remained standing, staring hard into the darkness trying to make out what they could be. He bent down slowly and drew his dagger. Heavy footsteps came sounding beyond the room, rapidly approaching from some dark entrance beyond their sight. A second pair of footsteps accompanied it just as fast before silence fell all together. Sabrina and Edlen were both frozen, careful not to make a sound.

Sniff! Snifff! "Grraaaaaaah!" The footsteps began again carrying a heavy weight with them and quickly growing louder and louder.

"Run, Edlen! Into the light!" Sabrina shouted as she took off towards the column of sunlight that shown down. Edlen stayed still in shock. He could hear the creature advancing towards them, and it made no sense that Sabrina would charge after them as though to meet them at the sunlight cast down into the cave.

"Come quickly!" she shouted. "If you want to live, get over here!"

Edlen snapped out of the fear and took off running. His heart pumped hard and the tingling fear shot waves of pain in his limbs, as he bolted as fast as he could across the bones. Stumbling here and there, slipping on rolling limbs and tripping over cracked ribs, he could see what was racing towards them.

Sabrina stood tall in the center of the light with her arm reached out towards him, yelling panicked encouragements. Edlen leaped into the sunlight, landing in the center of it. A ring it had formed around them with no more than a foot of space on any side. As Edlen stood at his feet, just beyond the edge of the light, he met a large creature nearly eight feet tall. It was horribly hideous with pale grey skin on its face, but much of its body covered in thin dark hair. Its mouth dropped open with rotten teeth like a human, only sharpened and a blackish grey. Its nose was bulbous, and eyes very dark. It stood like a heavy man, but wore no clothes. It was very muscular and thick. Its arms hung down, hands large and strong, tipped with cracked yellow nails. It stared down at Edlen and released a horrifying roar.

Spit flung out, spraying Edlen in the face which made him cringe. Yet there it stood, not making any advancements, and seeming quite angry. Its breathing was heavy, and smelled horrible of rotten meat and staleness.

Sabrina held onto Edlen's arm.

"Hold fast, Edlen. They can not enter the light."

"What is it?" Edlen said in a whisper, not trusting it wouldn't lunge suddenly.

"A cave troll," Sabrina replied. "These mountains are crawling with them, as they make caves like these their homes." In the distance, faded in the shadow, the second troll stood, also breathing heavily and studying the situation.

"They used to be like us," Sabrina continued. "Until darkness took them over and drove them mad. They grew to fear the sun, and sought out shelter from its wrath." The troll only stood there, huffing and puffing, staring straight at Edlen. Then suddenly it turned away and retreated to some shadow in the large room.

"As it consumed them, the sun's light became harsher, burning them and drying them out. Eventually becoming so intensely painful that it hardened any surface it touched on their body, as hard as stone."

Edlen gazed up at the sky above. It was blue now, without a cloud visible through the small opening they had. He looked down at their feet and stared at the ring of light they stood in. As he looked, the edges of bones being lit up shifted. Some edges began to fall out of the light, while others on the opposing side became revealed. Then Edlen's concerns grew.

"What happens when the sun rests beyond the opening? When the light fades to night? What will we do then?!" The panic returned to his voice.

Sabrina looked at Edlen with fear and anger. Fear of the situation they were in, at what would be to come. Angry for the loss of what simple protection they had then. Although not seen, the breathing and grunting of the two trolls in the shadows served a realization that they were simply waiting for that time to come.

Edlen and Sabrina sat in the sunlight, shoulder to shoulder in silence. Thoughts ran through their heads, though of different nature. While Edlen had his thoughts focused on what they would need to do in the coming hours, Sabrina grew angry at where they had ended up. Dwelling on the recent, she grew discouraged. As her thoughts continued down the path of what the foolish boy next to her had done, so did her opinions of him darken. Annoyance had turned to hate, and in her mind their current situation suddenly had a source of blame.

The longer they sat in silence, the further these thoughts ate away at her. Hope had been drowned in the increasing shadows of their fate. Each moment that passed crippled her heart. The cave they had fallen into seemed to be working a dark curse on her mind. Before long, she couldn't stand it any further and broke the silence.

"You shouldn't have done what you have," she said echoing off the cave walls. "Did you really think you could have made a difference? Do you think your petty actions could have altered our destiny?" Her voice saddened and intensified. Edlen sat in silence, not knowing how to answer. Her outburst continued.

"Look at what you have done! A swift death by a dragon tooth, quick in pain I could have had! Stolen away from me by you and your need of approval. Your weak attempt of heroism. For what consequence? To buy me a few more hours of life?

"And now you are also bound to the same death. Trapped here in this cave, with hungry creatures lurking in the shadows. You haven't given me anything better! You've brought only a count down to an inevitable end. I would have rather spent my last hours not waiting to die," she stared intently at him with disapproval and a half-turned head.

Edlen's bottom lip began to quiver as he fought to hold back his tears. He could say nothing in response to such an outburst of truths.

"Weakness and shallow," she said to him. "That's what I see in you," she ended. He could only get a small squeak out from under such heavy emotions.

"I'm sorry," he said under his breath.

Sabrina took a deep breath and exhaled with force, not accepting anything he could have said. He felt crushed and helpless, and quite like dying. The pain in his heart was unbearable, and the familiar desire to undo his actions set in heavy. The regret returned, though not losing its potency. He grew sick of the feeling, but found it difficult to alter his thoughts on anything but sorrow. And even the dark shadows of the cave they sat in had no comparison to the darkness that fell over him.

Hours had passed. The column of light had moved across the cave floor some distance to a far side. It was clear now the direction the sun was crossing the sky as the sunny circle traveled from one side of the room to the other. Through that time, Edlen sat in the light with Sabrina, trapped in their imaginary cage of safety. It was an odd feeling. The feeling of being in such an open space, so vulnerable. No bars or walls kept him there. Air flowed freely as it mixed the fresh above with the stale around them, and it would take only a step to remove himself from such a constraint.

But to remove himself from such safety, he would not risk. Not when the danger lurked just yards out of sight. No, he was trapped in his cell, unable to leave for fear of his own life.

Despite being in the cave for some time, his eye sight could not adjust to the darkness, not while remaining in the sun. His eyes gave no hint, no shadow of a figure to the two trolls that sat remaining on the edge of the room. Yet he knew they were there for the sound of their heavy breathing continued, and the occasional scratching or sniffling gave away their presence.

The longer they waited, the stronger the dread fell over him. They were playing a standoff game with two creatures intending to kill them. Before long, the dreaded outcome would be decided, and it was heavily in the trolls' favor. Edlen thought hard of their situation. What did they have to fight against such creatures? Primitive bones under their feet? A small steel dagger?

He unsheathed it and held it in his hands. The tip dug into his palm as his opposing hand twisted it around, spinning it as he gazed upon what little hope he had in such a small weapon. It shown bright in the sunlight, almost polished as a testament to how little action it has seen since Edlen had become its new master.

As he spun it, he could see the reflection of the opening above. The sky blue reflection grabbed his attention as he very much wished he could escape above and out. With a slight twist, the intense brightness of the sun shown in his eyes at which he squinted. Such brightness, it almost hurt. Then it struck him.

"Sabrina! I got it!" he shouted in a whisper. "The dagger!" he said as he stood quickly.

"Hey!" Edlen shouted, trying to get the trolls' attention. "Hey, you big galoots! Come over here!"

"Edlen, *what* are you doing?" Sabrina whispered. "That dagger won't sink deep enough to kill them! You'll only anger them! And if you stick your hand out of the light they'll pull you out and crush your bones before eating you alive!"

One of the trolls grunted loudly in annoyance. *Thump-thump-thump-thump.* Its footsteps grew closer until its figure could be made out. It stood feet away from the edge of the sunlight, then let out a loud *Graaaaaaaw!*

Edlen lifted his dagger sideways in front of him, in the strong sunlight. Rotating the edges around, he found the sun's reflection above, hitting the ceiling of the cave. Turning it down, he shown the reflection straight into the troll's eyes.

Immediately a hissing sound came from the face of the troll, followed by smoke rising. It let out an incredible scream and bellowed pain as it covered its face with his large hands. Hunched over, the hissing gave way to cracking, and the screaming halted as the now stone-heavy head fell over with a *thud* on the pile of broken bones, taking the limp body with it.

"Rooooooooooooh!" The second troll shouted in anger to see its kin collapse to the floor, and charged towards Edlen and Sabrina. The sounds of its footsteps were rapid, and it was clear it had no intention of slowing down. In a berserk fit of rage, the second troll leaped off the ground even before being within sight. Edlen saw out of the darkness two outstretched arms, tipped with yellow nails, reaching for him, followed by the most terrifying anger expressed on the troll's face.

Edlen ducked low and forward, and as the troll passed over him and into the light, the same hissing sound came. Dust and smoke swirled around in the trail that the troll had left through the air. On the other side of the column of light came a hardened stone troll body that quickly fell to the ground, plowing a trough through the carcasses on the floor.

Edlen stood up as the sound of crumbling bone fragments settled down into the pile beneath the stone troll. The sounds echoed into a silence. He looked over at Sabrina, who kept her attention on the troll. She walked up to it to ensure its lifeless state. Indeed it was no longer a living thing. Edlen smiled wide with pride.

"You *are* incredibly foolish!" Sabrina shouted as she turned to him. The smile fell from his face and was replaced with a sense of shock and a bit of anger.

"Fool!" he shouted back. "They're dead because of *my* idea! You only sat there sulking and pouting, doing nothing to help!"

The two of them only stood there, staring at each other, not saying any more. The cave fell silent and felt empty. Being free from their light cage brought little relief, but knowing their lives were not immediately going to end at dusk brought a stronger will to continue. Edlen looked at the troll laying in the bone pile to his right, then the one with only a stone head on the other side of the light. Its body was mostly in tact, still of flesh as only its face was exposed. Enough to kill it, but not to spoil the rest. He then glanced back at Sabrina.

"So what do we do now?" he asked.

She looked up at the opening, but even a short glance would tell you it was far too high to even consider an attempt. She glanced in the direction in which the trolls had made their appearance and sighed. She walked towards Edlen, then described what was going through her mind.

"Trolls, even cave trolls, cannot live off of meat alone. They too need water," she said as she grabbed the dagger from Edlen's hand. She walked towards the troll on the edge of the light.

"Take off your shirt," she commanded.

Edlen was shocked at the request, and began blushing. But his sense told him her intentions were not of what his heart had barely dared to dream. He began to unbutton his shirt as she knelt in front of the partial-stone troll.

Driving the dagger deep into its gut, she grunted with force as she sliced its belly open, spilling its innards onto the pile. Edlen stopped, with two buttons remaining, dreadfully shocked at the sudden gruesome scene.

"You done yet with that shirt?" she said back at him without breaking her focus on the creature. He stumbled the last two and handed the shirt to her.

She grabbed it with blood-soaked hands and stabbed cuts into it with the dagger. Tearing it into multiple pieces, she piled them next to the body. Continuing to slice through the skin, she folded a large piece up, exposing the jelly-like fat on the underside.

Then one by one she pressed the torn shirt pieces against the flesh, soaking up the fat into the fabric. Edlen felt sick in his stomach, like a heavy rock settled low. He also felt saddened that his shirt was being abused in such a way, and least of all, felt a bit chilled. Yet he knew they would need lights to make it through the cave tunnels, though how to spark them he knew not.

"Find some longer bones we can tie these on," said Sabrina, as she continued pressing more cloth pieces into the troll fat.

Edlen began looking around the pile for some large bones that would make for well-fitting torches. He found two that he felt would do, and brought them back to Sabrina, laying them at her side. The sound of the pressing was sickening. Wet and warm, and it smelled horrible. Edlen could hardly stand it. Despite being used to the smells of carcasses from hunting, the troll's smell was far worse than any other creature he had opened up before, so he had to take his leave for a moment on the outer edge of the room to catch a fresh-enough breath.

After a moment, Sabrina came over to him. Edlen was sitting against the far wall with his head between his knees. He looked up at her as she stood, waiting to be acknowledged. Her hands and wrists were stained dark red in their creases, but she was able to wipe most of the blood off. The column of sunlight shown bright behind her. Her dark hair long down her back, a few strands dangling in her face. Her emerald green eyes peered down at him. She was still as beautiful as he could picture her. But he felt as though he had failed her in too many ways.

"Are you ready?" she said. Edlen looked out across the room.

"Let us leave this place," he said, then glanced back up. A small grin formed on one side of her lips before she moved to his right. She felt around for a stone, then brought it back into the sunlight. It was black, and held little glamour in the sunlight. She pressed the dagger hard against it, and the the rock itself against one of the fat-soaked cloths. Rubbing the edge of the dagger against the rock, a single spark shot out.

Scrit! Scriiit! Scrat! After several attempts, a large outburst of sparks came, and the cloth began to smoke. She cupped it in her rough hands, and blew gently. An orange glow formed from the palms of her hands and lit up her face. Without tilting her head, her eyes looked up at Edlen and she smiled, blowing again.

With a single torch each, they began their journey into the shadows. The large room had a single exit which led to a single tunnel. It wound back and forth, up and down, and proved to be tight in some passes. The torches lit well enough to see their immediate surroundings, but the darkness surrounding them felt thick and heavy.

After some time, they found a small passage that led to a small room. It was short in length, and the ceiling was low. In there, they found a collection of items in which the trolls must have found interesting or valuable. Some were useless, as a troll's judgment is far from accurate. But weapons they found, and a pile of various clothing items too. Edlen found a shirt that fit him well enough, and despite the unknown amount of time it had spent in the dark cave, it brought warmth almost immediately as he buttoned it up.

The rest of the items varied in both usefulness and value, but it was not what they needed at the moment. They continued on, making their way deeper into the heart of the mountain. Before long, they heard the familiar sound they had hoped so much for. The trickling sound of fresh water echoed from some distance down the path they were taking.

"This way Edlen!" Sabrina said with excitement. The sound grew louder as they rounded each corner. Hopes ran high, and in Edlen's mind he expected to see some source of outside light. They came around the last corner before finding the source of the sound, and their hopes were crushed.

They found themselves in a large room, complicated in structure with rock corners and piled boulders, and a non-uniform ceiling that nearly escaped the light of their weak torches. High above, in a unseen emergence came down a small trickling waterfall. Splashing against a slimy rock face, it collected in a small pool in the floor. Where it left the room could not be seen, as it was apparently some place beneath the surface of the pool. Although they had found the water source, they found no traversal exit.

Edlen felt crushed. His face felt heavy, as though gravity was pulling him down. His grip loosened as he stared at the pool of water, shimmering in the fire light of their torches.

"Fortunes of evil!" Sabrina shouted, throwing her torch on the ground. "This place is cursed!"

"Maybe there is a second way? We have not seen all sides of this room yet," Edlen said in hopes of calming her down.

"Not likely!" she retaliated in a shout. But this did not alter Edlen's optimism. He took his torch and began circling around each odd corner of the room. Moving the torch back and forth to chase away shadows only revealed dusty stone corners that led nowhere. As he progressed around, his optimism began to fade. He made his way back to the entrance they had come through, and feeling disappointed and defeated, sighed a deep breath.

"Let us get a fire going, at least we can keep some light while we think about our next option to take," he said, trying to keep his hopes alive. There was little to burn save the carcasses of the trolls, and some odd items found in their plunder room. The fire they kept low, as it was not very cold in this cave, and their eyes needed little light to see anything.

It was not long before small fish and other odd creatures were discovered in the pool. Large enough to eat, and plentiful enough for a while. As they placed their small catches on the fire, puffs of white smoke rose to the ceiling. Edlen noticed it followed a different path than the entrance they came in, and bent around a jagged rock sticking out near the top of the room, disappearing.

"Where is the smoke flowing out to?" he said, looking up. Sabrina glanced up.

"There must be an exit somewhere up there!" she replied, a slight sound of hope carrying on her voice.

"Can we get up there?" Edlen thought out loud. "We have to try!"

The two inspected the walls and boulders surrounding the ledge, looking for a path they could climb. Difficult it was, to traverse over smooth rock and leaping from ledge to ledge with little to grip on to. Edlen found a path, and made it to the top of the ledge.

"I cannot see where it leads, though it looks small and dark," he shouted down at Sabrina. She tossed up a torch, landing next to him on the small ledge. He lifted it in front of him to show a very shallow opening, the smoke rolling along the top and disappearing in a short distance. It was hardly tall enough for a person to squeeze through, and it was impossible to tell for how far it would lead with sufficient space.

"It looks tight, but I believe it may lead somewhere! I will go through and see how far it leads. If it continues far, I will come back."

Holding the torch while crawling through proved to be a challenge alone. Although at points his back rubbed against the top as his belly slid across the bottom, the opening was plenty wide. Swinging the torch at arms length like the sweep of a bat wing, he slowly made his way through the cracked pathway.

To say it was tight would barely give justice to the constraints of this space. He felt tight and trapped, not able to take a deep breath, for his body ran out of room to fill up with air. It was dusty, and each breath forced a cough, but coughing required more breath than he was able to take. His mind began to fog, and he felt a sense of panic.

He longed for open air, for twisting around to catch his breath. He did not *need* a deep breath, only the need to know he could take it. But it could not be given, and he began to feel crushed. He pushed up on the rock ceiling and the incredible feeling of an entire mountain above him soon became realized as it gave no movement. The mountain above would take no command from him, no notice despite what desperation he felt.

In a panic, now breathing rapidly and deep, he laid in the small slit through the rock. He had room to move forward, and room to back out, but he felt paralyzed. His mind would not focus, and as he laid still trying to regain control, his torch flickered lightly in his left hand. It pulsated, as though finding a new part of the fuel to burn. A small heated ash floated off and fell onto his hand. It was red hot, and burned where it landed. In a quick reflex, he thrust his hand back. In doing so, his elbow slammed against the rock hanging above him. The pain echoed through his arm, and such a painful focus allowed him to break free of the panic he felt.

With his head clearing and knowing he must go on, onward he went. Moving side to side, the crawl continued tight. No signs could he find of any other visitor through here before. It was incredibly dusty, dark, and small. He had no idea how long he was in there, but it felt like he would never find the end. He knew he was on a slight incline, which helped keep his head straight a bit. The smoke trial continued to flow past him, leading him in the direction he thought would be best to go.

In the dim light of his torch, he could see the sides of his small path come to an end. They converged to a point that remained black and empty, and the smoke from their fire flowed through it. It appeared he found some sort of exit, though nothing could be seen on the other side. It was hardly large enough for him to squeeze through, his shoulders being the tightest part to get out. But beyond was an opening far larger than any he had been in since he had awoken on the bones.

He stood with relief and took a deep breath. Although stale, it felt good to be freed from such tight spaces. He held his torch up high, but could not see a top. He was standing on top of a large rock face, a cliff that dropped ten feet before finding another surface.

As he stood on the edge to peer down, rock crumbles fell. Hitting the next landing down, they echoed through the room. Although he could see no other side, the echo gave way to the immense size of where he stood. No other sound could be heard. No water running, not another soul. Only space that had not been disturbed since its creation. Isolated from the outside, Edlen felt very alone.

He headed back through the way he came, now knowing that he had done it once before, it helped to remove fear and uncertainty of finding a dead end or getting stuck. Although the way back provided different challenges, he did not feel comfortable going headfirst, as the decline proved too steep. Spinning around, he continued backwards for a while, but the lack of sight became too difficult to navigate, and so switched back. Eventually he made it back to where Sabrina was anxiously waiting.

"There you are! I almost came up there after you!" she said.

"It is a bit of a way to get through, and tight! But it leads to some large room of which I cannot tell where its boundaries are. My torch could not fill it, but it sounded large and empty," Edlen explained.

"Let us collect what we can. If you are right, Edlen, we may be able to find another exit yet!" Sabrina told him with a bit more cheerful hope in her tone.

The two collected what items they could manage, remembering the tight path they would need to traverse. From the storage room they found an old chest, which broke apart easily to provide light firewood. Digging through they also found a goatskin water bag in which they filled at the pool.

Packed and ready, Edlen led Sabrina through the route he had taken. He found even having been through this space before, it still gave him the feeling of being closed in, but it was easier to bear as he knew he would fit, and knew that the other side was open.

Their baggage had to be drug in a line, tied together with strips of clothing in order for it to fit through, though it was light either way. Edlen also found that the trip became shorter each time he made it, which came as a relief as it was most uncomfortable.

Emerging through the small opening, Edlen found himself back in the large room. He pulled the rest of the baggage out, allowing Sabrina to make her entry.

"*Gasp!* What room is this..." she said in a whisper. Her whisper echoed through the emptiness, as it was spectacular in any sense for being so deep under the mountain. She stepped towards the edge of the cliff face they stood on and looked down. Like Edlen had explained before, the bottom was out of sight. She broke off a piece of tinder and lit it. Glancing at Edlen, she tossed it into the darkness before them. Down it fell, lighting no walls around it. Their focus was hard on the ember as it landed hard on a flat surface nearly forty feet down. A cloud of dust swirled out and around the small piece of burning wood, and the *smack!* it made echoed through the entire room.

"Not as far as I had thought," Edlen said still peering down. "But far enough!"

Edlen and Sabrina worked their way down. The path was easy to find given the size of the room, and no ropes were needed to traverse to the bottom. They explored the great space around, as the room seemed to be as large as a great hall in some castle. The floor was perfectly flat with no cracks or odd inclines. It seemed odd, and almost perfect in shape. As they continued to explore, the great room became more peculiar.

"It is almost as though this was not made by the mountain," Sabrina said out loud. Her voice echoed far back. "As though it was made by some man ages ago."

Edlen approached the far wall and worked his way around. Lit with his torch, he found an exit. Bordered around were two pillars topped with an arch. This set

Sabrina's suspicion, as they were carved directly into the rock itself.

"Sabrina! An exit!" he shouted. She rushed over and with their two torches, lit up the entirety of the carvings. The pillars were beautifully carved. Large with sharp edges, perfectly straight up, holding perfect angles. The arch above was cornered with extensions of the sides, and held a name carved deep:

ᚺᚠᛚᛚᛗᚠᛉᛏ
ᛣᚠᛏᛣᚠᛗᛒᛣ

"What does it say?" Edlen asked. He knew the carvings looked familiar, but couldn't put his mind hard enough to know where.

Sabrina paused for a moment, staring at Edlen intently.

"They are catacombs," she answered, returning her attention to the carvings. "Catacombs of a civilization long ago. A place of great warning," she said, redirecting her attention back towards Edlen. "A place we should never enter."

At that moment, his memory recalled. He had seen similar markings above the dungeon in the Eastern Watch Tower nearly a month ago. The horrible events he recalled sent a shocking fear through his limbs as he *gasped!*

Sabrina looked at him at once. He remained silent, not making eye contact. Only focusing on the letters.

"What do you know, Edlen?" she said with great concern. As he thought through what he remembered, he also remembered the odd markings below, ones made by the Great Amarok. They looked vastly different, and were absent from the wall in front of him.

"Nothing," he replied. "I thought..." he stopped.

"Thought what! Answer me what you know!"

"I saw these at a tower, a very old tower, but there were also other markings...letters from the great wolf," he replied. "I see no such letters here though."

Sabrina fell silent, but unsatisfied.

"We must be wary, nonetheless," she said, as she headed through the passage way and into the darkness.

The next several weeks they spent exploring the passages they had discovered. The way forked in several locations, making it difficult to follow at times. However, all passages were very clearly carved out by man, making their traversal easier than a natural cave.

They kept a base camp in the pool room they had first discovered, allowing them to replenish their water supply as often as they needed. The entrance they had fallen through proved to be invaluable, as some mountain-dwelling critter or creature fell to their death often enough to keep them fed and supplied with fat and fur for burning. The skylight also helped with moral, as it was the only way they could separate day from night.

Each morning, they would set out to explore a new part of some uncharted leg. Each morning, they would crawl through the long, thin crack into the great room. Each night, they would return, and etch their new findings into the wall of the pool room, expanding their map little by little.

It was tedious and exhausting, and so very important to not become lost. Markers helped as they found new forks, but it was astonishing how empty such long walkways could be. After several weeks, though, their journeys began to prove to be too long to make in a single trip. Nightly camps became more common, so they could reach further into the heart of the mountain. And such depths ate away at Edlen's mind. Spells of dizziness fell over him, and he dreamt of endless cave dwellings, the feeling of being trapped in an endless maze of rock and dirt. Until one day...

A wooden door, untouched by any hand for centuries, stood sealed shut in the dark slumber at the end of a long corridor. For centuries, not having the warmth of any light shown on it. Its aged wood still held its strength, bound by iron with no signs of rust in the dryness of the mountain's depths. Its handle caked in dust, and a gruesome ancient face stamped in iron hung on the front. Nothing had passed through it as far back as one could remember, yet its very existence told of who its masters were.

It was a gateway. An entrance to which residents remained lurking inside.

Then a disturbance came to the door, breaking its centuries of silent rest. Footsteps echoed as though a realistic dream had begun. Closer and louder they became, until the iron face on the door lit up by Edlen's torch.

"Sabrina! A door! A door!" he shouted. Sabrina came running around the last bend of the pathway and held her torch up high. She immediately took a step back.

"No..." she said under her breath. She was very clearly frightened.

"What is it? What is wrong?" Edlen asked.

"No. We will not enter here. We will find another way," she answered.

"What is this place?" he asked, "What could be beyond this door other than a way out?" He placed his hand on the handle. As his skin touched, his hand felt ice cold. Wails and cries echoed in his head. Terrifying howls, of nothing he had heard before, paralyzed him. *SMACK!* Sabrina smacked his hand off the handle.

"NO!" she said sternly. He looked at her with fear.

"We will *not* enter that place," she concluded. "Only if there is no other way."

A week went by since they had made that discovery. Their search for a second way out proved fruitless, however much Sabrina had wanted it. Edlen grew a strong fear of the door, and found it difficult to stay focused any time they came near the place. But eventually, each fork they had marked on their map led to a dead end. And even after a couple of days of contemplating, it was only then that they decided it was the only way which had a chance of having an exit. The night before, Sabrina felt it best to prepare Edlen for what they were about to encounter.

They sat around the small fire next to the pool of water. It took courage to even talk about what she knew laid beyond the door. Knowing how close it was made the feeling even more uneasy, but it must be talked about.

"Beyond the door," she said, taking in a slow breath, "is the catacomb. A place of the dead."

"But if only the dead reside, what is there to fear? What curse lay over them?" Edlen asked, knowing what he felt just a week ago, but still fresh in his mind.

"The people..." Sabrina paused. "Well, they are no longer people, but once were. They are restless, bound to the room beyond that door by some unrelenting will, waiting for their chance at revenge. They were once soldiers, from what I can recall hearing about them. Soldiers of a war long ago, during the first age, whom were all killed wrongfully in their sleep.

"A treasonous act of jealousy by the King's brother and his men. Ancestor of your "*Good King*" Valdór," Sabrina paused at this moment, suddenly as though she caught herself off guard, intending to keep secret what she was closely guarding. She could not keep her eyes focused on Edlen, and shifting in discomfort, directed her eyes toward the fire.

"The history I do not know. I have only heard these warnings through tales on the street and strangers I've met. One stranger whom was a long descendant of such, and still claimed the name today. But the warning was clear, and I remember vividly the sigil of the clan in which he bore. The sigil mounted on the front of that door."

"So, they're still alive?" Edlen asked, fully afraid of passing through.

"Not exactly, as they have already died. But their souls were too restless to leave this earth, not ready to join their ancestors in the great halls," Sabrina explained.

"How will we pass through without harm? Do they not know we are not responsible for their deaths?"

"I do not know. I know little of these things."

This did not sit well with Edlen, but they had no other choice. He now understood her precautions, but hoped that any doubt in her memory or the tales of old might prove to be too old. Perhaps things would not be an issue, and no trouble would be found.

Yet in his heart, his fear remained real. What he felt and heard at the door kept the flame of shadow flickering in his mind. He had the most uneasy feeling that horrible things were about to happen. He slept not a moment that night.

The next morning, as ready as they could be, Edlen and Sabrina set out for the door that haunted their thoughts all that night. It was an evil which they very much wished they could rid of. Like a painful snap of a joint out of place, they knew they must get through it. They made their way to the front of the door, which lurked in the darkness as though knowing full of their intentions.

Edlen stared at the sigil of the slaughtered clan. It seemed to stare back at him with anger and vengeance. His heart pounded hard and eyes clamped shut tight. His mind fled and desired to take his body with it. He felt more vulnerable than a mouse in an open field. His trembling was audible as he held tightly his torch in one hand, and sword in the other.

"Quiet and swift," Sabrina said. "I do not know what exactly is beyond this door, but the longer we can go about unnoticed, the better our chances of making it out alive," She took a deep breath and clamped her eyes shut tight as she placed her hand on the handle.

Edlen ceased to breathe. His eyes open wide focused hard on the edge of the wooden door. It *cracked!* Loud and echoing through the halls behind them. Dust shot out from the edges and hinges as they *creaked* and *squeaked*. The door swung slowly open, revealing nothing more than a small tunnel much like the one they stood in. Slowly they progressed down the walkway. As they walked along, Edlen noticed the ground changing to dirt. Slowly, there began to creep up long thin piles of very fine dirt, almost dust-like. The slightest disturbance would wisp them into a cloud. Even a foot step was enough to give flight, swirling around like a fog.

Broken pieces of pottery also began to show. Sticking out of the fine dust like jagged rocks in the ocean, and they began to show more frequently the further they traveled, until they came to the foot of a long stairwell.

The top of the stairwell could not be seen. It was wide, as wide as the tunnel, and steep. Edlen and Sabrina looked at each other. A bit of relief was found in their eyes, as the place they stood in seemed unoccupied. Sabrina gave another deep breath and took the first step of what would become thousands.

The bottom part of the stairwell was covered in broken urns filled with ashes.

They piled at the bottom, spilling their contents across the steps below. But the higher they climbed, the fewer urns they found. Soon enough, they were alone again. Not able to see more than a dozen steps above, and seeing nothing but the most recent of steps below, leading into blackness.

Edlen felt extremely vulnerable. He felt as though the darkness behind them had eyes watching, that at any moment, some creature or being could lunge out from the shadow below them. He stumbled on the next step, keeping his eyes behind him and collapsing on the steps in front of him.

"Careful!" Sabrina shouted in a whisper, "A bad step would land you at the bottom, and with a fall like that you'll be joining the dead!"

Edlen did his best to gather his courage and stand on his feet again. Further and further up they climbed. Not entirely straight, as there were several flat landings for rest and turns, which they found quite helpful despite the collection of urns and ash at each. But Edlen's legs felt tired and weak, and he wondered if they were ever going to find the end of this horrible climb.

After nearly three hours of climbing, they came to another passageway. This time, it was without door, only framed for such. It was overly large, standing nearly twelve feet tall and eight feet wide. This one was not carved into the rock, but trimmed with metals of brass and silver. It shimmered beautifully in their torches.

As they approached, the air about them shifted. A breeze blew from behind them and through the door. A sound also was heard, like the rushing of wind and water. A dull roar was coming from the room beyond the door, and for once, what laid in front of them beyond was not entirely black.

A faint light glowed in front of them, almost enough to make out the shapes of the walls beyond. Edlen's hopes soared at the thought of reaching the other side of the mountain, and filled with the hope of a way out. He nearly took off running through the door if it were not for Sabrina catching him by the shirt.

"Edlen! Do not be a fool!" she whispered. "This is what we have feared! This place in front of us is what I have warned about! Stay alert and careful!"

Sabrina led with Edlen carefully following behind. Both had their weapons drawn and carried their torches outward. As they passed through the door, they found the walls to be lined with carved out resting beds stacked three high. Column after column, these were filled with skeletons of past war heroes still clasping their decorated swords, still bearing their helmets. All were motionless, resting in peace.

Edlen kept a watchful eye on each one, looking for any signs of movement — any sound at all. His heart pounded in his throat. His hands clammy with sweat. He was breathing shallow and rapid, fearful of a trap. There seemed to be too many of them, and he couldn't watch them all. The further they walked, the worse his nerves became. He soon realized that an ambush would mean the death of them both, as the walls were covered with the dead, each with their own weapon.

"Calm yourself," Sabrina whispered, placing her hand on his arm. "I do not think these souls are without rest."

They continued down the great hall. Each step they took, the light in the room seemed to grow brighter, until they could see the end of the path they were taking. It turned to the left where the source of light seemed to be coming from. As they made their way around it, Sabrina *gasped*!

Edlen stood next to her, a big smile grew on his face. Opened before them was a grand hall, over fifty feet tall and wide open. On the far side was the source of the light, an opening in the cave wall where an ice-cold river flowed into the cave and down the wall, forming a white waterfall. At the top the rock was covered in ice and snow, and the opening was blinding being so bright. It was a beautiful thing to see. The river crashed at the bottom just before a large platform carved into the cave itself. The river flowed to the right and disappeared into some crack that swallowed it up whole.

On the platform were three tombs, each with a stone slab sealing it as a lid. The floor before them was laid out in patterns of stone, carved symbols and pictures to tell the story of those who had been resting there. Monuments were erected on all sides with tokens of memory and respect. Gold coins, fragments of long dead flowers, carved wooden symbols of the ancient gods. The sight was spectacular to see.

"Sabrina! Look!" Edlen said with excitement as he pointed off to the left. Along the wall, carved into the rock was a set of stairs that led up almost as high as the grand hall itself. At the top was a door.

"That surely leads us out!" he said with excitement. Sabrina smiled.

"Let us leave this place and return to the land of the *living*!" she said, sharing his excitement.

They took their first steps out onto the stone floor when Sabrina lost her balance. The floor shifted down as a group of tiles they both stood upon dropped two inches. A loud *clank!* echoed through the hall as an iron gate fell behind them, landing upon the stone with sharpened beams, locking itself into place. The sudden *SLAM!* shook the walls, breaking free ancient dust in the ceiling as it fell in a fine faint cloud.

Sabrina and Edlen were both on their knees and looked up with a sudden shock, not moving. Listening for any movement. Only the sound of crumbling dust echoed in the grand hall, quickly being drowned out by the roar of the waterfall. They looked around and found no signs of immediate danger.

"Let us hope there are no other surprises!" Edlen said with a smirk. Sabrina was far too suspicious that the trap was not alone in a turn of ill-favored events. Uneasiness fell over her.

"Draw your sword," she whispered, remaining hunched down, looking toward the base of the falls at the three tombs.

"Beg your pardon?" Edlen asked in full voice, unsure of what her caution was.

"Draw your sword, Edlen," she whispered again, turning her head towards him to show the seriousness and fear in her eyes. His eyes widened as a chill crept up his spine. The hairs stood on end on his neck, and shivers shot out over the back of his head as though a chilled air blew over him and down his face. It was almost painful, and it echoed through his arms and into his fingers. He grabbed onto the hilt of his sword and quickly pulled it out. Although it had seen many battles in appearance, it was still new to him. He had a brief moment of grief as the thought of his father's sword, of Dragonsbane, passed through his thoughts. He missed it, and with that missed his father.

But the thought of his father brought courage. He felt as though his father was watching over him, encouraging him, and wanted to make his death not be in vain. Bravery began to overcome fear, and he felt he was ready for the next test.

They stood in a motionless silence, waiting for what ever enemy might have been awoken to reveal itself. Edlen took a step forward. Suddenly the wails and cries he heard upon touching the door handle came back in a loud shriek. Like the sound of dozens of creatures in pain, they echoed in his head, hurting his ears. Though as he covered his ears, the pain remained as it came from within his own mind. A great wind blew from behind them and seemed to swirl at the center tomb just before them.

The cries began to cease, giving way to the loud sound of his own heart pounding. *Thump-THUMP. Thump-THUMP.* It was far louder than he ever remembered it being, and after a moment, he realized it sounded more like battle drums than his own heart. And it began to startle him with every beat.

But no relief could come from it, as it all seemed to be coming from *within*. His eyes were opened wide, never ceasing their stare at the center tomb. He could not look away despite the terror he felt. As though a curse was over him, despite what ever sort of will he possessed, he could not turn away.

As he stared, as the battle drums pounded away in his heart, his eyes witnessed the rising of two horn tips from the top surface of the center tomb. First the right, then the left, and they were wickedly unnatural. Curving from the outside inward before curving back out and in, as though a deformity of a natural horn, the right was far longer than the left. As they began to converge, they met their end being mounted into a darkened steel helmet, of which rested securely upon its owner's skull. The beating continued...*thump-THUMP*.

The helmet continued long on either side of the skull, revealing the darkened eye sockets with dots of glowing bright blue. These eyes seemed to be locked on Edlen, as he could feel the attention of the creature rising in front of him through the very stone he was meant to be encased within. Below the helmet showed crooked and rotting teeth, fully revealed in both the top and bottom jaws. Every continuous moment, the beating grew louder. *Thump-THUMP!*

Trailing down was a long beard braided in three with the middle trail being the longest. Gold and silver rings were woven in between each braid, and the beard itself kept its color of the life before: a mix of red and aged gray.

Standing tall out of the tomb, the creature before them held his great sword and was covered in chain mail and other battle-ready armor. What cloth it wore had faded in decay, and missing pieces revealed the skin-wrapped bone underneath. Little skin remained on the rest of the body, and was a pale gray. It stood before them with the tip of its sword resting on the top of its tomb. The sword was nearly six feet long, but rested at no angle even with the hilt firmly in place of its master's palm. A horribly foul stench filled the room, stinging at Edlen's nose.

Edlen and Sabrina stood frozen, not moving. Though their presence was certainly acknowledged, they didn't dare to move. Yet the *draugr* which stood before them showed no immediate signs of attack, only careful watch.

"What do we do?" Edlen whispered to Sabrina. Sabrina stood still for a moment, staring at the draugr as it stared back.

"I..." she hesitated, unsure of the situation. "I think it is waiting for something," she concluded.

"Waiting? Waiting for what?"

"For us to decide what our intentions are, I believe," she explained. The draugr stood tall, looking back and forth at the two invaders of his catacombs. It seemed upset to be woken up, but made no advances towards them.

"Maybe if he knows we only mean to leave, he will leave us alone?" Edlen suggested in a whisper. Sabrina agreed, although they had little other choice. She took a step towards the staircase on the far left. This brought the draugr's attention to her. She kept a tight focus on him as she took another step.

The draugr tightened his grip on his great sword and let out a labored grunt. Another step she took, this time the draugr shifted his body towards her, and lifted his large sword's tip off the stony floor. Without taking breath, the draugr spoke out loud.

"No rich man may depart. Not a coin. Not alive."

It spoke in the ancient language that Edlen did not understand, but it was though he was chanting with anger. A threat as his sword was held steadily pointed towards Sabrina. Sabrina made no further advances, instead took her place back where Edlen stood. The draugr returned his sword to its resting place at his side.

"What do we do now? He will not let us leave!" Edlen said attempting to keep his whisper from cracking under his fright.

"I do not know!" Sabrina snapped back. We cannot return to the caves even if we wanted to!"

"We are no match for him, even with two! Look at him!" Edlen said as his options were exhausted. At that moment, a sparrow flew through the opening of the waterfall. It swirled around the cave chirping, grabbing the attention of both Edlen and Sabrina. It perched on a rock shelf high above, continuing its chirp.

The draugr looked up, acknowledging its presence. The chain mail and armor it wore clinked at it shifted its head upward, then it returned its gaze back at Edlen and Sabrina.

The sparrow took off flying with great speed towards the base of the waterfall. Edlen and Sabrina watched it bolt across the room while the draugr kept its attention on them. *Sploop!* The sparrow plunged straight into the crashing waters, disappearing behind the falls. After a moment of staring, the draugr took a step to the side and pointed his sword towards the falls, and spoke once more in the ancient language: *"Go. Go and never return."*

Sabrina looked into the falls. They appeared ice cold and clear. The sparrow had not returned. She looked at the draugr then again at the door at the top of the steps.

"Edlen! The falls! The falls must be the way out!" She grabbed his hand. A sudden flutter of excitement filled his chest. It was the first time she had touched him, and it chased out all fear and concern from his mind. He felt weak and without will. He felt her presence fill his being, and it gave him comfort beyond expectation. She was pulling him out of their stone circle, and even if he willed to fight, he would not have been able to.

In a fog, he followed her. With every fast-paced step she took, his feet met. He could only watch what his body was doing and felt no control over it, as though her touch had taken over his mind, and he loved it. He watched as they approached the platform, the draugr that stood upon his tomb.

It followed them with its eyes, keeping its sword pointed at the falls. As they passed, Edlen's eyes focused hard on draugr. It no longer seemed a threat. As it towered over him like a great statue, Sabrina's fingers slipped from his hands. All of the warmth and comfort they fed him vanished, and he was shocked back to fear. He stood before the draugr, fearful to move.

"Edlen! Come!" Sabrina shouted back at him. She stood before the crashing falls. The draugr continued to stare down at Edlen. It began to grow impatient. Then silence fell over Edlen. The sound of Sabrina's calls faded and the crashing waters ceased. He heard nothing, save the breathless silence of the undead commander before him. Dry and deep, it seemed to whisper a rumble through his heart. *"Go,"* it spoke to him.

This broke Edlen of any fear as his mind began to understand. This was no creature of evil. This creature was once human. A human with kindness in its heart. Though restless, it was *letting* them pass without harm. The man, this draugr used to be, must have been well respected, yet ended in tragedy. Edlen took a step back towards the falls as their sound became clear again.

"Who are you?" he whispered. The draugr tilted its head in a slight downward angle, almost as it was curious or taken off guard by the question Edlen asked.

"Go." it whispered back, returning the tip of its sword to the stone lid it stood upon. This time, Edlen fully understood what it had spoken.

He took several steps back, keeping his gaze upon what was once a great war leader. He heard a loud *splash!* as Sabrina jumped through the falls, followed by Edlen as he broke his stare with the draugr.

Splash! As he entered the water, his breath was stolen from his lungs. It washed over him like a painful wave, stinging at his skin and sending aches into his muscles. It felt colder than ice, and robbed him of any warmth he may have had. He collapsed to his knees against the wet rock behind the falls. Before him was a short incline of slick stone surface, Sabrina standing above and reaching a wet hand out. He grabbed it, and was hoisted to dry ground.

They were both soaked in water, and through the crashing falls, they could still see the silhouette of the draugr standing on his tomb. Slowly, it began to sink back down into its resting place, and they knew the danger was passing.

Steam flowed off Sabrina's hair as she was catching her breath. Edlen also was fighting to keep a hold onto his, as the shock of the cold began to wear off. Before them was a tunnel, and light brightened the corner turn just up ahead. A strong breeze flowed in. As cold as the waterfall, dry and sharp, it kept the warmth from returning.

Stinging at his eyes, Edlen covered his face with his arm, as he and Sabrina made their way down the tunnel. It was natural, no laid stones, no carvings on the sides, and vacant of any signs of recent visitors. Low at times, they were forced to crouch, and it was at these points the wind blew particularly forceful.

They turned the corner, and found the corners where the walls met the floor were beginning to be filled in with snow. It was blindingly bright, yet deathly cold as they took their final steps back out into the world.

CHAPTER X

KUONI'S CABIN

— 11th of Frostfare, 1867 —

The wind blew relentlessly cold. Snow swirled around every open space in a confused panic. The sun was risen but hidden behind a dense storm of wind and ice. Every second that passed stung any exposed skin, and numbed the rest. Every step taken drained strength like walking waist deep through a marsh. As the two made their way through the snow drifts, their water-soaked clothes stiffened and froze. Icicles hung at a sharp angle off dangling fabric, and Edlen's hair grew hard.

"We have to find shelter!" Edlen shouted, fighting the noise of the blowing wind around them. Sabrina took no notice of his alarm.

"Sabrina!" he shouted again. She turned with her head tilted down to keep the snow from freezing her face.

"I cannot continue like this!"

"We must get down the mountain!" she shouted back and returned her focus to the pathless route they had to take.

It was likely, that buried somewhere under the feet of snow, there existed some sort of trail. But if it did exist, it had not seen the light of sun for ages. They were far above the cloud line on some tall peak of the Rhim Mountains. However, it appeared they were on some north-eastern side of the mountain, though it was uncertain to them at all where exactly.

Edlen and Sabrina continued down the mountain as best they could manage. It was a slow and painful trek, each step becoming more difficult than the last. The storm around them pounded the mountain side with all its fury, raging against it in some attempt of breaking the mountain's spirit. To be caught between such a battle between two forces of rock and wind would ultimately prove too much for any living being. As though the gods were clashing themselves, the storm commanding the mountain to move, and the mountain firmly rooted to the earth, it was treacherous for a fragile human to be caught in.

Time moved slowly and progress was little. Edlen kept his eyes closed as often as possible. The longer they were held open, the greater pain he felt in them. Once again, he glanced up with hopes of a small relief foreseen, but he found it not. He found nothing, only a wall of white swirls. Sabrina was no where to be found.

"Sabrina!" he shouted. The harsh wind absorbed his cries and quickly dwindled them down to nothing. No echo, no calls back.

"Sabrina!!" he shouted with what strength he still had. No answer.

His next step was a fault, and as his hands were tucked under his arms, he could not catch his fall. His body hit hard against the steep decline he was on, and he slid down further and further. Waving his hands in any direction, trying to grab on to something to halt his tumbling, he grasped only at soft snow. Waves of white flew by him, and he could not tell which way was up as he rolled down. The confusion became too much to bear, and his trip down seemed to never end.

His sliding slowed and he eventually came to a stop. At this point, though, he was far too weak to stand. The tumble had bruised him badly, and the cold had numbed everything about him. He lay helplessly in a snow bank, far up some unknown mountain face.

A strange feeling came over him. The feeling of warmth, and it started from within. His eyes remained open, but told him he was still in the storm on the mountain. It made no sense, but the warmth spread. It grew uncomfortable, as though he was over-dressed on a warm summer day.

Instinctively, he began to unbutton his shirt. He felt no wind or breeze against his chest; the warm feeling did not leave. The snow blowing around him seemed to blur. He could not make out the blowing flakes, and even his own hands were beginning to fog. Edlen laid back in the soft snow, ready for his end.

Something threw him off balance. Though he was barely conscious, he felt suddenly dizzy and weightless. Very little could he make out, all he could see was only a blur. Like fading sparks between sleep and reality, he felt movement as though being dragged along or a disturbance in his solitude. But the sparks faded too quickly and he remembered nothing more until a few days later.

Dull aches resided in every corner of his body, and the surface numbness on the skin was still present. But he felt warmth again. Not a deceiving warmth like on the mountain before, but a true warmth from outside and in. He was dry and indoors, but knew not where.

He managed to shift his head to the side and moved his feet around. His breathing was labored, and he began to feel an urgency in answering his questions. Where was he? What happened to him, and where was Sabrina? He tried to open his mouth, but felt a burning pain as his lips cracked in multiple places.

"Hush, boy. Rest for now." He heard an unfamiliar voice speak up as the pressure of a cloth was dabbed across his forehead. He took a deep breath and returned to sleep.

Edlen woke, feeling much more refreshed than previous. The aches had resided and only stiffness remained. His skin felt little on the surface though, but began to itch in an intense dryness. He opened his eyes and managed to sit up.

He found himself in a stranger's bed resting in a stranger's home. It was warm and well decorated. And well-stocked with a plethora of herbs and goods. He recognized little save some large jars of honey and comb, and some dried herbs hanging on the cross beams near the ceiling.

The bed he was in was extraordinarily crafted with beautiful natural designs in the wood. It was large, far too large to be suitable for just himself, and was covered with an arrangement of different pelts and furs. He had never rested in such a comfortable bed before, and knew it had aided in his recovery.

The bed itself sat in a sunken platform off the main room. A thin smoke filled the air as a roaring fire burned hot in the fireplace on the far side of the home. The hearth in front was made of beautiful natural stone. The rest of the floor throughout the home was wood, save the open bedroom in which he found himself. That also was floored with beautiful mountain stone.

In the main hall was a tall table with large matching chairs. On the table were several bowls of various foods. Cheeses and dried fruits, biscuits encircling a jar of honey, and one bowl filled to its limits with dried salted nuts. In the center stood a lantern with a large wax candle, burning bright. The table looked well-used, and the entire house smelled of dried herbs, teas, and cheeses. It was all warm, welcoming, and very relaxing.

Edlen took a deep breath. It felt wonderful to be indoors again, and for the first time in a very long time, felt almost as comforted as he was at home. As he continued to study his host's sanctuary, he found a small round window on the far wall. The muntin within the window formed a single cross, made of natural wood. All around the window, frost had begun to creep in. Outside, Edlen could see nothing but hard blowing white.

Questions began racing in his head. From what he could see, his host was not present. Where was Sabrina? He felt suddenly anxious and fearful that she had not made it out of the terrible storm, and could not recall how long ago that time was. But before his mind could drive him to madness, a shadow passed by the window.

BAM! The large door next to the window flung open. A gale of snow and ice came racing into the cabin, along with a very tall man wrapped in furs, caked in snow. *Ka-BAM!* He slammed the door shut as fast as it had opened. The tall figure stood still for a moment, looking at Edlen who was sitting up in his bed. In his hands he held a wrapping of firewood, and after a moment, fell to the floor unwrapping itself. Firewood rolled across the hard wood floor.

"I see you have come to!" the man said with excitement, though muffled by his scarf. He took heavy steps towards Edlen as he unwrapped the scarf, revealing a very aged man.

"My name is Kuoni. I am very happy to see you have returned to your health!" He unbuttoned his thick fur coat to reveal an astonishing long beard, thick and silver-gray, it hung down past his belt. Well-groomed and decorated with several rings of gold, brass, and silver, it was braided into two long strands almost immediately below the chin. His eyebrows matched his beard in color, and were scrambled in wild directions. He had a bit of madness in his eyes, but kindness seemed to be their source as they were a sharp green and he spoke wide-eyed at all times. The top of his head also was covered in silver-gray hair, though it was short and thick.

"What in the names of the gods were you doing out in such unfortunate weather, young master?!" he asked as he finished removing the last of his snow-packed clothes, placing them on the warm hearth to dry.

Edlen shifted in bed as his memories were returning.

"But, oh! First tell me your name! How rude of me to rob you of your own introduction!" Kuoni remarked.

"I am Edlen, son of Eldor," he responded a bit shy and unsure of his host.

"Eldor..." Kuoni replied. "...no, it rings no bells in my head. But that says not much, my boy! This head is far older than I would like to admit!" he said with a wink, tapping the side of his skull with his long index finger.

"It is a very nice pleasure to finally meet you, formally, Edlen! Welcome to *Kuoni's Cabin*! Home, as I would call it. And I hope you find it as comfortable as I have!" he said, pulling a chair across the open room and down to the bedroom's level. Although the chair appeared to be quite too large for Edlen, Kuoni fit perfectly within it.

"So, Edlen," he said seeming excited. "Tell me! How did you manage to find yourself so far up this side of the mountain?"

Edlen wasn't sure where to begin, and he was anxious to know where Sabrina was, so he answered as short and simple as he could.

"We came out of the catacombs, behind the waterfall," he replied. Kuoni's smile dropped as he sat back in his chair, and a look of surprise and concern fell over him.

"The catacombs you speak of...Jall-dökk?"

"I do not know their names. We found ourselves trapped in a cave weeks ago. It took all of our strength to get through them..." he stopped. Edlen's eyes began to tear up as he remembered the fear and doubt of ever escaping, and of his lost band of friends prior to his awakening in that terrible cave.

"Oh...Edlen, you are safe now. Nothing can harm you here. Not in *this* house. But, you say *we*?"

Edlen nodded.

"Who else was with you?" Kuoni asked, growing concern that perhaps he had missed someone.

"A girl name Sabrina. She also shared the terrible burden of those caves. A member of our party from the days before. She emerged from behind the falls, but I lost her in the storm. I called for her, but received no answer back."

Edlen fought the tears, choking on his emotions, swallowing them down enough to finish his thought.

"That's when I fell. I lost my footing and remember little until moments ago."

Kuoni took a deep breath then stood from his chair. He walked to the fireplace and put a large pot of water over it for tea, leaving Edlen to catch his emotions. Moments later, he brought a cup of a strong tea to Edlen.

"Drink this. It will help to calm, and help to strengthen your mind," He handed Edlen the cup. It was filled with an orange-tinted tea, and smelled strong of warm cinnamon and pine. Edlen began to take a few sips, and felt its warmth spread through his heart.

"Now.." Kuoni said, "tell me everything." Edlen proceeded to start from the very beginning, from that very dark day that would always haunt him. It was the first time Edlen had talked about it in such detail, a trial of his emotions; a test he did not want to take. Emotions poured out over the lost of his father and uncertainty of where the rest of his family were presently. Like a scab that was not healed, his heart bled over the grief he uncovered.

But through it he talked, and began talking about the morning he awoke in the Grassy Knot in Leafenfell. Then he began to talk about Radholf. Kuoni perked up in curiosity at the mention of his name.

"Radholf?" he asked, leaning back in his chair as though digging through deep thought. Edlen grew concerned, as it seemed Radholf's name had brought unfortunate consequences with it. Kuoni smiled.

"That is a name I have not heard in a very long time," he said, still in deep thought. He snapped back to Edlen's attention.

"You are a friend of Radholf, yes?" Kuoni asked, seeming excited.

"I am," Edlen replied, feeling more comfortable now to reveal further information. "He saved me from imprisonment, at the time, and healed me under the hospitality of his beautiful friend Dargmara, keeper of the Grassy Knot." This threw Kuoni into an outburst of excitement and joy.

"Dargmara!" he yelled in excitement. The sudden outburst startled Edlen, and to see such a large man release that much excitement made him a bit nervous, though brought a bit of emotional warmth to his heart.

"What a wonderfully guided world we live in! You certainly are being watched over by someone in your favor, Edlen!" Kuoni said as he settled back down in his chair. "This certainly bodes well for your well-being! Please! Continue your story!" he said with a smile.

Edlen began to talk about the morning they left, and of Oatikki.

"Oati! O' Fadir! What have you foreseen to place such a young man in my care!" Kuoni shouted out loud. "Keep going, Edlen! You may not know it yet, but your story *must* be of importance. Let us hear the rest of it!"

Edlen grew suspicious that this man knew all of his friends thus far. It seemed to almost be of trickery, but could not imagine any motive for such, so he continued his story. He told of their tedious trip through Bjornwood, the first encounter with the wolves, and imprisonment by the Imperials.

It was this part of his story that he felt his emotions erupt again. He talked of the man his heart was still filled with hatred for, Colonel Remus, and what he had described to Edlen of his mother and sister. Though in details he could not stand to tell, it needed to be not as Kuoni had stopped him before, sharing that it was perfectly acceptable to move past.

Then Edlen told of his escape, and of Luno. He expected another outburst from Kuoni of Luno's name, but no response was given, only a continuous attention of eagerly wanting to hear his entire story. So the rest of the story he told, describing what details he could, until he told of the night of the dragonling. At this point, Kuoni's face told of a different thought. He no longer had a look of wonder, but of sudden realization. He asked no questions though, and spoke not a word, as he knew many more questions would come. And his storyteller would not be able to answer most of them.

The night of the battle at the mouth of the ancient road was particularly exciting to hear, and Edlen left no detail out. Kuoni seemed particularly interested in the actions of Edlen's sword piercing the hand of the dragon. Though Edlen made no mention of Dragonsbane, Kuoni noted the peculiar abilities of his sword.

Eventually, he talked of the day he awoke in the cave with Sabrina, another test of emotions as at this point, as he had left his friends behind. He did not know how this part of his tale would end. At this moment, his memories were exhausted, and his tea cup empty.

"Very well told, Edlen," Kuoni remarked, taking his cup to be refilled. "I am saddened to hear of the loss you have taken, both of the known and not known. I am afraid I do not know where *any* member of your party might be."

"I was hoping you may answer a few questions of my own," Edlen said, ready to get his answers.

"Of course! I will hide no truth and pass along all I have in knowledge that you may request of me!" Kuoni replied.

"Well," Edlen began. "How did I end up here? I only remember falling in the snow." Kuoni returned with a fresh cup of tea for Edlen, and one for himself. He placed his cup on the table and walked to the far end.

"Two days ago, the mountain side was hit with a terrible storm. Wind and snow blew with might, and Ol' Kuoni sat here bundled up with a roasting fire to keep warm. I was enjoying a bit of a snack when I heard something *FUMP!* on the roof. Concerning myself that it may have been a small rock, and wanting to ensure it was not the first signs of many more, I found myself outside in the storm looking for what could have caused it." Kuoni picked up a small cloth folded up around something small. He brought it over to Edlen to show what he found.

"But the bump on my roof was of no rock, but this poor little messenger bird," he said as he revealed a small sparrow, lifeless and cold.

"The sparrow," Edlen said under his breath. He looked up at Kuoni, feeling mournful for the small creature's fate.

"He is the one that met us in the cave. He showed us the way out!"

Kuoni grew a half smile.

"This little messenger knew you needed saving, and he desperately tried to tell someone of your presence on that mountain top," Kuoni said as he refolded the cloth to cover the bird. "Although it took his life, it seems he was successful in his purpose."

Edlen sat in bed, sorrowful for the demise of such a little thing. He knew not why the sparrow cared for him or his wellness, but felt forever in debt for the sacrifice it made for his sake.

"So knowing a messenger such as he would not be caught in such a storm unless the message he carried was of great importance, I knew there must have been *someone* up there!" Kuoni continued, placing the wrapped up bird back on the table.

"I dressed as quickly as I could and headed out. I spent close to an hour before finding a trail of disturbed snow, quite messy at that, and figured it was the result of a fall. Of course it led me straight to you, and you were nearly frozen solid by the time I had found you!"

"I remember feeling hot," Edlen said in response. "Towards the end of my memories, I do remember that, of which I found strange."

"Yes, you were quite bitten with frost and your mind began playing tricks on you. But of any one on this mountain to have found you, I am the best!" Kuoni said proudly with a smile. "I know the best herbs, teas, and recipes to speed up your recovery! I am proud to say that, thanks to my summer bees and winter-time gathering, I have chased away nearly all that frost on your skin! Another day or so and you'll be better than fresh born! Ho-ho!"

Edlen smiled at this, and gave many thanks for the kindness Kuoni had given him. He certainly was feeling much better with each passing moment. But then his next question came to mind.

"What about Sabrina? Did you find her? Or any other tracks in the snow?" Edlen asked.

"I am afraid that after I had found you, I believed to have fulfilled all the little messenger was trying to send word for," Kuoni answered. "I did not see any other tracks, though my mind was not expecting any either."

Edlen sat in the bed, fighting back tears of the thought she may be out there still. He had wished with so much anger he had not lost her in the storm, that they had stuck together. After some time in silence, Edlen broke it with his next question.

"So where exactly am I?"

"Apart from my cabin? Or do you mean the mountain?" Kuoni answered, fishing for the best he could. "If you mean to place yourself to the nearest location, that would likely be Skydale, if you are familiar with the name. You find yourself deep in the Rhim Mountains!" At this, Edlen perked up as this was not all bad news to hear.

"Although my cabin rests outside the borders of any boundaries," Kuoni continued, "the edges of Skydale are less than a week away. I do not visit much. Do not fancy myself with magic and wizardry, but now and then I set out to make a visit."

"Skydale! That is where Luno was heading! The party! Radholf was trying to get to the Elves on the other side of the mountains, and Luno said he *must* pass through Skydale to get to them!" Edlen suddenly poured out excitedly. It was light on his heart to know he was not entirely off course from their plan, and began to hope that perhaps he might find Radholf there.

But as soon as his hope came flooding in, it retreated back again at the realization that it was entirely too possible his party was consumed by the fierce beast that threw him.

Edlen's face turned sour as he stared into the distance in horrible thought. Kuoni, picking up on this, continued the conversation in the direction of hope.

"Hmmm," Kuoni said in deep thought. "You last saw your party at the mouth of the ancient road, yes? And this was several weeks ago, yes?" Kuoni verified. Edlen nodded in confirmation.

"Yes..yes it is entirely possible that if we set out in the morning, though slim in chance, we may find your party just arriving as we do. That is, of course, if Radholf, and the rest of your party, decided to abandon the ancient road and continue east to the main entrance. Otherwise we would be out of luck." Kuoni's words gave great hope to Edlen, and it felt as though his journey would begin to become easier to bear again. A much needed relief to recent events.

But there were more questions Edlen wanted to know. The heaviest on his mind, at the time, was Kuoni's history with Radholf, Oatikki, and apparently Dargmara. When inquired, Kuoni seemed vague in his response, but was more than willing to share some non-specific stories. He told of several battles and trips they had taken long ago, and his descriptions of their actions seemed fitting, though Edlen found the lack of time placement puzzling. Even if Kuoni himself seemed old in age, and perhaps Radholf, but Dargmara certainly did not. Orcs were too hard to judge in age, but this lack of detail still left a hint of suspicion in Edlen's heart.

That night, Edlen was sound asleep. The snow blew gently outside the cabin while the fire burned warm, keeping any cold at bay. The cabin was peaceful, quiet, and warm. Edlen stirred at the sound of a sword being unsheathed, and he opened his eyes. He saw the silhouette of Kuoni by the fire, inspecting Edlen's sword, looking it up and down in the fire light.

Turning it around, feeling the edges. Feeling the handle. He mumbled something under his breath, something Edlen could not make out. Edlen sat up. Kuoni, taking notice to Edlen's awake, turned in a half-startle. He looked down at the sword.

"This sword has not pierced any dragon's palm," Kuoni said, looking back at Edlen.

"No, that is not the sword I used. This sword I found in the caves," Edlen replied.

"And the dragon-piercer?" Kuoni inquired, sounding nervous of the answer.

"I lost it," Edlen answered, still saddened by this thought. "It must have been tossed with me from the dragon's clasp and found a different landing."

Kuoni sighed deep, and sheathed the sword he had false hopes of.

"That is of ill-fortune. Quite unfortunate indeed. Very few weapons are strong enough to pierce a dragon's skin, and only one sword that I have met before, only one I am aware of. But it seemed to have served its purpose thus far, since you are here before me alive," Kuoni said.

"But..." he continued. "You must answer me this: by which means did you come by such a weapon?" Kuoni's voice had become very serious, and it was clear that Edlen's answer would carry with it great importance.

"It was my father's sword," he said, speaking what truth he knew, and full of sorrow as this wound on his mind was still quite sore.

"Radholf made sure to have taken it from our home the night after my father's death, and brought it with him to Leafenfell. For when I awoke in Dargmara's inn, it was lying there on the dresser."

Kuoni smiled a relief at this news.

"And I suppose your father received it from *his* father?"

"That I cannot answer," Edlen said. "For it was only a few months ago now that I was even aware of its existence! My father kept it well-hidden, a secret from all of us until an ill-fated night of a bear attack..."

"Ho-ho! Killing a bear with such a sword would be like squashing a bug with a boulder!" Kuoni laughed. He leaned forward in his chair in anticipation.

"Tell me, young Edlen. Did this sword have a name?"

"Dragonsbane," Edlen said, curious but without hesitation. Kuoni smiled a big smile and stared at the floor. His eyes filled with tears and his cheeks began to rose. Looking up at Edlen, he took a deep breath.

"My boy," he said. "I knew one of your ancestors. A great man who lived many generations ago, a great-grandfather of sorts, though too many greats to be counted. His name was Edelmar, and he was one of my closest friends. Radholf knew him too, as well as Oatikki and Dargmara. Together, we were the five protectors of the Gronndelon, the Verndari of this realm. It is an honor to meet you, Edlen, son of Eldor, heir of Edelmar and of Dragonsbane."

"Verndari? The protectors of the Gronndelon? Protectors against what?" Edlen asked, as this was the first of these tales he had heard of. He had no idea who Edelmar was, as his father had never mentioned such a man.

"Why against all things evil! And your ancestor Edelmar, ho-oh boy! He was tasked with the greatest challenge of us all! Protector against dragons, yes! It is why he carried the one sword that held with it the strength to pierce a dragon's scales! The *only* sword with such a gift, and a great gift it is!"

"A great gift it *was*." Edlen said now realizing what a terrible tragedy it was to have lost such a sword. Kuoni sat by the fire in silence. The fire continuing to crackle as neither of the two knew how the story of Dragonsbane would continue, as it seems Edlen's unfortunate events had led it to its end. In a sudden realization of the late hour, Kuoni broke the silence.

"That should be enough story for the night. Now get some rest. We have a lot of hiking before us in the 'morrow."

Edlen laid back down and shut his eyes. His thoughts dwelled on the events as he was parted from his company, of losing Dragonsbane and the importance it had carried. Feeling torn between a chance to meet his party again and leaving Sabrina behind, he knew the trip to Skydale must be made. Little hope remained in his heart that Sabrina was still alive, but he knew nothing was for absolute certain. And although his heart yearned to daydream of meeting her again, his mind was a cage that kept the reality of her end close, and he became afraid to dream of such dreams.

Within that moment, Kuoni had begun humming a melody not familiar to Edlen. His deep voice rumbled quietly in the firelight, carrying a song of relief and healing. Low in tones, yet very soothing, it was easy to relax. Yet even with such lullaby, Edlen's heart and mind continued to pull back and forth until they wore his body out, and he eventually fell back to sleep.

CHAPTER XI

SECRET LIES IN THE DUNGEON

— 23rd of Kaldagger, 1866 —

Hellen awoke the next morning, hatred and revenge brewing in her heart. Her intentions driving her to silence, her focus unbreakable. She could feel the end coming, and fully expected this to be her last day. But if she was giving up her life, she would take the one that drove her to this.

"Leaving so early?" Eira asked, stretching out her arms with a yawn, still in their shared bed. Hellen stood a few feet away, heading towards the common room.

"The bells have not yet chimed!" Eira added.

"Stay safe, dear child. I am sure Bard will look after you," Hellen said without glancing back, then continuing her walk to the common room. Eira sat up in bed recalling the last words Hellen had spoken to her the night before, the realizing what was about to happen.

"Ma! Wait!" Eira shouted as she threw off the blanket, hurrying to catch Hellen in a hope to stop her. Hellen gave no acknowledgement of her attempts.

"Wait!" Eira said, grabbing her hand. "Please do not leave me! You cannot do this! You will not be able to!"

"I must," Hellen replied. "This sort of evil should not be allowed to flourish as it has in this place. In that man's heart, there is only darkness. It must be stopped before it spreads."

"But is not the killing of a man only furthering the darkness of our days?" Eira asked. Hellen paused for a moment. This question challenged her, and it seemed this eight-year-old drove a conclusion that she could not argue against.

"Sometimes lighting a small spark in the bushes is the only way to stop the spread of a raging wild fire. It is painful to do, yes. But necessary to save the thousands behind you," Hellen answered.

Eira stood in silence, as Hellen pulled her hand away and continued through the arching door.

"Will you not at least say goodbye to Bard?" Eira shouted in a last attempt. But Hellen was done talking with her. Yet she found it in her heart a desire to see Dahlia one last time, to give her some hope that the cause of all her heartache would soon be stopped. So instead of reporting to her post, she headed down into the lowest chambers of the castle's prison.

Hellen found her way to the stairwell that led down into the darkest parts of the castle. The smell coming up was horrendous, reeking of death, blood, and foul odors. A smell she found difficult to stand as it stung at her nose. Step by step she followed down. Drips of water echoed through the well as mice scurried busily up and down the steps along the edges. Few candles were lit to give only the slightest light, just enough to see, and they were spread far with great shadows in between. Eventually, she reached the bottom.

Before her was the landing and ahead, a single wooden door with a single guard, asleep at his post. He sat on a three-legged stool, his spear leaning against the right corner, his snoring soft but obvious.

Beside him a small wooden crate sat on the floor. On the front was a worn painted clover flower, the symbol of the Cloverfield Meadery. Inside were three empty bottles, the fourth unopened. Beyond the door, silence sat in the dark, absorbing any echoes that traversed into it.

Hellen stood quiet for a moment, then cleared her throat.

"Ahem," she audibly said. The guard startled awake, leaping to his feet and scrambling to fix his helmet so he could see what officer may be before him. He immediately grabbed his spear to return to his proper position.

"Oh!" he said, seeing Hellen stand before him. "I thought—" he stopped, feeling recomposed and seeing she was not some superior that he feared may have caught him sleeping.

"Um," he continued, "no visitors in this wing. You should know better not to come down here!" he added, feeling quite embarrassed to be caught sleeping.

"And you should know better to not be sleeping at the post..." Hellen added, knowing she had leverage. The guard just glared at her with disapproval.

"If you do not want your nap to go noticed, I suggest you allow me this one pass. I will not be long, and have only a few words to share with my friend before our departure," Hellen offered, knowing there was not much to lose in the agreement except on the guard's end.

"Scoff! Very well...but be quick about it! Only guards are allowed in there, except for rare occasions." The guard took out a large iron key and inserted it into

the keyhole. *Ka-chunk!* The door unlocked and creaked open.

"Then let us hope your nap is such a rare occasion..." Hellen said with the subtle tone of threat as she passed him, reaching for a single torch next to the entry way of the dungeon.

As she stepped into the room, the darkness seemed to absorb all light the small torch tried to give off. It was terribly humid, the walls lined with water and a sticky humidity of stench. Even the echoes of her footsteps on the stone floor did not carry far.

As she held the torch out ahead of her, squinting her eyes, she found the far wall to the right. It was made of stone, the entire top half with stacked stone blocks giving a short, wide opening at the bottom only a few feet high.

She leaned down on one knee and held the torch into the opening. She found a cell, empty but only a couple feet high. It dug down into the ground, with no room to stand. The floor was natural dirt with little straw to help with what ever mess the prisoner may make through life or upon death.

She moved on to the next cell down, crouching down to see if it was occupied. This one was also empty. So to the next one she went, but unlike the previous, here she found a body curled up in the far corner. This prisoner's back turned towards her, and she could not tell who it was. So she called out Dahlia's name.

"Dahlia?" she whispered into the cell. The prisoner gave no motion. "Dahlia?! Is that you?" she called. Still the prisoner made no movement.

"Hello?" she heard a call from the other side of the chambers. Hellen startled at the sudden sound of voice behind her, but before she left the cell she was currently looking in, the prisoner slowly leaned back to reveal his face. It was a young man, horribly beaten and bloody. His eyes showed strong and clear behind his mask of dried blood and dirt. Sharp blue eyes, however swollen they were. Hellen's eyes locked with this young man's stare.

"Help..." he whispered. Yet he had so little strength it was impossible to roll himself over and face her properly.

"Help..." he whispered again behind his cracked, bleeding lips. Something about this man seemed peculiar, something calling out to her about him. Yet she could not make sense of what it was.

"Hello?" Dahlia called out once more, breaking Hellen's focus. She backed away from the man, still having difficulty breaking eye contact. Turning around, her torch slowly revealed the opposing wall of cells. Kneeling down, she found Dahlia chained to the back wall on her knees, having to bend her head down from the low ceiling.

"Hellen!" Dahlia called out. "What are you doing here?"

"I came to say goodbye...to tell you I plan on assassinating the king!" Hellen explained, tears beginning to flood her eyes with emotion. She could feel the end coming, that her actions would mean her death. Even speaking the words she just had, if heard by the wrong ears, would mean her end.

"What?!" Dahlia replied in shock. "You cannot! How are you going to? He is too well-protected! You will not be able to get close enough to do anything...and if he finds out, you will end up like me or worse!" Dahlia was frantically trying to talk her out of this.

"I cannot let this continue," Hellen answered back. "I am doing this for the good of all the people of this kingdom and mine. He needs to be stopped, and I wanted you to know this so you may be at peace about him. That he *will* reap for the actions he has done to us, to you, and to all whom he has inflicted."

"Thank you, dearest Hellen. I am glad to see there are still people like you who mean to right all that is wrong in this world," Dahlia replied.

"Please help me..." the man across the dungeon hall cried out again in a raspy whisper. Hellen looked back into the darkness, hearing his chains rattle. He was trying to get closer, desperate for help.

"Who is he?" Hellen asked Dahlia before departing.

"I do not know," Dahlia replied, the man still crying out for help. "This is the first I have heard him speak. In fact, I was not aware anyone was there until this moment."

Hellen returned her attention to Dahlia.

"Farewell, Dahlia. Remember what I have told you. So, if you happen to make it out of this place, that you may tell others my deeds." Dahlia nodded with saddened eyes looking up at her.

Hellen began to stand up, then crouched back down once more.

"Oh," she said, remembering one last departure request. "And if that is the case, please go and find my daughter. Her name is Gracie. She escaped before we were taken here."

"Of course," Dahlia answered without hesitation.

"Thank you, sweet Dahlia," Hellen said at last before standing up again. She took a few steps towards the door, ready to leave, when the man cried out again.

"Please do not leave!" he cried out. "I need help! I do not know why I am here!" Hellen paused in her steps and looked over at the blackened cell. She could not see the man, and his voice struggled to carry even that short of distance. Still, something tugged at her about this man. Something that pulled her curiosity in his direction, and she could not forget it.

As she approached his cell, she asked, "What is your name?"

"Ronan," he answered with a struggle. He was beginning to feel faint, having spent what little energy he had to call for help.

"Ronan..." Hellen said. Then the familiarity struck her. "Ronan, son of Rannver?" she asked. Ronan nodded, his eyes beginning to close as he laid his head down on the ground.

"Hurry up in there!" the guard shouted outside the door. "You have been in there far too long, lady!"

"Of the late Jarl of Furskarth?" she asked with sudden urgency. But Ronan had passed out and remained silent.

"Come on!" the guard said, now having taken a step into the dungeon himself. But Hellen was frozen in thought. She was frantically trying to figure out why the son of the recent Jarl of their capital was in the dungeon of Gammal Keep. She knew, as she could feel deep in her heart, that she had discovered a terrible secret here in these cells. A secret she was not meant to find by the Empire, but perhaps one that *needed* to get out.

"What are you *doing* in there?!" the guard shouted as his last warning.

"I am coming! And quiet yourself, dreamer!" Hellen threatened back at him, reminding him she still had a reason to not be pushed.

"Ronan!" she whispered back in hopes of waking him, but he remained motionless. Hellen stood and began to make her way to the door, then paused. She thought deep for a moment in silence. Then faced the cell Dahlia remained in.

"Dahlia..." Hellen said, breaking the silence save the quiet breath of her torch.

"I have found something more important that needs tending to before I carry out my plans. I will see you again," she concluded.

"Be careful..." Dahlia wished her as Hellen left the room and the dungeon door slammed shut with an echo that settled the dark cells.

"Sure did take your time in there!" the guard commented.

"Only what I needed!" Hellen snapped back. "I will speak no word of anything that has happened in these past moments as you agree to the same..." Hellen said wanting to settle their agreement.

"Yes, yes! Now be gone, maiden! Rid me of your presence..." he said, waving his hand at her.

The rest of the day, Hellen attended to her duties as she was required. Throughout the day, Ronan carried heavy on her heart. Her thoughts, as often as she could spare them, pondered on what possible reasons he could be here. Surely he was not a fugitive or once a captured servant as she had become, and sent down in that horrible hole in the ground for some offense. There had to be more than what it appeared. She knew there must be answers to all of her questions. And it was at the end of her day she decided this was her new task.

As the workers collected in the common room for their evening meal, Hellen found Eira and Bard already seated and enjoying their warm plates of food. Eira was surprised to see her come down the stairs, but was filled with joy as she approached.

"Ma!" Eira called out. "I am so happy you can join us for supper!" she said, her eyes nearly filling with tears as she ran to her and wrapped her arms around Hellen.

"Yes, dear child. My day went very different than I had expected," She sat down at the tables as a server placed a warm plate of supper before her.

"Different, eh?" Bard said, taking a big bite of bread. "What did you expect to happen?"

Hellen sat quiet for a moment with a smile, keeping her manners about her.

"I met someone I did not expect to see, and re-united with a friend. It was a good day," she said in hopes to keep any suspicions at bay.

"Oh! It is always nice to make friends!" Bard said with a smile, looking at Hellen and glancing at Eira as he finished chewing his bite.

"Indeed..." Hellen responded. Then her face fell serious and she leaned in to Bard.

"I have a question, young Bard, that I hope you may have some answer for," she said. This got Bard's attention, and he placed his roll down on the table.

"Of course...what ever I may know I will gladly share! What is it?" Bard replied.

"This person I found...met rather," Hellen continued. "I do not know why he is here. But he has some sort of importance, and I am sure the reason he is here might reveal a dark secret about this place..."

"I see..." Bard replied. "Well, what kind of importance is he? Is it possible I may know him?"

"Maybe," Hellen replied, "but I would prefer to keep his name to myself for the time being."

Bard nodded in agreement.

"But his family is of importance, I believe. But his presence here makes no sense to me. He really should not be here."

"Well," Bard thought for a moment. "If you need to find out more about a family, you may need to look in the castle's library."

"The library? Where is it?" Hellen asked.

"It is not hard to find as it is what fills the castle tower, but it is impossible to get in," Bard added. "Only authorized scholars are allowed there. Those books are for the King only...but I have heard of the many books they have there! And when family lists are compiled, including you and your daughter, that is where they go."

"So, how do I get in? Is there no way?" Hellen asked.

Bard took a bite of roll as the urgency in their conversation seemed to be settling, at least in his mind.

"Well," he said between smacks, "Unless you are a scholar, I see no way," he concluded.

"So, to become a scholar..." Hellen said in thought.

"But you are already a servant!" Bard said. "You cannot just *switch* jobs like that! Besides, only another scholar or the King himself can permit new scholars into the library..." Hellen's face fell, as it seemed this answer was proving too difficult to carry out.

"I am sorry, Hellen. I wish there was another way," Bard said, finishing his meal.

"It is fine, Bard. You have helped more than you may realize," Hellen said with a sigh.

That night, Hellen thought hard about how she may find a way into the castle's library. This man's presence began to haunt her, unable to let it go. The longer she dwelled on him, the more she felt that she was *meant* to find him. A man of her own homeland, of her own history. She soon developed an allegiance to him, and a sense of purpose that he deserved to have his secret discovered. And it was during this night, sleepless as it was, that Hellen thought of an idea that could get her into the library.

The next morning, Hellen awoke and quickly left to begin what she had planned. Her hope laid in the willingness of someone she despised almost as bad as the king himself. As she had spent time in the king's quarters, the king let out a very small detail in which Hellen bridged together with her immediate need.

Edgar, having told all of his tales that day, was sent back to to the castle tower for, what Hellen could remember, cleaning. It did not take long for Hellen to find the man lurking in the shadows as he seemingly did too often.

"Edgar..." she said, approaching him during their breakfast time, finding him standing by himself in a darkened shadow of the servant's dining hall.

"Hellen," he said in response, nervous that she was speaking to him willfully. "I...I am sorry for what I tried to do that day," he said. His apology sounded sincere, but whether it was or not, Hellen accepted it.

"It is in the past now, and I should thank you for relieving me of that secret. But if you truly mean it, I thought I might ask a favor of you."

She was not entirely sure how willing Edgar would be to this request, and thought it may be dangerous to trust such a request to someone who seemingly uses any information to his advantage. For this reason, Hellen was sure to word her request carefully.

"An act of kindness, what ever it may be, would be a just request for what I could have done to you," he said with a slight bow.

"And what you *have* done to Dahlia!" she said with a sudden tone of anger.

"To Dahlia? Yes, I have not seen her in some time..."

"She was sent to the dungeons for what you told the king about her!" Hellen said, her heart beating heavy and face turning hot.

"I did not send her there myself," Edgar said defending himself, "It was *her* actions that were judged, and the judge himself sent her there. I was merely... echoing what was said," Edgar ended with his eyes squinting.

"Well, if you want to make things right as I do, then you will do this request for me," Hellen replied.

"I cannot agree to a request not yet asked," Edgar answered back.

Hellen paused for a moment and listened to the room. She did not want to appear suspicious, and looking around for listening ears could warn Edgar of fouler intentions. But hearing only distant chatters and breakfast-eatings, she continued.

"I need to find a book in the library...a special book about the laws of this land. You see, I am unfamiliar with what rules the king has laid before us, and if there is any hope in trying to lessen the torture he has put upon sweet Dahlia, I want to be able to pay what ever price I may." This was her reason, the best she could come up with. It was innocent, and did not appear treasonous in the least sense.

"You have helped put her there, Edgar," she continued. "The least you could do is help get her out again. I ask not of much, and the only efforts you will have is to let me in that library. I know that is where you clean, where you are assigned," she concluded.

"Hmmm..." Edgar said, thinking about this. "And if you find your answer?" he asked.

"I would place myself in her dungeon before willfully returning to the king," she said. "But if there is a lesser way, a trade or limitation perhaps..." she paused for a moment. "I know not of what I ask, nor am I sure there even *is* an answer for what I seek..." At this statement, she was speaking from the heart. She did not know if she could find the answer she truly sought after. But for these reasons to Edgar, as innocent as they appeared, could buy her enough time to be sure.

"I should agree that you may not find what answers you are searching for, but I will not risk myself for the sake of someone who wronged themselves," Edgar answered. Hellen's face fell as this seemed to be her only hope, and it was not going as well as she had planned.

"But..." he said with a grin. "It would seem much less suspicious to the scholars that the woman whom entered with me was there to also clean," he said. Hellen's face lifted a bit. "To help me do my duties...that would be enough incentive for me to take that small risk and let you come with me. But your excuse to your post need be yours and yours alone. I will not be involved with that," he concluded.

Hellen thought for a moment.

"Agreed. This would relieve us of most excuses we would need to come up with. I will take care of my own assignments. Tomorrow morning, I will join you in your cleaning duties." Edgar nodded in agreement, then took his leave from the dining hall and up the steps.

Hellen left to report to her post and found the same hustle had been going on. She changed into her dress to match the other servants and went to reach for the first plate of hot food she could find, a ceramic plate full of hot bacon. As she pulled it off of the counter, she let her fingers slip just enough to have the plate begin to fall. To give herself credit, she attempted to catch it with her left hand, which guided the plate to the stone floor, crashing in pieces and cutting her hand in multiple places. The crash startled several other servants as all attention fell on Hellen.

"My hand!" she shouted as she grasped it with her right, blood running out between her fingers.

"Ma'am, are you alright!?" one servant rushed over. "Quick! Get a bandage!" she yelled at another, who rushed into the kitchen to retrieve a cloth for wrapping.

"The plate was too hot when I grabbed it! I could not hold on, but I'm afraid I wasted the bacon..." she said, sounding disappointed in herself.

"Oh, do not worry about that!" the girl said. "You need to get this hand wrapped up and healed quickly!"

"What has happened here?" an elder woman said as she approached. She had silver hair braided behind her head, and a dress of similar design as the other servants, only a shade of pale yellow.

"I dropped the plate of bacon and it broke, cutting my hand," Hellen admitted.

"Dropped the plate!" the woman said. "You are a servant! This is your only job! How could you be so careless?!" she yelled at Hellen. Though Hellen had done this on purpose, so nothing this woman could say would be taken to her heart. In fact, Hellen was hoping to push the situation a bit further so to get re-assigned. She needed to prove she was no longer fit for this job, and if she could have any influence in what her assignment should be, she wanted to give it.

"Perhaps your years are starting to catch up to you," the woman said in a nasty tone. Hellen pulled a sour mask over her face. She had to sell this act. She had to feel hurt by these remarks.

"I am sorry!" Hellen replied. "I can do better! I just...I need another chance!" The other servant returned from the kitchen with a torn cloth. The first girl began pulling pieces of ceramic from her cuts as they prepared to wrap her hand.

"This is the service for the King himself!" the woman shouted. "He will not tolerate second chances! You will find other work more suited for your age," she said.

"So, I will not be allowed to serve our King?" Hellen said, pulling any tears she could find into her eyes.

"A fool like you should be no where near the King! You are more suited for cleaning after him and his guests! Out of sight and away from the most impor-tant!"

"As I am commanded, Ma'am," Hellen said, hanging her head low.

The woman took a deep breath in, calming her anger. She watched as the three of them finished dressing Hellen's hands. Then in a regret of the outburst, and feeling a sudden sense of pity, she asked her, "What can you clean? I suppose dishes are out of the question..."

"Yes, I suppose so, and it may take a week for my hand to heal completely. But I do not want to burden anyone!" Hellen said, playing off of the pity she was getting, but seeing the opportunity she had.

"Well what about dusting?" the old woman said. "No need to get your hands wet. But we cannot have you around anything fragile! I will not be responsible for your clumsiness!"

"Of course not," Hellen agreed. "But where can I clean that has nothing to break?" Her questions were more of a guidance into the one answer she was hop-ing to get.

"I will put in an order to have you reassigned to the castle's book keep. It would be hard to break a book! And there is no water or wine allowed in there anyway."

"The book keep?" Hellen asked, trying her best to keep her success contained.

"Yes, the castle tower. It is where the library resides," she said as she walked to the dresser at the end of the room. From the top shelf she pulled down a small parchment and a quill pen.

"Take this to the tower," she said, scribbling on the parchment. "It is there you will find Úlfgeir, keeper of the tower. He will tell you what to do," she said as she rolled it into a scroll, tying a thread around it.

"I hope you serve them better there than you did here," she said to Hellen, handing her the scroll with disapproval. "You will have little elsewhere to go if you fail again."

Hellen was filled with excitement. The hope that, however small of a victory this was, had now become a strange feeling. That a single thread of light was so blinding being trapped in darkness for so long. It seemed now she had the authority to be in the place she needed, even without Edgar's help. Hellen took her leave and headed for the castle's tower.

As she approached the entrance to the tower, she found herself in a grand hall, three stories tall, leading to two oversized wooden doors. On each door were various carvings of symbols and histories of the five states of Nýland. Flags and banners hung from finished support beams across the hall. Stained glass lined the walls, filling the hall with beautiful colors of sunlight. A light dust filled the air.

At the end of the hall sat a large desk with a beautiful stone top. At the desk, an elder man focused on his scribbling on various scrolls scattered across the top. Hellen approached the desk, assuming this was the man she was supposed to see.

She stood at the front of the desk, waiting patiently. No notice was given to her as he continued to write furiously on his papers.

"Sir Úlfgeir?" she inquired with a quietness in her voice. Still no notice was given.

"Excuse me, Sir Úlfgeir?" she said louder, taking a closer step to the desk.

"Whoah!" the old man jumped backed in a sudden startle. "When did you get here? What do you want? Can you not see I am busy at the moment?!" he said, going back to his papers.

"Ahem, Sir Úlfgeir," Hellen said, holding out the transfer scroll.

"What is this then?" he said, looking up and plucking the scroll from her hands. He quickly unraveled it and muttered the words to himself.

"Ah, very well then..." he said, rolling the scroll back up and stuffing it into a small drawer on his right side. "Head in through these doors, you'll find a man named Edgar somewhere in there. He will show you what to do. And please! No more interruptions!" he said, making no eye contact with Hellen.

"Thank you," she replied as she went around the desk and towards the large wooden doors. She placed her hand on the large iron handle and pulled, but it did not move. She pulled harder, but it still did not move. After pushing and pulling a few more times, her efforts became quite audible.

"Use the left door!" Úlfgeir shouted in anger without looking up from his desk, then muttered under his breath, "for the sake of all things holy..." shaking his head in disapproval. Hellen pulled on the left door and it swung open, echoing the creaks of the hinges into the great tower before her.

The sights took her breath away. Before her stood tall a towering room, many floors high. Each floor a ring around the outer walls, and each wall lined with shelves. There were thousands of books within the tower. The library as a whole smelled rich of parchments and papers.

Two sets of stairs connected each floor on opposite sides of the ring they formed. Each floor having four windows that wound around, each one offset by several feet from the one below it so the sun's rays swirled around as the tower stretched high above.

In the center of the tower on the floor, a beautiful mosaic lay of a map of the realm. Scattered across were several desks for studying and note-taking.

"Magnificent, is it not?" Edgar said quietly as he approached Hellen from the side.

"I have never seen anything like it," she admitted, still in awe.

"It is why I love coming here. No matter the task, even cleaning a place like this feels like an honor."

"Indeed," Hellen added, still taking in every detail she could. Her endeavors have proven to be more rewarding than she had realized, and for a moment, she thought about where she found herself, and her motivation to find answers escaped her.

"Well, we better be quick if you want to find your answers!" Edgar said. He seemed quite willing to help her, which came off as a bit suspicious to Hellen, seeing as before he tried so desperately to take her down in front of the king.

"Oh! I have officially been transferred, permanently," Hellen said with a tone of authority.

"Permanently?" Edgar asked, surprised.

"Yes, they feel my skills be better suited here. I have officially been transferred to the library to help clean."

"Well, well!" Edgar said, still surprised. "Looks like you've bought yourself all the time you need! And for what price?" he asked, looking down at her hand. "Ah! With the price of blood, I see," he said, reaching for her hand to inspect it. Hellen pulled her hand away, bearing a face of extreme disapproval.

"Do not touch me!" she said sternly. "You have no right! This was my sacrifice for what you did to Dahlia!"

"I beg your pardon, Hellen. What *I* did? We have already discussed this...*I* had done nothing wrong," Edgar still defended himself.

"Just keep your distance from me," Hellen replied, still angry. "I am only here to help my friend."

"Very well!" Edgar replied. "But you will be needing to know exactly what your duties here are, yes? Did Úlfgeir not say to come find me?"

"He did..." Hellen admitted. "So what is it I must do? Seeing as I am to be here for a long while, I should at least be able to do what I am assigned."

"Yes! It is not difficult, but more tedious than I would like. Still, though, I cannot imagine a more wonderful place to do it!"

"Out with it!" Hellen demanded. She very much wanted to end her conversation with this man.

"Hastiness will not lead to proper cleanliness!" Edgar told her. He smiled smugly at her, knowing his annoyance was eating away at her patience. Hellen stared at him with disapproval.

"Well then!" he said, walking across the main floor. "Welcome to the library!" he shouted with his arms stretch high. His voice echoed up the stone walls, resonating at the top of the tower. His hard footsteps on the stone mosaic also carried an echo.

"We clean each floor, one per day! There are seven levels here, which means each level will be dusted, swept, windows cleaned, sills polished, chairs organized, and banisters wiped once a week!" he explained as he approached a small wooden door on the far side of the tower.

Hellen looked up, counting the floors. Seven floors indeed towered over her. Each one seemingly small enough for a single person to handle on their own. She followed Edgar across the mosaic. As she approached the small door he was ready to open, she saw another door, worn in wood but with polished brass trim to her right.

"What is in there?" she asked. Edgar looked over.

"Oh...you must not enter that door. That is the king's private collection. It is locked anyway! No one, not myself nor even Sir Úlfgeir is allowed in there."

"Private collection?" Hellen asked. "What sorts of books would a king want to keep private?"

"I do not know!" Edgar replied. "Important books, I would imagine! Now..." he said, opening the small door they had arrived at. "Here are the cleaning supplies. A duster for you," he said handing her a wooden handle with a large bunch of peacock feathers tied to one end.

"The feathers are light enough to not move anything other than dust! Start on the top shelves and work your way down until any dust you can find ends on the floor. Then use this," he said, handing her a straw broom and an iron pan.

"Collect what you find! I typically use the window over there," he said, pointing at the window closest to the bottom of the staircase.

"Do *not* toss dirt outside any window above us!" he warned. "It tends to blow back towards the castle wall and cling to its wet surface! If you are caught doing that, I am afraid you will not have many other jobs they will find you useful for!" Hellen nodded in understanding.

"How will we split the work?" she asked, only seeing one duster and broom.

"You will do the dusting, and I will do the polishing. I hate dusting, and it brings some satisfaction to me to polish the brass to something shiny and clean..."

Hellen agreed to this without hesitation. Dusting bookshelves was much easier than the job she had before, and she did not need to wear any ridiculous clothes to do it. In addition, it appeared she would be mostly alone, despite having to share the same tower floor with Edgar. It was definitely a trade she was happy with. And before long, they both set out to start their cleaning for the day.

CHAPTER XII

RED INK

— 30th of Kaldagger, 1866 —

Quietness filled the tall tower, day after day. Much knowledge was contained within this space. Much history lined the stone walls. Each book resting, waiting to share what its pages told. Although their spines saw many sunrises and many sunsets, many moonless and moonlit nights, rarely would any move from their spot on the shelf.

A few days passed with each day a new floor to be cleaned. Hellen studied the books and scrolls on each shelf, looking for anything that could shed light on the possible family history of Ronan and his ancestors. But shelf after shelf, day after day, she found nothing useful. The library was indeed filled with many books whose topics spanned vast subjects of study. Many books on medicines, old battle tactics, and literature. But nothing that seemed extremely relevant for what she needed.

On the sixth day, Hellen arrived to the library, ready to start cleaning. However, Edgar had not shown up yet. It did not matter much to her since she had a good grasp on what to do, and the closet was always unlocked. So she took her broom and duster, and began to head up to the sixth floor.

A couple of hours had passed and the whereabouts of Edgar grew heavier on her mind. She wondered why he had not shown yet, and eventually it became too much to bear.

Hellen headed down to the first floor and walked through the main doors to find Úlfgeir at his desk.

"Excuse me, Sir Úlfgeir?" she asked politely.

"Yes, yes, what do you want?" he asked, continuing his study.

"Edgar has not shown up yet, and I was not sure what, if anything, should be done..." she said a bit sheepishly.

"What should be done!" he said a bit angry, looking up and making eye contact with Hellen.

"What is your duty?" he asked.

"To clean the librar—" Hellen began to reply.

"To clean the library! Yes! Now go clean it!" he shouted at her returning his focus to his desk top papers.

Hellen's face turned to a puzzled look. Úlfgeir seemed quite uninterested in Edgar's absence, and it seemed the entire responsibilities of that day's cleanings now fell solely on her. So she returned to the sixth floor to finish her dusting.

Hours went by. Hellen tried her best to speed up the process knowing she had twice the duties now that day to complete. It was nearly mid-afternoon before she finished her dusting and sweeping (and not entirely thorough either). She then gathered the rest of the equipment and began polishing the brass and cleaning the windows.

Before long, dusk fell. Hellen grew exhausted with such a long day of work. As the top floors of the towers glowed with an orange color of the fading sun, the bottom floors rested in shadow. Hellen sat against the far wall under a window to take a rest before finishing the last brass rail. The tower was peaceful at this time of evening. The books rested in their quietness, settled snug in each of their own corners of the shelves. The air was still in the large open space of the tower, and Hellen found herself staring at the flat space on the shelf next to her in front of the row of books, watching the fading orange sunlight lose its luster and fade into the coming night.

Ka-chunk! The main door on the first floor creaked open. Hellen leaned forward to see what the commotion was about, fearful it might be Úlfgeir upset at her delays in completing her duties. But it was Edgar that had walked in. He carried a lantern with him in one hand, and in the other, a set of keys jingled as he walked.

Hellen sat back, careful not to make a sound and stay out of site. She listened to his footsteps walk across the mosaic floor before they stopped. The sounds of the keys echoed through the tower as they unlocked a door, followed by the creaking of its hinges.

She waited for his footsteps to fade for a moment before peering over the edge again. The door to the king's private collection was left open, and a fading lantern light died out of site as Edgar disappeared into some unknown room.

Hellen sat for some time, waiting for Edgar to return. Her concerns about him grew immensely as did her suspicions. She felt a sense of danger in that her presence there could be costly if he were to discover her, so she remained as quiet and motionless as possible.

The evening light lost its luster and the tower grew dark. This darkness gave Hellen a sense of safety as it would be very difficult to spot her up on the sixth story now from the ground floor. But it seemed like a full hour had gone by as she waited to hear anything from that doorway. Eventually, Hellen's eyes grew heavy and she found it difficult to stay focused.

A shift in papers echoed across the tower as Edgar's lantern revealed itself from the dark corridor the doorway had led to. He emerged with several scrolls tucked under his arm. As he emerged, he held his lantern out to shed little light on the library in front of him. Satisfied in his solitude, he turned around, shut the door, and locked it. He then left the library with Hellen in it to ponder what he was doing, and why.

Hellen returned that night more puzzled than ever. The mystery of Ronan in the dungeon, Edgar's access to the king's private collection, and even Úlfgeir paying no attention to his absence, none of it made sense to her. She slept little that night as these thoughts ran over and over through her mind.

The next morning she found Bard eating breakfast at his usual spot. In the same corner of the room, Edgar stood, watching the comings and goings of those around him. Hellen took a seat close to Bard, knowing Edgar's eyes were upon her.

"Good morning, Hellen! How has your endeavors to the library come?" he said with a smile.

"I have been transferred there, Bard, but please keep your voice down..." she said quietly and close to him.

Bard continue to chew at his morning muffin.

"Why?" he said between bites. "Are we in danger?"

"We might be...I saw something last night, something that has raised great concern in my heart," she continued.

"What is it?" Bard whispered, looking rather frightened.

"Someone I know has lied to me, someone in this very room," she said without breaking eye contact with Bard. "He has deceived me. Someone I thought was like us, but I watched him in secret last night entering the king's private book collection."

"The what!?" Bard asked in shock, nearly choking on the food in his mouth.

"Contain yourself, please!" Hellen asked again.

"Hellen, only two types of people go in there..." Bard continue. "The King himself, or his dirty, sneaky sewer rats! It sounds like to me you've found one of his rats..."

"You mean he works for the king?" Hellen said, glancing over at Edgar who remained standing in the shadows, watching people come and go.

"I have heard of these tellers of tales before, reporting back anything suspicious to the king. But they are hard to come by! Such an accusation could lead to severe punishment!" Bard warned.

"I have seen public executions over such things..." he continued. "Hellen, you *must* be careful with this man. They are dangerously sly and very witty. The mind-games they play are beyond what a common folk such as myself would be able to pick up on...so I do not even know if I have ever met one! I would not be able to tell I would guess!"

Hellen sat in silence. The fear she had felt the previous evening became much more real and far stronger. Her arms lined with goosebumps knowing how close she had already come to getting caught with very dangerous information. She certainly could not tell Edgar now what her true motives were. But she felt all the more urgency in completing her task.

Now, however, she knew where to look for the information she needed. And she knew who had access to it too. But it was how she would get there that left to be seen.

"Thank you, Bard. Once again you have proven yourself more helpful beyond what you could understand," Hellen said.

"Please do be careful though, Hellen. I have grown rather fond of you and your daughter!" he said with a smile. Hellen smiled back, and left for her morning cleanings. It appeared now that Edgar would be joining her again.

Edgar caught up with Hellen as they both headed toward the library.

"Good morning, Hellen!"

"Edgar! You have decided to show up today!" she said. In her mind, she *had* to act as though she did not know anything about who he truly was. To remove all suspicion in her, she had to act suspicious of him.

"What happened to you yesterday?" she asked.

"Oh, yesterday was such a bizarre day!" he started off. "I woke up without being able to speak! My voice was completely gone! I was taken to see the healers and they fixed me right up! But it took a full day's rest to get there..." His story was weak but she went along with it.

"Well, I had to pick up your work too!" she said sounding rather annoyed. "I barely got out of there on time!" This was the line that sealed her secret, and Edgar swallowed it without hesitation.

"You mean what I had to do every day before you arrived?" he replied back with a smirk.

"*Humph!* Well, now I can at least appreciate the help of a second hand as you do I am sure..." she said, turning the corner and making their way down the main hall before the library doors. They both approached the doors, entered the library, and went about their cleaning of the seventh floor that day.

The king sat at his dining table alone. The late evening sun cast rays of light through the stained glass windows, lighting the entire hall with a shade of yellow-orange mixed with various colors. His chewing and smacking echoed loud through the emptiness all around him. No servants stood at his side. No guards close enough to hear a whisper of a command. His plates were half empty as one of his *sewer rats* approached.

"My King," Edgar said as he bowed his head.

"What do you have to report?" the king asked without looking up from his plate, sucking the duck fat off of his fingers.

"Her suspicions in me have diminished, quite rapidly, I am afraid. She did not question the story I fed her, despite its ridiculous nature. I also found out about a recent visit she had in the dungeons. Seemed like she wanted to talk to that Dahlia girl, but the guard I spoke with said she spent quite some time down there."

"Can you get what we need to take care of it?" the king asked once more, still not looking up from his dinner.

"She is after something in the library, but her hunt for it has ceased. I am beginning to suspect she means to find a way into the King's library," he finished.

This grabbed the king's attention. He placed what carcass was left of his meal down on the plate in front of him and wiped his hands clean on the cloth next to it, then wiped his mouth.

"If that is what she is hunting for, a dangerous trophy she must be after." The king picked up his goblet and drank deep of the wine it held. Placing the empty cup back on the table, he wiped his mouth again with the napkin he held in his other hand.

"Find out what it is, precisely, she is looking for. There is a question that haunts her mind, and an answer she believes she knows where to find it. But she must have found out about the *King's* library from someone. It appears you need to open your ears a bit further, Edgar."

"Yes, My King," he said, lowering his head in respect.

The king took a bite of cooked apple as the start of the end to his meal.

"Let her find what answer she seeks," he added. Edgar's eyes opened wide at this permission.

"You mean to let her into that library?"

"As soon as she finds it, bring her to me. We will make sure the secret will not leave her lips," he ended, taking another bite of soft apple.

"Yes, My King!" Edgar said, taking his leave.

The next morning, Hellen and Eira awoke ready for breakfast. They found Bard sitting in his usual place, a plate with an untouched muffin sitting before him.

"Good morning, Bard!" Eira said sitting down across from him.

"Bard..." Hellen said as she sat down next to him. "I do not think I have ever seen a muffin go untouched before you..."

"He came to me last night," Bard said, staring only at his muffin.

"What? Who came to you?" Hellen asked.

"Shh!" Bard replied. "He is watching, always listening, always close."

Hellen looked around slowly but saw no sign of Edgar.

"He woke me in the night, holding a blade to my throat. I had to tell him everything. He was ready to take my life!"

"What did you tell him?" Hellen demanded an answer.

"That you knew he works for the King. That you were trying to get to the library for some answers. I told him..." Bard paused as he began to choke on his own words with regret.

"What, Bard..."

"I told him you met Dahlia in the dungeons. And that had something to do with what you sought after."

"And did you mention the other? The other one I met down there?"

Bard paused for a brief moment.

"Oh, stupid Bard!" he said to himself. "I had completely forgotten you mentioning that!"

Hellen took a deep breath of relief. She wrapped her right arm around his shoulders and kissed the top of his head.

"Bless you, Bard! Your failed memory may have saved us all!" she said, releasing him as he regained composure.

"He knows, though, that you know more than he had realized. And you can be sure he knows now all that I have just told you. Be cautious, for this is when traps are set!" Bard warned.

"I know, dear friend. And thank you," Hellen said as she got up from the table. "I am thankful for you, Bard," she said looking back at him before heading to the library.

The day was similar to the day Edgar never showed, for he did not show that day either. Hellen knew a trap was being put in motion, and the entire day she spent cleaning the first floor, she kept her guard upon her. Every creak, every small sound had her startled. Her eyes constantly darted towards every shadow in the tower, worried that at any moment she would be seized.

But the day was spent without another soul being seen. She began to finish up her cleaning for the day, carrying her supplies to the cleaning closet. As she entered the closet and hung her dust pan and rags, the library doors suddenly opened.

Her instinct kicked in and she ducked down quickly in the closet. Between the chairs and desks, she could see Edgar walking across the floor, towards the King's library. He paid no attention to the rest of the library, not looking around, not making any announcement or question.

In his hand was a red leather book. He opened the door to the King's library and disappeared for only a moment. Suddenly he reappeared, and in a hurry, swung the door to close. The door's latch hit its mark, but failed to shut completely. Yet Edgar seemed to be in such a hurry, he did not take notice. And without so much of a second breath, he was gone and the tower returned to its quiet state.

Hellen remained silent, without movement. Her answers were just beyond the door that now remained opened. No one was in sight, and she seemed to have a way into what she had hunted for.

But something did not seem right. Edgar was in way too much of a hurry. And it all seemed too easy. Her suspicions grew, and it was then she had made her decision. Her plan had finally formed, as she knew how she would get her answers.

She stood from the closet, walked across the mosaic floor, and approached the ajar door. From behind a bookshelf on the second floor, a pair of eyes watched as she stood before the door to the King's library, her hand on the handle of the door. The trap had been set, and she was taking the bait.

Cla-clink! Hellen pushed the door shut, the echo of the latch giving tell of its security. Edgar lowered his head in frustration from behind the spying shelf, then continued to watch as she returned to the cleaning closet to finish putting away her supplies.

As she left the library, she found Edgar standing just beyond the library doors, his hands folded behind his back. His sudden appearance startled her, sending a wave of deep fear through her heart.

"Come with me," he said as he turned around, leading her away. Hellen, knowing what danger she might be in, followed.

He led her down the hall and to a flight of stairs that led up to the King's chambers. The two guards stopped him before he could open the doors.

"I am expected," he said to them, and they lowered their stance and let him pass through.

The king stood outside on his balcony, watching the birds flock in the evening sky. As they entered the room, the cool evening breeze blew in strong now having an escape through the bedroom doors before they were shut once more by the guards standing just beyond them.

"My King," Edgar said, approaching the entrance to the balcony. The king turned and stared at Hellen.

"And what has become of our Hellen?" he asked Edgar.

"She has passed the test," Edgar said, smiling and turning towards her.

"Ha! Marvelous!" the king said, his hands open wide as he approached her, placing them on her cheeks. "Marvelous."

"Edgar tells me you know of his deeds," the king continued as he returned to the doorway of the balcony, returning his gaze outward. Then turning to look back at Hellen with a smile.

"He tells me you can be trusted with this secret. I hope my trust is not placed in an ill-fate," he added, his smile falling and his face revealing a much more serious look.

"Of course, My King," Hellen replied. Her heart pounded as her nerves were fully tensed, every muscle tight, and her breathing labored.

"Good! I am relieved to hear that!" the king replied. "So, of these questions you had. A way to save your friend from what I hear," the king continued. Hellen looked down at the floor, as though all she had to keep secret was now revealed.

"It is honorable to struggle so far for someone you care about. To work so hard to save another. Though you had gone about it in a careless way..." the king continued. "Still though, honorable.

"But you see, my dear Hellen," he said as he returned to the inside chamber, walking slowly in deep thought around the end of his bed. "There is nothing you could find in the tower, nor anything in my personal library that could reject *my* commands." He approached her closely, locking eyes with her, nearly touching the tip of his nose to hers.

"*Nothing.* Besides," he said, breaking his stare and moving around her, "there is nothing you could be interested in my own private collection! It is just tales I find fascinating, old paintings, ancient scripts that perhaps need more care and attention to...nothing you could possibly find of interest!"

He walked back to his fireplace and stared at the dancing flames as their glow began to overtake the dimming light of the setting sun.

"I think we can settle this matter, yes?" he said, looking at Hellen.

"Yes, My King," Hellen replied. She knew not what game they were playing, for it seemed far too easy of a way out. What she had done was nearly treasonous, and they very much seemed to want to have her simply stop. Almost cowardice to give her such an easy way out. It simply did not *feel* right.

But there was nothing more to be said than to agree with the king. She felt far too out of her sense to keep up with what they were saying, what they were planning. And it did not matter anyway, for she had already found a way to getting the answers she sought.

That night, while all was quiet and resting, a mother lioness prowled through the castle in secret, returning to the library tower, careful to have no followers, no shadow, no eyes watching. To the door to the King's private collection she returned where the latch had been stuffed with a cleaning cloth, and a quick jolt of force upward undid its security.

And for the next several hours, unknown to any in the castle, she skimmed through the shelves deep in the basement of the tower. Down further and further it went, passing book after book, until she found a trail of absence of dust from one particular book. She removed it from the shelf, and in the dim light of her single lantern read the title.

The Lineage of Kings of the Realm of Nýland

As she studied its contents, nothing appeared out of the ordinary. She took it to a central table where she placed the lamp near the corner. It was here she found a large sheet of paper, as large as a map. The top of it reading:

A Quest of Heirs to the Throne of Nýland

She touched the top of the sheet, feeling the old ink as family trees were drawn out. As she wiped her hand down the page, the ink markings became less faded, changing in hand writing styles with different branches of family, until she found a red marking. Like a red bolt of lightning, it shown in the dim lantern light.

Following the line down, it led to a final entry of King Gunvald, current king of the Freeman Empire. But off from the red marking, a dotted line branched out. For generations it led down, names of heirs, of firstborn sons whose names had never been placed with royalty.

But at the end of this branch, with the freshest of ink still pure in black, she read the last name at the bottom of the tree. A name she certainly recognized.

And it was here the pieces fell into place. Her mind put together the motives that had caused the pains in her recent life. For it was on this paper that was described the conspiracy of the breaking of heirs, linked all the way through centuries of generations. The final entry, Rannver of the Gronndelon, recently deceased, the 39th generation of Jarl of Furksarth. Father of Ronan, who being the nephew of the current Jarl Sigurbjorn, now prisoner of Freeman Empire.

CHAPTER XIII

TO SAVE A LIFE

— 14th of Frostfare, 1867 —

High up on the mountain side, covered in deep snow, a thin smoke trailed upward in a windless morning sunrise. The air was still, frozen, having all heat robbed of it. Nothing moved outside of the cabin (save the smoke of the chimney), for nothing was freed from the harshness of winter's grasp. No sound, only the glistening of the yellow sunrise against the freshly fallen snow.

Inside the cabin proved to be a haven of warmth and comfort. Shielded against any biting the cold could attempt, Kuoni had refueled the fire, and it roared hot and bright. The inside was filled with a wonderful aroma of crispy bacon; a hearty meal to prepare the soon-to-be travelers of mountains! It was this warm scent that first awoke Edlen's stomach, then the rest of himself.

"Oh-ho!" Kuoni shouted at the first sight of Edlen's awakening. "Looks like my breakfast has finally gotten you out of bed!" He smiled as he placed an over-sized plate of bacon, biscuits with honey, and a variety of dried fruits down on the table as Edlen's share of breakfast.

"Fancy yourself for a cup of breakfast tea? My own blend!"

"Thank you very much!" Edlen said with his spirits high. He had fully recovered, and found himself to be quite fortunate to be waking in such conditions. For the time being, it felt as though any darker thoughts had been chased away, and his hopes were high for what lied in front of him. Kuoni plated a breakfast for himself and joined Edlen at the table, bringing two mugs of a strong blackened tea.

"Drink up! It will put stamina in your muscles and wit all about you!" Kuoni took a big mouthful of biscuit as honey dribbled down his beard. "You'll be need-ing it today!" he said with difficulty as the biscuit proved dense and the honey thick. Edlen grinned as he was very much enjoying his host.

Throughout breakfast, they discussed the plans for the next several days, as it would take roughly five before they made their way to the gates of the City of

Stone. The paths they would take, the challenges they would face, but in all, it did not sound like a terrible walk.

Their first leg would take them off the mountain side as this is where most of the danger resides. The loose footing, deep snow, and dangerous cold was all to be avoided as soon as possible. From the base, they would follow the valley around several mountain bases and around a few small lakes. The trails existed, but were not constantly maintained. And although it was not the *quickest* route, it was the easiest for the valley's descent was far more gradual, until meeting the city's borders.

"However," Kuoni continued. "The city rests high upon a small valley, in a bowl surrounded by three mountain peaks. The city streets themselves reach far into the sky from where we must enter, at the gateway near the base of Festning Mountain, the gateway into Skydale."

"A mountain?" Edlen said out loud with surprise. "A mountain is the gateway to the city?"

Kuoni smiled.

"Oh, yes! A wonderful way to protect the city, no doubt! But oh! It is not like any other dwelling nor cave you have ever seen! The inside is a beautiful place! You will surely enjoy it, I doubt it not!"

Kuoni continued to describe the insides of the mountain as a wonderful market place of all sorts of interesting gadgets, enchanted jewelry, herbal remedies, just about anything one could be looking for, and for any occasion. The halls were tall and spacious with several levels of markets, inns, places to eat, and other dwellings.

"Of course you need to see this place for yourself! I fear that my words simply are not enough to describe it proper!" Kuoni said. And with that, they both finished their breakfasts and began packing. Before long, they were dressed and ready to open the cabin door to the outside winter.

"Never forget," Kuoni said as a lighthearted warning, "do not lose sight of me! I will lead the way as the paths surely are buried, but I know them better than the strands of me braided beard! Ho-ho!

"We need to make it to the base of the mountain before night fall, which shouldn't be much of an issue. Onward!" he shouted as he burst the door open. Swirls of cold air surrounded them and hit Edlen's face, what little was exposed. His eyes hurt in such cold as his body's heat battled the biting frost.

Like a fearless force of man and beast, Kuoni headed straight into the knee-deep snow. Of course at this height, it met Edlen's waist even with Kuoni plowing a path through. With the help of a long walking stick, Kuoni continued down the path as he found it. Knocking the bottom of his walking stick through the snow, the sound of hard stone told of the right way to go.

As the travelers journeyed down the mountain, the sun continued to rise up the sky. Edlen's breath left a trail of steam that rose steadily up as it broke through his scarf. The sky above was a crisp blue, and all around them were large pine trees heavily draped in layers of snow.

Their path wound through the woods, steadily down in absolute silence. It was only broken by the occasional crow call in some distance, or a clump of snow breaking free from some top branch as it was warmed by the rising sun. It really was beautiful if it was not so horribly cold.

With their scarves wrapped around their faces, conversations were minimal. They did not break often, and the deep snow wore Edlen out quickly. Every so often, Edlen could see glimpses of white wisps blowing between the trees. It almost looked as though snow packed against the branches broke free and rode the wind through the forest, yet no wind blew. Curious, Edlen lowered his scarf inquiring.

"What are those?" Edlen asked after seeing a fourth wisp float through in some distance. Kuoni paused and turned his whole body as he was heavily dressed in furs, making it hard to turn just his head. He stared into the distance and lowered his scarf.

"Ah! Winter-wisps! Yes, these woods are home to many! Harmless unless provoked, probably waking up in the golden sun!"

"But what *are* they?" Edlen asked, confused.

"Oh, their origin is far beyond my memory. I believe they are some creation of snow and spirit. Magical beings that bring coldness and frosted beauty where ever they go. Of course they love it up here!" Kuoni returned his focus to the path without pulling his scarf back up.

The morning was aging and their progress down the mountain was noticeable. By the day's end, they had reached their goal at the foot of the mountain. There, a winding river would lead them to the front door of Skydale.

At this point, much of their view was shadowed in gray as the sun had long passed over and behind Kuoni's mountain home. The sky above was clear and dots of stars began waking up. The temperature was cold, and the ground still covered in snow.

Their path continued and the snow had gradually shallowed to only a few inches deep. The forest around them was now thick and crowded with pine, evergreen, and spruce. Little could be seen as Edlen gazed out around them. The forest all together felt close and cluttered, and no wind was breaking through that night.

The two travelers turned a corner and the sudden sound of the river became clear. Muffled to a silence until only feet away through the dense forest, it was larger than Edlen expected. Still free-flowing, although without a doubt freezing cold, it roared past them and into the coming night.

"Ah-ha! Our accommodations for the night!" Kuoni said breaking through the roaring sound of the river. On the opposite side of the trail from the river was a small wooden shack with a small stone chimney. As they approached, it reminded Edlen a bit of the hunter's shack they had found in Bjornwood, although this seemed a bit larger and much better kept.

They both entered the cabin and found it to be cold and dark. Split wood was stacked next to the hearth and it took little effort to light it. Before long, the crackling fire had chased away the darkness and was beginning to spread its warmth.

It proved to be nearly as cozy as Kuoni's cabin up on the mountain side, and it was far better than Edlen had expected. After getting settled in and a hot supper cooking over the fire, the two sat down for a much needed rest.

"Kuoni?" Edlen said having taking his last bite of supper. "Could you tell me more about my relative? Of Edelmar? I know nothing of his name as my father had never told me of such stories."

Kuoni smiled with a mouth full of potato, and leaned back in his rickety chair and placed his fork down.

"Of course, Edlen! It is only proper that one knows his own family history!"

He moved his chair at an angle so to face Edlen and leaned on the table. Folding his hands, his mind dove deep in thought and memory.

"Centuries ago..." he began, "many centuries now, huh-huh," he chuckled at the thought as though now realizing how long it had been. "...when King Valdór destroyed the Draugrthrall in battle, and thus bringing dawn to the second era, he had a vision before his death. A vision that one day, the spirit of Draugrthrall should choose a champion to bring back the will of all evil to our earth. That this champion, through powers beyond our imagination, should bind the evil forces now scattered throughout our world to one purpose. It was this vision that led the Good King to make a calling. A request for the best of fighters, and of purest of hearts, to make a vow to protect the realms of Men from such horrors.

"Through vigorous tests of strength in muscle, mind, and spirit, twenty-five men were chosen. Of these, five clans were formed. One clan was sent in each direction, and the last were to remain in, or near, the Gronndelon. This last clan, I am one of. Radholf also, and Oatikki. Dargmara as well, and the fifth was Edelmar, your ancestor. We called ourselves the Verndari, or *the protectors.*"

"How could this be if the oath was taken centuries ago?" Edlen asked, concerned over the validity of Kuoni's story. "How could you have known Edlemar?

Wouldn't that make you..."

"Oh, just shy of two thousand years old...if I'm counting correctly," Kuoni said, stroking his beard. "If my memory is working properly, I was 84 years old when I took *the oath*."

"Two-thousand years!" Edlen shouted in disbelief. "That cannot be! I am no fool, Kuoni!"

"Of course you are not! But I said *shy of*, not quite *that* old yet!" Kuoni replied. "But this was part of *the oath*..." he said, holding out his hand to reveal a golden ring with a bright blue gem encased. It glowed a light blue, as light as a bright day's sky and all the more clearer.

"This is *Alder*. Each of us that has taken *the oath* received one. An enchanted ring, that as long as the master of it wears it, should not age another hour. It is not until our *oath* is complete that we may remove it."

Edlen stared at the ring, then looked back up at Kuoni, who then continued.

"It serves as a good reminder of our oath, but if I were to remove it before my oath is complete, the aging of all these years it has saved from me should be thrust upon my being in a single moment."

"So, what happened to Edelmar?" Edlen asked. Kuoni's face told of a changing thought as he became saddened. He could only reply at first with a simple answer.

"The world took him, I am afraid." A silence fell over the small cabin. After a moment, Edlen spoke up again.

"What happened?" he asked quietly. It was another moment before Kuoni could finish gathering his memories, but continued with what he could recall.

"There came a time when the five of us had to make a decision. War was upon us, but we had taken an oath. To protect *all* against any evil that showed its ugly face. But what we could not have foreseen at the time of taking these oaths was the twisted corruption that had already begun.

"When we thought of evil, we thought it be easy to find, easy to recognize. A dark shadow that with the power of light we chase out of every corner. Like a hunter and its prey, that was our task. But the prey has become tricky. We never thought it was capable of doing what it did.

"Infecting the hearts of our own kind, corrupting Men, we suddenly were faced with a decision. To betray the Men of the Gronndelon of whom we never imagined would *become* the enemy, or to break our vow and side with our own kin, our own brothers. Our own sons." Kuoni paused in deep reflection, staring off into some distance, then looked back at Edlen.

"We chose to honor our oaths," he said proudly. "And thus found ourselves siding with creatures of the forest. Greed had overtaken the minds of our own kin. They longed for precious power at the cost of painful torture, enslavement, and death."

"The Arborian War..." Edlen whispered under his breath, remembering the stories Radholf had told him a month ago around that fire in Bjornwood.

Kuoni nodded.

"Radholf set out for aid from the Woodlen Elves. If anyone would help us, it would be the *Children of Arboran*. The rest of us joined the fleeing keepers of the woods, trying to escape to the wild through what is now Bjornwood. But —" Kuoni stopped.

Even after so many years it was difficult to recall the horrible events that transpired during those days. He still felt guilt of betrayal, guilt of failure. He gathered himself and continued.

"- but it was a trap. We did not foresee it, but they were ready for us, just before we reached the Vanalta river." He looked over at the crackling fire in the fireplace. Pain was written over his wrinkled face. Without breaking sight of the fire, Kuoni asked the next question.

"Do you know what happens when an Arborian is set aflame? Among the shrieking and crackling, the horrible pain...what sight one sees?" He suddenly shifted his focus to Edlen, waiting for an answer. Edlen shook his head, fearful of what would come.

"Their blood burns a bright gold. A testament of its richness and power within the honeycomb. As the fire reaches their hearts, they are bathed in golden flames." Kuoni became restless, his leg jittering up and down, fighting the horrible sights his mind had uncovered. His shaking intensified as the battle being replayed in his mind worsened. Then all at once he stopped and broke his endless stare.

"Edelmar, your ancestor, lost his life during this battle. He died defending the Arborians. He died fulfilling his oath."

"But the ring! Did he not have his own ring of life?" Edlen asked.

"Of course! But the ring does not defend us against death! Only aging. Each of us may still die if taken by actions of evil. But foolish he was not. Nay, but honorable, a fighter among the best of them. He fulfilled his oath better than any of us have yet."

Edlen was proud to have come from such a honorable warrior. One so well respected and befriended by so many. If these tales were true, and he hoped with the deepest corners of his heart they were, it meant that he was in good hands. The tales Kuoni had told settled most of Edlen's curiosities and questions. And ending on such notes of bravery left his heart feeling full.

The rest of the evening was quiet, and stories of lighter happenings were told by Kuoni (who loved to have this chance to share). Eventually, the talks between the two weary travelers began to space out, until they were both asleep.

The next morning they awoke to another cold sunrise. Although they had traversed down into the valley, winter had freshly settled into the mountains and laid down a blanket of snow. The air was once again crisp, with crystallized water droplets dancing in the golden sun's rays.

They took their leave as the first of that golden sun shined through the small single window of the cabin. Bundled up, their path was easier to find as the snow was not as deep, and the river flowing strong gave a good indication of where it was laid out.

As the river wound back and forth, snaking its way between mountain feet, so did their walk for that day. Much of the valley was densely forested, with a bit more variety than just evergreen. Naked aspen trees, cottonwood, and willow began to appear. Freshly dead grasses towered out of the snow banks along the river, tan and brittle. But the roar of the river kept the feeling of loneliness at bay.

"What is the name of this river?" Edlen spoke up, looking for something to talk about as the morning hike was beginning to bore him.

"Oh! This is the Big Bristlecone River! Ice cold but it never freezes! At least not as long as I have walked on its shores. Great spot for fishing in the summer time, and the surrounding lands blossom into something spectacular! Green foundations colored bright with summertime wild flowers! Yellows, purples, reds, and blues! And you can almost hear the entire valley buzzing with bees and thirsty insects. Makes sense now why I chose to build a cabin up here, does it not? Ha-ha!"

It was clear Kuoni was passionate about these valleys and mountains, and seemed he loved living up here. It also made Edlen a bit saddened to think his journey had brought him through on such a grim and cold time of the year, missing the peak of the valley's beauty.

On either side of them, the feet of the mountains rose up to tall white towers in the sky. The valley floor felt in itself just under the sky dome, but the mountains reached up much higher, the peaks of which seemed to escape the air and reach into the heavens.

The rest of the day went by quicker than before. The sights of the mountain giants never ceased in their awe, the sun was warm for such a cold winter day, and all in the valley was bright.

Their path led to the north, away from the river until some time further down. At this point, the path inclined up a single mountain foot. Not a difficult climb, even in the snow and ice, but at some points it wound back and forth to make the incline more gradual. Eventually, they came to the top where a second path had joined.

"That path," Kuoni said, pointing up the joining way, "comes from the far side of my mountain. It has been many years since I have traveled it, but it eventually ends high on the slopes. A faster route, if we had begun our journey there, but much more difficult."

"By how much faster?" Edlen wondered, looking up the rocky and uneven walkway.

"We likely could have arrived at this point last night, if we had taken it. But treacherous it is, and quick to wear you down. Only in urgent matters have I ever taken it."

They continued to walk down the path another mile, high up on top of the foothill. It commanded a beautiful view of the valley to their right. The setting sun, still just above the rims of the mountain peaks, cast a golden-orange light across the white snow. The river shining bright flowed east and around the next mountain foot. Far in the distance was a wide flattening that shimmered lightly.

"Ah! Starlight Lake in all its splendor! We must hurry to get there before it becomes too dark! For that is our next stop and only shelter within reach!" Kuoni said. They picked up their pace as the sky began to shift to beautiful shades of oranges, reds, then purples. The coming dusk began showing its shadows above the eastern peaks and the brightest stars revealed themselves as they had their first glimpses of the cabin in their sight.

As they approached, Kuoni noticed a depression in the snow in front of the door. He walked up carefully, studying all around.

"Someone is here, or has been, within the past few days. I see no signs of recent footprints..." he thought out loud. The cabin was about the same size as the last, loosely held together with old planks, but a solid small window in the front and a well enough roof to keep from blowing off in the wind. Kuoni approached the door and knocked hard. No answer came, no sound from within. He glanced back at Edlen and shrugged his shoulders.

Thrusting the door open, they found an empty mess of a cabin. Dust lingered in the air, and throughout the entire space were signs of a sloppy yet recent guest.

"Humph! Whoever stayed here last did not have much courtesy! Look at the place! It is as though they cared not for cleanliness or tidying up! Bah!" Kuoni said, shedding off some of his anger.

"And look! They didn't even take out the ashes! There's bed sheets still on the floor, and food on the table!"

It was at this moment that he noticed something rather odd about certain items left thrown about in the mess. On the wooden floor boards under the table, was a small stone mortar lying on its rim. Kuoni inspected it curiously, lifting it up. A brown sticky substance stretched out between the lips of the mortar and the floor boards. It was thick like honey, but far too dark.

Kuoni brought the bowl to his nose and sniffed. His eyes were deep in thought, then he noticed scattered scraps across the table. He picked up a small broken twig, some sort of spruce, robbed of its needles. Winterthistle stems, and stains of red snowberry he found also on the table and floor. He returned his attention to the mortar and dipped the tip of his finger into the sticky goo. Touching it to his tongue, he had identified what it was.

"Frost-keep!" he said turning towards Edlen, who had come inside, leaving the door open for what little light there was left.

"But why would someone..." Kuoni suddenly dropped the mortar and with a few heavy steps in his boots, ran to the back door of the cabin and thrust it open. He darted out into the snow banks in the cold dusk.

Edlen quickly followed, running past the table and out the back door. He found Kuoni on his knees, ten yards out the back, just on the edge of the sleeping thicket. He was throwing snow left and right, uncovering what was at the base of a small mount. He slowed down, carefully brushing off the snow from a young lady's face.

As Edlen approached, he grew nervous for not knowing what they had found. But even in the dim light of dusk, there was no mistake who lied there. The long dark hair and beautiful young face suddenly took all life from Edlen's mind. His heart stopped and clinched tight. At that moment, the mountains surrounding them collapsed, all stars fell. The lake behind the cabin fell into a void, and the land flattened to nothing. The world grew completely dark save the pale blue shades of Sabrina's face encased in frost.

His hearing ceased and legs grew numb. This had to be a nightmare, a terrible dream his horrible mind had fabricated. In a single moment, his heart was yanked into the dark depths of despair. So sudden it was, it took several moments before he could react to anything else.

Slowly, a low rumble began to grow in his mind. Muffled, it caught his attention. Kuoni was shaking Edlen, trying to get him to snap back. But Edlen could not understand what he was saying, nor did he care. What his heart had always feared and hoped so much against, his eyes were telling him they had found. He collapsed to the snow.

Kuoni, feeling rather frustrated, hauled him out of the snow and into the cabin, leaving Sabrina's body in the snowbank. As soon as he had set Edlen down on the bed, Edlen jolted in an anger of rage. Denial had hit him hard, and he would not accept what was just outside.

Amid the screaming and flailing of arms and legs, Kuoni continued to shout at him the same thing he had been.

"She's not dead! She may still be alive!" Kuoni yelled. This was almost too much for Edlen to understand, but it broke his angry fit.

"We may still be able to save her!" Kuoni shouted, ending all yelling as silence fell upon the cabin again. Edlen composed himself. Tears had soaked his cheeks and scarf, and his head was burning hot.

"I take it you know this young lady?" Kuoni asked Edlen. "It would be my guess this is your companion from the catacombs, yes?"

Edlen only nodded. He could not bring himself to speak yet, as the fear of reality was still trying to settle in. Yet now it was being rocked again, and his emotions did not know how to handle such extremes.

"This potion that was made, the potion found in the mortar. It is a recipe called Frost-keep, and if used at the right time, can preserve life if frozen." Kuoni tried to explain as best he could. Edlen was still trying to catch his breath.

"But it is not as easy as bringing them inside and warming them up, I'm afraid. And the potion does not last long."

"Then what must we do?" Edlen said, his voice wavering with strong emotion.

"She needs another potion to unlock herself. Frost-breaker, as most call it. But it is not something I can craft here."

"So, we must take her back to your cabin?" Edlen said, hoping there was at least some answer to the terrible riddle they found themselves in.

"The recipe calls for a special berry that I have never seen grow upon the mountain sides, a wild berry that, for what I know, only grows in the arid dry deserts far to the south. Our best chance, Edlen, is to take her with us to Skydale."

"But that is still three days away!" Edlen said with fallen hopes.

"That it is, but..." Kuoni continued, lowering his head, revealing his own hopes were falling. "I have only heard of Frost-keep lasting three days at most. And we do not know how long she has been here already. From my best guess, it has already been at least two days, maybe three, as she was covered in the snow that fell before we left." Kuoni said, saddened by the need to deliver such news.

"So..." Edlen said, his voice cracking under the weight of his throat swelling. "we are already too late?"

"It is difficult to say, and we will not know for sure unless it is attempted," Kuoni answered. "But indeed, each hour spent without the remedy harms her chances of an awakening. Haste *must* be taken! And our path around the bases of these mountains will prove too much."

"But what choice do we have!" Edlen retaliated, willing to fight anything that would stand in his way.

"We can take the path that leads north over the northern crest of the twin mountains. The path we were planning on taking goes south, and around the bases of these mountains. The entrance to Skydale is just beyond this crest and across a narrow valley. I believe we could be there by sunset tomorrow, if we leave now."

"Then let us take our leave!" Edlen said without hesitation.

"Edlen! This route is dangerous and difficult to traverse! I can carry your friend the entire way, but you will need to keep up. If you fall behind, I should not slow down. Though I do not believe you would want to find yourself alone on this trail. To be honest, you would find our original path much safer and more comfortable. I believe you could complete that journey on your own, if you must."

Kuoni was simply explaining all options to Edlen. He had some concern over Edlen following on the path that leads north, but was only trying to inform him the best he could so Edlen could decide for himself.

"Of course, I will leave this decision to you, Edlen."

Without any time to think, Edlen knew he could not be separated from Sabrina a moment longer. Not if there was hope left, however thin, of bringing her back.

"This girl has saved my life, more than once even. I will not leave her side. I will not leave the chance to repay what she has done for me."

Kuoni had already known what Edlen's answer would be. He nodded in approval, then pointed to a small cabinet on the far wall.

"Grab what you can from there. You'll find several small bottles of old potions and ointments. Also, be sure to grab the rope and any jars of dried goods. This will be a difficult climb for both of us!"

Within moments they were ready to set off again. Kuoni held Sabrina in his arms, who appeared smaller in comparison to the large man he was. To Kuoni, this would be no more to bear than an extra pack of supplies. A journey he had made between his home and Skydale many times before, but the first like this over the crest.

"We cannot expect the moon to rise over the eastern peaks for a few hours more, so I am afraid we will have little light until then. But once it reveals its face, its light should last us until the first of dawn again. By then, we should be at the slopes of the crest." Kuoni wanted Edlen to be fully prepared for the journey through the cold night.

"Please stay close, Edlen. I will be walking with haste!"

For the next several hours the land around them certainly was in a shroud of darkness. Even with the white blanket laid over the lands and the bright stars above, it was difficult to see beyond the immediate distance.

In Edlen's mind, the world had closed in around them. The darkness about them felt fitting and bothered him none as his only concerns were of reaching Skydale in time. Each minute that passed felt painful. Each moment a possible failure unknown. It was the not knowing if the seconds that passed by had just become the "*too late*" to save her that took its toll on his heart and mind. The trek was long and tedious, but it was not the physical toll that wore Edlen out. It was the not knowing.

Each time he looked up, he could see the black shapes of the mountains cutting into the starry sky with hopes of seeing the moon rising. A risen moon meant the sun was on its way, and a risen sun would mean they were within the day of arriving. But those long moonless hours seemed to have them trapped in a forever of empty steps.

Over time, a gradual brightness began to glow beyond a single peak, and within moments, the bright white face of the moon came out from behind its hiding place. Suddenly the earth grew wide again, and the slopes and peaks of all mountains around them shown in their slumber.

The rising of the moon did well for Edlen's mind, as it now gave him a way to keep track of their time and efforts. The higher it rose, the closer to dawn. And the light it shed made it easier to visually see the progress they were making as the crest that lied ahead grew steadily closer. He suddenly had more to dwell upon than the passing moments of unknowns.

The night aged as the moon passed over head. Over time, Edlen had forgotten to check its progress, and the sleepless night had begun to wear him down. His urgency had worn off, and his eyes tired. The step after step through cold snow ached his legs. He was beginning to really feel the challenge of keeping up, though Kuoni himself showed no signs of slowing. It was difficult to keep this notice from dragging his spirits down.

Every so often, Kuoni would look back to check on Edlen. Though his main concern was the precious life in his arms, he only half-expected to find his follower still behind him. Each time, though, Edlen was right there, and his endurance brought warmth to his heart.

After several more hours, the sky began shifting into color. The blackness in which the stars laid upon slowly came to life in dark blues and purples. As the Rhims to the east silhouetted against a glowing red and orange dawn, Kuoni and Edlen found themselves face to face with the steep slopes of the crest before them.

Kuoni gently placed Sabrina on a small snow bank. He stretched his arms as they were becoming sore and tight in spots. He glanced up at the steep trail that led high up the slope.

"We must be careful, Edlen," he warned. "There will be many places where ice covers our footing. And never trust a snow bank! It can be deceitful and bottomless. I will continue to lead, of course, so step only where I do, when possible." Edlen nodded in agreement. It was clear now that he had a difficult time keeping up to this point, but the physical challenges were only to begin.

Their trail was hardly visible in the snow, but bare at extremes where the wind had wiped it clean. It was very steep, and in many places had logs or flattened stones half-buried into the frozen ground to act as a stepping place. Finding good footing proved even more difficult.

As they began, Kuoni grabbed a tall stick, dead from at least this past year, and used it to find his footing ahead of himself before trying it with his next step. This proved to be a slow way up the side, yet necessary for their own safety.

As they slowly climbed, so did the rising sun on the other side of the crest. Their path was in constant shadow, but the lands behind them lit up far to the west. The light slowly moved closer as they climbed higher and higher. The top of the crest came suddenly at an outburst of sunlight as it appeared both the sun and their small party had reached their peaks at the same moment.

"Wow," Edlen spoke up in sudden awe of the sight before them.

"Indeed!" Kuoni replied, taking a deep breath of relief as the warming sun shone on their faces.

"Indeed..." he said again, exhaling.

Indeed it was a beautiful sight that lay before them, for they were high above the narrow valley, face to face with the towering Festning Mountain. Its immense size, taking moments to grasp, blocked much of the sky and yet incredibly rested behind a great deal of space between it and the small, fragile lives that stared upon it. Its slopes clothed in white, its peak like a black spear bursting forth from the earth, piercing the sky. Wild winds swirled off the top, carrying whipped up snow from the other side with it.

At its base, a winding road led up to a small collection of buildings and eventually two tiny pillars carved into the rock itself with a matching arch over the top of it.

"It may be in sight, but we must still use caution until we reach the bottom," Kuoni warned. And right he was, as their path was still covered in snow and ice. Edlen nodded, and the two continued down the path.

As Edlen took his first few steps down, he found his knees were sore from the climb up, and the steps leading down pushed the strength of his legs to a new limit. He found it hard to control and bear, but kept Sabrina's life above all thoughts.

Back and forth their path wound, and progress continued to be slow. They were nearly a third of the way down when Edlen's foot found a patch of ice hidden beneath the snow. His foot shot out from under him, and not expecting such a fall, had little control over which direction he fell. As he collapsed, he tried his best to catch himself. His foot slipped beyond the ice and off the ledge they were traversing, and the rest of his body followed.

His arms stretched up in an attempt to catch a hold of the ledge, but they found only the same ice in which his foot had met. He had no way to stop his fall, for it was a straight cliff that he fell down until finding the next rounding of the trail, some thirty feet below.

He yelled as he fell, grasping at nothing but air. Dust clouds of snow followed him, and as he watched the edge rise high above him, he saw Kuoni turn and watch in horror as he plummeted down. Without being able to keep straight, he could not see the bottom quickly approach, and thus did not brace the impact of the catch.

Ka-THUNK! His legs twisted in odd ways as they met the hard stone and ice. What little snow did remain on that path did nothing to help cushion his fall. His head whipped back before meeting the same cold, hard ground...crack! The sound echoed in his head, and he felt a sudden burst of cold pain in his legs and the back of his head.

Kuoni ran to him, snow flying out of his way, and laid Sabrina's body back down on the cold ground.

"Edlen!!" he shouted, looking him all around to see what might be his most urgent injury. Edlen's eyes had a difficult moment to focus, and his ears rang loud.

"Edlen! Tell me what hurts!"

"Ma..." he muttered. Edlen lifted his hands up to his head.

"Your head?" Kuoni asked. He lifted Edlen's head and felt around the back under his hood. His hands returned with patches of blood across his fingers. Kuoni reached into his small satchel he carried on his side and pulled out a long bandage.

"What else, Edlen?" he said, then lowered his voice with care. "How are your legs?" he asked without looking down at them.

Edlen nodded with the look of pain on his face.

"Painful," he managed to get out, his breathing labored.

Kuoni first wrapped Edlen's head in the bandages.

"A nice bump you will have back there for some time, but I do not think anything up *there* is broken. But for your legs..." he said, taking more care to inspect them properly. He lifted the bottoms of his pant legs on first the Edlen's left as it appeared to have taken the hardest hit.

Just above Edlen's ankle it began to swell. It firmed and became discolored.

"I'm afraid you may have injured your left ankle. A sprain, likely," Kuoni informed him, looking out into the space just off the slopes and to the valley.

"A wonderful place to have such an injury!" he said with sarcasm. Edlen did not appreciate it, and knew he was going to have to get himself down that slope.

"Let us take a look at your other leg," Kuoni said. He inspected it carefully, poking the skin lightly and rolling his ankle around.

"Well, this one seems to still be working fine..." he concluded. "Though I'm sure it will also be sore for a while. And as for your ankle..." he continued, "I will go and find some wood to splint it, and see if I can find a sort of crutch while I am out there, for although I am large for a man, I do not think it would be safe to try and carry the both of you!" He said as he stood. He looked at Sabrina, still frozen and lifeless on the trail, then back at Edlen. Taking a deep sigh, he concluded, "Don't you two go anywhere," with a wink. Then he turned and headed back up the trail.

For Edlen, this was the darkest part of the journey. He found himself just feet from the one life he was trying so hard to save, fearful of their efforts never finding life in her again. Exhaustion had settled in, and now he had become a burden rather than a help to their cause. He felt as though he had failed her. That they would never make it to Skydale in time to save her.

He stared at her body, at her pale face. He called out to his own heart for one last search of hope, that perhaps in it, he would know she was still alive. But he found silence. He felt a lifeless void in his heart, and at that point, he truly felt she was gone.

And for the next hour he sat on the cold mountain side, the wind blowing snow dust all around, feeling truly alone. Alone with nothing but his darkest thoughts of failure and worthlessness. He very much wanted to end the pain in what ever way he could. And among the sounds of the wind howling and small bush branches waving in the air, he heard a familiar sound.

"Caaaw," he heard, carried on the wind. "Kra-caaaaw!" he heard it again. He looked up at the bright blue void of the sky in search of the source of the sound. High up, a black raven had its wings spread wide. Its flapping and *caw*ing brought sudden memories back of their time before the caves, during his journey through Bjornwood again, and of that terrible day when this all started. Visions of the falling flower, of the cold hard raven beak, of the loss of his father. With so much suffering and foulness around him, Edlen's world began collapsing.

He recognized the struggle he was enduring, and dwelt on the ending of life, and what would come after. He remembered the lone man in the prison and his song, and the feeling of wanting to defeat all things evil, to rise again at the final war, and he called out:

"Valdór! Purest of heart, hear my cries," Edlen began. "I am desperate for relief from this evil that haunts me. I do not want to hide, I do not want to run. Command this evil to let go, and relieve me of this pain!" His eyes began to water as he felt exhausted from his emotions, from the terrible things he had been thrown into.

"Release me, O' Kriger. Release me, gift me freedom and strength to crush that of evil, and I will serve your purpose to destroy all of ill-will," Edlen was crying uncontrollably at this point, his cheeks soaked and voice cracking.

Suddenly, out of the east came a large bird. A brown mountain eagle soaring through the emptiness with great speed. It flew through the air toward the raven, whose view of the eagle was difficult to spot as the eagle's brown feathers matched the dark bare patches of the Festning mountain behind it. Before the raven could react, the eagle collided with its talons out front.

In an explosion of black feathers, those released on the impact slowly fell from their place in the sky as the eagle clamped down onto the raven. With a few rips of its beak, the eagle slaughtered the horrific bird hundreds of feet in the air, releasing its grip on it. A mess of torn black flesh plummeted to the ground, landing in the tall grasses that covered the valley floor.

The eagle released an echoing cry of power and dominance, making a show of its greatness in swirling flight high above. After a moment, it turned east and returned to some hidden nest high on the slopes of the Festning.

As though the eagle's kill had some sudden impact on his mind, all of Edlen's foul thoughts and feelings fled. A weight of relief fell over him, and his mind cleared.

"Bah! Thank the Creator for eagles, yeah?" Kuoni's voice suddenly spoke up. "Oh, how I hate those ravens! Awful creatures they are! Always bringing with them something horrible in the mind...woof!" he said as he shivered off the last of the memories of the foul bird. Edlen grinned as he was happy to have his friend return.

Kuoni proceeded to strap two thick sticks to his injured ankle and wrapped them with more bandages. Edlen then realized how well-prepared Kuoni had been for this trip, and was thankful for such foresight. As Kuoni tightened the bandages around his foot, a shock of pain came back, but settled nicely as it now felt strengthened. The swelling had numbed the pain down to a dull, and Kuoni even offered a small droplet of what appeared to be hardened candy.

"This will help mend any tears, and keep the pain at bay," he said. It was a golden ember color, and tasted incredibly bitter, but he got it down.

"Also," Kuoni continued, pulling a large forked tree branch from behind himself, "I managed to find you a perfect crutch! Use this on your left side until we can get you something proper in the city." Edlen took the branch and managed to stand back onto his feet. His backside was covered in snow, but it felt good to stand again.

"Please keep a careful footing, Edlen. Another slip like that and I may have to leave you here!"

"I will certainly be careful, but I do not want to burden you any further..." he said, revealing the dwellings of his thoughts.

"Hm!" Kuoni responded, without much argument. "You will keep up just fine, my boy. Look! Our path has already begun to shallow out. Our remaining walk is not so steep anymore," he said pointing outward towards the valley.

Edlen looked out and found that the slopes did indeed begin to shallow, and there was not much more of the winding back and forth of their path as it was able to find more gradual routes down. The snow also gradually grew thin, and the trees also. More rock faces shown, larger boulders, and at the very base were wide grass fields with bare trees dotted through out.

Kuoni took Sabrina again in his arms as they resumed their travels down. The sun had passed over them and was beginning to set beyond the crest they had traversed over. Shadow crept from its peak, but the warmer valley below remained mostly in sun, and kept the cold winds of the higher mountain slopes away.

The walk down didn't seem to be as bad as Edlen had thought it would, even with his limp. The footing was much easier to keep, and the makeshift crutch Kuoni had gifted Edlen was a strong wood and perfect height for his shoulders. Kuoni had chipped away the point at the end of the crutch to also help with the loose gravel they were beginning to find. Before much time had passed, and without further incident, they had made it to the base of the crest and found themselves on the edge of the woods, facing an open field.

As they gazed out, a warm breeze blew across the lightly snowed grasslands. The yellow sun lit up the entire field and might of the Festning mountain before them. At this view, it had only grown in splendor and amazement. The mightiest mountain Edlen had laid eyes upon. A single buck and his three doe galloped through the grasslands, and sparrows darted here and there. Even on the dawn of winter, the valley was still buzzing with life.

"Just a few more miles, my friend! We are not far now!" Kuoni said in encouragement. "Hang in there my child," he said in a low voice at Sabrina, then looked back up towards the Festning. "We are not far now..."

The walk across the valley was almost pleasant as it was a great deal easier than the climbs and descents of the mountains behind them. It was easier for Edlen to keep a quick pace, especially with the added medicines that had taken their full effect. It seemed that their pace had quickened at such a speed, that rather than being passed over by the shadow of a setting sun, they were creating distance in between. And in full bright sunlight and the quickly approaching gates of Skydale, Edlen's spirits began to rise.

As they crossed, Edlen spotted something black in the grasses. It was the dead raven, fallen in a broken blanket of snow on a bed of dead grass. Its body mangled, blood stained the snow red, and its lifeless eyes staring off into an unknown direction.

He stared at it, knowing it would not possibly come back to life, but not fully content in that trusting. He took the tip of his wooden crutch and pressed down hard on its body. Its bones cracked under the heavy pressure, blood spilled out of its open beak. Edlen's face cringed at this site, but still, he had not had his fill of closure.

He moved his crutch to the birds head, right under its left eye. He leaned hard on the crutch, pushing the bird deeper into its grassy grave before he heard a cracking pop under the weight of himself, smothered deep in snowy grass. Edlen needed not to look at the mess, and suddenly feeling fully satisfied, looked up to see Kuoni standing ten yards down their path looking back at him.

"It is dead, Edlen. You may leave it now," Kuoni said. Edlen took a deep sigh of cold air, exhaling out steam that was carried away on the midafternoon breeze, and continued down the path. After a few moments, Edlen looked down at the end of his crutch and saw the remaining raven blood which had stained the end of it. Like a scar to remind him of what had been, he was happy to put a final distance to the recent deceased.

Not much after, they approached the main road that ran north to south. It was well-paved and clear of any snow.

"To the south, the road takes you to the troll tunnels, far south of here, then deep into the Old Forrest," Kuoni explained in a hurry, nearly out of breath as he continued to make haste.

"And to the north..." Kuoni paused a moment to catch his breath. "That takes you to the valley of the Elves." Edlen looked north at the path that followed the valley beyond sight.

"But!" Kuoni said, almost startling Edlen. "Let us go see what we can do to save your friend here!" And they took the beautiful stone path in a continued eastern direction. It wound around like a snake through the grasses before leading them into what looked like a small town of stone buildings.

At its entrance, just outside the first building on the right was a beautifully carved stone sign hung on large evergreen tree trunks:

Welcome to

Festerling

Kuoni took little notice to the surrounding buildings, nor the people that watched as they approached. Their faces turning to horror to see a frozen body in his arms and a limping Edlen tagging along, and they departed towards the gates.

"Never mind these folk," Kuoni said back at Edlen. "They can offer us little. This town merely serves as a resting place for those not permitted to enter the city. An inn, a trading post, and little else remains out here..."

They passed through the town and found themselves facing the beautiful entrance to the mountain. Carved into the rock itself, giant squared pillars rose high into the sky with beautiful blocks joining them together in an arch. At the peak, the emblem of Skydale shown with fiery light and a white-glowing star at the very top.

The pillars bordered two giant doors made of bronze and trimmed in steel. The contrast between the brownish-gold and silver made for a beautiful sight. The doors appeared to be fifty feet tall when reaching their highest, and opened from the center.

The bottom half of the doors were cut into a smaller opening that swung inwards. They were already open as there was no need to keep them shut. The city had not fallen under siege in hundreds of years, and there were no signs of turmoil anywhere around. Kuoni and Edlen passed through the doors and into a different world.

At the doorway, the road turned to solid stone. Behind the doors was a great hall carved out of the mountain. Grand pillars lined the sides with beautiful carved swirls of natural vines and leaves. They were carved to resemble giant trees, their bases like roots that spread out into the rocky floor. The inside was sparsely crowded with only a few groups of individuals conversing of their own business. Lamps were lit throughout the hall, giving it plenty of light to gaze upon its immensity. At the far side of the hall was a set of tall gates of golden-colored metal. There, guards of Skydale stood at multiple openings.

Kuoni and Edlen raced across the hall as quickly as they could, their footsteps barely able to keep their echo off the rock floor. As they approached, the hum of the market place beyond the gates grew.

"Welcome to Skydale!" one of the guards said with a smile at first, which dropped to a concern when he saw the condition of the new arrivals.

"We seek medical attention," Kuoni said immediately, knowing their reasons for visit would be questioned, as is the routine to permit entrance.

"Oh, of course!" the guard said, looking quite concerned. "You have visited before, yes?"

"I am Kuoni of Dökk Mountain. This is Edlen, son of Eldor of the Gronndelon," he said, nearly out of breath and as quickly as possible, trying to speed through the required information.

"And this-"

"Do not worry, just go!" the guard interrupted. "We only count the living..." he added as he stepped out of the way, permitting entrance.

"But she!" Edlen began before Kuoni interrupted again.

"Thank you, sir. Thank you!" Kuoni concluded their business and quickly moved past the gates. Edlen, taking the hint, followed.

The road opened to a wide market place with center pillars holding up the mountain ceiling. They towered hundreds of feet, providing the market with seven floors around the outer rim. As each story widened, the floor of each provided the ceiling for the one below it. The walls of each were carved into the sides of the mountain which acted as shops, inns, restaurants, and services.

In the center of the grand hall was Skydale's waterfall. It poured from an opening at the top of the grand market, through the center, and crashing down into a large circular pool of which had no visible exit. Around its edge on the base floor, it was lined with a circular wall only a few feet tall, trimmed in gold.

The market was dotted with lamps and benches, and the place as a whole was as warm as a summer day. Each pillar bearing similar carvings of tree-like features, only these were lined with beautiful gems, stones, and fossils. On the far side, in the distance, was a tall ramp that wound back and forth against the far wall. It led high up into the mountain and disappeared beyond another set of gates clear at the top.

"We must get to the third floor, and quickly!" Kuoni said as he quickened his pace. "That is where we will find the medicine shop. We must get the remedy in her before she thaws in this warmth!" Edlen began to have a difficult time keeping up, but knew he would find Kuoni if they became separated.

Dodging around the crowd of diverse groups and eager salesmen, they made their way to the first staircase on the right side of the market. Climbing the stone stairs was not easy for Edlen, but he felt the urgency had suddenly become real again.

At the top of the first set of steps, they crossed the brief walkway and to the base of the second flight. Quickly, they made their way to the third floor and continued deeper into the mountain's market. Edlen began to fall behind, though Kuoni was much taller than most, so it was easy to keep his track.

At once, he saw Kuoni turn sharp right and into a larger storefront. Above the door hung a wooden sign with a carving of a vial on the front, bordered in swirls of vines. Edlen followed.

The store was quiet, and smelled of herbs and extracted natural ingredients. It was stocked to the ceiling with bottles of potions and medicines. The shelves lined with tools, utensils, pottery, and fresh ingredients. The store was empty of customers save Kuoni, standing at the back at a stone-carved counter, urgency echoing through the store.

"Yes, Frost-breaker!" he said to the store's owner. "You must have some!"

"Hmmm, I believe I do..." said the owner with little urgency in his voice. He seemed to take no notice in the young woman Kuoni held in his arms.

Slowly, the owner walked around the counter and to a shelf on the left. He was an older man, sickly skinny and had little kindness in his face. He looked up and down, scratching at his scruffy chin.

"Ah!" he said at last, reaching up and grabbing a small glass vial of bright red liquid. It was encased in a small wooden stand and a miniature cork on top. He hobbled back and placed it on the counter.

"Ah yes! Should be enough to bring your little guest here back to health I should think," he said rubbing his cheek with the palm of his hand. "Now, of payment. This is not easy to come by..." he looked at Kuoni.

"How much?" Kuoni was losing patience.

"Mmmmm..." thought the old owner. "Four-fifty ought to cover it."

"Are you mad?!" Kuoni retaliated in a furious fit. "For such a small bottle! That cannot be worth more than twenty silver tops! The berry alone is only worth fifteen!"

"Ah, I am sorry!" said the owner. "But you are not buying the ingredients, yes? You are buying the life of your friend back! And I mean not silver, but gold."

Kuoni's face turned hot red. He took a step back so as to not kill the owner right then and there.

"You, sir," Kuoni continued, trying to keep himself from exploding. "Can you not see our need? Can you not see what precious life is clinging to hope?! I have not that kind of gold! Not with all in my possession could I trade enough to meet that absurd amount!"

"Precious, yes! And precious brings value! I am sorry, cheap giant," the owner insulted. "That is what I will accept. If you cannot meet it, I will ask you to take your leave!" he shouted as he grabbed the vial of potion and placed it on a hidden shelf under the counter.

"Bah! We have no other choice, shop owner! No other shop sells this! You *must* see the desperation we are in!" Kuoni argued in hopes of finding a shred of decency in the old man's heart.

"Desperate indeed if you think you have any more business here! I bid you a peaceful leave before I call the guards!" the old man shouted back.

"Bah!" Kuoni ended in a rage as he quickly turned around, heading for the door. "I should call the guards myself at such greed and stupidity!" he shouted back as he stormed out of the store. Edlen followed, shocked and angry at the owner. His heart began to fill again with rage, finding it hard to believe at the heartlessness of a business owner when it was so clear the importance of their needs. But yet desperation flooded his mind, and his motive changed from hatred against what was stopping him to that of finding another way to save a life.

Kuoni sat on a bench near the entrance of the store, holding Sabrina. Edlen approached, taking no seat next to him.

"I am afraid we may be too late now..." Kuoni said, studying Sabrina's face and running his finger down her cheek. "She is beginning to warm, the blueness is giving way to pale, she will be unreachable within moments..."

Edlen's tears began falling from his eyes.

"What can we do?! We cannot give up! What we need is in *that* shop. There must be a way to convince the owner to sell or trade it! What if..." his mind raced with possible solutions. "What if we worked it off? I could give myself as payment! I could be a servant of his until the debt is cleared!"

"He is done with us," Kuoni said. "If we step foot in there again, he will have us arrested for sure."

"But this cannot be it! This cannot be her end when we are so close!"

Kuoni looked over at Edlen, painful emotions poured from his eyes.

"We have exhausted our options, Edlen. I am afraid she is lost."

Edlen collapsed on the bench next to Kuoni, sobbing uncontrollably. Kuoni, though strong he was, shared in Edlen's grieving and he held tight to the life he failed to save.

The crowd of people that walked by took no notice of the two. Walking by without so much a glance, no one wanted anything to do with a crippled boy, an old half-giant, and a young woman slipping from life.

CHAPTER XIV

STARDUST

— 16th of Frostfare, 1867 —

From some distance in the crowd, among the chatter and business, a familiar voice cried out.

"Edlen? Edlen!" it shouted. Edlen looked up with watery tears and saw a man approaching, cloaked with a hood, holding a tall staff with a dragon carved into the top.

"Luno!" Edlen shouted as he recognized the tattoo markings on Luno's face. Luno ran up to him in excitement and surprise.

"Edlen, you are alive! By the stars, what a wonderful thing to have found!" Luno said, placing his hands on Edlen's shoulders. Then he looked over past Edlen to see Kuoni sitting on the bench, holding Sabrina.

"What have we here..." Luno said, taking a closer look at Sabrina. "What happened?" he asked Kuoni, then looking back at Edlen.

"Luno! We need help, she needs help! She needs medicine!" Edlen said full of panic.

"Oh, I can see that!" Luno replied. "But I have not any medicine, it is not my practice!"

"We need something called Frost-breaker," Kuoni added. "It is in this store here, but the owner is blinded with greed and will not sell it to us."

"Oh, is he?" Luno said with a smirk. "Such is the ways here in Skydale, which is uncommon and a bit unfriendly to outsiders." He took a few steps towards the store front, past Sabrina and Kuoni.

"Let Luno handle this keeper..." and he disappeared into the store.

"So, that was your friend Luno of your party?" Kuoni asked.

"Yes," Edlen replied. "That must mean..."

"Your party has already arrived," Kuoni finished the thought.

"But where —" Edlen began.

"One problem at a time, Edlen. And she needs you now more than ever," he said looking down at the paling face. Edlen remained standing, staring at the shut-eyes on Sabrina's face. Despite the loss of color, she still remained as beautiful as he had ever seen her. Within a moment, Luno returned from the store.

"Is it this that she needs?" Luno asked, holding out the vial of bright-red liquid.

"Indeed it is!" Kuoni shouted, taking the bottle from Luno.

"But how did you talk him into selling it?" Edlen asked.

"Never mind that, my young friend," Luno replied, smiling with a bit of deviousness in his eyes.

"How can I repay you?" Edlen asked, wanting to leave no debt remaining.

"Let us call it...a welcome back gift," he answered returning his attention back to Sabrina and Kuoni. Kuoni had uncorked the vial and opened Sabrina's lips. He poured the thick liquid into her mouth. It coated her tongue and throat, finding its way down as the vial was emptied.

"Luno?" Kuoni asked. Luno gave him his attention. "I am Kuoni, a friend of Radholf and Oatikki."

"My! What a small world we do live in!" he said smiling.

"Sabrina needs rest, and it will take some time before we will know if the medicine has worked. Do you have a place where we may rest?"

Luno's smile fell, then looked at Edlen.

"You also have found misfortune, I see..." he said as he looked at Edlen's splints and crutch. "I have very little to offer. A place of my own, but made for only my own."

It was clear Luno did not want to sacrifice what little he did have for three more people, especially one he had only just met. Edlen's face dropped in sadness.

Luno studied their reactions, then looked out across the crowd and the market entirely. "But..." he continued. "It would be more comfort than any place you could find with enough coin," he said looking at Kuoni. "What place I call home, you may too for a short time..."

He was afraid to make any commitments, and this offering was unusual for a wizard. It made him uncomfortable to invite them in, but he knew Edlen would have further questions about the party, and felt his own home would be the most comfortable place to talk about it.

Luno led the three weary travelers through the market and to the entrance to the city at the back. They walked up the wide ramps that wound back and forth, carved into the far wall, leading higher and higher. At the top, stone pillars trimmed in gold and silver led to a wide and tall tunnel.

Their path was fully lit with lanterns, the floor made of laid stone, the walls and ceiling carved in similar fashion as the market. The sides decorated in carvings to remind its guests of a dark and dense forest. Shapes of trees towered in stone leaves above, and everywhere along this path the walls glistened with gems. It climbed higher at a steady pace, their footsteps echoing up and down the long halls. As they turned a final corner, a cool breeze blew in strong. Before them was the City of Stone, marvelous and beautiful, opening up to a crystal clear night sky.

The stars above were far brighter than anything Edlen had witnessed before. The blackness they rested within pure and flawless. He saw stars he never knew existed, flickering in wonderful color beyond imagination. Their brightness never fading even as they approached the horizon, and he felt as though the entire city was lifted *into* the heavens themselves. Such a sight had stolen his breath.

In the high of the sky, Edlen could see the warrior constellation in its full form, spreading its twelve bright stars across half the sky. Each one twinkling far brighter than he had ever seen them, as though they were ready to burst with life and shine down upon the face of the earth once more. Each one in a demanding stance, commanding awe in its brilliance and power.

"This way," Luno said, giving Edlen a moment to take witness of the new sights. He led them down a stone-laid path that found its way through towering stone towers built on top of cliffs. Bronze doors gave shelter to homes and dwellings carved into the cliffs themselves. Lamp lights shown through the bottom of the doors and small square windows.

As they made their way through the labyrinth of small cliffs and stream bridges, Edlen soon became lost. It felt very closed in, and there seemed to be no attempt of an organized layout of the city. And there was not, as the city simply *was* taking form around the natural shapes in which the valley had provided. Although seemingly chaotic, he still found the city to be full of beauty.

At the end of their walkway, they were faced with a set of stone steps. A roaring water fall fell on their right, and a small stone wall kept the water from spilling over the steps. A short climb led them to a landing, and another short set of steps to their left. At the top, they found themselves surrounded by cliff faces on three sides, each side with a matching metal door. Luno approached the one on the left and pulled a key out.

Click! He opened the door and invited his guests in.

Inside the house it was warm but small. The ceiling was low and rooms narrow. He had a fireplace carved into the side of the rock and a small round table in front to serve as his kitchen. The main room was stuffed wall-to-ceiling with shelves and hooks, all full of interesting rocks, gems, and small pouches filled with enchantments. At the far end of the main room was an entrance to his bedroom.

It was here that Kuoni took Sabrina, and laid her down on the bed.

"It may not be much, but you are welcome to stay for the next day," Luno said to Edlen. "I have plans to leave the day after tomorrow, but can delay my departure by a day or two if you need it."

"Thank you, Luno," Edlen replied. The smell of works of metal and dusty stone lingered in the air. Quite a different place to stay in than what he was used to, unlike any he had been in before. But it was warm and very quiet.

"I suppose you must be wondering where your other friends are," Luno said as he took his seat next to the fireplace. "And I sure am curious as to how you are still alive!" He stared hard at Edlen, wanting to hear the story.

"Yes, I am anxious to find Radholf! Now that we have done all we can for Sabrina, I would very much like to find him!" Edlen said, then paused in silence. Luno gave no answer, only stared back at him with little expression on his face.

"He is not here, is he?" Edlen said quietly, knowing what he had feared was likely true.

"No," Luno said sternly, without breaking eye contact.

"He has moved on, went to see the Elves?" Edlen asked. He suddenly became afraid of the answer, that perhaps Luno was the only one that had made it. That Radholf's absence could only be from finding some demise, that perhaps the dragon had taken him, or he abandoned hope for finding Edlen and returned to the Gronndelon. His mind raced with possible outcomes.

"Rest is what she needs now. There is nothing more we can do," Kuoni said as he returned from the bedroom. "I cannot say for sure if we had made it in time, and my heart carries little hope even now. But we can say we have done everything in our abilities to help her. The rest is up to her, and to the gods." Kuoni then realized he was interrupting a serious discussion between Edlen and Luno, and took very little to guess as to what it was about.

"Where is he?" Kuoni asked as he stared hard at Luno. "Where is Radholf? And Oatikki?"

"Not here!" Luno replied, feeling quite defensive and a bit insulted as to the sudden aggression of such guests in his own home.

"Tell us what happened on that mountain side. What happened after Edlen was thrown from the dragon's clutch?"

"He is alive!" Luno admitted, but did not go into much detail willingly. He seemed to not want to disclose such information, but neither Kuoni nor Edlen could guess as for what reason. They began to grow in frustration.

"Tell us all you know, Luno! We have been desperate to meet them again!" Kuoni spoke for Edlen on these matters.

"I do not know if you *should* know..." Luno admitted. "What dangers would I be putting him in to tell of his direction? A half-giant stranger! What proof do you have to show that you are indeed a friend and not foe? My telling you his whereabouts, I may be killing him!" He turned to Edlen.

"Edlen boy, I do trust you, but how can you trust this...*Kuoni* as he calls himself?" He very much felt as though he was on defense, and in his own home.

"He is a friend, he has proven enough to me. He knew my ancestors, and has earned my trust. He saved my life, and has proven far more caring than most I know in his attempts to save Sabrina. You can trust him!" Edlen responded.

"If there is still a dragon south of the Rhims, it is of extreme importance that I speak to Radholf!" Kuoni said trying to convince Luno to tell all he knew.

"Radholf made me promise not to speak of it, *to no one* he said."

"Even to me?" Edlen asked.

Luno paused for a moment, looking at Edlen with saddened eyes.

"We thought you had passed," he admitted. "When we saw you thrown from the dragon, after leading her astray, we searched for you but found you not." The room sat in silence for a moment, now realizing that Radholf did not know Edlen was alive. Although not a surprise, Edlen felt terrible as to the false sorrow he had brought upon them.

"The only trace of you we found was your sword..." Luno said. At this, Kuoni perked up in great interest and approached Luno closely.

"...but nothing else," Luno said, focusing only his eyes on the approaching half-giant.

"You found the sword? Dragonsbane?" Kuoni asked anxiously.

Suddenly, Luno realized such need of information they were desiring, and felt very content in the control over the conversation he had again.

"Yes, we found the sword," he concluded the questioning.

"We continued to traverse the mountain side as best we could find before discovering a cave entrance. Knowing these mountains are riddled with caves, we took our chances."

"And you found a way through?" Kuoni asked, very much wanting to keep the conversation moving, and quickly.

"Oh, yes indeed! It was not difficult, I must say! It took us a little less than a week to make it through!"

"So, you led the entire party through the cave system? Adelmar and Brandr? And their refugees?" Edlen asked, having a hard time visualizing such travelers making their way in the dark.

"Oh..." Luno said suddenly realizing the pieces of the story Edlen had missed.

"No, many of their refugees did not make it to the cave. That beast of fire bathed them in her flame before we led her away. Brandr also, as he foolishly charged the beast, was swallowed whole by her incredible jaws."

"And Oatikki?" Kuoni asked. Edlen was suddenly without speech as to this news. His eyes watered and throat swelled to hear of the loss of innocent lives.

"That big Orc continued with Radholf, Adelmar as well," Luno continued. He sighed heavy, knowing he was about to give up all he knew.

"After a brief visit to the market to gather supplies, they continued north towards Arboran. This was over a week ago, I am afraid."

"They would be within the borders of Arboran by now," Kuoni said, staring at the fireplace. He turned at looked at Edlen.

"We could not catch up to them now even with ponies."

The room fell silent again. The crackling fire was the only thing to break the silence as the three contemplated their situation.

"What do we do now?" Edlen asked Kuoni.

"Well," he said in deep thought. "Our host is kind enough to let us rest for the next day. Let us sleep while we can, let these thoughts settle in their places, and we will talk more in the morning."

Kuoni looked back into the back bedroom at Sabrina, motionless on the bed. Sweat had covered her brow, but the color had not yet returned to her face.

"We all need rest," he concluded.

Luno found a few large furs tucked away in an old chest he had in his bedroom. They laid them out on the stone floor for Edlen to rest on. Kuoni insisted he would remain in the bedroom to watch Sabrina's progress closely, and Luno rested in one of his dining chairs.

It was a quiet and restless night. Edlen's leg continued to throb in pain, but his thoughts and worries weighed too heavy on his heart to allow his mind to take much notice. He slept little, as well as everyone in that small carved-out home, only drifting in and out of light sleep.

The hours drug by slowly. It was difficult to tell how long the night had progressed, but every moment he awoke, he felt as though he was lost in some firelit night, unable to guess how long he had been lying there. Every moment awake, he sat up enough to glance into the back room, and every time he saw a resting Kuoni hunched over on a chair next to the bed. Eventually, the awakenings became enough, and Edlen's eyes shut for several hours.

The wind blew hard again, carrying a blinding snow that swirled out of nothing. Grinding against his face, it flew past him into an empty void. He was knee-deep in a frozen slope, high up on the same Dökk Mountain he had emerged from. The blowing was silent, though, and only feet in front of him he could see Sabrina. She took steps without progress, walking down an infinite plane of snow and ice. He called out to her.

"Sabrina!" he shouted, though he felt so overcome with emotion, that his voice only gave a harsh whisper, and it did not seem to be enough to grab her attention. He tried again, struggling to give it any volume as he chased her. She slowly grew more distant. His heart pounded as he tried so desperately to catch her, yet into the blinding white she fell.

The snow at his feet washed away by a river of raging waters. He now stood upon the shores. The whiteness faded to night and stars twinkled above him. His breath shown in the coldness, yet his body was numb to it. In front of him was the cabin where they found Sabrina behind. There was a commotion within, the sounds of breaking dishes and things being slammed. The back door of the cabin flew open and Sabrina soberly stepped out. Her skin was already pale cold. She shivered violently, unable to control herself. She stood at the entrance of the door, just outside the cabin. Edlen slowly walked up.

Her attention was on him, but she spoke not to him. Tears rolled down her eyes as she watched him approach her. Her lips were glossed over with a brown liquid, though ice blue underneath. Her face showed signs of great pain, both of her body and her heart. The silence between them was like a clear wall. Physically keeping them apart where no touch nor words could penetrate through. But the emotions between them flowed as strong as the cold winter wind. She knew she was dying.

Sabrina took a few steps beyond the cabin, and like great leaps of distance, quickly approached the horizon. Her being faded to a sparkle that followed the mountains into the sky, where it forever remained in the darkness of night.

Edlen opened his eyes slowly, feeling very tired still as a result of a restless night. He looked around at the same dimly lit home of Luno's and found not much had changed. Sitting up, he noticed Kuoni was gone, and Luno was sitting in a different chair now, wide awake as though waiting for Edlen to wake up. Edlen sat up straight.

"Where is Kuoni?" he asked Luno. Luno had a serious, almost angry look on his face. "He has left to the market, to resupply," he responded.

"Resupply?" Edlen asked, a bit confused.

"Edlen..." Luno continued. Edlen felt a wave of fear fall over his body, and it almost ached. "Sabrina did not make it through the night."

Edlen leaned back as his arms became weak. The reality would not hit him, and his mind denied these words to protect his heart. After all they had tried, after the two days of wrestling with the thought, fighting it back, never accepting, he was forced to give in. As though he had already been mournful, this news was no harder to swallow than the moment he saw her in the snow bank. Deep in his heart, he had always known this was going to be true, though he clung to a thread of hope. Finally, the hope had diminished, and was forced to accept it.

Edlen wept at the loss of his friend, and worse still was the absence of Kuoni. Luno proved to not be the best companion in mourning, though he did what he could to help ease the news. He offered Edlen some mead, stiff for the morning but it was all he had to offer other than water. Luno partook as well. Edlen's fallen tears, like an early spring rain, slowly washed away his emotions. It felt good to weep, something he needed to do for days now but would not allow himself to.

After some time, he recomposed and felt as though he could talk again.

"So why would Kuoni need to resupply? Do you know what he plans?" Edlen asked Luno.

"We discussed it during the night," Luno replied. "Skydale is not meant to be your home, and with nothing holding you here now, he believes you are best to be reunited with Radholf and...the Orc," Luno answered. "You will be departing later today, after Sabrina's parting..."

"Her parting..." Edlen said in a half-curious question.

"She will be taken outside the city and buried in her own place, some way up the road," Luno answered.

"Does she have no family? No kin? She was from Skydale, was she not?"

"She had only passed through Skydale, having come from the east, further than I know of, for she was certainly not born here. Though she does not belong here, as she was banished nearly a year ago."

"Banished from Skydale? What did she do?" Edlen was very curious now and it felt good to talk about his recent loss.

"You know of her abilities, of her magic. She tried to use them on one of our counsel members. She was with several others, mostly men all looking like they were of her family. Dark hair, green eyes, all of them speaking in a tongue I have never heard before among themselves.

"And what she did speak of ours, she spoke little. Though enough to make her way to the counsel. I was there in the meeting halls when she approached Alfgeir, one of three head members.

"Her questions made no sense. No one understood what she was asking for, though she believed us to be hiding something. So, to get her answers, she laid hands upon him in an attempt to convince him to release his answers. But what she got out of him was wasteful nonsense, only a few murmurs of senseless words before the guards pushed her back. Under threat of death, they banished her from Skydale in that moment."

"You said there were others? Other men with her?" Edlen asked curious.

"Yes, three others. Though *she* was banished, they were simply asked to leave. From what I heard, they returned to the east where she decided to head west. I assume to continue to find her answer to the questions I still do not understand."

"What was her question?" Edlen asked, extremely curious now to know what secrets she may have hidden.

"She kept asking the whereabouts of something, or someone, or some time. I really am not sure. In her broken language, none of us could understand what this was. One of her brethren tried giving reasons behind their inquiry.

"In an attempt to help solve this puzzle, " Luno continued. "Alfgeir asked where they were from. They simply said 'the nocturnal city,' and they had awoken. So, they were looking for night time." Luno had a most puzzled look across his face, still trying to make sense of their questions. Frustrated, he shook his head in a fit as to rid flies buzzing around.

"It does not matter though! Lost their minds they had! And I do not believe we will meet them on our road north as we continue our travels," Luno ended.

"*We?*" Edlen picked up on Luno's inclusion of himself in that last statement.

"I will be going with you, Edlen," Luno said in a curious fashion. "I was going to be leaving tomorrow in my second attempt of reaching Nýland, as Jarl Halvar got in my way during my first attempt. Instead, I will travel with you north into Arboran, making my way to the shores in hopes to avoid your Gronndelon all together!"

Edlen did not further inquire about Luno's intentions, or what business he had in Nýland. He was only happy to have another friend to go along on the journey. And although Luno's reasons were pure and true, he did not give hints to the additional motives behind traveling with Edlen. Luno did not entirely trust Kuoni's caretaking as he knew little of him. And as he would never admit again, Luno was still very happy to see Edlen alive.

At this moment, Luno's door creaked open. The morning light shown bright into the small home, silhouetted by a tall Kuoni carrying several packages of supplies.

"Edlen..." he said, seeing Edlen awake and sitting at the small round table.

"It is okay, Kuoni. I know..." Edlen paused a moment, keeping himself under control. "We did all we could."

"Though it was not enough. I am truly sorry, young Edlen," he concluded. Edlen lowered his head in thought. Kuoni quietly laid his items down and shut the door. Walking over to Edlen, he embraced him to show comfort. As a big man, he had warmth in his arms and emotions. A comfort Edlen had long needed.

"Luno has told me of our plans, and that he will be joining us." Edlen said wanting to leave the subject of Sabrina's loss. Kuoni nodded as he looked at Luno.

"As soon as we are ready, we will depart, and take Sabrina with us until we exit the city. Edlen, you will pick a place along the north road to be Sabrina's resting place. I feel it is only appropriate that you be the one." Kuoni had placed his hand on Edlen's shoulder. Edlen agreed without speaking.

After some time, Luno had packed up and Edlen's leg was redone with more stable splints. It was rigged nicely, now that Kuoni had access to the right supplies, so Edlen could put most of his weight on that leg with little discomfort.

Each one took a share of the supplies in addition to their own belongings. In the market, Kuoni found some new warm fitting clothes for Edlen as well as a new elk-skinned pack. Sabrina was wrapped in soft deer fur and tied around with a beautiful gold ribbon. Kuoni picked up Sabrina as they departed, and stepped out of Luno's home. Luno turned around, pulled out a small brass key and *clink!* The door was locked shut.

The morning was as beautiful as the previous mornings had been. The city took a new look in daylight, settled in a different beauty than the previous night. All around, people were coming and going, walking on odd walkways at odd heights, leading through the maze of sidewalks, bridges, and underpasses.

The three travelers made their way to the market, down the large ramp, and to the bottom floor. It seemed as though the market never slept, that the crowd had not changed and the business never broke. But through the crowds they made their way, past the roaring waterfall in the center, and to the other side where the gates were open just the same.

A different guard of similar uniform nodded at them as they passed through, saying little, but noting Sabrina's body. He bowed his head in honor of the fallen, keeping his respect as they passed through.

Passing under the front doors to the market, they continued through Festerling. The small outpost was all quiet as most kept indoors during the morning hours. Without talk, they made their way to the fork in the road and turned right. After several moments, Kuoni spoke up.

"Edlen, as I had mentioned earlier, I will let you choose the place." He looked down at Edlen, who nodded and focused his attention on the horizon. They continued to walk north on the well-maintained road. As they continued, a small outcrop of stone appeared between the roadway and the foot of the Festning mountain to their right. At its base were several trees in their winter sleep.

"There," Edlen said as he pointed towards the outcrop. "That will be her place."

Kuoni smiled.

"A fine place to rest," he said as he looked down at Edlen. Edlen returned the smile, then looked back down at their footing.

They followed the road as far as it would take them without passing the outcrop. They then left the road, making their way through the tall grasses as they approached the bare trees. They were a cluster of tall maples, and would prove to be beautiful in any season. The soil was also fertile, and being the only outcrop they had seen thus far, would make it easy to find if any returning visits could be had.

Kuoni laid Sabrina's body down and begun digging a hole of perfect length and width. At the same time, Edlen found a large stone to place at the head of her grave. With Luno's help, they carved her name into it using one of Luno's picks. Kuoni laid her on the ground next to the hole, uncovering her face. He looked over at Edlen as tears returned to his eyes.

Edlen approached her, kneeling at her side. His tears rolled down his cheeks as he spoke to her through his heart. It was difficult to say goodbye, a reality that he felt had not yet fully hit him. She laid there, never losing her beauty even in death, her eyes shut as though she was sleeping. He leaned in to kiss her forehead, which felt cold and lifeless. Even so, it left his heart with closure. His tears fell from his eyes and landed on her cheeks, rolling down into her black hair.

He noticed a silver-white chain around her neck. A necklace she had always worn, yet he only now noticed. He placed his hands around the back of her neck and unlocked the necklace behind. Pulling it out, a beautiful white gem encased in swirls of silver revealed from under her cloak. He gazed upon it, and looked back at her face. He felt like he wanted permission from her to keep it, and in the silence that fell over them, he knew she would have freely given it to him. He clasped it tight in his hands, wiped his tears, and brought himself back to his feet.

Kuoni proceeded to lay her in the ground, then slowly covered her with the fresh soil he had recently dug up. At the end, he placed the stone Edlen and Luno had named at the head of the pile, and the three stood in silence for several moments more before returning to the road heading north.

CHAPTER XV

A FAILURE TO BREAK

— 18th of Frostfare, 1867 —

With every breath I take, each passing light of day,
Every time I look up and see you not there, I break down and weep.
But I remember the things you said, the trials and tests ahead,
And the warning that you would be taken way.

But I never thought the trials would be this hard,
What you told me, it did not prepare me for the deepness of this shadow.
I walk through night, through catacombs in fright,
And find only the little courage needed to continue.

Watch over me, father, give me sight to keep my footing in the right
Shed me light to guide my nights so I may break free into dawn.
Break me free, father, give me strength to crush my fears to dust,
So they may fade, blow away with the wind,
That I may face what needs to be done.

The fire cracked warm in the cold night air. Sparks rose from the embers high
into the sky, becoming lost in the stars high above. The three travelers rested
just outside the borders of Arboran, still between the northern-most edges of the
Rhim Mountains. Just off of the main road that was leading to Solum, the capital
of Arboran. For this was where Radholf was headed, and therefore, where Kuoni
was taking Edlen.

Beneath the moonless sky, Edlen was fast asleep. His leg continued to heal,
giving him little ache. Kuoni too slept soundly, and even Luno found a comforting rest that night. Among the crackling fire, a noise came from nearby. It blended
well with the sound of the fire, and was only brief.

Edlen awoke, opening his eyes. He faced the red glow of the fire. The embers still hot and comforting however small the fire was. At first he questioned the sound, unsure if it was real or his mind echoing some past memory of a sound. He changed his focus from the fire to the darkness behind it, not moving. Breathing lightly, making as little noise as possible. Nothing more came from the night.

Feeling unsure, his certainty that they were alone slowly returned as the silence wore on. His eyes heavy, they slowly shut again, and he returned his head to the most comfortable position it could find.

He awoke again, just on the edge of sleep, like a jolt. The sound was similar to what he heard before, and this time, Kuoni and Luno woke as well. All three sat up and stared into the darkness in the same direction. The sound they heard was that of rock crumbling. As though a small boulder had found rest in a bed of gravel, a sound so clear it could not be mistaken for anything else.

"What is that?" Edlen asked in a whisper, becoming nervous that danger was just beyond the reaches of the firelight. No answer came from Luno or Kuoni as they sat waiting in the night, tensed up like a trigger ready to escape in a burst of urgency.

In a sudden explosion of sound, a horrible bellow came from the mountain side. A sound that had haunted Edlen since that night of their battle. One that Luno also recognized, and Kuoni knew immediately of the danger before them.

Luno leapt to his feet, grabbing his staff and bags.

"To your feet, boy!" he shouted. Kuoni also leapt up and quickly gathered his things. Edlen scrambled to his feet, grabbing his things as best he could. Kuoni took a torch in one hand, lighting it and taking off towards the road.

"This way!" he shouted as Luno and Edlen followed.

"Mother of light, send us your guide!" Luno shouted as the tip of his staff shown a bright white, lighting the grasses around them and casting an outburst of shadows, for the grass was tall where they had camped.

Behind them, Edlen could hear heavy wings beating as the beast leapt off the mountain side and towards the prey it hunted.

"Hurry!" Kuoni shouted as he gained distance ahead. Edlen began to fall behind as his leg was still strapped with splints.

"Wait!" he shouted, growing fearful of what chased them. Luno, who had kept up well with Kuoni, glanced back and found Edlen was just on the edge of his staff's light. He halted, and looked forward to Kuoni, whose torch flickered in the distance.

"Fah!" he shouted in disgust, and quickly turned back to Edlen. The dragon caught up to Edlen, and as Luno approached, its face was revealed in Luno's light, soaring overhead and turning quickly around. Edlen stumbled to the ground as Luno's staff was thrown over him, shielding him in light.

"What fools you must be to believe you could out run the *Ashblood!*" the dragon shouted as it landed in the road with a *THUD* that shook loose gravel and stone from the surrounding mountains. Its forked tongue whipping out between long teeth.

"For weeks, I have hunted your scent. Never resting! Never forgetting! Killers of my children will never be forgiven!" Its voice thundered down the road, echoing off the rock walls that surrounded them and into the night sky.

"You cannot bring death upon what you cannot catch!" Luno shouted back, clutching a white stone, and quickly slammed it down on the ground, breaking its shell and unleashing the spell within. In an explosion of darkness, he and Edlen completely disappeared. Even his staff's glow vanished in the eyes of the dragon. It stalled in confusion.

Edlen and Luno remained in the same spot, concealed in a dome of the spell. To them, Luno's staff still shined bright all around them. They could see the creature clearly, but it could not see them. Edlen shifted in disbelief. Before he could say a word, Luno shushed him quietly. The spell he cast concealed only their sight, not their sounds.

"Trickery! O' how I hate the tricks of your devices, wizard! You pull a mask over my eyes, but you cannot mask your scent!" the dragon lowered its head to the ground, sniffing deeply. Step after step walking towards the wizard and the boy, moving its head back and forth.

Slowly, Luno unsheathed his sword, making every attempt in silencing the grind of the steel blade against the iron ring of the sheath. Laying his staff down carefully on the ground, he pulled out of his satchel a small vial of a deep blue liquid. The dragon approached the edge of Luno's spell-dome, nearly touching them with its forked tongue.

As Luno tipped his sword in the blue liquid, the beast's head fell closer to them, only a few feet away from where Luno stood. He picked up his staff again, waiting for the right moment to strike.

Edlen's heart raced as he made every attempt to silence himself. He could feel the fear reach deep into his legs and his heart pound against his chest. It was like he had awoken in some nightmare, but he knew this was all too real, and he only wanted it to end.

"Hoooo!" they heard Kuoni shouting in some distance. Edlen looked down the road to see Kuoni's torch, now realizing his followers had disappeared, running back in some last-effort act of heroism.

This caught the dragon's attention, and it immediately turned its head towards the commotion. This was exactly what Luno was waiting for, as he thrust his sword out, jabbing the dragon in its left eye.

As his sword escaped beyond the dome of protection, the spell failed altogether, revealing Luno and Edlen now completely exposed next to the great beast.

His sword made contact, and a flash of light came thundering from the tip. Like lightning making its mark on the beast, bright blue veins suddenly appeared, spidering out from the tip of the sword. In a sudden clap of thunder, they cracked at their marks and crumbled the scales surrounding the large yellow eye, blackening the eye itself, forever blinding the beast on that side.

The creature collapsed to the ground, wailing out in pain and horror. Kuoni halted in shock. Luno grabbed Edlen by the cloak and drug him to his feet.

"Quickly now! I have only disabled her, and I am sure she is quite upset at me now!" he shouted as they ran past the beast, who was trying to recover and cope with the pain it now suffered from.

Luno and Edlen rejoined with Kuoni, who was now determined to remain at the back of the party. They quickly continued down the road as the beast stumbled back to her feet.

"The pain! You will not die quickly, wizard!" the dragon shouted, and with a few flaps of its wings became airborne once more.

It was a race to the edge of the mountains, to the borders of Arboran. Where the mountains ended and the deciduous forests began, that marked the entrance to the realm of the Children of the Arborians.

"We must make it to the edges of the great forest!" Kuoni shouted. "We will find safety there! It will not dare to enter the land of the trees. Not unless it looks to be torn apart and fed on by the roots of those who guard it!" Kuoni said with a grin.

A loud *whoosh!* overhead blew Edlen to the ground as he stumbled. Kuoni and Luno managed to keep their footing, but did not realize the fallen Edlen for some steps down the road.

Fwoooosh! The dragon sprayed a line of fire between the boy and his fleeting help, separating them and leaving Edlen in darkness. As the dragon circled, she laid another line of fire that cut them off, trapping both Kuoni and Luno between walls of fire.

"Kuoni!!" Edlen shouted, tears began falling from his cheeks. In his heart, he knew he could not bear to watch the fall of his two friends like this, to see their end in a wall of flames, but he felt powerless to help.

THUD. The dragon landed on the southern edge of the fiery entrapment, its tail whipping high above the wall of flames at its back, just overhead where Edlen was lying.

But above the roaring and crackling of flame, Edlen noticed the sound of rushing footsteps coming up from behind. He turned behind him, having lost all hope, to see two men rushing up to him.

"Radholf!" he shouted as the familiar face came into the light of fire. Adelmar followed quickly behind.

"Edlen!! I knew we would find you!" Radholf said, sliding across the gravel to join Edlen low and hopefully out of sight. He looked up at the dragon, then back down to Edlen with a face sour of fear.

"Who has she cornered?" Radholf asked.

"Kuoni, and Luno too!" Edlen said, his cracked voice wavering with sorrow. Radholf stood to his feet and pulled Edlen to his, and took a deep breath while taking in the horrific sight before them. Then, he looked at Edlen, his face not wanting to break the difficult news to him.

"Edlen, there is only one ending to a creature such as this," he said. "Only one way to bring that end," he added, as he removed Dragonsbane from within his cloak. He held it out to Edlen to take.

Edlen's face fell with shock, his tears like streams down his ashy cheeks, shaking his head.

"No! I cannot! I cannot kill that dragon!"

"Edlen! You must! You are the keeper of this blade now. No one else may wield it!"

"But how will I get close enough? She will bathe me in flames before I can reach her!"

Radholf pushed the blade into Edlen's arms.

"Your friends are about to die in there. You must go. Now!" he said as he looked up at the wildly swinging tail above them.

Edlen took the sword and unsheathed it. His breathing was in a panic, but he knew he could not stand by and listen to the dragon's prey cry out in their final moments while he stood on the side, holding the sword with the name of her ending.

Edlen walked under the tip of the giant tail, still swaying back and forth, as close as he could to the wall of flames before him. His heart pounded with nerves, and his stomach churning. He fought every instinct to flee as it seemed foolish to reach out to such danger.

At once, her tail swung low, low enough for Edlen to grab onto one of the scales near its tip. As light as he was, and as thick as its armor, the dragon took no notice to the young man climbing up its back.

"What is the matter, O' Wizard? Have you no magic left? Have you ran out of tricks to play?" the dragon teased.

"Cast your fires and get this over with!" Luno shouted back.

"Ha-ha!" the dragon rumbled with laughter. "Oh no! Not for you. I will cook you slowly. First by burning off your armor, your hair, and then your skin! I want to enjoy your taste as much as I enjoy your crisping..."

At this point, Edlen had climbed to the arch in the dragon's back. He had to get her attention and away from the helpless prey before her. He took a deep breath, but held it. He wanted to shout, but his fear overtook him.

"Hey!" Edlen squeaked out in such a quiet whisper, it faded quickly among the crackling of fire around them. He needed to shout louder. Another deep breath, this time intending to let the world know he was there. He shut his eyes tight.

"Hey!!" he shouted loudly and with force. His voice echoed off the sides of the mountains surrounding them, a boom that surprised even himself.

The dragon turned its head to find Edlen standing between two of its largest plates of scales.

"What is this?!" she shouted in anger. "You are so bold to disrupt me while I feed? How foolish you are!" she yelled as her head came swinging around, jaws open wide to crunch Edlen between her jaws.

Edlen fumbled, shaken by the quickly coming of teeth and fury. His footing lost their marks and he fell backwards, landing in a crevasse between the two plates of scales.

Crunch! The dragon's jaws landed on either side of her back, though her teeth did not puncture her own hide. She drug them up, grinding their sharp points along her back scales until they freed themselves beyond the top edges of her plates, then *CRUNCH*. They clamped down with nothing between them, just feet before Edlen's face.

As he looked up, he saw nothing but the interlocking edges of her teeth. Again, with anger she opened her jaws and tried to pull Edlen out from his hiding place, but she came up empty with a *CRUNCH* just before him.

"Raaaaah!" the dragon shouted with anger and frustration as it took one more clamp down around its back. This time, it whipped its tongue in between the small cracks, looking to free the nuisance from his hiding place.

Edlen looked down as the dragon's slimy tongue groped at his feet and legs. The warm, wet saliva dripped down over him, and coated his pants. It felt hot.

But the dragon continued to struggle to loosen Edlen's grip from where he was hiding. Having exhausted its patience, it took a deep breath. Edlen looked up and down the throat of the great beast, his face beginning to glow yellow from the stoking fires from within her belly. The dragon was ready to blast him with her fury.

Edlen's eyes flowed strong with tears. His breathing constant, having very little left in him to suffer. Sweat soaked his body from the hot breath surrounding him, his hair wet and dangling in front of his eyes. His lips trembling, and arms felt weak, he had nothing left in him, only a desire for this torture to end.

Echoing in the back of Edlen's mind, he could hear the voice of his father returning to him. In a single blink, he found himself back home in the old fishing shack behind his house on the same peaceful night in which he and Gracie had fed the fish of the lake old stale bread.

"To be tested, Edlen, is to face trials of both danger and hatred," Eldor said to him, giving his full attention to Edlen at the moment.

"It is in these times that you must make a decision. To face your unseen adversary despite every instinct telling you to flee, or to let the fall of your heart guide you further into darkness.

"For if you let into the wrong doing when you know what is right, then the corruption strengthens its grip on you. And if you let it take you in the wrong moments, it will claim your life, or some part of it."

Edlen sat deep in thought, trying to imagine facing such a trial.

"It will come at you from every angle, my son. Cunning it is, and you may find yourself filled with rage for an action or word that comes from someone else, perhaps even someone you hold close. But the monster inside will curse your thoughts, and try to spew out its poison through your own words and actions. You must not let it!" Eldor said sternly.

Edlen nodded, trying to understand the importance of what his father was telling him. Eldor paused for a moment, shifting his thoughts.

"But other times you will face trials of great fear. Fear of danger and of pain. It is only in these moments do we grow in courage. For you cannot walk around and say 'I have courage.' No, it is something you must find within yourself during these trials.

"But know this, son: when the most foul of thoughts and vile creatures surround you, it is the darkness trying to take down a heart of strength and will for good. For the strongest of towers takes the hardest blow to crumble. And the wind blows strongest from the most furious of storms."

Eldor looked at his son, a smile beginning to form as peace rested across his face.

"That is our calling, my boy. To anger the storm, make its thunder cry out in desperation. Be the tower it cannot crumble."

As his father's smiling gaze faded into memory, Edlen's sight returned to the growing light of fire and rage before him. Fear had presented itself before him, a greater fear than any he had encountered. And it was in this moment, Edlen needed to make his decision. To let it overtake him, or to fight against it.

Edlen tightened his grip on the sword and swung it wildly above him, severing the dragon's tongue in half.

The sudden sting from within its mouth forced the dragon to instinctively pull its head back. But the flames were already on their way out, and so it spewed a fiery spray into the night sky as it wailed in pain.

Edlen leaped off the dragon's back, sliding down the side and falling to the ground with a *thump*.

The dragon swung her head around to the other side, burning with anger.

"You will die now!" she yelled as she blasted her own back with flames, not realizing Edlen had already made his escape.

No sooner had the flames reached her back scales did Edlen swing hard at the back of her front-left wrist, causing the dragon to collapse on her left side.

Blood poured out of her wrist and onto the road. As it left its host, the blood instantly evaporated into black ash, carried off by the cold winter wind.

The dragon cried out in pain and anger.

"Where are you hiding? Show yourself and face your death!" But everywhere she looked, she found nothing. Edlen had disappeared, as well as Kuoni and Luno.

As she frantically looked around, the three had crouched down behind her upper back, quiet as mice.

"Edlen..." Luno whispered. "The dragon was wrong about something..." he said, pulling out a leather pouch filled with some grainy material.

"I do have one last trick," he said with a sly grin.

Edlen looked up at the beast behind them, then looked back at Luno. He took a deep, quiet breath, and gripped the hilt of his sword tight. He swallowed hard, and thought all of his situation. The dragon was injured, blind in one eye and crippled. He had to finish it. This was the only end to his fears. He glanced at Kuoni, who nodded back. Edlen, turning to Luno, gave him the nod.

Luno stood to his feet and hurled the pouch with all the strength he could muster. As it reached the peak of its arch, Edlen leaped to his feet, placing his good foot onto Kuoni's ready hands. Kuoni launched Edlen up and over the beast's shoulders as the pouch landed on the edge of the wall of flames.

As Edlen used his left hand to guide him over the scaly shoulders of the beast, doubts began flowing through his head. The reality of what he was doing hit him hard, and the wave of fear fogged his thoughts.

Ka-BOOM! A large explosion of white and yellow sparks shot out from the pouch's landing, grabbing the dragon's attention and swinging its head to the left. This explosion snapped Edlen out of the fog he was in just as he reached the top of the dragon. He thrust his sword deep into the base of the dragons throat, holding tightly to the hilt and letting his weight drag him down, drawing a long line of spilled blood.

Edlen landed hard and fast, for the sword had no difficulty making the cut. The dragon collapsed to the ground like a fallen tree, writhing in pain.

Coughing out pools of blood, it squirmed and struggled to breathe.

Edlen was out of breath, his heart unsure to trust the hope that it was done. His guard was not yet completely down. He began to weep uncontrollably.

For weeks the dragon had haunted him. Showing in his dreams, always forcing him to jump at anything over his shoulder. He did not want to have to kill anything, but he was the only one capable of ending such a terror, and he hated it.

As the creature squirmed in pain, struggling in the losing of its life, Edlen continued to weep, his stomach churning. But he stood to his feet, his clothes dark with the ash of the dragon's blood. Even his sword shined clean as the wind blew off the last of the dragon's remains from its edges. He took a deep breath, his fear and grief turning to anger. Anger of the tragedies the dragon had executed on so many of the innocent. Tired of the nightmares, of the running, he walked up to the head of the dragon, ready to make his claim as triumphant.

"Your time has ended!" Edlen shouted, his voice cracked and tears still falling.

"My time!" the dragon spoke out between wet curdles of blood spray. "The days—" the dragon coughed, struggling to breathe as her throat bled slowly. "The days of my blood line...have not yet approached!" The dragon struggled to talk.

Edlen grasped tightly to his sword.

"What do you mean your *blood line?*"

The dragon grinned, revealing its red-soaked teeth, not able to lift its head off the rocky ground.

"The *Ashblood*...have been reborn. My kin..." the dragon paused, struggling to take her next breath. "They will find you...all of your kind. The day of man, of Elf and greenery is approaching its dusk." The dragon wheezed heavily. "The world will turn black, scorched by our fire and all you call precious will diminish before your eyes." The dragon released another deep-chested cough, taking a slow breath in. Its time was limited now.

"That is our purpose..."

"You tell of lies..." Edlen said in disbelieve.

The dragon quietly chuckled, struggling in its pain.

"But that will only be the beginning, for that is how we will prepare the world for...." the dragon struggled.

"What!" Edlen shouted at the dragon. The dragon's eye rolled back into its head as it whispered out its final words.

"...Heir...of the night..."

Silence fell over the beast on the road. As its blood poured out into puddles on the stone, it quickly dried into a black ash, blowing away on the lightest breeze. With it, the fires diminished, and the night returned to quiet.

"Edlen!" Kuoni shouted as he and Luno ran up to him. "Edlen, my boy! You have done it!" he said laughing with joy.

"You sure have..." Luno said in disbelief, looking at the lying dragon now lifeless.

"Radholf!" Edlen said, dropping his sword and running over to embrace his long-lost friend properly now that the danger had died.

"Haha!" Radholf said, patting him on the back. "Just like Edlemar used to!" Radholf said with a grin looking at Kuoni. Kuoni nodded in agreement.

"Well!" Kuoni said as he approached Radholf. "What a way to find each other, huh? Ho-ho! Whew!"

"So, you were right, Radholf!" Adelmar added as he approached. "We have found that of which we have hunted for weeks!" Adelmar said with a smile as he passed into the dim light of Kuoni's torch.

"Kuoni..." Radholf said, hugging the half-giant as best he could.

"My dear, Radholf!" Kuoni replied, giving him a bear-hug, nearly crushing the poor man, then placing his hands on Radholf's shoulders.

"What has it been, my friend? Several decades since we have last seen each others faces?"

"I should venture a guess to be longer than that!" Radholf replied.

"But far too long at any guess! Ha!" Kuoni replied. He then looked at Adelmar and smiled with a nod, then looked back at the trail.

"But uh..." Kuoni continued. "By the stories our common friend here has told me..." he said, giving a glance in Edlen's direction. "...it appears we are missing one more?"

"Ah, yes..." Radholf replied. "Oati scouted ahead some days ago. It was our agreement to meet just inside the entrance of the wood. He should only be less than a day's walk inside —"

"Less than a day! Less than enough to have missed what I have!" a grumbled voice echoed out from the dark forest. Joining the group came Oatikki from down the trail, and his voice had given Luno quite the startle as Luno was the closest to the borders of the woods.

"You should know better to startle a wizard!" Luno scolded him, not liking the fright nor the return of the Orkken.

"Haha! And you shouldn't have allowed such a clumsy Orc sneak up on you!" Radholf teased back.

"Even *I* could hear him moments before he appeared," Adelmar commented with a grin.

"Kuoni." Oatikki nodded in what honor an Orc could display. After all, they had been long-time companions from some ages ago, and even the Orc could not swallow all the joy he had in seeing an old friend again. Kuoni returned the nod, keeping a respectful silence of emotion, but knowing Oatikki was just as happy to see him.

"So, here we all are again! Three of the five Verndari!" Radholf said.

"More like three and a half!" Kuoni smiled as the group looked upon Edlen. The sudden attention upon Edlen made him bashful, and he felt as though the compliment was above him.

"So, I take it Kuoni has told you all the tales of your family's past?" Radholf said, quieting his voice and moving closer to Edlen.

"Although it does not surprise me..." Radholf added with a grin, looking back in a sarcastic blame at Kuoni. Kuoni avoided eye contact as he knew himself to have a hard time keeping good stories from being shared.

"But how did you find us?" Edlen asked, still having a hard time believing that his friends were all there with him.

Radholf stood up straight.

"After we parted from Skydale, we reached where the road forked North. Something tugged at me, tugged at my heart. I did not feel right going into Arboran, as it felt premature.

"In my stutter of steps, dear Oatikki stopped as well." Radholf looked over at Oatikki. "Do you remember what you said, Oati?"

Oatikki kept a solid face, giving no expression. He took a deep breath.

"We would not leave you behind. We knew you were somewhere between where we stood, and where we lost you."

"And we were determined to find you, even if it meant uncovering every stone in all the Rhims," Radholf said.

"And I had no where else to go," Adelmar added.

"So, Adelmar and I hurried back, now knowing the way, and searched again. It was agreed upon that Oatikki should quickly head north towards the woods of Arboran, to catch you if we somehow missed you.

"So, Adelmar and I, we took the road south around the feet of the mountains to the west. We had guessed this would be the route you would take, as it is the only road worth taking if not in a hurry. For days we walked, until we met the Lake Starlight. Nearby was a cabin, and it was here that we picked up a trail. Two sets of foot prints in the hard snow. One set so large only a fool could mistaken it..." Radholf grinned again in Kuoni's direction.

"And the other gave us hope," Adelmar continued. "We were unsure of who the second set belonged to, knowing both you and Sabrina were gone. And at this, we were saddened."

"Adelmar and I continued to follow the trails, and quickly, in hopes of catching up. But there seemed to have been a change in urgency at this cabin along the Bristlecone River. We could only guess as to what it was, but you had likely already arrived at Skydale upon that day."

A look of grief fell over Edlen's face, and silence upon the rest of the group.

"Sabrina..." Edlen spoke up.

"We know," Radholf said, stopping Edlen from needing to continue. "We found her honorable resting place. A very nice stone indeed you had chosen for her," Radholf paused for a moment in silence.

"But within the grief of this, a light of new hope shown in our hearts. We knew you were alive, Edlen, and not far!

"So Adelmar and I rushed as quickly as we could north, even just as last evening was falling upon us. It was not long before we heard the rocky rattling of the recent creature that hunted you, and knew you were in danger. So, we rushed in, and well, here we are!"

Edlen was filled with relief that his companions had found him. He was surrounded by friends, and felt safer than he had ever since the day he left his home. He took a deep sigh of relief as joyful tears fell down his cheeks.

"Well! No sense in standing like fools in the middle of the road in the dark of night!" Oatikki said, breaking the silence. He walked past Kuoni and Radholf feeling rather uncomfortable with the emotions that were coming out.

"For once, I agree with the Orc..." Luno said, his staff illuminating the path in front of them, and taking a turn, following the Orc. Radholf smiled at Kuoni, who shrugged his shoulders.

"Come boy," Radholf said. "We are heading into safe lands for sure!"

"Wait!" Oatikki said as he walked around the dragon's head. He knelt and pulled an unbroken tooth from the dragon's mouth. As long as his hand was, he inspected it briefly before tossing it over to Edlen.

"A trophy," he said as Edlen caught it. "Something you can keep as a warning to others, o' dragon-hunter," he said with a wink.

Edlen smiled, but the subject of the dragon brought back concern over what it had said to him. And it appeared that he was the only one who had heard it. He did not know what the dragon meant, and was afraid of what could come. But as Radholf had said, they were surely heading into safe lands, and that settled his thoughts into comfort enough to let it go.

"And you should be proud," Radholf said putting his arm around him, recognizing Edlen had many thoughts running through his head.

"What you did was a brave thing, something we are all proud of." Edlen smiled, and slipped the dragon tooth into his satchel.

As they headed into the forest, Edlen's mind began to clear, allowing for the subtle changes to take notice.

"The air is warm here," he said out loud, his voice echoing a short distance. "What happened to the coldness of winter? Does it have no grasp here?"

"Not in Arboran!" Kuoni answered. "This land was the promised land given to the *Children of Aboran*, promised to always be fruitful and lush!"

"Yes! A perfect harmony of plant and creature alike," Radholf added. "The Gods who created this land fell into an agreement, that the earth should provide an eternal warmth. A warmth that should melt any attempts by the wind and darkness to shadow this land in a cold death, for the light sheds the darkness at will, and the earth holds fast against the wind."

"It is here, Edlen, that the balance of the world still remains as it was meant to be," Kuoni continued. "Here, evil does not prevail, and you should not find yourself in any danger unless you are the enemy of peace."

As they continued to walk, the forest floor began to light up in sparse little spots. These lights rose up, floating through the night air, glowing a faint yellow. Before long, the entire floor around them was carpeted in waves of small lights. They rose and fell in unison, like gentle waves on the ocean.

As they rose, they clicked quietly, followed by a whispering hum as they fell back down towards the ground. The clicking-humming surrounded the traveling party in a rhythmic song that seemed to sooth the mind and chase away any thoughts of fear or sorrow.

"Fireflies!" Kuoni said with a smile.

"What a sight!" Edlen said, amazed at what he was seeing. It was peaceful and beautiful to watch. Luno closed his eyes and took a deep breath in, slowly exhaling. He loved the fireflies, and found their light shows to be mysterious and magical. And as they continued down the road, the sides began to line with small, green-glowing mushrooms as to light their path. It became easy to see them in the darkness, and the road ahead was clear.

"So, where does this road lead? Other than more forest, I imagine." Edlen asked. "Where are all of the Elves?"

"This road leads to one city, as one city alone has been built within Arboran." Radholf answered.

"This land is not like your Gronndelon," Luno interrupted. "The Elves do not concern themselves with settlements scattered across the land. Although this land *belongs* to them, they see the construction of cities as a scar on the gift they would rather leave untouched. A waste of opportunity, if you were to ask me."

"It is not a waste to leave your gifts unchanged," Kuoni replied. "They have taken only what they need, never in excess. Although you are right about one thing, my wizard friend, this is not like any settlement of Men. For Men are what you may consider to be opportunists, I would say the Elves have made a smarter decision."

"What is smart about leaving so much of this land untouched? Laid waste and undiscovered! Who could know what precious gifts lie just under our feet? Or beyond the reaches of sight from this very road?" Luno argued back.

Kuoni stopped and turned his attention towards Luno. The rest of the party came to a halt as the attention was now focused on their conversation.

"What you are failing to see, wizard, is the respect the *Children of Arboran* have for their lands. This gift was designed by the Gods themselves, and it has only been in thanks to their foresight that it remains in such harmony and balance.

"If it had been taken by the greed of Men, this land would have been stripped and war-torn long ago, and the last safe haven of the Western World would have been lost. Then, where would we be now?" Kuoni said, clearly growing impatient.

"Dead, likely," Adelmar thought out loud. Kuoni raised a single eyebrow and pointed in affirmation.

"Or never have been born." Kuoni added, then looked the wizard straight in the eyes.

"I would dare to say you have more to thank the Elves for than you have ever realized." At this, Kuoni returned to the road and continued walking.

Scoff! Luno did not care at all for the lecture Kuoni had just put him through. But with no other arguments coming to mind, he could only let it hit his walled off mind and try to keep it from resonating in his thoughts.

Edlen only stood in the background, having watched the argument resolve, was left wide-eyed and unsure of Luno's reaction. But it was best left alone, and he returned to following Kuoni. Luno, having paused in dissatisfaction, waited for the rest of the party to continue before reluctantly following as well.

The night swiftly aged to early morning, and the tops of the trees high above began to glow. Although the forest was dense and thick, it was not long before a light mist filled the space under the canopy. As the treetops brightened, the fireflies returned to their hidden places to rest for the day, and the mushrooms lost their fluorescence. It was their time to rest as well, and focus not on showing off their light, but to continue to grow. Before long, bright yellow beams of sunlight broke through small openings between commanding trees.

Everywhere they looked, they were surrounded by these columns of light that faded into the distance. The heavy morning mist settled in the windless forest, and it was cool and refreshing. The forest was waking up for the day.

Snifff! "Ahhh! What a beautiful morning it is in Arboran!" Radholf said, taking in a deep breath of the fresh forest air. "Rejuvenating, is it not?"

"It is tolerable," Oatikki said, who was a bit annoyed at the humidity as it made his leather straps stick tight to his body. He was accustomed to dryer air, but found that even he could not find much flaw in the sights around them.

"It *is* a beautiful land..." Adelmar said. "I am also a first-time visitor," he said with a smile at Edlen, who was walking at his side at the moment.

The birds sang echoing songs through the forest. They seemed to harmonize in a common chorus, each bringing its own voice of shrills, chirps, and twitters. But each a necessary voice in the common song they sang. It was hard to not notice how perfectly synchronized their songs were, and to bring such cheerful thoughts to those passing through, even the hardest of the travelers could not contain the slightest smile.

On what gentle breeze would occasionally pass, carried a sweet smell of blossoms. Though not often, the smell of sweet honey could also be caught, as could a buzz from a busy morning bee making his rounds.

All around them was green. Beams of yellow sun broke through the trees and dotted the forest floors around them. Although mostly flat, in the distance hills were revealed as the mist lifted. The forest was quite lively, with rabbits hopping through towards the neighboring berry patches, chipmunks chasing one another in a playful fit, and an occasional family of forest deer picking the lowest broad leaves from the lowest of hanging branches. Soon, the sound of rushing water grew as they approached a narrow river.

Radholf, leading the party, approached the river. He waited for the others to approach as he gazed over it. The waters were as clear as daytime air, giving bends to the shapes of stones and riverbed rock under it. It looked cold and refreshing, flawless and pure. The sounds of its sprinkling and leaping over rock was soothing yet exciting.

Edlen studied it as it played with the smaller pebbles in smaller pools spun off near the shores. No litter was found, no dirt was carried by it. It gave a fine mist that soaked the air around it with life and freshness.

"Here we are!" Radholf said, breaking through the sounds of the river.

"What? The *river?*" Luno asked, unsure of what Radholf's point was.

"No, my fine wizard friend! We are *here!*" Radholf replied, opening his arms towards the far bank of the river. Silence fell over the group again as the sound of the river continued. Over it, the birds carried on their songs. Edlen looked over at Adelmar, who shared a puzzled look. Then, he glanced at Kuoni, hoping for clarity. Kuoni rolled his eyes.

"*Ugh*...every time..." Kuoni muttered under his breath.

Radholf looked straight at Edlen and smiled with a large, goofy look on his face. Then he took a big step off the edge of the river bank and right into the river.

But water did not meet his landing, for Radholf knew precisely where the crystal bridge was set just above the surface of the river flow. Edlen (as well as the other first time guests) had completely missed spotting the clear walkway that crossed the river.

"Come, my friends! We are at the borders of the great city! And I can assure you, our arrival will be most welcome!" Radholf took a few more steps above a solid (yet still hard to see) walkway and onto the far banks.

"Come, Edlen, I will help you find your footing," Kuoni said with a wink. Edlen crossed the borders into the great realm that is Arboran, and thus did his new friend Kuoni. Adelmar followed, and Luno as well. Lastly, their Orkken companion brought up the end of their party, and they were safe at last.

To have come so far, to have gained and lost so much, Edlen was relieved to have arrived safe in such a wondrous place. His haven to be had now, a reality he had hoped for, and clung to through so much struggle. A haven he could then call his new home. A new home for his heart to take rest in, for the one he once had was taken so wrongfully from him.

Taken from him, but it had failed to break him.

Book II

The Awakening of Rhim

CHAPTER XVI

CHILDREN OF ARBORAN

— 19th of Frostfare, 1867 —

Morning had aged to what seemed to be nearing noon, as so the beams of bright sunshine shown nearly straight down through the breaks in the trees would tell. The sights and sounds of the lively forest never grew old in Edlen's eyes. He wandered down the road in a blissful haven of peace and good being.

As they rounded a wide corner of the road, far in the distance Edlen could see something formed. The end of the road was approaching, though what structure laid at its end did not seem out of place, nor unnatural. And it wasn't until they approached closer that Edlen could make out really what it was.

"Allow me to take the lead," Radholf asked of his group. "My face will be well recognized at the entrance." He continued to lead them as they met the arch over the road. Tall and made of the living trees on either side, it was covered in climbing ivy and towered before them. Long purple bell flowers dotted the ivy, and the entire arch buzzed with thirsty bees. At the top, the living emblem of the *Children of Arboran*: Three spear-shaped leaves blooming out from the center, encased in a small perfect circle of sapling branch that ran through the leafy centers.

At the entrance stood two tall figures cloaked in beautiful long fabrics. Each with intricately woven designs that swirled around like the vines climbing the arch. A hood paired with their cloaks, and neither of them bore any weapons. They stood tall and elegant, with their hoods down and peaceful smiles on their faces as the arriving guests approached.

"Welcome, Radholf Verndari," the guard on the right spoke out as they stopped at the arch. "Many new moons have passed since your last visit. Lord Halldór is waiting for you." He shifted his focus to the travelers behind him.

"Kuoni Verndari. Good to see you have come," he said as Kuoni smiled with a nod. The guard shifted his attention to the party behind them, expressing concern of their presence.

"You have brought great evil to our doorstep," he said as he returned his attention back to Radholf. "A great beast of wing and fire such that we have not seen since before the Great War."

"Yes, it is why I must speak to Lord Halldór immediately," Radholf replied. The guard gave a single nod of affirmation.

"Of your companions," said the second guard approaching, "we have every reason to welcome friends of Radholf, and have places for each of you to rest and recover, for your road must have been long." He turned towards the way the road led.

"Please, follow me," he added as he began walking through the arch.

As they entered the city, Edlen saw more and more Elves going about their day. They all looked very similar, as they were all close in kin. Fair skinned with spots of brown freckles. Some with straight blond hair, some with straight brown hair, and some with hints of a fiery red that shimmered in the golden sunlight.

"Kuoni..." Edlen spoke softly so to not bring attention to his questions. "I have noticed that some have green eyes where as others have blue, but no brown?"

"Oh, certainly not! For these are the two families of which the Elves have roots of. The blue eyed Elves are those who take closer after their mother, the *Mother of the Seas*, of the streams and rain. The green eyes are of those who take after the *father* of earth and green life. And although they live in peace today, they are still held up as a purer line of Elves, for they are the true *Children of Arboran*.

"Yet, in this land, these two classes coincide in peace. But you will notice that neither intermingle, nor marry within the other."

Edlen continued to observe the city around them, the people and their glances at the travelers. The road he walked on was of solid stone, swirling with beautiful colors within the marble. There existed no buildings, only flat landings of earth and stone, each surrounded with stacked stone and rock with various ivy's and flowers growing all around it.

Throughout the city, small shaded streams of crystal clear water flowed. Frogs *creeeeeked* here and there, and the city buzzed with the sounds of bees coming and going, and of birds chattering just above the walkways.

Where there was shade, it was from overhung tree branches with dense broad leaves. And it seemed like every time he glanced up, there was a new type of fruit he had never seen prior growing just within reach over his head. It was then that it dawned upon him, and Adelmar spoke aloud his exact thoughts.

"It is though this city was not built *on* the earth, but has grown *of* the earth!" Adelmar said in amazement, taking in the sights and sounds surrounding him.

Their road had forked into different trails left and right like veins of a leaf laid out across the lands. With each trail, its own stream flowed, and each one twisted and turned so that none revealed much in a single glance down its lane. It was not long before their stone path, the main vein of the city, began its incline up.

As their path rose, so did the earth around them. At first it was only the right as they entered around a small cliff. It dripped with fresh rain water and was covered in a hanging moss. As their path wound around, the left side became a wall of stone. All along the cliff were inlets carved with small statues of past Fathers of Elves, Lords in their own time. Each with their name carved in their own language. Each lit from behind with ever-burning candles, clean and pure.

Luno took particular notice of these as he wiped his finger along the rock behind one such figure. The rock face, which towered directly of the candle, wiped clean with no soot.

"How does one burn such light so pure?" he asked aloud noticing the dry rock face. He looked ahead for a response, but no one gave him his answer. Oatikki followed behind him, passing him.

"The Elves have their ways..." he muttered, not wanting to get into the details of *how*, although never taking the time to learn for himself.

"Orcs do not care for such things..." Kuoni said with a wink at Edlen. Edlen grinned, and was perfectly happy with Oatikki's answer. It gave a sense of mystery and magic, for which Edlen was filled with joy to be able to experience.

As they reached the top of the summit they found themselves effortlessly climbing, they came under a wide ceiling, high into the trees, made of intricate vines and broad leaves. The floor they stood on, made completely of stone, was dry of any moisture. Between small holes in the openings of leaves, thin strands of sunlight shown down like a thousand stars beaming down from the heavens. The breeze was calm and sweet here, a place for comfort in those who gathered, for this was the main hall in which Lord Halldór and his brothers waited for their guests to arrive.

As Radholf revealed himself around the last bend of path, Lord Halldór rose from his throne with his arms open wide.

"Radholf, my old friend! How good it is to see you." He approached Radholf and embraced him gently. His robe shimmered of violets and reds as he stood in several sun beams. His crown was beautifully woven of a living vine. Small three-speared leaves complimented the various gems and stones the younger vines grasped onto. He was tall and thin, with emerald eyes and a very white smile.

"Your friends are welcome here," he said as he gave attention to the travelers, now all arriving. "But you come from a darker time..." he said to Radholf.

"Dark indeed..." he replied. "We have been exiled from our lands once again, Lord Halldór. The Great Grizzly from the West has been hunting us, pushing us into the wilderness," Radholf paused for a moment, then looked back at his companions.

"Lord Halldór, my fellow travelers are quite weary. Let us find a place of rest for them before we continue our conversation," Radholf requested.

"Of course," Lord Halldór replied with a bow. A single Elf approached, wearing similar styles of robes but in a dark shade of blue.

"If you would, please follow me and I will show you to your quarters," he said in a calming voice. Leading them to the left, they followed a stony trail down from the main hall. Their surroundings were entirely of stone, save the constant leaf ceiling high above. Though this hall was not narrow by any means, as the entire party could have walked at each others sides with comfort. Their steps echoed down as they approached the landing.

Before them was a wide open space, far larger than the hall they had just come from. The top was difficult to see in the mist that filled the space, but the same golden beams of light shown down forever into the distance. Several streams flowed in naturally carved impressions into the stony floor. Towering giants of tree and vine walled the great space as birds flew from branch to branch high above.

The branches hanging out, reached as far as they could into the open air above. Chirping echoed through, giving compliment to the sound of trickling water in several directions.

"Wow..." Edlen spoke under his breath. "This is amazing..." he added as he looked up, taking in the beautiful view, trying to comprehend its immense size.

"These are the quarters of any guest to Arboran, and you are welcome to stay as long as you need," the Elf ahead of them said, continuing to walk down the path.

Though the floor was wide, swirls of pink stone marked the walkways. On either side, moss grew where it could take grasp in imperfections of the stone, and in scattered divots where enough rich soil could be gathered, flowers bloomed joyfully.

At their first fork in the pink stone, their Elvish host led them left to a row of wooden doors. They had no handles but opened with ease as their rooms were revealed to them.

As Edlen looked down the row of doors, they were all carved into the base of trees growing in a semi-uniform line. Not all trees were the same as the barks varied in textures and colors. But each tree was an ancient giant, and what hollowness came from having a full sized room big enough for even Kuoni's size seemed to be of little notice to the living towers of wood and leaf.

"Each guest is welcome to their own room," he said, indicating the first six rooms to be theirs. "My name is Matías, and if there is anything at all I may be of service to, please do not hesitate to ask." He looked at each of the travelers, making sure to appropriately address their presence as a silent, but personal introduction.

"Your road must have been a difficult one, so does your faces tell. But you can rest now, for you are safe in this haven of ancient trees."

Edlen looked up at Kuoni and smiled. Kuoni smiled back as he entered his claim to a room, and Edlen took the first one to the right of Kuoni's. With relief and gratefulness, each room was claimed by the remaining members of their traveling party.

As Edlen entered, he found a room whose walls were the insides of tree bark, as though the room itself was carved into the trunk of a living tree. The floor was smooth stone, the bed large, and a dresser with a washing basin sat on top. He walked over to the bed and sat down. The mattress felt as soft as a cloud, and the sheets of silk were lighter than any he had touched before. There was no fire place, for it was never cold here.

Above the door was the symbol of the Arborian realm carved into the wood to give a view to the outside space. Sunlight beamed through, lighting the room and placing the symbol's shape on the far wall.

As Edlen studied the room, he noticed a small outlet of water on the wall above the wash basin, refreshing its water supply constantly. With every trickle that flowed down, a matching trickle spilled over the back edge of the basin and into a small collecting pool in the stone where it disappeared under the wooden walls. The room was peaceful. And he already felt the burdens and worries melting off of his mind. Here he laid to rest, and with the sounds of the trickling water, he quickly fell asleep on his own private cloud.

Edlen awoke from a deep sleep in which even his mind was far too relaxed to conjure up any dream. He sat up in bed and found himself still in the same room. But instead of golden rays of sunlight, he found the soft white light of the moon shinning through the emblem opening above his door. The quiet trickling of his wash basin encouraged him to return to his sleep, but in his heart, he missed Radholf. He stepped out of bed and opened the door to the great space before him.

All of the birds that echoed before now rested quietly in their hidden nests somewhere in the nearby treetops. Frogs *croaked* and *creeeked*, echoing through the space. Crickets chirped here and there, and the fireflies had returned to their waving dance just above the ground. No fires were lit, for the moonlight shed plenty for Edlen to see.

Edlen glanced down to his left at the countless trees containing restful guests. No signs of light or disturbances came from that direction. He approached Kuoni's door to his right and pressed his ear against the outside. Sounds of deep rumbling snores came in a constant pattern with deep exhales in between. Everyone else was catching up on some much needed sleep.

Edlen slowly followed the trail back up towards the main hall. As he approached, he noticed the hall empty save the sound of conversation echoing from another path to the right of the thrones. The voices they carried sounded unfamiliar save one that belonged to Radholf. Edlen headed towards the path before he was suddenly stopped.

"They are having a private conversation," a guard said, suddenly making his presence known. Edlen startled at the sudden appearance of the guard as he had been standing in plain sight against the back wall just next to the opening to the pathway, but had remained unseen until he moved.

"I can shed light on their questions," Edlen said, only guessing at what they were discussing, but knowing his experiences were important in their own to talk about. The guard thought for a moment.

"I am instructed to not allow anyone through," the guard said, placing his hand on Edlen's shoulders. At this, the guard's face turned concerning, and his eyes lost their focus as though he was suddenly in a deep though.

"But you may have a point," he said, removing his hand and letting him through.

Edlen paused for a moment, finding the guard's sudden change in mind suspicious, but took the invitation. He made his way down the path, listening to the words being exchanged as their clarity became easier to understand.

"You do not believe me..." Radholf replied, sounding disappointed. "You do not want to see the same signs I am telling you!"

"We understand your concerns, dear friend, but we cannot come to aid for sake of your land," Lord Halldór answered.

"We once fought side by side, you helped us rid those lands of the evil that infected it. I only ask you do the same in our time of need!" Radholf argued.

"We fought for the lands of our mothers and fathers. And when it was done, the land was returned back to them. Yet, the sons and daughters of your kin have once again swept through and reclaimed what was not theirs! And now you ask us to wage war against the West?"

"No! I do not ask to challenge the West, Lord Halldór. I ask you to open your eyes and see what is on the brink of the horizon," Radholf warned.

At this moment, Edlen stepped in and found a large round room with a fitting round table in the center. Here, candles were lit all along the walls as the ceiling was low and let little light through.

"Do you remember the prophet Valdór had written in the Book of the Good King?" Radholf asked.

"The ancient scripts of the Good King were lost long ago. We only know of a hand full of visions he saw," Lord Halldór answered.

"One of which was the return of the Ashblood, was it not?!" Radholf shouted. "You have the first of many signs to come lying dead at your door step and you want to ignore it?"

"The sighting of a dragon means nothing. If you were to recall the words he spoke, the dragon's origins has a very specific name! A name of pure evil, full of hatred and foul will.

"But you once again raise your warnings at some creature that has been wandering the wilderness for ages! You were deep in the wild where you found it, not at the origins of darkness! It simply was by chance you found her roaming the night skies. It did not come to destroy us all. Your imagination is getting the better of you, Radholf, my friend. I suggest you take control of it."

"It is as Radholf says," Edlen said, speaking out as he approached the table. The Elves shuffled uncomfortably in their seats to have an unwelcome addition rudely barge into their conversation. Radholf stared hard at Lord Halldór.

"What do you know of the dragon?" one of Lord Halldór's brothers asked. Edlen suddenly felt embarrassed at his outburst and defense of his friend, pausing in his answer.

"He killed it..." Radholf said, shifting his attention towards the brother.

"Killed it? But only one of a few Verndari swords could *kill* a dragon..." the brother added.

"Yes!" Radholf answered. "This is Edelmar's descendent, rightful heir to Dragonsbane." Edlen stood still, watching the Elves, waiting for approval.

"Then welcome, Edlen, member of Edelmar's bloodline. Be seated, please," Lord Halldór said, holding his hand out to an empty chair next to Radholf.

"Tell me, Edlen. Did you speak with this beast you slaughtered?" Lord Halldór asked.

"I did," he replied. "She spoke of a horror, something to fuel nightmares with. Her intentions were clear, though. Her warning felt too real. A warning that all things green will come to an end. That the time of Men and of Elves is approaching its dusk. That the Ashblood had been reborn..."

Edlen's memory began to fail him, as he could remember little else of the conversation between himself and the dragon.

The room fell silent. Even the light of the candles seemed to dim at the words he repeated from a creature so foul. Before long, Lord Halldór broke the silence.

"It is difficult, now, to know if what was said holds any truth. After all, dragons are among the least of humble creatures. They find joy in placing fear in others, and it is entirely possible she was only speaking on that motive."

"But we cannot —" Radholf said, suddenly being hushed by Lord Halldór.

"No, we cannot, my friend. We cannot let this warning settle without taking heed of it. We can only watch for the other known signs before the return."

"What other signs?" Edlen asked, curious to know what could be coming.

"The sights the Good King witnessed were spoken by him during a time of great weariness," Radholf explained. "For he was dying when he began to see these things, so many of them are interpreted differently based on who you ask."

"So, what is the next sign to look for? What is supposed to happen next?" Edlen asked.

"*A sea of pale from a land forgotten, in flown a tide to tip the balance of war.*" Lord Halldór spoke with his eyes shut.

"A sea from a land? How does that make any sense..." Edlen thought out loud.

"Hence the interpretation conversations!" Radholf said, smiling.

"It is for nothing to engage in this argument," Lord Halldór continued.

"That I agree!" Radholf added. "We know nothing will come of the darkness until the City of Rhim is found again."

"Found!" Lord Halldór argued. "*Rhim* is a fairy tale, Radholf. Your people may not have accepted it, but *you* have not sent forth generations searching for it!"

Radholf slumped back, not accepting Lord Halldór's argument, waiting for the rant to be over.

"Where *was* it? Can you point on a map where we should find it? Where is the evidence? Where are its people? Have you rummaged over every stone, every boulder, searched every valley or climbed every peak? How long have you hunted for this city, holding on to what little hope there might be to find it?" Lord Halldór's face grew red with frustration.

"But —" Radholf tried to get a word in.

"But only to be let down! To find nothing! I want *Rhim* to be found as badly as you, my friend. But my kin have mapped out the entire Rhim Mountains and have found nothing. I am afraid if Rhim ever existed, it is long lost."

"Rhim will return!" Radholf said, standing up, defending his beliefs.

"Do not be a fool!" Lord Halldór insulted back. "Your trusting in hope is blinding you."

"Hope is all we can rely on!" Edlen said, standing up next to Radholf, wanting to defend his friend. As he stood, the gem necklace he wore from Sabrina slipped out of his shirt and hung low, swinging forward and backward as his hands were placed on the table.

The stone it held shone bright and commanded attention in its reveal. Everyone, even Lord Halldór sat in silence, staring at its beauty.

"Where did you find this gem?" Lord Halldór asked.

Edlen stood still, feeling overwhelmed by the sudden focus of attention upon himself once more. His immediate reaction was of guilt, wanting to cover up where he had taken it from. But in his heart he knew this was not right.

"From a friend who did not survive our journey," he answered.

"A young woman who was found traveling out of the East," Radholf added, knowing Edlen was talking about Sabrina.

"A woman from the East?" Lord Halldór questioned. "How far East?"

"We do not know," Radholf answered. "Much about her is shrouded in mystery and questions we will never know the answers to."

"Perhaps you will..." Lord Halldór added, turning his head off centered. "Tell me all you know about her."

"She had black hair and green eyes," Edlen spoke up. "And fair skin. She first came to Skydale with several other men, all looking similar to her. They claimed to be from the city Nocturnal."

Radholf turned his attention to Edlen, taken by surprise of the information he had about her.

"She spoke little of our language," Edlen continued. "They were searching for something, or someone. Or some time."

Edlen looked up at Radholf.

"Luno told us about her, when she first arrived in Skydale nearly a year ago." Radholf smiled and placed his hand on Edlen's back, encouraging him to continue telling all he knew.

"Searching for something..." Lord Halldór shifted to a more serious focus. "For what reasons?"

"Luno said he was confused by their inquiry. He said the men were looking for the night time," Edlen explained as best he could.

Lord Halldór sat back in his chair, taking a deep breath.

"And this gem around your neck..." Lord Halldór asked. "This was with the young woman?"

"She wore it around her neck until she had passed. Then I took it for myself as a token of remembrance," Edlen admitted, unable to maintain his focus on the Elf Lord. "I feel guilty about it now..."

"No..." Lord Halldór denied his guilt. "You may have the only evidence we have known hanging around your neck...

"But the *city Nocturnal*, you are sure?" Lord Halldór asked for confirmation.

Edlen nodded.

"A city cursed in slumber until the coming of night," Lord Halldór thought out loud. The room fell silent as minds digested this thought, trying to find where it could lead.

Suddenly, Edlen silently gasped in a memory.

"The dragon..." he said in a loud whisper. All attention turned towards him.

"The dragon said she had come to prepare for the heir of the night." His eyes were wide with fear.

"The inheritor of the night, you are sure of this?" Lord Halldór confirmed.

"Yes, my Lord," Edlen said with respect and assurance.

"Then this could explain the missing city," Lord Halldór continued.

Radholf shifted his focus again to Lord Halldór.

"You believe the young woman is from Rhim?"

"Tell me, Edlen, how did you get past the guard at the entrance?" Lord Halldór asked.

Edlen stalled, but knowing his truth to be more important than any honor he could falsely hold on to, he spoke.

"Well, at first he did not let me through. But he placed his hand on my shoulder and seemed to have a change in his mind."

Lord Halldór tilted his head back, his eyes widening.

"This is of ancient magic," he said under his breath. "This gem you have around your neck allows you to influence the minds of others, simply by contact of the body. A spell too powerful to be cast now in these days. One that comes from only ancient times."

"So, now do you believe Rhim is real? After you have hard evidence?" Radholf asked with a tone of disapproval.

"I believe," Lord Halldór answered, "that perhaps Rhim has had its awakening."

Radholf returned to his seat, placing his face deep in his palms, dragging his hands back over his head to pull his hair back again.

"If this is true..." Lord Halldór added. "Then dark days certainly are before us."

"If this is true," Radholf replied, "then the hope we have hung on to is all the more real, and the name of the Verndari will be put to its final test."

"Indeed. But there is another quest we must focus on," Lord Halldór added. "Rhim *must* be found if we are to keep the hope of our salvation."

Radholf nodded in agreement.

"It is a tragic loss of your friend to have passed in such a dire need of her presence, Edlen," Lord Halldór commented. "Her knowledge would have proven to have saved us for sure, but it is now up to us to find her home.

"I will assemble my finest questers for a purpose such as this," Lord Halldór continued. "Kaltag, our best tracker will help lead you through the wilderness. He has attended most of our previous quests through the mountains, spending much of his life searching for the lost city. It would be only fitting he be the leader of your expedition.

"Moli, a promising Guardsman who has proven himself worthy of any task given to him, I send as a protector of your party, and of the third of my family to join you," Lord Halldór said as he held out his left hand to the young woman sitting several seats down.

"This is my eldest daughter, first of my children, and your third party member, Camila."

This was the first moment Edlen had noticed her. A young Elf woman only a year or so older than he, though it was difficult to tell.

Like her father, she had emerald-green eyes and beautiful red hair that waved down past her shoulders. Even in the dim candle light of the room, her freckles shown against her fair skin.

"It will be an honor, father," she answered.

Lord Halldór looked back at Radholf.

"It would be wise to send a member of your party as well, someone to represent your Gronndelon."

Radholf smiled and looked at Edlen. Lord Halldór also turned his attention to Edlen.

"Well, Edlen..." Radholf began. "Are you ready for another adventure?"

"But we only just arrived..." Edlen said, denying the request. But he looked at Lord Halldór, and realizing the honor of the request from the Elf Lord to join their party, he slowly lowered his head.

"It would be an honor," he answered.

"Do not worry, Edlen son of Eldor, master of Dragonsbane," Lord Halldór said. "You will be with great company. "

"Of course he will!" Radholf said. "He will have half the Verndari with him!" Radholf smiled. "Per your acceptance, my Lord, I would like to join you. Oatikki as well."

"I will match your three with three of my own," Lord Halldór answered in acceptance.

"Edlen, you will get your rest. The party will leave after ten days of rest and preparation," Lord Halldór said at final.

"Thank you, Lord Halldór," Edlen answered politely.

"Come, Edlen. Let us return to our rooms and complete this night in slumber," Radholf said, standing from his chair.

Radholf bowed in respect to depart. Edlen followed, bowing and acknowledging several of the Elves before him. The last sights he took in from the room before rounding the corner was of Camila, the Elf Lord's daughter, who watched with a friendly smile as he left.

Later that night, only hours before dawn, Radholf awoke to the sound of weeping. As he approached Edlen's door, he gave it a gentle knock. The sobbing stopped, and Edlen opened the door, eyes swollen red.

"The night has turned to a quiet rain," Radholf said as he sat down next to Edlen on his bed. Outside the door, a gentle shower had been washing clean the leaves and branches of the trees of Arboran, and giving all things green a refreshing drink.

"What lays heavy on your heart, my lad?"

Edlen sniffled, and wiped the last of his tears from his cheek.

"This is a wonderful place, Radholf. Safe from any dangers. Filled with peace and of joy." He took a deep breath filled with sorrow.

"Why can we not now return to find my mother and sister?" he said, emotion cracking in his voice. "Can we not bring them here too? I miss them..."

Radholf took a deep breath.

"Edlen, you have a kind heart. And a desire to share your comfort with your close loved ones is understandably right. But what do we know about their fate?" Radholf asked.

"We know they are in Kathlon, so the Colonel told us," Edlen answered.

"No, we do not know that for certain. That may have been their intention, or may have been where they were going, but we do not know for certain where they are at the moment.

"I am afraid that by the time we might arrive, they will have long since departed."

Edlen sat in silence, feeling the same defeat from Radholf's logic and sensible thinking as the first day in Dargmara's inn.

"But your role in what is about to come is far more important than to save two of your own family, Edlen," Radholf continued. "Though noble it is of you to want to bring them here, doing so would provide only a taste of safety from what is to come.

"You are meant for much more than that. What you are about to embark on will save thousands of people across multiple nations. And it will not be a simple taste of a green haven, but a deliverance from what plagues our hearts, and hunts the insurgents of greed."

Though Edlen's tears had ceased to fall, his heart still laid heavy to be reunited with his family. Although his tests had already been many, and many of them difficult, he would not fail this one either.

"Thank you, Radholf," Edlen said. "I am honored to be part of this expedition."

Radholf smiled, and leaning over embraced Edlen with a warm hug of comfort and reassurance. Then leaving him for what remained of the night, he slowly latched his door shut and returned to his own room.

The sun shown bright as it was midmorning in the realm of Arboran. The company of travelers had gathered at the city gates as one of their party was now prepared to leave. It had only been a couple of days since they had arrived, just enough time for Luno to have gathered his strength and rest, and replenished what he could for the trip ahead of him.

"Farewell, Edlen," Luno said, placing his hand on his shoulder. "You stay safe!" he added.

"Thank you," Edlen said with a grin. He knew Luno did not care for the Elves, and even though he was shown incredible kindness and welcoming, had tolerated them long enough.

"Safe travels, dear friend," Radholf said, shaking his hand.

"Thank you. I am very much looking forward to this journey, however delayed I am by now," he said sounding a bit annoyed. But with his staff in one hand and satchel hanging around his neck, he headed off to the West in his second attempt towards his destination.

"I sure am going to miss him..." Edlen said as they watched the wizard disappear into the lush woods before them.

"Bah," Oatikki said. "His foul moods were infectious," he muttered. Edlen turned his head with a smile.

"And yours are not?" he asked. Radholf laughed loudly at this, as so did Kuoni.

"I am in a much better mood when he is not around!" Oatikki defended himself.

"I had not noticed!" Edlen said, chuckling.

"Perhaps we need to work on your friendliness, my dear Oati!" Radholf said laughing, throwing his arm around Oatikki's shoulder. Radholf led Oatikki back into the city of trees. Edlen remained, watching his departing friend in the distance, trying to catch any last glimpse of the wizard's cloak from between the trees.

"Come, Edlen," Kuoni said, placing his large hand on his shoulder. "Let us return with the others. You have much to prepare for."

Edlen took a deep breath. Willfully departing from a friend was difficult. He would miss his wizard friend, but he knew he was in the best place he could be. Thus he turned around and entered the city once again with Kuoni at his side. The best place he could be. The safest place he could be. Like a breath of fresh spring air after a long, dark winter, it rejuvenated him in body and spirit. He was ready to face his next test.

CHAPTER XVII

A SORROW LEFT BEHIND

— 21st of Kaldagger, 1866 —

A thick wooden door swung open on its large iron hinges as it *creaked* and ended with a *SLAM!* Dust blew around in swirls as the daylight shown into the small house. In the doorway stood Stelli with the still frightened Gracie wrapped in his cloak.

As her eyes adjusted to the dim light of his home, she found a small fire burning in its place at the back. It was a single room house, large enough for just a single man. A small, round stained-glass window let a beam of colored light shine in from the south side of the house and onto a spot on the floor where a reflection of the glass pattern was clear to see. It was shades of blue and red, and gave hints of purple where they met. The house smelled the same as Stelli's cloak, and the walls were lined with herbs, flowers, and oils.

"Welcome to my home, little Clara," he said to her as they stepped in. He released her from his cloak to let her explore if she wished, but she only stood still near the entrance, studying the room from that point. Odd things she saw, as she looked closer at what was on the shelves. Small skulls, bird feathers, and jars of bits and pieces of what she could not identify. The whole place was troubling and concerning, and made her feel very uncomfortable.

CLICK Stelli threw the lock in place. He hung his cloak on a single wooden peg next to the door, then walked past her.

"Do not be afraid!" he said to her. "Please come in! Nothing here will bite, least of all me!" She still remained silent and without movement.

"Ah," he said, sticking a single index finger out to indicate an idea. He turned around and headed to his fire pit where he pulled a plate with a cloth draped over it off the mantel.

"I was saving this for after tonight's supper...but I think it may be better spent on such an occasion as this," he said as he approached her. He lifted the cloth to reveal a sweet bun with raisins baked into it.

"I had been keeping it warm above the fire all morning. It should be perfect at this moment! Please! Do not let it go to waste!"

Gracie held out her hands to hold the plate, for the bun certainly looked appetizing. The iron chains rattled around her wrists as the cuffs shifted.

"Oh, how could I have forgotten!" Stelli exclaimed. "My dear let us rid you of those!"

He took her to the side where he had a work bench with various artifacts of strange origins all about. Broken small bones, plant stems and mortars of crushed powder. Very little room was left on this bench, but he was in such a hurry to make any please of her, he cleared half the bench with one swipe of his arm, pushing all that was in its path to the floor. A few of the items found their landing in a basket on the floor while the majority came crashing down to the ground, rolling around in a frenzy before finding their temporary resting places.

"Here!" he said, taking the plate and setting it off to the side. "Keep your hands still! These locks are not so difficult if you have found your way out of them before," he said with a wink.

He pulled a small drawer out of the wall above the work bench and rifled through, looking for a specific tool. Pulling out a small, crooked iron pick, he quickly began to work on her cuffs. Within moments, they had both come loose.

"There we are!" he said, returning his tool to its drawer. "And here _you_ are, my little Clara!" handing her the plate once more, smiling an awkward smile.

Gracie looked down at the roll, studying it. She brought it closer to her face and sniffed in. The smell immediately awoke her stomach as it growled audibly.

"Go on! It will be delicious! Though I had not baked it myself. It is from a wonderful bakery just down..." he stopped for a moment as Gracie studied him. Finally catching the hint, he smiled.

"Take your time, little Clara," he ended as he left her to eat at her own company, and returned to the fire to stoke it.

Gracie took a small bite at first, unsure of the safety she was in. Though as her mouth salivated over the warmth of the baked good, her mind began to unlock her guard. It made no sense for anyone to have a poisoned roll just sitting on their mantel for no occasion. And content with this logic alone, she continued with larger bites, taking little time to savor it.

Stelli smiled knowing he had finally built some trust with the little girl, satisfied in his ability to offer her something she needed. Without looking back, knowing she was coming close to finishing her roll, he walked to his small dining table and poured a glass of milk.

"You will be wanting something to drink too, I imagine," he said, handing her the glass. Gracie looked up at him with crumbs scattered across her face, licking her lips and taking the glass. She took a few sips, and it went down smooth. A perfect compliment to the dense dessert she just enjoyed, filling her tummy better than it had over the past week.

"Thank you..." she squeaked out, trying to remember her manners.

"Ah-ha! So it *does* talk!" Stelli shouted with a grin.

"You had Stelli nearly convinced you have not understood a word I have been telling you! I was beginning to wonder what distant land you had come from! Oh, but what a relief you can understand old Stelli." Gracie's shyness began to return as she said nothing more and breaking eye contact.

"You need not to fear Stelli," he said. "I will admit, I have never had the care of a child in my past. Nor do I care to impose myself onto others much. Most people here...well. They do not understand, will not understand. I may seem strange to most, but most seem strange to me," he said. His purpose was not to frighten Gracie, but to open up and show her she had nothing to fear, even though he may be coming across as odd.

"All of this..." he said, opening his arms to the room around them. "This is Stelli! This is who I am. I want to help people. Help heal. Help to fix the broken."

Gracie looked around. The mortars of dust, the dried plants and jars of oddities began to make sense.

"You make medicine?" Gracie asked, trying to piece everything together.

"Medicine! Yes!" Stelli replied. "But strong medicine, more potent than what most people know how to make! You catch a cold, and what do you do?" he asked her.

"My momma..." Gracie started off, but a sudden wave of sorrow fell over again and she stopped. A long pause fell over their conversation as Stelli picked up on a painful past, perhaps fresh still.

"She would make you some tea, yes?" he asked her. Gracie nodded.

"Yes! But what if you could have that cup of tea ten times in a single sip! How must faster would your cold leave? That is what I do...but more! I have found..." he continued, as he gathered raw ingredients from his shelves to show Gracie.

"I have found the most potent ingredients and discovered new things! Things that strengthen other things! I can have a cold leave you the same day, the same *hour*! I chase it away!" he said as he threw his arms out in an exciting passion. A pouch of powder flew from his hands and crashed into his shelves, knocking over a few vials of liquid and sending their contents splashing on the ground.

Gracie giggled. Stelli, realizing what had just happened, blushed and grinned.

"But not always in perfect ways, I must admit!"

"Well..." Stelli added, looking around. "If you are to be staying here, which I think would be wise in your... situation...you will probably be wanting your own place to sleep. And a few other things... little girls... need," he said, unsure of what the answer was exactly.

"Luckily!" he said, pointing to the ceiling but keeping his eyes on the ground in some deep thought. "I have saved away quite a bit of coin, unsure of what I would use it on."

He walked over to the end of his bed where a trunk sat under a wool blanket. Tossing the blanket aside, he opened the lid and dug through various articles of clothing. As he reached the bottom, he pulled out a small chest, locked tight. Walking back to the table, he placed it down hard as it was heavy and made mostly of iron.

"Now..." he said, tapping a single finder on the lid of the chest, darting his eyes back and forth. "Where in the west did you hide the key?" he said to himself as he quickly moved across his small home, looking through drawers and under any small trinket he had placed as a decoration or other means.

"Found you!" he said, opening the lid to a small urn on the mantle. Gracie looked at him with concern and surprise.

"Oh, do not fret! That is only Clarence. He keeps guard over this place while I am out." Gracie's face turned puzzled, losing no concern in her mind, but found it more curious now.

Ka-chink! The lock threw open and the lid revealed a beautiful purple satin bag with a black draw string. Stelli lifted it up and the sound of heavy coins could be heard as they shifted down in place. He dropped the bag in his cloak pocket.

"Fine then!" he said to her as he headed to the door. "I will be out gathering things to make *my* home a place *you* may also call home." He paused for a moment as Gracie remained in the same place, not having moved since he unlocked her chains.

"Uh..." he said, unsure of leaving a strange girl in his home. "It would be wise not to touch anything on the shelves..." he said, more concerned over her safety than the safety of his own things.

"And please, do not leave. I have rather enjoyed your company. You are a good listener," he said with a smile. Gracie gave the slightest grin, looking down at the floor.

"I will return after a while, and we will be sure to get you set up proper!" he said as he opened the door and quickly shut it behind him.

Hours passed as the stained glass circle of sunshine moved across the floor, and now formed a thin oval on the far wall. Gracie had slowly come out of her shell, taking confidence that she was alone, and had begun to explore the house at her own pace. For some time, she stared out the front window and watched as neighbors came and went about their business, careful not to be noticed. But this was easy as the window had needed a good washing for some time, and there was little other light coming from within the home.

There was not much to explore in this house so small. But in every corner was something in its place. Some container or trinket, an artifact or things she had never seen before. Things she really could not imagine what their purpose was. But at this time, the fire had died down to glowing embers, and the outside world started to lose its daylight.

Click! The front door unlocked and swung open wide. Gracie's heart raced again at the sudden appearance of noise in such a quiet corner of the city. She was getting comfortable with just herself being alone, and with a break from the strange Stelli, his reappearance brought back to life some sense of suspicion.

"Ah! You *did* stay!" he said as he saw her now standing by the fire pit. "I am glad! It won't make waste of all *this!*" he said as he put down sacks of items he had purchased. After closing the door and hanging his cloak, he turned his attention to the sacks.

"Come, come! All of this is for you!" he said, inviting her over. Her interest peaked as she approached to see what gifts such a stranger could give her.

The first item he took out was a beautiful dress. A pattern of small violet flowers and green leaves on a white background.

"I...I could only guess at your size. The woman who made the dress helped me figure it out as I roughly knew the top of your head came up to about here," he said holding his hand at his stomach. "I do hope you like it though. These violets I use in a tea that tends to cheer me up. I thought it would make sense for you to wear them..." he said as he handed her the dress.

"Several more I have too, seeing as you probably should have some changes in clothes." He pulled out three more dresses all of similar size, but all of different patterns.

Gracie was speechless. She had never gotten so many new dresses at once before, and the fabric was beautiful to her. Her emotions began to swell as she attempted to hide them.

"And for you to sleep on..." he said as he pulled out a thick, rolled up mattress stuffed with wool. It was smaller than a normal bed, but perfect for a girl her age.

"And..." he continued, as the last thing in his sack was a warm blanket to go with it. It was a forest green made of tundra cotton.

"They had not any pretty colors, I am afraid," he said as he placed the folded blanket onto the now rolled out mattress. Gracie smiled as a tear fell down her cheek. Her emotions began to show.

"Now in *this* bag...I found a few little things you may enjoy to keep you busy!" He reached in and pulled out a small doll with a head made of wood and the body of stuffed fabric. It was quite a bit different than the one she had lost back home, but the sight of it brought with it a flood of sadness she could not contain. Tears bursting from her eyes, she sobbed as she took the doll, studying its form with her fingers before clutching it tight with her eyes shut.

Stelli did not know what to do.

"Did..." he began, before changing his question.

"Do you not like it?" wanting to make sure she was happy, wanting to fix the situation. Gracie sniffled, trying to choke back her crying.

"No its...I like it," she said.

"Good..." Stelli replied, not quite satisfied with the answer. He then pulled out a book. A very old looking book with a worn leather cover. On the front were worn out carved letters of an ancient language, pressed into the leather but losing their depth from age. Below what appeared to be the title was an imprint of a crude dragon figure, and at the mouth of the dragon, a small red marble pressed into the cover.

"I also found a story book for you..." he said, handing the book to her. "I think it is about dragons! Do you like old stories?" he asked.

Gracie paused for a moment, peering down at the book in front of her through her teary eyes.

"I cannot read," she said.

"Oh! No matter...I will read it to you then! Perhaps we can use this book and I might teach you!" Gracie did not respond, only held on tight to her new doll.

"I will put this book up on the shelf for now. Perhaps we may start a story tonight after supper," he said as he placed the book on a low shelf, well within reach of Gracie's height.

"Supper!" he said with a sudden reminder of the late hour. "Supper is what is in the last sack!" he said as he ran back over and opened the last bag on the ground. He pulled out a large clay pot with its lid tied tightly with twine to keep its insides contained. Carrying it by the small handles on either side of the opening, he placed it on the small wooden table and returned to the sack. The last item he pulled out, a large loaf of bread wrapped in cloth, filled the house with a wonderful smell.

"I sure hope you like stew! There is no meat in it, I am afraid, if you prefer that kind. I enjoy a good vegetable stew over anything with cow or lamb in it. Adds too much gristle. *This* will taste much more fresh." He pulled out two bowls, one much newer looking than the other, and two spoons. Filling Gracie's bowl first, he placed it on the opposing side of the table with her half of the bread loaf.

Gracie sat down with her doll and peered over the bowl of warm stew. It smelled much different than her mother's that she was used to, but the ingredients all looked the same. Pieces of carrots and potato, crushed tomato and caps of wild mushrooms. The smell awoke her stomach once more as it let out an audible growl.

"Yes, I am also hungry! What a day we have had," Stelli said as he sat down in his chair. Gracie waited for Stelli to start eating before taking her first few bites.

Much of their dinner was spent quiet. Stelli paused for a moment to build the fire back up again as the house begun to grow cold. Dusk had fallen outside and the bustling sounds of the city had died down for the night. Lanterns were lit up and down the streets, and the late autumn breeze blew chill across the roof tops, carrying smoke trails with it off the chimneys.

Stelli laid down the mattress on the floor near the fire pit. Gracie had changed into one of her new dresses, and though it was a bit larger than Stelli had planned, it was fit enough for her to grow in to, making it quite the comfortable night gown. She laid down and covered herself up with the warm wool blanket. The mattress did a fine job of keeping the hardness of the stone floor from discomforting her. As she laid down, Stelli walked over to the bookshelf.

"Would you like to start one of our stories?" he asked, pulling the book off the shelf and glancing over at her. She looked back at him, holding her doll, and nodded.

"Hmmm," he said with a smile, walking over to his bedside. He lit his lantern to see the writing on the pages more clearly. He opened the front cover and looked at the first few pages.

"Oh!" he said as he studied the pages. "This is not at all what I had thought..." he flipped through the pages, passing paragraphs and sketches.

"This is not even in our language!" he said with his pale eyes wide open. Gracie looked down at her doll, feeling a little disappointed as a bedtime story sounded rather pleasant.

"Ah-ha! But Stelli *does* know what language this is! And I can be your translator for the night!"

Stelli cleared his throat, and leaning back to sit comfortably in his chair, he crossed his legs as he turned to the first pages of the book.

Skimming across the pages with his fingers, he studied the characters and murmured words to himself. Gracie sat patiently waiting for the story to begin. Looking to the side, she was unsure if he was ever going to start, or simply forgot she was there to listen to the stories.

"Ah!" Stelli said at sudden, startling Gracie with the outburst of volume.

"This, my dear child," he continued, "is the tale of the great Warriors decent from the heavens!" He said with a smile, returning his attention to the book pages.

"Yes, uh..." he cleared his throat once more before officially beginning, as though what he was about to read was some official document or decree.

"During the time of King Valdemar's reign across the vastness of his mountainous kingdom, he was blessed with the coming of twelve guardians upon the brink of war. For his kingdom, finding favor by the Great Warrior Kriger, who rests among the others of stars, sent down his twelve of brothers, each as a piece of his own to guard the great city capital.

"These warriors having the blessings of Kriger fought viciously, becoming well-known as the greatest warriors to have ever descended down onto the West. Whereever they traveled, their enemies shuttered in fear, for no foe had the strength or endurance to make match against a single one of them."

Stelli looked down at Gracie, whose eyes were already shut. He then blew out his lantern and put himself to bed.

After a moment of fire glow in the small room, the little girl broke the silence one last time that night.

"Gracie," she said out loud. Stelli stirred in his bed to look over in her direction, Gracie's eyes still shut.

"That is your name?" he asked. Gracie took a deep breath and exhaled slowly, feeling relieved of much of the sorrow that she was leaving behind, and fell asleep for several hours.

Gracie sat up straight, screaming in fear, tears rolling down her eyes. Stelli leaped out of bed and sat down next to her.

"What is it?!" he said, placing a comforting hand on her shoulder. "What is wrong?"

Gracie clung to her doll, not wanting to open her eyes for fear of what she had just seen would still be in front of her. For a few moments, she sat on the mattress, rocking herself forward and backward, whimpering and trying to forget it.

"My mama..." she said finally.

"You miss her?" Stelli asked.

"She was under an ax. Her hands were tied. I heard bells ring out as snow blew hard. Then..." she paused in fear of continuing. Stelli rubbed her back in comfort.

"Go on, dear child...what did you see?"

"A big man. He held up his ax high above my mama...then the wind stopped. The snow fell straight down like it was holding its breath..." Gracie let out her tears, unable to speak. This was all she had dreamt, and it took all of her emotion to get it out.

"Oh, dear child..." Stelli said, holding her. "It was only a bad dream..." But in his heart he knew what this was. He knew of the gifts of prophecy within dreams, and knew this was likely something that was going to happen, if it had not already. This is what he had feared, that it was already too late.

Stelli continued to rock her back and forth, comforting her as best he could, pressing his palm against the back of her head to give a sense of security and protection. And after some time, Gracie had fallen back to sleep. Gently guiding her back down onto her mattress and covering her back up, she remained quiet for the rest of the night, showing no signs of the vision's return.

CHAPTER XVIII

THE DAY THE EARTH SHOOK

— 27th of Frostfare, 1867 —

Nearly three months had passed since Hellen had made her discoveries in the King's private library. And since then, she had been extremely careful to let no word of her plans be known to anyone it did not involve. But for weeks she had made these plans, and she scrounged enough gold to make the necessary payments. Carefully scheduling the series of events to make Ronan's escape possible. It just needed to be triggered.

The morning bells chimed out in the basement of the castle. It was time for a quick breakfast once again, so Hellen and Eira made their way to the round dining hall and found their friend Bard, already nearly finished with his.

"Good morning, ladies!" he said as they approached.

"Good morning, Bard," Hellen said in return with a smile. Bard leaned in close to Hellen.

"Do you think today will be the day?" he whispered.

"Bard!" she said. "We have already discussed this! We will not talk about it any further. You know what to wait for. You will be ready, yes?" she said.

"Of course! It is just causing some anxious nerves in me to shout out...each morning I wonder!"

"Soon enough, my friend..." Hellen said, ending the conversation.

Hellen left her friends behind and headed towards the library, as she had done for months now. The sunrise had been slowly delaying each morning, and what rains should have fallen had already begun to fall as snow. Winter was on the brink of starting, and the castle grew colder and more damp from when Hellen had first arrived.

As she came upon the hall that led to the doors of the library tower, she could see Edgar standing next to the desk that sat just in front. With him were several guards, completely dressed in armor.

In Hellen's mind, she hesitated to keep walking. But she had been so careful in her planning, and she knew she had to act as though she had nothing to hide. She had to act innocent, for that is what they needed to believe.

"Good morning, Edgar..." Hellen said as she approached.

"Morning indeed, but whether it is good or not is yet to be seen," he replied. One of the guards approached her, revealing shackles in his hands.

"What...what is this?" Hellen asked, sounding surprised and caught off-guard.

"This is just a precaution," Edgar said. "The King has some questions for you. It would be best if you came without a fuss."

Hellen's face grew concerned. In her heart, she knew they discovered something. But how much of her plan was spoiled, she did not yet know. Her heart pounded and her face turned blush. Yet she went along with his request, and held out her hands as the guard locked the shackles in place.

She was led up to the main dining room where the king sat alone. No plates were on the table, no servants other than a few fully armed guards and one of the king's servants.

"You may tell Remus he may pursue his endeavors at this time," the king said to his servant. His servant bowed and quickly took his leave.

"Ah! There she is!" the king said, standing from his over-sized chair.

"My King! What have I —" Hellen began before the king struck the side of her cheek with the back of his hand. The gems of his rings digging deep into her soft skin, leaving broken lines to bleed out.

"Several weeks ago, I found disturbances in my library. Disturbances caused not by any of my trusted, but of someone else. Things not left where they should have been.

"But I —" The king raised his hand again, holding it in the air.

"You will not speak, lest you desire pain," he said sternly. Then he walked back to the table. That is when Hellen noticed a familiar piece of cloth. A cleaning cloth, the same she had used to jam the door with. The one she had left just inside the door way to the King's library.

The king picked it up, and rubbed a single sheet of its fabric between his fingers.

"So, you know of the completion of *The Quest*," he said, looking down at the cloth, then glancing back at her.

"You have the answer you were looking for, yes? The same answer to a different question that has plagued me and my fathers for generations?" He placed the cloth gently onto the table.

"And yet you have told no one?" he asked.

"No, My King," Hellen said.

"Why not!?" he shouted at her, angry that he could not figure out what other secrets she was hiding.

Hellen trembled with fear. It was in this moment that instinct spoke for her. Her mind turned numb and the words she spoke, she felt little control over. Yet it was the only answer she could give that could keep her plan in motion.

"After discovering what I did, I realized what dangerous information it was. So, I tried to forget it. It was a ship too large to seize. I did not want to put anyone else in danger from simply *knowing*."

"I see," the king said, not entirely swallowing what she was feeding him, but not having enough doubt to continue to question it.

"My King..." Hellen said, knowing she was about to poke the bear in ways she should not.

The king turned to give his attention to her.

"Why keep him alive?" Hellen asked. The king chuckled, then shook his head.

"You know little of the games we must play with crowns upon our heads," he replied. "I could have killed him, yes. Months ago! But why be the King of Nýland when I could be the King of the West? Everything from the Rhims to the Western Sea. Without Sigurbjorn's beloved nephew as leverage, he would have never given me control of the Gronndelon so freely. It has never been so easy to take the land beyond the mountains.

"But once every Jarl is within check, once I have won over the hearts of your pathetic people, this secret will die with *the rightful heir*." He looked grimly at her. "And every mind that holds that secret will die with it. And there will never again be a challenge to my claim to the throne."

Tears fell from Hellen's eyes. The guards jerked her back, causing her to lose her balance as she fell to the floor.

"To the prisons with her!" the king commanded. "Tomorrow will be her last day! Send for the executioner, make ready the chopping block in the market. Let her sing her fowl songs where all may hear and make example of what a treasonous word will bring."

Kicking and screaming, Hellen was drug out of the hall, through the cold castle, blood still running down her cheek, and to the prison cells below.

"Bard!" Eira yelled the next morning at breakfast. Bard was halfway through his morning muffin, crumbs still on his lips.

"Bard! She never came to bed last night! It has happened!"

Bard coughed on his breakfast.

"Are you sure?" he asked.

"Yes! Today is the day, Bard! I will meet you outside the stables!" Eira said grasping onto a small pouch of gold coin she had brought from under her mattress, then running up the stairwell and out of sight. Bard wiped his mouth, took a deep breath, and left the unfinished muffin at the table.

As Bard made his way to the kitchen, he put on his apron as he had every day for years. He walked to his station and began making breakfast muffins, just as he had always done. Flour, sugar, eggs, blueberries. All swirled around in his bowl.

Then from the far back corner of the shelf, he pulled out a small glass bottle of pale-green powder. He poured the powder into the mix. It blended well with the swirls of blueberry juice and dark wheat flour.

Four muffins it made, plated on a silver plate. He took these muffins and left the kitchens, making his way to the deepest, darkest dungeons of the castle, where he found two guards standing in front of the door that held the worst of prisoners.

"No visitors!" the guards demanded.

"Oh, no! I mean not to enter! I simply came down to see if I can offer any muffins. Seems we made far too many this morning and, well, we cannot seem to get rid of them! I hope you like blueberry..." he said, holding the muffins out to the guards.

"Well, we can certainly help with that!" one of the guards said with a smile, taking a muffin and stuffing a big bite into his mouth. The other guard watched as he savored the warm baked good, smelling delicious with steam rising from the opening.

"Thank you," the other said, taking a second off his plate and biting into it. "Oh, these are good!" he said, eager to finish it.

"You are welcome!" Bard said with a bow and taking his leave. Though he did not walk far up the stairs, only out of sight, waiting for the sounds he was expecting.

Within moments, two thuds of collapse echoed up the stone stairwell. When he returned, he found two dead guards on either side of the door. As he approached them, the tower bells rang out. He knew this was his best time to get the prisoners out. Taking their keys, he opened the door to the dungeon and with a torch in hand, rushed in, and began searching for Dahlia and Ronan.

Cell to cell he searched, and found a beaten prisoner, barely able to speak, up against the far wall.

"Ronan? Are you Ronan of Furskarth?" Bard asked.

Ronan turned meekly with eyes barely able to open.

"Yes..." he whispered. Bard hopped down into the cell, placed the torch on the ground and unshackled his wrists and ankles.

"My name is Bard. Please come with me! We have little time!"

As Bard leaped out of the cell, he called out for the other.

"Dahlia! Dahlia, are you here?" But silence echoed back. No answer came. With his torch he continued from cell to cell.

"Dahlia?" he spoke into a cell opposite from Ronan, who was just now able to crawl out. A lone woman laid motionless on the ground. Bard entered to inspect closer.

"Dahlia, wake up!" he said, shaking the young woman. But Dahlia had found her limit just days prior. For she was cold and pale, giving no answer, for no breath she held anymore. Bard took a deep sigh of grief.

"Rest now, Dahlia. Your sacrifice will lead to the salvation of thousands..." he said, placing her back down on the cold floor of her cell.

"Come, Ronan, we must make haste! A cart is waiting for us outside the stables. Hurry!" And although weak and exhausted, Ronan was a strong man. He gave what little strength he had left as he tried to keep up with the chubby baker boy. Together, they made their way through the castle, careful not to run into anyone unfriendly.

Hellen, tied down in the back of the cart, felt the cold winter wind cutting away at her skin. She had little on, especially for the time of winter they had fallen into. She was being taken to the market place to be made a public example, and to get the collection of townsfolk. The castle bells rang out. Tears fell from her cheeks, knowing the cart was taking her to her end.

As they pulled up, two guards came around to the back and pulled hard on her chains. She was thrown down onto the cold stony road, bruising her elbows and scratching up her knees.

"On your feet, traitor!" one of the guards commanded. But her will was too exhausted, and she took the beatings of disobedience without hesitation. Without any will remaining, she was dragged to the center market onto the same platform she had first arrived on, a trail of tears and drips of blood leading from the back of the cart.

The sky was grey, overcast with ominous clouds. The large snowflakes, picked up from the angry sea to the north, charged through the marketplace, winding around on-lookers, reluctant to find a landing. It was bitterly cold.

As she took the three steps onto the platform, seated at his throne upon the stage was the king, fully clothed in furs, his golden crown showing bright. All around him were guards and other highly ranked officials, men he trusted, men he wanted his kingdom to know. But Edgar was not there.

In the center of the stage was the chopping block, freshly cut, never used. Standing next to it, a tall man wearing a black robe. His face bore a beard as black as the robe and a look of disgust. The guards walked her across the stage, stopping her just feet from the section of tree trunk that sat before her.

Hellen peered out over the crowd, hundreds of eyes upon her. The wind blowing directly into her face, her eyes watered from its relentlessness, her sorrow fueling the flood. Down on the ground, just beyond the edge of the platform, she found Edgar. One of the crowd, blending in as well as any, making no indication that he knew her.

"Attention, all!" shouted an official, walking to the front of the stage while holding his arms high. His shouts were thrown back in the strong wind.

"We give to you a *traitor!* An example of what speaking a doubtful word of the rightful heir your King has to the throne! Her blasphemies have cost her the life she cherishes!

"Know this! Any word muttered against the King will be punished the same! Gaze upon the horrible ending she has brought upon herself!" He looked back at her. Then keeping his volume for the crowd to hear, asked her a question.

"Cowardice woman! Do you have any regret in the false accusations you lashed out at our true King?"

Hellen remained quiet. She saw Edgar watching, then turned to look behind her. Still seated, waiting for an answer was the king. Comfortable in his own warmth, satisfied with the ending she was about to receive. Tears continued to fall.

Only in her mind did she know that her plans were complete. The trap she had set, using herself as the bait, were taken without hesitation by all they were intended for. For the king and his *sewer rat* were here, and not where they would have been to have foiled what went on in the castle. The careful placement of the cloth, the raising of suspicion in herself, the playing of mind games with those deemed too brilliant to challenge. They had all fallen for it. They had all taken the bait, and it was now that it would be completed. It was now that it would all end.

"Stelli!" Gracie called out, picking up a fresh custard pie from the local baker's shop. "Can we please have this for supper?" Stelli walked over to take a look at what Gracie was holding.

"Haha!" he chuckled. "We cannot have only *pie* for supper! But yes, I think something sweet would be a lovely way to brighten up our cold and gloomy day."

Gracie smiled, happy to have such an easy way to get sweets, and a caring friend to want to make her happy.

After a bit more browsing, Stelli paid the baker for the pie and the two of them took their leave out into the market streets.

They walked side by side, Gracie skipping across the broken lines between stones under her feet. The wind blew strong and cold as the snow raced down the alleyways.

"I have a surprise for you, Gracie..." Stelli said, breaking the silence between them.

"A surprise!" Gracie replied with a big smile, looking up at him. "What kind of surprise?"

"A guest! A visitor I have long awaited...someone very dear to me, whom I believe you will enjoy the company of."

"Who is it?" Gracie asked, curiously. But before Stelli could give his answers, the sound of bells came echoing down the streets. It grabbed the attention of all those around.

"What is that?" Gracie asked. Stelli's face drew concern as he gazed into the distance at the tall castle high up on the cliff.

"The castle bells..." he said, then looked down at Gracie. "The King is calling us all to the center market place." He looked around at the sudden shift of shoppers and shopkeepers unifying in a single direction.

"He has some announcement to make."

"Oh..." Gracie said, not wanting anything to do with the king. "I wonder what..."

"Well..." Stelli said, wanting to protect the innocent mind of his six-year-old friend, but also wanting to make sure she was prepared for what it could be.

"Hopefully nothing...but sometimes..." he looked down at her curious, timid face. "Sometimes it is not a pleasant thing for a little girl to watch..."

"But if we are supposed to go, should we not?" she asked.

"We should," he said with a sigh. "Stay close, little one. And if anything is frightening, you do not need to keep looking."

This warning put fear into Gracie's mind. For the first time since their meeting, she grew afraid of what Stelli was telling her. Her trust in him was being tested, and he became a source of protection unlike she had felt in him before. Closely, she followed him down the streets, around corners, and to the edge of a largely forming crowd.

As they approached the crowd, the cold wind continued to blow hard and carried large snowflakes off the angry sea. Their view of the center stage was blocked by the numerous people around them. Stelli struggled to see what they had setup.

Gracie stopped in her tracks, her head tilt down as though she was focusing.

"Stelli..." she said to him. Stelli stopped and looked down.

"Stelli...something is not right. This feels familiar," she said. She looked up at him with a puzzled face. "I...I have seen this before," she said, trying to figure out why this was all so familiar.

Stelli's head turned crooked, as though he himself was figuring out what she was saying. A look of fear fell over his face as he quickly looked up at the stage to see a woman, shackled and wearing too little in this cold weather, standing before a chopping block. A man was walking back and forth across the front of the stage, but what he was saying, they could not hear. Not over the strong wind.

Filled with fear, Stelli looked down at Gracie. Gracie's face moved from puzzled to sudden realization as she looked up to meet Stelli's eyes.

"My mama..." she said, tears filling her eyes. She darted towards the stage, screaming.

"Mama!!" she cried out, pushing strangers aside, thrashing in what ever way she could to get to the woman on the stage.

Stelli raced after her.

"Gracie no!" he called out, unable to catch up to the small child weaving through the dense crowd. But Gracie was too fast, able to move quickly, and she threw herself to the ledge of the platform.

"Mama!!" she cried out, tears fully flowing from her eyes, soaking her cheeks. The sudden sound of the child startled everyone on stage. Edgar, only a few feet away, suddenly looked at Gracie, having solved te mystery Hellen had carried. Hellen looked down at her child.

"Gracie!" she shouted, and felt a sudden wave of regret that her daughter was there to bear witness to her horrible ending.

"Kill her!" the king commanded, standing from his throne, pointing his finger at her. Edgar quickly moved, reaching for the six-year-old girl.

The executioner lifted his ax, following his king's orders. As he did, a whisper came rushing along with the wind. Faint words carried with the snow, and as the executioner's ax rose, the wind died. Snowflakes suddenly halted, nearly floating in their place. A hush fell over the crowd.

Hellen looked in fear at the man before her, who only then began to notice the odd change in wind. It was just enough oddity to cause him to pause for that brief moment, a hesitation as he held her end high in the grey sky.

As she stared at him, the world around paused except for one small change. At first, only the corner of her eye did she catch it. Something silver and small, followed by a wooden shaft, then a black feather. A single arrow cut through the still space between her and her executioner. Still in shock, they continued to stare at each other as the arrow followed its intended path across the stage, ending in a *thunk*.

Both Hellen and the man in front of her turned their heads to see where its landing had been made. Standing with his finger still pointing was the king with an arrow deep in his chest, his breath taken from him. He took a step back, losing his balance on the edge of his thrown, collapsing into his seat and looking down at the quiver sticking out.

Then a second arrow came, cutting through the same small space between Hellen and ax-bearer. But this arrow made a different marking. Just as ill-intended, but much more effective. Another loud *thunk* as the arrow cracked through the forehead of the king, just below the brim of his crown, pinning the back of his head to the wooden back of his throne.

Like an echo of the thud, the earth suddenly shook violently. The deafening rumble brought everyone to their knees, collapsing to the ground.

Hellen dove down to the floor of the stage. The wind suddenly roared being held back with such force by what ever spell had been spoken. The crowd fled in an intense panic as a wave of men spilled into the market place. Strange men all bearing the same armor. Armor with markings of a pale face. Men of an ancient time, unseen for centuries.

Their arrows sang in the wind, their blades cold steel and clashing against the guards of the Freeman Empire. But these guards were no match for the soldiers of Pale Faces. Though their numbers few, their mission was already accomplished.

Hellen crawled to the edge of the platform. Edgar had disappeared, scurried away to some place unseen. There, for the first time in months, she held her daughter's hands.

"Gracie, I am so happy to see you alive!" Hellen said with tears rolling down her broken cheeks.

"Mama!" Gracie cried back. "I have missed you so much, Mama!" They held each other in a loving embrace stronger than either one had ever felt. Quickly, Stelli approached, pausing only to let Gracie and her mother have this moment despite the urgency they were in.

"You must be her mother," he said. "Please! Come with us! I can help you!" he asked her.

Hellen looked at Stelli, unsure of the help of a stranger in this realm.

"It is okay, Mama, he is a nice man! He has taken good care of me!" Gracie promised. Hellen looked at Gracie, still crying with joy and relief. But in the back of her mind, she knew she was given a new chance. That this had happened for a reason, that she was meant to take this gift of time and use it not for herself. She knew she could not go with her daughter. Her voice began to crack, upset at what she had to do next.

"I cannot," she said. "Please, take her and make sure she stays safe," she said to Stelli. "When the dust settles, come find me. I am taking a very important person south. We will be in East Nýland within a few days. From there, we will be taking the White Mountain Pass into the Gronndelon. Please, come find us!"

"You have my word," Stelli said, wrapping his arms around Gracie to protect her from the chaos that swirled around them.

"Mama no!" Gracie called out, as Hellen began to release her hold on her hands.

"It is okay, Gracie! We will be together again soon! And in a much safer place! Please trust your new friend!" Hellen stayed on her knees as she crawled across the stage, keeping out of the flying arrows around her. As she reached the western edge of the platform, she rolled off and into the crowd where she disappeared.

"Come, child! This is no place for you to remain!" Stelli said, holding Gracie close as they made their way through the chaotic fighting and clashing of men.

That evening, Gracie and Stelli sat in his home with a fading fire. The custard pie they had bought earlier that day sat untouched on the table. Gracie had no appetite, for the emotions that had spilled out had robbed her of any desire for food. She sat there holding her doll, thinking nothing but being held again by her mother.

"Do not fret, dear child. Stelli is all packed and ready. We only need to wait for my guest to arrive. I am sure he will come with us too!"

Gracie remained quiet for a moment, anxious to leave so they could sooner be with her mother.

"Who is coming?" she asked. "Who are we waiting for?" she asked. Stelli smiled.

Thud thud thud! The knock on the door came sudden and loud.

"Ah-ha!" Stelli said, standing up in a hurry. "He has arrived!" He quickly made his way to the door and opened it. Gracie looked in anticipation.

"Ah! Brother!" Stelli shouted, wrapping his arms around a dark figure, cold wind blowing in from the late evening.

"Well, are you going to let me in or freeze out here?" his brother asked, not at all happy with the cold weather he found himself in.

"Come in!" Stelli said, leading his brother into his home. "It has been far too long since you last had a visit!" he said. His brother wore a dark cloak, the color unseen in the dim firelight of the house, and carried with him a tall staff of complex design, though also difficult to see.

As he dropped his hood, he revealed his face. Similar to Stelli he looked, his eyes opened wide and a pale blue. Markings over his face revealed he too was into the arts of unusual natures.

"My, my!" his brother said. "Who do we have here? I do not remember hearing word of a *daughter*, young brother! Though I must say..." he said, studying her face. Gracie grew uncomfortable, but his strangeness felt oddly familiar as the first time she met Stelli. He stood and looked at Stelli with a grin.

"She does not look a bit like you!"

"Oh, no!" Stelli replied. "She is only in my care...temporarily. Her name is Gracie! Her..." he paused for a moment, his voice moving from cheerful to serious.

"Her mother was a prisoner of the king...escaped recently as we had fallen under attack by an army I have not yet seen. They killed the king of these lands...and I am afraid we must leave. Tonight."

"Leave?" he asked. "But I only now arrived!"

"Yes! But her mother is headed south, making her way to the Gronndelon. We must take her there to meet with her on the road, as I gave my word I would."

"Interesting..." he replied.

"Of course, you are welcome to stay here if you are too weary from your travels..." Stelli teased.

"Bah! Too weary!" he looked at Gracie. "What a fool to think his older brother too weary to keep up. Ha! I think not! I am already packed! Let us head out tonight!"

"Good! We will gather our things and be ready within moments then!" Stelli answered.

His brother approached Gracie and knelt, his satchel sliding out from under his robe. Gracie stayed back, not giving any hint of approval.

"It looks like we will be road partners, little one..." he said to her quietly.

"Oh, where are my manners!" Stelli said. "Gracie, this is Luno. He is my brother."

"Nice to meet you, Gracie," Luno said, bowing his head a bit. His staff now leaning forward into the fire light, revealing the dragon-face carved into the top, holding no gem in its mouth at the moment. Gracie gave him a small smile back. Her anxiety began to wane now knowing they were readying to leave. And within moments, they had all of Gracie's things packed, and the last few items of Stelli's ready to go.

"Shall we take our custard pie?" Stelli asked Gracie, Luno waiting patiently by the door. Gracie looked at it, then nodded without saying a word.

"Good decision! I would hate to waste such a wonderful looking pie..." he said, carefully covering it up with a cloth and placing it at the top of his bag. "Let us hope it survives until we reach our resting place tonight!"

With that, the three walked through the door and into the young night. From within the home, the sound of the latch throwing echoed quietly through the empty room. The fire left to die on its own, and all the trinkets on all the shelves to rest untouched for many nights to come.

CHAPTER XIX

A QUEST SOUTH

— 1st of Winterhold, 1867 —

"To take a quest as noble as this
in a time of the most dire need
is to give us hope in all that is good
ere the birth of the end of our world."

These words of Lord Halldór echoed in Edlen's mind as they walked further from the edge of trees behind them. Words of encouragement, of recognition in the importance of their mission.

"To fail this quest is to fail the free world. To end in defeat, is to defeat all that is good and green."

Though only fragments of Lord Halldór's parting speech could be recalled in his memory, it were these lines that stuck out the most.

Such kindness was shown to him, and to Radholf and Oattiki. A kindness that was bittersweet to leave behind. Knowing he always had a home in Arboran, a never-ceasing welcome to the land of the Elves. But knowing they put their trust in him to help find their hope felt like an honor not deserved.

As they traveled out of the wood and into the valley between mountains, their surroundings brought a flood of emotional fear back to Edlen's heart. Though with the sun having just crested, the light of day changed this familiar place to one much less threatening.

It was not long before the warmth of the forest behind them lost its grip, and thick snowflakes whipped around in a frantic dance on the wind. The cold was a bitter reminder of his tragedy he faced upon the mountain side, the last place he had seen Sabrina fully alive.

As they continued to walk into the wind, the path before them began to turn to black. The snow blowing was dry and had little grip on the rocky surfaces around them. But before them, just off centered to the west on the road, sat a large mount of frozen dragon flesh.

"Here lies the beast of flame," Radholf spoke up. "Lay your eyes upon the trophy of the heir of Dragonsbane, and let the world know her fire has turned cold."

The three Elves that led the expedition approached the dead beast.

"I have only heard of such creatures in my father's tales, only have read about them in old pages," Camila spoke, gazing upon the mound. Snow lightly clung to the most extreme southern faces of scale and horn.

"A heroic accomplishment indeed," said Moli. Kaltag nodded in agreement.

Like his cousin, Camila, Moli was fair skinned, though little did any freckle show. His hair was straight and blonde, with only hints of a reddish tint.

He was tall, however, taller than any other in their party, and seemingly stretched thin in his arms and legs.

Kaltag was much older. His hair had begun to turn to silver with few hints of any red it may have had. His skin shown little worn, as it was still fair, and he was quite trim, though appropriately tall, only slightly taller than Radholf.

"Let us leave this beast behind. I would rather make it to Skydale before the cold really settles into my bones," Oatikki said, taking no moment to pause or glance at the dragon.

Edlen paused for a moment, not turning fully towards the dragon, but only looking at it with a turned head as he continued to follow Oatikki. It was dead enough for him, and he knew it would return not.

"You killed that creature?" Camila asked him as she caught up to him. Edlen gave a slight smile, though displeasure of the memory hid behind it.

"That is most impressive..." she said, smiling back at him. "I feel as though I would have froze up in fear should I have ever faced such a creature," she remarked, looking down at the stone road before them.

"You may still have your chance," Edlen replied, returning her humble compliments with a slight tease.

"You better be there with that sword of yours if I ever get caught up in an unfair fight such as that!"

Edlen smiled, feeling bashful of the attention he was getting from a pretty Elf of such high class.

"There will never be a need for that," Moli said as he approached from behind, interrupting their conversation. "Not as long as I can still grasp the hilt of *my* sword."

"I was unaware your sword also had blessings of our Elders to pierce the hide of a fully grown dragon!" Radholf spoke up from behind having listened to their entire conversation.

Edlen grinned as he smiled back at Radholf's support.

"But it is my duty to protect you, my lady," he said towards Camila with a bow of his head.

"And grateful I am of it! But as you can clearly see, Edlen has already taken care of the danger on this road," she said, smiling at Edlen.

This proved to be too much for Edlen to remain comfortable in, and so he quickened his pace to catch up to Oatikki to help take the lead.

"Don't care. Don't care to know," Oatikki said, keeping his focus on the road ahead.

"I know. I am only looking for some quiet," Edlen responded.

Oatikki gave a slight hint of a grin and exhaled through his nose forcefully, the biggest sign of amusement Edlen had ever seen in him.

As time went on, the wind continued to blow relentlessly cold. Though the snow was not heavy, it still proved to be quite the discomfort for travelers working their way south.

The mountain sides all around them were blanketed in white where permitted, with jagged black and grey rock faces piercing out in their own command. The sun was beginning to lose its influence of daylight through the chilling clouds on the valley they traveled, though haste had been made since their departure.

As the clouds eased off, the wind calmed, and breaks in the clouds began to reveal the dark violet skies dotted with icy-cold stars.

It was at this time they decided to stop for the night. They made a small shelter on the mountain side with some dead logs and large branches. Radholf got a warm fire going, and they rested their eyes and legs as best they could before setting out at dawn once more.

The day went on in much of the same haste. They wanted to reach Skydale before nightfall, as another night in the cold valleys did not sound comforting at all. But the day aged, and Edlen's mind swirled with sights of boulder after boulder, of an endless rocky road under another cloudy gray sky.

Soon the valley widened, and the sun sank deeper behind the mountains to their right. Moments later, they approached a familiar grove of leafless trees to the west.

"Do you wish to visit her?" Radholf said quietly at Edlen's side.

Edlen thought for a moment. Sabrina's death still brought too much regret for him to handle as a warm tear rolled down his cheek.

"Perhaps another time," Edlen said as he continued south.

"Who are they talking of?" Camila asked Moli, picking up on their conversation even from some distance behind.

"I am unsure," he responded. "I can only assume the loss of a close friend or loved one, whom now rests in this grove off to the side."

"I am going to go look," said Camila. Without a moment for Moli to answer, she disappeared silently into the shadows of the tall grasses that led to Sabrina's resting place.

Further south they continued until they finally arrived at their destination for the night. As they approached the Rolling Stone Inn, the warm fire light within glowed bright from under the front door.

Kaltag entered first, followed by Radholf and Edlen, then Oatikki. Behind them came Moli, and just as he was about to shut the door, Camila had finally caught up with the group.

"Good evening travelers, and welcome to the Rolling Stone," a man said in a half slumber, leaning back on the two back legs of his wooden chair, his feet up on a three-legged stool close to the fire place.

His hood covered most of his face, but a thin silver beard, well trimmed and pointed down from his chin bobbed up and down at any movement of his lips.

"Rooms are of your choosing tonight, as you are the only ones to have made it in from this cold," he said, leaning his head back to see who exactly had come in.

" Six of you, eh?" he said, sucking the last of his dinner from between his teeth. "Well! Should you be wanting six separate rooms then?" He stood from his chair and approached the group.

"That would suffice," Kaltag answered him, holding out several coins to pay for all six beds.

"Ah-ha..." said the man, accepting the payment and counting to ensure a complete amount was given.

"Well, like I said, choose any of the open rooms, as this place is now to yourselves..." he muttered as he dropped the coins into his pocket and returned to his chair, tipping it back to its previous position.

"We will take the three closest to the front," Radholf said to Kaltag. Kaltag nodded.

"My lady..." Moli said, holding his hand out towards the staircase, indicating a suggestion that she sleep upstairs. Camila gave a stern look in return.

"You have no one to impress here, Moli," she answered back. "My father's eyes cannot see this far. You do not need to watch over me like a doe her fawn."

Moli's face turned red with embarrassment as she walked past him, taking to the second floor on her own volition.

"I am only doing what your father sent me to do, Lady Camila," he answered.

"You were sent to help seek the answers we hunt," she said as she stopped midway up the stairs. "To help us find what once was at rest. Not to buzz around my head like a fly," she concluded as she turned, continuing up the stairs.

As her footsteps echoed on the wooden walkway that was opened to the large center room on one side, the five companions she left remained speechless, waiting for the slamming of her door. But Camila was not quick to anger, and so a gentle *click* of the latch was all that was heard of her.

"Well!" Radholf said, stretching his arms to break the awkward silence. "I sure could use a good night's rest! Come, Edlen, let us go and find our beds..."

Oatikki followed, passing Moli who remained standing at the foot of the steps, his mind working on the things Camila had just said to him.

"Don't let it eat away at you," Oatikki said to him as he passed by.

"Good night, Verndari," Moli said, breaking his heavy thoughts. And as the three Men found their rooms, Kaltag walked up and placed his hand on Moli's shoulder.

"Take the room at the top of the stairs. I will be on the far end," he said. Moli took a deep breath and climbed the stairs to the first room on the left where he entered for the night. And as Kaltag did the same, they left the owner alone in front of the warm fire, who had already began to doze off in a snore.

Edlen laid in his bed, staring at the wooden ceiling of his room as he had for the past several hours. He was once again restless, and found it difficult to shut his eyes to find peace.

Feeling worn from the constant tossing about in his bed, though comfortable it was, he got up and left his room to sit in the main hall of the inn.

As he approached the bottom of the stairs, he found the owner snoring loudly in the same chair as he had left him in. Edlen took a seat at a nearby round table.

The sound of the wooden chair scooting across the floor startled the owner awake.

"Boy!" he shouted as he was thrown forward from the settling of his tipped back chair. "My, you gave me a startle!"

"My apologies, innkeeper," Edlen replied. "I meant not to disturb your slumber."

"Oh, it is of no matter," he said as he found his way to the same table, weaving back and forth in his drowsiness.

"What keeps you up after a hard day of travel?" he asked Edlen.

Edlen took a deep breath, staring only at the wooden table before him.

"To be honest, I have not been able to sleep for many nights," he admitted. He looked up at the innkeeper, who sat quietly, listening.

"She still haunts me. The creature I slay many nights ago. Her face I see in my dreams and I cannot out run her."

The innkeeper was not sure what Edlen was talking about, but to give what support he could, he stroked his beard and nodded with concern.

"I am sorry," Edlen said. "I mean not to burden you with my own troubles."

"No need to apologize! I see quite some interesting characters come through here, many of them far more troubled I am sure than you are. Many who keep to themselves, as their presence is rather kept than shared with anyone else."

Edlen and the innkeeper sat quiet for a moment. The fire snapped loudly a timber of pine, which broke the silence.

"I need not to know the business of my guests, but if I can be of help, I am glad to offer what I can. Even if it is a simple ear to listen," he said kindly.

Edlen thought for a moment.

"Actually, there is something you may know. My fellow travelers and I...we are on a quest to find something. Perhaps you may have heard of a city we are searching for?" Edlen began to inquire.

"Perhaps! I have heard many tales from travelers passing by. By which name does your lost city go by?"

As Edlen took his breath in preparation for his answer, the blade of a knife came flying across the room and *thunked* into the table in front of him.

"Not another word!" Kaltag shouted from the balcony of the hall. He came quickly down the steps as Edlen sat back, watching him approach. Radholf emerged from his room, his hand on the hilt of his sword.

Kaltag furiously walked up and yanked his knife from the surface of the table. He pointed the tip of it straight at Edlen's face in a scolding manner.

"Say another word and I will remove you from this party," he said sternly.

The tip of Radholf's sword slowly came into Edlen's view, sliding on the edge of the knife, and lifting it up and away from Edlen's face.

"Threaten a brother of mine again, Kaltag, and I will remove any grasp of life that might be holding on to you."

"I will not risk the success of our quest because one member of our party couldn't keep his mouth shut," Kaltag answered back.

Edlen felt terrible at this remark. The feeling of pain in his heart ached as he felt irresponsible, as though he suddenly was more of a burden and threat than a help on their mission.

"Rhim! Our foretold salvation, or the city of Nocturnal!" Radholf said to the innkeeper, who was accustomed to the roughest cut of travelers finding his inn as the only place accepting of their kind. This outburst served only as entertainment to the keeper.

"There now," Radholf answered back to Kaltag. "Now there are two of us that cannot keep our mouths shut."

Kaltag scoffed at this, and headed back to his room on the second floor.

"Such ignorance and recklessness will be the downfall of our success!" he shouted in anger, not looking back before slamming his door shut.

"I am so sorry, Radholf," Edlen said, unable to look him in the eyes.

"Oh, do not shed a flake of worry about him! He has his own ways, where we have ours," Radholf replied, sheathing his sword and pulling up a third chair to the small round table.

"In-keeper!" Radholf spoke as he sat down and put his hands on the table, dropping a few coins in its center. "Do you have anything that might help ease a troubled mind and lead it to sleep?"

The innkeeper picked up the coins cheerfully and replied, "It's a bit strong, but I do have something that will knock you out!" He stood with a smile and went into a back storage room, returning with a tall, thin-necked clear bottle of a light brown drink.

As he placed three small glass cups on the table, he poured the strong-smelling spirits into each cup.

Radholf was the first to pick up his glass. He smelled it at first, but took a sip as the innkeeper sipped himself.

"Starlight in the heavens!" Radholf shouted, squinting his eyes as he placed it back down on the table. "That is strong stuff!"

"Ha-ha!" the innkeeper laughed. "Strongest drink you'll find in Festerling!"

"So, tell me, innkeeper," Radholf continued. "Have you an answer for my friend's question?"

"About your lost city?" he asked. Radholf nodded.

"I have only heard of the name of *Rhim* in old fairy tales, I am afraid. And no other name you mentioned has rung any bells," he said, looking Radholf in the eyes.

Radholf took another sip. Edlen held onto his glass, unsure if it was a good idea or not to take part in this.

"Very well!" Radholf replied. "So, what kind of folks do you usually get coming in here? Anything interesting happen recently?" Radholf asked, changing the topic.

"We have not had many guests of late, but most that do come in usually keep to themselves, and I tend to not share much of their happenings with others," the innkeeper answered, taking another sip of his stiff drink.

"Oh you must have at least one good story to tell us...we are in quite dire need of a good story!" Radholf continued, winking at Edlen.

After taking another sip, the innkeeper began to grin.

"Well, there was a time, oh, several months ago..." he began as he was trying to recall. "Ha-ha," he chuckled at the return of the memory.

"I had one man come in, looked pale as a ghost! He was a larger man, eyes glazed over. Came barging in here talking about seeing a dragon!" The innkeeper could barely contain his laughter at the absurdity of the story he was telling.

"A dragon! What nonsense!" Radholf said, laughing along.

Edlen found this to be peculiar, and did not know what Radholf had planned, but began to think perhaps his drink was beginning to take over his mind. And not entirely wanting to be there for this, feeling as though his struggles and night-mares were something to be laughed at, he lifted his glass to his lips.

Radholf, without ceasing his laughter along with the innkeeper, laid his hand gently on Edlen's forearm, hinting at his desire for Edlen to put the glass back down.

Edlen looked over at Radholf, who did not look back. But then he noticed Radholf's glass was still full.

"He swore he saw this giant flying beast soaring between the mountains!" the innkeeper continued, laughing and sweating from the commotion he was causing.

"So what did you do?" Radholf asked, tears in his eyes from the humor.

"I kicked him out to deal with his ghost-white self!" he replied, barely able to breath in between giggles. "I wanted nothing to do with a crazy drunk like that!"

Radholf appeared to take another sip of his glass, as both he and the innkeeper caught their breath and let the humor settle.

"You know..." the innkeeper continued. "I do recall hearing the word *Rhim* floating around about a week ago..." he took another sip, approaching the bottom of his glass. Then he continued.

"There were only two of them. They came in late one night much like you fine gents. Needed a place to stay, asking similar questions. I told them nothing as I know nothing...but they went on their way the next morning."

"Do you know which way they went?" Radholf asked gently. He was getting to the answers he knew the innkeeper had, but it took some time to get it out of him.

"They entered the city gates, but shortly after returned to the road south," he answered, emptying his glass between his lips.

"Thank you, friend. And thank you for this wonderful drink!" Radholf said, emptying his drink as a whole into his mouth, setting his empty glass on the table. Edlen's eyes opened wide in awe at the knowing he just completed his entire glass in one heavy gulp.

"Oh, my," the innkeeper yawned. "I really must make it to bed before my eyes shut completely!" He stood from his chair and carefully made his way to the back master room, and shut the door.

Radholf looked over at Edlen and smiled.

"...and we have our own ways," he said with a wink. Edlen smiled back, but his face quickly turned to deep thought.

"Radholf," he began, "why are we searching for Rhim? What salvation do they hold for us?"

Radholf took a deep breath, folding his hands as they rested on the table.

"We do not know what lies within the city, only that they are destined to save us. That is the truth we know."

"But how do we know?" Edlen asked.

"Through faith," Radholf answered simply. "Because we believe what the prophecies the Good King spoke of. That our salvation is found in Rhim."

"But what could it be? A weapon? An army? I find it difficult to be passionate about finding a lost city without knowing for myself what it is exactly we hunt for," Edlen admitted.

"The truth is what we hunt for," Radholf answered. "It is dangerous to guess at what we cannot see. By doing so, we try to twist the truth into what we desire. This is the opposite of faith. Because if we set expectations for truth, it becomes not the truth. It becomes a falsity we search for.

"And then when the truth stands before us, and our minds are already expecting something else, here, two things can happen. Either we cast down the truth as being false, a mistruth, and we miss it entirely. Or we become angry at it and do not accept it, because it was not what we hoped it to be."

Radholf picked up Edlen's still full glass of drink and walked over to the fireplace.

"Both of these paths lead to conflict. Torn between what is true and what is not. These conflicts lead to wars. Wars bring to us death," he said as he tossed the liquid into the fire, which erupted in furious flame, flashing a bright yellow light to fill the room for a short moment.

"Do not fabricate your own version of truth," he said as he returned the glass to the table in front of Edlen. "It will not bode well for any."

He walked to the door of his room, but before entering, turned and looked back at Edlen.

"Try to get some rest, Edlen. We have some men to track down in the morning," he ended with a smile, then entered his room and quietly shut his door.

Edlen sat at his table for a few moments in solitude. He listened to the crackling fire, falling entranced in its dance of orange light that filled the room. He took a deep breath, ready to battle the nightmares that waited for him on the other side of sleep.

But as he was ready to stand from his chair, he heard the *creeaak* of a door on the second floor. Light footsteps followed, and he did not need to turn around to know who was coming.

Camila approached Edlen and took the seat next to his, and leaned into the table, putting her forearms on the edge.

"You cannot sleep either?" she asked, looking over at him with only her green eyes.

"Not for some time," he answered.

She nodded.

"This adventure we have started, it is my first time leaving home with such a small party," she admitted, hinting at some doubt and possible fears on her mind.

"Sadly, it is not my first. Nor does it seem as dangerous as my previous endeavors," he replied in hopes of giving her some peace about their quest.

"I still feel though as I am being watched over like a child..." she said, looking back at Moli's room.

Edlen watched her glance in disapproval.

"You do know," he continued, "that you should only be who you want to be."

"What do you mean?" she asked, taking slight offense with her tone.

"Your father only loves you, and wants to make sure you are well taken care of," he answered.

"Yes, but does he have to send along my own bodyguard to watch my every move?" she asked, feeling frustrated.

"You are very precious to him," Edlen answered. "To lose you would be devastating to many, and not just your family," he said. She smiled as she took this as a compliment.

"And I know he wants you to be safe," Edlen continued. "But not doing what your father wants will prove nothing. If what he wants is not what you want, it does not mean that the opposite is what you are meant to be either."

Camila sat, listening to Edlen's advice, surprised in how insightful it was.

"You have no one to prove you are brave, Lady Camila," he said with respect. "Just be who you are, and I refuse to believe a beautiful flower such as yourself is as audacious as you are trying to prove to Moli," he ended, "or whomever else may be watching."

Camila was in full smile at the politeness and flattery Edlen had given her. She leaned in, wrapping her arm around his shoulders, and gave him a light kiss on the cheek.

"Thank you, Edlen," she said. "Your words are very kind, and mend a troubled heart."

She stood from her chair, satisfied with this being the conclusion of their brief conversation.

"I bid you a good night, and do hope your troublesome dreams take their leave," she said.

Edlen smiled, his face still blushing from the light kiss, his cheek still warm from the touch of her lips.

"I think they might tonight," he said with a half smile.

As Camila headed up the stairs to her room, she paused for a brief moment at the top to glance back down to Edlen over the banister, giving him one last smile as a memory for the night, then disappeared into her room.

Edlen returned to his room, and for the first time in many nights, slept undisturbed by any hauntings of his recent past.

Thunk-thunk-thunk! "Good morning, Edlen!" Radholf's sudden awakening of Edlen's deep sleep jolted him out of bed.

"We must begin our hunt, and there is no time for late-sleepers!" Radholf added as he headed across the main room on the first floor.

Edlen readied his things, and strapped Dragonsbane on to his waist. Having such a sword by him always brought the comforting memory of his father with it. And although he hoped he would never need to use it again for its intended purpose, he felt a sense of unaccounted strength knowing what it was capable of.

As Edlen emerged from his room, he found Oatikki standing by the fireplace, taking his last bites of a lamb leg for his breakfast. Radholf was tying up his pack, which was placed on a table near the exit, and Moli and Camila were sitting at one of the round tables, quietly finishing their breakfast of sliced fruits and tea they had brought from Arboran.

"Where is Kaltag?" Edlen asked as he approached Radholf.

"Oh, he felt he could better investigate the Festning market *without* our assistance..." he answered, giving Edlen a sarcastic look of disapproval.

"But you better grab some breakfast for yourself before it becomes too late!" Radholf added.

"Without us..." Edlen said, suspicious of the divergence their group was beginning to form. "I suppose he has lost some confidence in us after our openness with the innkeeper."

"Ha-ha!" Radholf responded. "I am quite certain he has a lowered opinion of our ways...but I certainly am not bothered by that," he said with a smile. Edlen smiled back.

Following Oatikki's lead, Edlen found a second lamb's leg still warm from the morning roast to be quite satisfying, and joined Oatikki by the fire.

"Radholf tells me of your findings last night," Oatikki spoke up. Edlen nodded.

"Two men we must now find along with Rhim. Certainly makes the hunt more interesting," he said.

"Do you believe Rhim will hold some aid in the coming of night?" Edlen asked him.

Oatikki nodded with a mouth full of meat.

"Either hold aid, or *be* of aid," he said, taking the last bite of the leg, then tossing the bone into the fire place.

"But if it is meant to protect the good of this world, then I will protect *it*. I hope you are willing to do the same," he said, placing his hand on Edlen's shoulder as he stepped away.

"I am," Edlen answered as he watched Oatikki's long black braid sway left and right with each step.

"Good!" Oatikki grunted, echoing through the main hall, and giving Moli quite the startle.

As Edlen took his first few bites of breakfast, the door rattled and creaked open. The cold winter's morning wind blew in strong with light dusts of snow swirling in.

Kaltag took a few steps in, his scarf covering his face, but his long hair draped over his shoulders.

BAM! He slammed the door shut quickly to keep the warmth of the inn from escaping, then lowered his scarf.

"Well, look who came back!" Oatikki said in mockery. "Find anything in your snooping about?"

Kaltag's face rejected the mockery, and showed great concern. Not wanting to deal with the sarcasm he was receiving from the Orc, he turned his attention to Radholf.

"I spoke with the guards of the market, and they confirmed what your innkeeper friend has told you." Kaltag began explaining with a very serious tone.

"There, see! I knew we could trust him!" Radholf replied.

"The guards told me they were from Nýland, of the Freeman Empire."

The room fell silent. Edlen stopped his chewing, and all eyes were on Kaltag.

"How can you be sure?" Radholf said, his face turning quite concerned.

"I questioned this too, and searched further for proof. These men were low on supplies, and their money, it holds no value here. So, I tracked down the one place they were able to make exchanges.

"Waking the store owner, I managed to bargain with him the same things these two men had bargained with," he said as he pulled out a long red fabric.

As he laid the red cloth on the table in front of him, it became clear it was a velvet-red cape with the grizzly bear symbol embroidered on the back.

Edlen approached the dreadfully red memory that laid before him. The last time he had seen such a cape, the wearer had a fully drawn arrow pointed as his father.

"Yes, that is certainly the Freeman Empire," said Radholf, aware of Edlen's approach. "And a cape of this magnificence could only belong to one type of man..."

Edlen, standing at the table's edge and not able to break his stare, answered,

"The Colonel."

CHAPTER XX

OF DREAMS AND VISIONS

— 29th of Frostfare, 1867 —

The cold wind blew hard down the stony road that night. The snow felt heavy being fed off the sea from their backs, and the Western Mountains to their left loomed in the dark, ominous clouds. No warmth could be kept in, and it proved to be a real test for young Gracie to continue in such harsh conditions.

The trust she had built up in Stelli was truly being tested, as she did not entirely trust Luno yet. But to follow them in the dark of night surrounded by the swirling confusion of wind and icy snow demonstrated well her desires to see her mother again.

She would go through anything to be held in her mother's arms once more. And even in a time as dark as she had come from, the shadows of a foreign land held no intimidation in her mind, as it was her mother that occupied all thought.

"How much further must we trek through this frozen storm, brother?" Luno shouted through the winds. "We have been on the road for hours now!"

"Another hour before we make it to Cloverfield, I am afraid!" Stelli answered. He looked down at a paling Gracie, shivering and weak.

"My dear! How are you holding up?" he asked her.

"I am cold," she answered with a wavering voice.

"Try to hold on," Stelli encouraged her. "We are almost there, dear child!"

"Here!" Luno shouted, reaching into his satchel and pulling out a very dark gray stone. He stopped in the road and pulled the white gem from the mouth of his staff. Inserting the stone into the dragon's mouth, he tapped the bottom of his staff hard against the cold ground.

Several sparks shot out from where the stone and the dragon's teeth met, and the stone began to glow orange.

Luno removed the stone and handed it to Gracie.

"Hold onto this, little girl," he said. "Keep it close to you, it will give you warmth well until we arrive at our destination."

Gracie took the stone, which was not hot as the glow would warn, but gave a soothing warmth that bled out slowly. It was also much lighter than she had anticipated, and she kept it cupped in both of her hands, which quickly brought back a soothing feeling.

As the night drug on, so did the brothers with their little companion. They saw no one else on the road that night, for no one wanted to brave the snow that lashed out in anger through the night.

It was certainly a night that would have been better spent bundled up in a warm wool blanket, sitting in front of a crackling fireplace with a hot cup of tea. Protected from the wind, from the sharp cold, from the biting frost that drains the warmth from one's soul.

And draining it was, for their pace had slowed quite a bit since their beginning. Gracie's tummy rumbled in hunger, her eyes heavy as they struggled to fight the late hours. The warmth of Luno's stone kept her body warm, but her legs ached in the cold, and her face chapped in the wind.

Despite Stelli's anticipated time remaining on the road, their arrival at Cloverfield came a few hours later.

The town was of average size. The first busy town south of Kathlon, whose fame was born from the large meadery that gave this town its wealth. The lands between the town and the foothills of the mountains to the east were vast, open fields of clover and flowering grasslands.

On the east side of the town is where the honey hives were kept. Large, silo-shaped structures lined the entire eastern edge, providing a home to millions of summertime bees. But at this time of the year the hives were covered with large linens stuffed with straw to keep the deadly cold out of the hive.

As the three travelers entered the town from the north, they could see these covered stacks in a never-ending line southward. Their presence in the night was almost startling, especially to outside visitors. Like resting beasts lying dormant in the winter wind, it seemed any disturbance to their slumber would awake them in a raging fit.

But as Stelli led on, the first of the town's buildings hid these ominous structures from sight, giving a sense of protection and relief to weary, wandering thoughts.

"Here! Here is the inn!" Stelli shouted in the harsh wind.

As he approached the doors, he grabbed onto the handles and pushed hard, opening the wooden doors to a small, dimly lit room. As soon as Gracie and Luno entered, Stelli shut the door and made sure it latched tight.

"My!" Stelli said, shivering off the snow sticking to his cloak. "What a horrid night to be out!"

"I should say so!" a voice called out as a large man entered from some back room behind the counter. The rest of the room laid quiet and empty.

"What in the West would have possessed your mind into taking a dear child out in this weather?" he asked, looking at Gracie, who stood hiding behind Stelli, still wrapped in the warmth she was holding onto.

"What indeed!" Luno remarked, giving a sneering look at Stelli as he stepped passed him, removing his hood from his head.

"We are meeting a woman here, she is expecting us," Luno said to the man behind the counter. Luno looked around the room, noticing its emptiness.

"Or at least that is what I was told," he added, looking back at Stelli.

"A lone woman you say?" the man asked.

"She may be with others," Stelli added. "This is her daughter, and they very much need to return to each other," he said.

The man behind the counter made no movement. He stared at Stelli, studying him. Then he moved his focus to Luno, trying to make some decision.

"I am afraid there is no one here of your description," he answered. "You must leave, for we have no more room."

"Ha-ha!" Luno laughed in mockery, his laughs echoing down the halls leading away from the small center room.

"No resident fits our description...of a *woman*? And yet your establishment is completely full? Of what!"

"Do you intend, my dear innkeeper," Stelli began as he approached the counter next to Luno. "To tell me that every single room here is filled with only men? If so, I must ask you to beg of us your pardon and rid us of your foolery."

The man put both hands on the counter and leaned forward, making direct eye contact with Stelli. Even in his posture, he towered over either of them by nearly a foot, and his blond hair that covered his knuckles were visible even in the low light of the room.

"Make any attempt at an insult of me or my name, I care not," he said, then directed his staring to Luno. "But you will not disturb any guest of mine."

Scoff! Luno snickered. He took a step back to center himself in the room, then looked at Gracie.

"Little child, what is the name of your mother?" Luno asked Gracie.

Gracie stared at Luno, then looked at Stelli for permission to answer, as Stelli was still the only one she trusted in the room, however much it was still being tested. Stelli gave a slight nod of his head.

"Hellen," she answered.

"Hellen!" Luno yelled, staring straight at the large man as a challenge to his commands. "Hellen! Come and receive back your child!" he continued.

"That does it!" the man said, jumping clear over the counter. Luno startled, stumbling back towards the door with a grin of enjoyment to have so easily angered the man.

The innkeeper quickly grabbed Luno by the cloak and held him tight with his left hand. Then pulling back his right, he formed a boulder of a fist, ready to fracture the face of the rude stranger.

"Stop!" a voice called out from the hallway closest to Gracie. There stood Ronan, his hand on the hilt of a sword, his face still covered in bruises and wounds.

"Give me your names," Ronan commanded.

"I am Stelli," Stelli answered first. "and this is Gracie, daughter of Hellen, who has been in my care for some time."

Ronan looked over at Luno, who was still being securely held in the keeper's grasp. Luno stared back for a moment, his thoughts still catching up after expecting a harsh beating, but realizing it was put on hold and may be prevented all together.

"Oh, I am Luno," he answered, breaking his stare, returning his attention to the innkeeper.

"Luno..." Ronan said, approaching the wizard. He looked him up and down, then looked at the innkeeper to give permission to release him.

The innkeeper scoffed at this, having been worked up and ready, found it difficult now to extinguish the fires that had built up inside himself.

Luno patted himself down to unwrinkle his cloak, then stared at Ronan, trying to figure out why he was being inspected so closely.

Ronan looked over at Stelli for a moment, then gave his conclusion.

"You two are brothers, are you not?"

"Yes!" Stelli answered. "Do you know where we may find this child's mother?"

Ronan gave one last look at Luno.

"We were expecting only one of you with Gracie, and we needed to make sure she was not being hunted by an enemy."

"We are only friends, Luno and myself. Never a foe to any friend of Gracie, or her mother," Stelli answered.

"Very well," Ronan said. "Follow me, Gracie..." he said, holding out his hand. "Let me take you to your mother," he added, smiling at her in kindness.

Gracie's face lit up. As she revealed herself from her cloak, she handed Luno back his magic stone and took Ronan's hand.

As Ronan took his first few steps, his strength began to fail him, and his left knee collapsed. He stumbled, grabbing onto the side wall for support with his free hand, still holding onto Gracie's with the other.

Gracie looked up at him, concerned and frightened that something may be seriously wrong.

"Forgive me, Gracie. My strength has not yet come all the way back to me," he said, standing upright as best he could.

Gracie looked back at Stelli for a final confirmation. Ronan was still a stranger to her, and although his face was of compassion, she still held reservations to go alone with him. Stelli, seeing her look back, followed closely behind.

As they passed several doors, they came to one that was cracked open. Ronan pushed it open slowly. It revealed a candlelit room glowing orange, and the first sights Gracie saw was that of two beds and a large table on the opposing wall. Sitting upon the first bed, waiting anxiously for her, was her mother Hellen.

The sight of her daughter brought a flood of tears from her eyes. She gasped for breath at the sudden impact of emotion, leaping up from the bed, her arms stretched out.

"Mama!" Gracie shouted as she bolted towards her mother, leaping into her arms.

"My little Gracie..." her mother said, barely able to speak through the rasp in her voice. She smothered her daughter, completely encasing her in a tight hug. For the first time since the day Eldor was killed, they were able to embrace one another without chains, without bondage. Without any foul eyes or darkened hearts near by, they were finally able to be together freely.

"My child," Hellen began, holding Gracie by the shoulders to inspect her. "How have you been so well taken care of?"

Gracie looked up at her mother, her eyes wide and filled with tears. Her nose ran and her cheeks had grown rosy. Sniffling, she briefly looked back at the three men standing in the doorway.

"Ma'am..." Stelli began, stepping forward. "Your Gracie has been under my care since the day I found her in the market. The day I presume was your arrival to the Kingdom."

"How can I ever repay you for giving my child such safety and well-care? How can I ever thank you enough?" Hellen asked, still struggling to keep her breaths controlled.

Stelli shook his head, waving his hand in front of him. Fighting back tears himself, he denied any offer of repayment.

"Your little one has brought much joy to Stelli's life," Stelli said, feeling overwhelmed with emotion. "Just having her with me the past couple of months has been the best gift I could have asked for."

Hellen smiled, still wiping tears from her cheeks, and held Gracie tight once more.

"Gracie!" Eira shouted as she came running around the corner from the second room in the back.

"Gracie, you made it!" she exclaimed excitedly.

With Eira came Bard, who was shy at first to meet so many new faces, and knew the reunion of Hellen and her daughter needed an appropriate time to happen.

"Hi, Eira," Gracie said, smiling at her.

"Thank you for lending me your mother!" Eira said to her, smiling.

Gracie looked up at Hellen, confused.

"A story for another time," Hellen answered. "Gracie, this is Bard," Hellen said, holding out her hand towards the husky boy still hiding in the shadows.

"Hello, Gracie! I have heard much about you!"

"Bard here is a great baker! And very friendly..." Hellen said to Gracie.

"And this is Ronan," Eira interrupted. She was very excited to have another girl near her age to befriend officially, now that they were no longer in captivity.

"He's real important," she added with eyes wide, nodding her head slightly.

"Let us not speak of such things here," Ronan said, giving his concern to the group.

"Oh?" Luno inquired, suspiciously. "And why is that?" He leaned into Ronan close, trying to break any barrier of lies in an attempt to uncover some malicious nature.

"We do not know who may be listening..." Ronan answered. "Or where others in this room may be from?" Ronan stood his ground, pure in intention, questioning Luno's reason for being there.

"Hee-hee! You need not to worry where *I* come from!" Luno snickered at Ronan's suspicion.

"Still though," Hellen continued, "we would like to know who you are, and why you are here."

Luno's face fell to shock as he felt singled out, as though he was some ill-intended and unwelcome guest.

"He is my brother," Stelli explained. "His home is in Skydale in the Rhim Mountains far to the East."

"Well, seeing as you do not appear to be a threat to us, dear Luno, then welcome to our party," Hellen answered.

"*Scoff!* Some *party*. It is as though you are running like fugitives of the Kingdom!"

The room fell silent as all eyes fell upon Luno at the truthful accusation. Luno's eyes widened at the sudden realization of his words.

"Oh, ha-ha! You do not need to fear me!" Luno said, laughing. "I am unwelcome in most Kingdoms myself! If from guards and soldiers you run, I would likely join you in the flee!"

Ronan stared at Luno with disapproval, but he was in no situation to deny Luno a welcoming to their group.

"I am curious though, brother," Stelli began. "What took you so long to get here? You were supposed to arrive in mid-autumn!"

"As were my intentions!" Luno defended. "However, it happened to be that my recognition was had in Brisrun and I was taken captive."

"What did you do in Brisrun that called for your imprisonment?" Ronan questioned him.

Luno smiled and tapped his staff on the ground. The white gem within the dragon's mouth lit up briefly before flickering and quickly fading. Luno shook his staff, trying to get the light to return to his gem.

"So, you are a wizard?" Hellen asked.

"Not a very good one it seems..." Ronan added. Luno scoffed at this remark, unable to return the gem to its vibrant glow.

"I was kept in Brisrun for only a few days before I met the most interesting group. A man and his young friend were both in the prison. But it was not long before their ugly Orc friend came and released them against the will of the guards.

"Of course, they would not have made it without *Luno's* help!" Luno continued. "We escaped the prison and made our way into the wild."

"What were their names?" Ronan asked, questioning every aspect of Luno's story.

Gracie yawned long, resting a very content and happy face on her mother's chest.

"Let us continue our stories in the morning, shall we? I think we could all use some much needed rest," Hellen said, most concerned about the well-being of her dear child.

"Hmmm," Ronan muttered, watching a very tired Gracie shut her eyes. "Yes, let us all get a well-needed rest," he said.

"Stelli, Luno, you may take the beds here in this room. Bard and myself will be in the left room, and Hellen may take her dear child to the right. Eira, you may join Hellen as would be most appropriate."

"Yes, sir," Eira said politely followed with a yawn.

"Thank you, Ronan, for protecting us so well," Hellen said, placing her left hand on his shoulder while still holding Gracie with her right.

"Anything for a sister of the Gronndelon," he said with a smile.

As Ronan headed towards the back room, he stopped and made sure all guests were settling in comfortably. Stelli and Luno began unpacking only what they needed for the night, which was very little.

"Keep a close eye on the hall, and a listening ear for anyone who may be looking for us," Ronan requested of the two brothers.

"Stelli is a light sleeper..." Stelli answered. "Not a mouse can scamper by without my knowing of it!"

Luno said little, giving no acknowledgement to Ronan's request. He simply collapsed hard into his bed, which was the closest to the door.

Ronan nodded at Stelli and took the rest of the night in his shared room with the baker boy.

And before Stelli was quite in bed, Luno blew out his candle and the room fell dark.

"What bothers you, brother?" Stelli asked in the dark as he found his way into bed.

Luno gave a deep sigh.

"I have missed you, and we have not spoken in years, and now that we are alone you only give me a deep breath?"

"It has been a long journey, little brother," Luno spoke quietly. "A very long journey."

Stelli thought quietly for a moment.

"Does it bother you that we are here helping these strangers? That you had little time to rest when you most expected it?" Stelli asked.

"No, it does not bother me to help strangers. I have spent the past few months doing just that! No, it is more of what I have seen that has me down. No trust in anyone. Here I lay with a heart intended to help, and I am questioned as though I scheme to gain something just for myself.

"But little brother, I do share your passion to help strangers, now. I had become fond of this young man on my journey, and I find he is on my thoughts often throughout the day. But I left him in the care of others. Perhaps I miss him, like a father should miss a son."

Stelli remained quiet and listened to his older brother talk in ways he had never heard before. He enjoyed hearing what was on his heart, and smiled at each thought in the dark Luno shared.

"Let us get our rest, Luno," Stelli said. "A restful heart can mend itself much easier."

Hellen laid in her warm bed with Gracie at her side. The room was dark and quiet, the howling of the wind outside whispering through the cracks of the window.

Concealed in darkness, a figure stopped just at the edge of the window, peering within. Only for a moment did the figure pause, then passed by the window quickly. Hellen watched intently, fear taking over her.

Footsteps came, down the hall, into the entrance. Nobody else seemed to hear them. Nobody else seemed to be around. Hellen continued to watch the door to her room, waiting for the dark figure to appear.

Like games from an illusion, her focus was intensely trying to figure out if her eyes were actually seeing what her mind expected them to see. Wisps of shadow leaned into the door, watching her watch them, then blurred as they quickly retreated. Like a haunting of something unknown, in her heart she could feel his presence. Her hunter, and she held tighter the dear child she cherished.

The dark shadow suddenly appeared at her bedside. Edgar's evil grin was the only thing she could see in the night. Overtaken by fear, she tried to scream, but not a squeak was heard. She forced a scream as hard as she could, but fear had taken a strong hold around her throat.

A shadowy hand reached out to Gracie, ready to yank her from Hellen's arms. It whispered to her, "Hellen...".

Panicked, she clenched her fist tight and pulled it as far back as she could. Again, the haunting shadow whispered to her, "Hellen..."

Screaming, she threw her fist at the figure, hitting it dead center in the face.

The sudden pain in her knuckles woke her from her nightmare, and found the room to be well-lit with a dull morning light coming in from the window. On the floor was Stelli, rolling around with his hands over his face, grunting in pain.

"Oh, my dear Stelli! I am so sorry!" Hellen shouted as she leapt from her bed. Gracie rolled over and rubbed her eyes.

"What a throw!" Stelli said, cupping his nose as a thin stream of blood dripped out, sitting up from the floor.

"I did not know it was you, dear Stelli!" Hellen said, feeling very terrible.

"Oh, no need to worry! I should have known better to wake you that close!" Stelli admitted. He looked at his hands to see what kind of damage he had taken.

"This will clear up on its own soon," he added. "But I came in to tell you that breakfast is ready, should you or Gracie be hungry. Everyone else is up and mostly eaten, but I did not want you two dears to miss any!"

"That is very kind of you," Hellen said with a smile, still worried about his nose.

"Ha-ha! Ronan even advised against waking you for this very reason! He said it is never a good idea to startle a mother out of sleep who has recently received her child back."

"Again, I am very sorry," Hellen apologized once more.

"Hee-hee! That *was* quite a hit!" he said, standing to his feet, taking his leave from the room.

Hellen looked around the room and was relieved to have woken up in the same peaceful room as she had fallen asleep in. A peace that her nightmare had failed to rob her of. She looked down at Gracie, who was still struggling to wake.

"Gracie..." she said, rubbing her daughter's back.

"Mmmmm..." Gracie muttered. The night prior had been long and late, and very exhausting on both her body and emotions.

"Come, Gracie, breakfast awaits us," Hellen spoke softly. The smell of sausage and potatoes came drifting into the room as Stelli had left their door open. The commotions of breakfast chattering could be heard from the main room.

"You mean to tell me you were in a battle with an actual dragon?" Ronan asked Luno, who sat at the large round table in the center of the room with an empty plate, leaving only a few crumbs scattered across the middle.

Hellen and Gracie walked in, and this question alone grabbed Hellen's attention immediately. She sat down to join the storytelling. Bard handed her a plate of food, filled enough for both her and Gracie.

"Oh, yes!" Luno answered. "It was quite the battle! A nightmare I hope to never relive! But it took most of the refugees, bathing them in its terrible fire. This, I did not witness as they waited for us at the end of the road.

"As the dragon found them, it screamed its flames at them. We also lost a brother of one of our companions. It was at this time we decided to flee."

"Where did you run?" Ronan continued to ask. All attention was on Luno.

"The dragon reached for us, trying to grasp onto Sabrina and the Orc. But Edlen stepped in to protect her."

Hellen choked at the mention of Edlen's name. She spat bits of potato across her side of the table, struggling to breath. Luno stared at her with a face of concern.

"Edlen??" she spoke out. Gracie looked up at her mother, then looked at Luno with hope. Eira handed Hellen a cup of water, which she cleared her throat with.

"Who is this Edlen you know?" Hellen asked with excitement, tears beginning to form in her eyes.

"Oh, he was a young man, somewhere around thirteen or fourteen years of age," Luno answered. Hellen's tears began rolling down her cheeks.

"He had a dragon sword with him too...a friend of Radholf's," Luno continued.

Hellen choked with an emotion of joy, holding back her crying. Her eyes had turned a watery red, and she could not stop smiling.

"Radholf found him?" she asked.

"That is what I was told!" Luno answered. "Should I assume you know Edlen and Radholf?"

Hellen's happiness had now gotten the best of her. Gracie continued to watch her mother.

"This man knows Edlen?" Gracie asked.

Hellen nodded, unable to speak, with a smile as wide as she had smiled in a very long time.

"Where is he?" Gracie asked, anxious to see her brother again. "Is he okay?"

"Oh, he is more than okay!" Luno said, now piecing together that Edlen was Hellen's son, and very excited about this happening to meet.

"Radholf and the Orc were leading him to Arboran for safety. We uh..." Luno paused for a moment, trying to pick up his story where he left off.

"We were separated for a while though, after the incident with the dragon. Edlen and this Sabrina girl ended up in a series of caves deep in the Rhims. It was much to my surprise though, to find them wandering the markets of Festning outside Skydale.

"Edlen was with a half-giant named Kuoni, who apparently knew Radholf from some time ago. They had with them Sabrina, who was badly injured. Unfortunately, she did not make it."

The room fell silent as Luno's story sunk deep into everyone's minds. Then he continued.

"I decided to go with him, he and Kuoni that is, to see to it that Edlen made it to Arboran as that is where Radholf was headed. Though on our road north, we ran into the same dragon. She had been hunting us, and finally caught up.

"We found ourselves in quite a situation! Edlen had been cornered by the dragon, but it was difficult to see through the flames."

Hellen's face had turned to horror, hearing what her son had gone through.

"And yet, he stood his ground! Not fire, nor tooth took your boy down! And within moments, the fires died. The beast laid slain on the roadside, and there stood Edlen with his dragon sword in a swirl of ash. Not a scratch or burn on him."

"Where is he now?" Hellen asked, anxious to know that Edlen was safe. And although it seemed dangerous to hope, the thought of being reunited with her son did not seem entirely impossible.

"Well, we did make it to Arboran, but..." Luno continued. Hellen grew worried again.

"It is a long story," Luno admitted, feeling a bit overwhelmed at this point and quite unsure of where to start, so he left out many details and explained what conclusions he had heard.

"The Elves, along with Radholf and his friends, believe that the ancient city Rhim has suddenly appeared again. I cannot tell you the details of why, but I am not entirely in doubt of this myself."

"Rhim?" Ronan asked, wanting to believe the tales of old and the prophecies of his ancestors.

"I know!" Luno shouted, spreading his hands out in disbelief. "But with the reappearance of the dragon, and this gem Edlen had found on Sabrina, and the questions, the banishment from Skydale, it all makes sense!"

Luno had obviously skimmed over some very important details, but no one at the table would question what they all were hoping to be true.

"So, the Elves sent a search party to look for the lost city. Of that party, Edlen was one of."

Hellen sunk into her seat, proud of the role her son had now took on, yet the worry of his well-being still rested heavy on her mind.

Ronan sat listening to the storytelling, staring down at the silverware they had placed before them. The end of the spoon that sat before him had a familiar design on it. His fingers ran down the spoon, feeling the designs that swirled back and forth before he was suddenly reminded of a long lost memory.

He fingered the metallic swirls on his father's crown that hung heavy from his hands. Six men approached the large cart draped with golden tassels and red velvet cloth. They carried with them an oak casket with carvings of symbols and swords. As they pushed the casket into the cart, Ronan's uncle walked up next to him.

With tears rolling down his cheeks, he looked up at his uncle and held out his father's crown. As Ronan was only nine years old, he was too young to take the throne of Furskarth. Therefore, his uncle would be taking his place as second in line as heir.

"Keep it," he answered as he placed a smaller silver crown upon his head. "You will be needing it some day."

"But I do not know to be a Jarl," Ronan said, his eyes still filled with tears. He looked ahead at his father's casket being secured down.

"You may shadow me if you would like," his uncle said, placing his hand on Ronan's shoulder. "I would be happy to help guide you to Jarl-hood."

With that, he climbed onto his horse, ready to follow the cart down Ravenrun Road to Brisrun for the Grieving March.

"Uncle Sigurbjorn," Ronan called out. His uncle paused for a moment, looking back. Ronan wiped his tears, trying to keep his vision clear, but saying nothing.

"Get your horse, young Ronan. It would only be proper for you to follow behind," Sigurbjorn said.

"—So, you know of my past, but let us hear of yours, *Ronan*," Luno said with a sarcastic end to his sentence. He did not very much care for Ronan at this time due to the amount of doubt he had received.

"Well, I am Ronan, son of Rannver," he answered. "I had been taken captive by King Gunvald of the Freeman Empire, and used as a leverage for his taking over of the Gronndelon.

"You see, my uncle, Sigurbjorn, is the current Jarl of Furskarth. When the King came to him with a deal to release me under the signing of his *treaty*, that gave King Gunvald all the power over the Gronndelon."

"But there is something more..." Hellen spoke up. "I found Ronan in the dungeons of Gammal Keep. It was a fateful day, indeed, for I had kept within me a hatred for the King, and had committed in my mind plans that day to kill him.

"But instead, after discovering Ronan in those dark dungeons, I took it upon myself to uncover the truth of his being there. And for weeks I searched, planned, and listened. Until I found my way into the King's private collection," Hellen continued.

"It was here I found a parchment, generations old, of a lineage of Kings of Nýland, laying out the true claims to the throne. But hundreds of years ago, the lineage breaks. And the claims were passed down to not the true heirs, but of the wrong descendents," Hellen explained.

"You see, it is Ronan here who I found at the bottom of the true lineage. Ronan is the true heir to the throne of Nýland, and of all the West."

"What proof do you have of this?" Stelli asked, as this was all difficult to believe.

"Other than my word that this parchment exists?" Hellen asked. Stelli nodded.

"I spoke with that awful man that called himself a king. He admitted to everything that was laid out there, and sentenced me to death for it! But besides that, why else would he target Ronan? He knew Ronan was the true heir of the throne, and thus wanted to remove the last of the lineage of the Good King."

Stelli looked over at Ronan, who said nothing but looked back at him.

"So, you are the rightful king to all of Nýland?" Luno asked, snickering in disbelief.

"I do not much believe it myself! I do not know how to be a Jarl, much less a King!" Ronan answered.

"Ha-ha! And how do you expect to lay *your* claim then? Are you going to just walk up to the throne and sit yourself down?" Luno giggled at the audacity of the idea.

Ronan looked at Hellen, then to Bard and Eira.

"If I would even want it, I cannot imagine how we would go about it," he answered.

"I should guess not!" Luno continued to laugh.

"But you must still try!" Stelli chimed in. "This is not just a claim as a King, Ronan. A claim is not an argument to sit on a throne over greed, that is not what a king does! These are your people, your kin, this is your land! And you say you want to *run* from it?" Stelli had fallen into a very serious conversation, in which Luno then understood the seriousness of.

"You are right, my friend," Ronan answered. "But let us for the sake of argument convince the peoples of Nýland that I am the rightful King, then what? I know not how to run a country! I doubt myself too greatly to tackle such a feat."

"These people are lost without a leader, Ronan. It is your responsibility to take it and guide them!" Stelli answered. "This late king Gunnvald was an awful man, causing conflict, wars, death...he conquered first by dividing. You must heal these people. Reunite the family that split long ago. Be not the ruler from the Gronndelon here to claim Nýland. You must be the ancestor of the Good King, here to help both realms heal. Remove the hatred that has festered between these two lands, break down the barrier! Then, you will win the hearts of both."

Ronan sat quiet, thinking deep of Stelli's insightful advice. After some moments of silence, he took a deep breath.

"So, what shall be my next action? To sit here as a fugitive of the very kingdom I seek to call in unity and lead as their king, that is quite a leap to make," Ronan said doubtfully.

"But a King would never run from his own country," Stelli answered. Ronan nodded.

"Come back to Kalthon, come and stay at Stelli's house," Stelli offered. "It is small, but we could use the close comfort of each other in these unsure times."

Ronan sat in silence, knowing he could not continue to run. It seemed that he had only two choices, and knowing the one was not the answer, it left him with only the return to Kathlon as his only path now.

"What say you, my King?" Hellen replied to Ronan's glance.

"Let us head out at dusk tonight. We could use a day to rest, and under the cover of darkness we will be less likely found."

"Well, then," Luno spoke out, standing from his chair. "This wizard needs a breath of fresh air!" he said as he left the room.

As Luno walked down the hall, he passed several other doors before finding the small entrance room. The innkeeper sat behind his counter, eating a plate full of sausage, scowling at Luno as he walked by. Luno gave him a quick wink as he headed out the front door.

But as he emerged, he did not find a welcoming bright sky. Even for mid-winter, the hour seemed darker than it should be. He stared up at the clouds overhead, and they were a far darker grey than they should have been. The sun struggled to show even the slightest light through the clouds above.

The ground was covered in layers of grey and white. It did not seem unusual, though, as it had snowed hard the night before. But as Luno wiped his finger on the banister of the inn's front porch, the substance flaked and fell apart like ash. Then he realized that it was not snow falling from the sky, but some sort of cold ash from dark plumes. Plumes that blanketed the entire landscape.

Luno returned inside, holding his finger stretched out with a stain of white-gray on its tip.

"We may not need to wait long for dusk," he said as he re-entered the room. "I believe dusk may have already fallen," he added, holding out his finger with a puzzled look.

The room emptied quickly as all eyes wanted to witness what had happened outside. As they emerged, they found Luno's guess to be plausible. The landscape was covered in ash, and the day was not growing brighter as it should have.

"What curse has fallen on this land?" Ronan said out loud.

"What can cause the sky to darken so? Has the sun forgotten to rise this morning?" added Stelli.

Moments went by as they all stood on the porch, trying to piece together what was happening.

"Let us pack our things so we may return to Kalthon quickly," Ronan said. "Perhaps it is not as bad on the coast," he added as he followed the darkening clouds south. The further towards the southern horizon he looked, the darker it seemed to appear.

"Something in the south is giving birth to this darkness," he added. "We must be quick," he said, redirecting his attention to the others.

As the seven companions packed their things and returned to the road, they found even for midday their route was empty of other travelers. It was as though the entire day was stuck in a never-changing dusk. The landscape around them was eerie, giving no comfort in any sight.

The falling ash continued, though it was light, still proved uncomfortable to have fallen upon. It colored every surface in a dull gray, and would choke any-one whose breath caught it. And as they progressed down the ever-gray road, the landscape began to stink of foul eggs.

Little conversation was had. Little joy was around them. The doubt of their plans, questions and unknowns, and the worrisome of their world around them all weighed heavy on their minds. The darkness that surrounded them was not only of a failing of light, but a failing of hope in their endeavors. They were walk-ing straight back into the enemy, of those who would have killed Ronan, and almost killed Hellen. It felt completely opposite of what they wanted to do, but under the leadership of the rightful heir, they placed their trust in their true King.

Even with a group of their size, the rest they had gathered the night before proved to be enough to keep a steady pace. And before the everlasting dusk could fade completely away to darkness, they had arrived back at Kalthon, making their way to Stelli's little home.

"I know it is not much!" Stelli said as he entered his home once more. "And it will be quite cozy with seven fish in a bag for one! But at least it keeps us from the ash-fall outside," he said with a smile, shaking his hood to get what ash he could off of it.

"Thank you again, dear friend," Ronan said, placing his hand on Stelli's shoul-der. "You are doing a great service to us, and I am proud to call you a friend."

Stelli smiled, his cheeks blushing in humility.

"Anything for the *King*," he added.

"We should take turns keeping watch outside the door. We know not of what eyes have been watching our arrival," Ronan said. "I will take the first watch. Stelli?" he said, grabbing Stelli's attention.

"Stelli, you have given so much already. But do you have anything here that may make a decent supper? Even if it is only for our ladies..." he asked.

"Right! Supper time!" Stelli said excitedly as he began pulling out different dried ingredients of flour and sugar, assessing what he had left behind.

"I should guess we will need more than just bread for a proper supper!" Stelli admitted. He grabbed his coin purse and left the house with a quick farewell.

As the evening progressed to night, Stelli had returned and made a proper meal of mutton and dumplings with carrots and onion. It was more than enough to fill everyone's belly with comfort, and the orange flicker of the fire's light brought some comfort back into their hearts.

And with warm bellies and warm hearts, each one shared stories with each other. Stories that were sad, stories of brighter times. And in the fire's glow of the little house, filled with the smell of herbs and the sounds of laughter, not even a darkening sky of ash could prevent the joy and fellowship that kindled bright that night.

In the darkness of the night he had found himself in, Stelli heard a voice. A feminine voice, like that of an angel. A bright light shown, and from it the voice spoke.

"Stelli," she said. "You have shown the purity of your heart and desire for the greater good. I come to you to ask of you, share this message with whom it is meant."

With a bright flash, the voice vanished and Stelli found himself in the middle of a great forest. He did not recognize where he was, but before him stood a young man.

The young man was turned away from him, studying a great oak tree before them. Looking up, the young man began to climb. He rose higher and higher, lifting himself from branch to branch. Stelli followed every step, every pull.

At last they reached a large fork in the tree where the center trunk split into three. There, a cup-sized landing filled with soil and moss gave the space a flattening.

Through the top branches, a beam of sunlight shown down towards the center and to the soil, warming it. Before his eyes sprouted a plant. At first, the leaves appeared. But rapidly it grew. Taller and taller, far taller than he himself, fueled by the warmth of the sun and the trickling rain waters that ran down the three extensions of the trunk.

As it reached its peak, the bulb of the flower burst into bright yellow petals that radiated light from the sun behind it. Facing the opening in the tree, the center was a dark brown, surrounded by a ring of hundreds of small bladelike petals.

The young man Stelli had followed, reached up high to pick the petals from the flower. One by one, he collected them into a mortar and crushed them.

As he finished, the branches behind him bent away and he entered a dark stone hallway. As Stelli followed, he found themselves in a tall round catacomb, the ceiling a large stone dome. In a circle on the floor lied twelve stone coffins. In a ring around the outer edge of the room was a shallow depression in which grew hundreds of dark violet flowers.

The young man carried the mortar to each tomb. As he approached each, the lid slid to the side and he dusted the gold powder across the remains of the one inside. For each he did this, and each one rose with the color of life being returned to them. Each one climbing out of his tomb. Each one bearing great weapons and armor.

Ding-ding! Ding-ding! Stelli was suddenly awoken from his dream to the sounds of the castle bells chiming. The pattern they rang out in was of a warning, and he leapt to his feet.

"What is it?" Luno asked, sitting up from his small corner of the home.

"Something attacks the city!" Stelli replied. Ronan sprung to his feet, readying his sword.

"Hellen," Ronan said as she too was getting off the bed and ready. "You stay here and watch over the children." Hellen nodded in agreement.

"Bard, you may come with us if you wish, or stay here. It is up to you!" Ronan said as Bard remained standing by the door as it was his shift that was ending.

"I would rather remain here as a protection for your home, Stelli," Bard answered. Stelli smiled and nodded.

"There is a sword you may use, if needed, in the trunk at the foot of the bed," Stelli said as he, Luno, and Ronan headed out the door.

"I wonder who would attack the city?" Luno said out loud as they briskly jogged towards the marketplace.

"It has been two days since the death of the King, perhaps the ones who sent the assassins believe they have their chance," Stelli said, looking at Ronan.

"I will not stand by and let an attack happen to my people," Ronan answered sternly, feeling a sense of obligation to the city.

As they rounded the corner of a building, it gave them their first view of the open ocean, and they stopped suddenly.

High above the water they witnessed three black beasts flying at some great distance, and with great speed. They dove in and out of the clouds with trails of black smoke and ash rolling off their great wings.

Cries and shrills echoed across the waters and onto land. As the smoke swirled off their skin, it gave birth to dark, thundering clouds. Within moments, the horizon was covered in rolling clouds of thunder, birthed by these horrific creatures.

"Dragons!" Stelli shouted.

"They look different than the dragon I met..." Luno commented. "Watch closely! They have no arms or hands, only wings."

"So, what are they if not dragons?" Stelli asked his brother, looking at him with great concern.

"They are servants of the evil one," Ronan answered, keeping his stare at the three beasts some miles off shore.

As the thunder clouds spread, they merged with the ash grey clouds overhead. Clashing, bolts of lightning shot out and the sun completely disappeared. The entire landscape was thrown into night, with even the slightest hint of a dusk-falling light vanishing.

The sound of the bells rung out again, this time signaling the arrival of ships. The ocean crashed hard, tall waves battering dozens of large vessels that approached the shore lines. On their flags was sewn the fish symbol of Brisrun. But yet, as they approached the shore, the sailors rose a new flag, one that bore the pale face of the assassins.

"It is them!" Stelli shouted. "They have returned in an attack!"

No sooner had Stelli said this, that the flying creatures turned from the skies above and began thrashing down onto the same ships that approached. They could breathe no fire, but used their harpoon-like talons to clasp and break the masts of each ship.

Though with every dive any had made, they were met with an outburst of white light, seemingly shielding them from making any contact with the ships, forcing the black beasts to turn and flee.

Stelli, Luno, and Ronan rushed towards the docks to see who it was that was arriving. As they made their way through the crowds of men, of guards, and of soldiers, the first of the ships had docked.

A tall, dark captain was the first off the ship, his swords sheathed. His hair was straight black and pulled back in braid, his emerald green eyes piercing through the crowds.

The commander of the Freeman Army approached from his guards, his hand on his sword and his men with blades pointed at the captain.

"What is your name, sailor? And where do you come from? For you are no man of the Gronndelon, nor of the great city Brisrun!" he asked the captain.

The captain looked around, studying the men and crowds behind them.

"Lower your weapons and I will give you my name," he answered, his accent thick.

"You fly the flag of our recent assassins! Men of your country killed our King! Speak quick, sailor, before I send you to meet him," the commander shouted.

"First, lay your eyes behind me, and see what wrath is waiting to be unleashed upon you," the captain spoke as every standing surface of the ship behind him held a foreign archer, hundreds of arrows pulled back and ready to be released.

"And second," the captain continued, "count the deck boards between your feet and mine. See there are precisely twelve, and your foot would not meet the first before your blood spills into the water under you, should you ignore my warning."

The commander loosened his grip on his sword's hilt, then looking around in a realization of being hopelessly outnumbered, he gave the command to stand down what men there were.

"I am Asbjørn of the city of Rhim. We did not kill your *king*, but the intruder that sat upon the throne and called it his own. We are here to correct this. We are here to find your true King."

CHAPTER XXI

A SHIFT IN THE TIDES

— 1st of Winterhold, 1867 —

The crowd erupted in fury, their fists swinging wildly in the air. Their voices calling out in anger and rage. Such treasonous accusations must be paid for, and the crowd wanted the head of the one responsible.

Asbjørn held aloft his sword in the air, his eyes clenched tight. It shimmered a bright white along the edges of the blade, rising from the hilt to the tip where a silence hushed from it, spreading through the crowd. Within seconds, the rage-filled hearts of every man, woman, and child in the market's center had died, fading to nothing.

The commander rested his eyes, trying to regain control of his own thoughts, and took a deep breath.

"If you would come with me, Asbjørn, we can take you to our center court in Gammal Keep and further discuss your absurd accusations," he said, looking at the barrage of arrow tips pointed at him.

"And we would take you and a few of your men, should you feel more comfortable with such an allowance," he added, nervous and careful of being vastly outnumbered.

"No, commander," Asbjørn replied. "This is not your city any longer." As he stepped forward, the men of his ships lowered their arrows and began to follow him, up the deck and into the market's center.

Asbjørn ascended to the main platform for all to see. He raised his hands into the darkening sky to gather everyone's attention.

"For too long," he yelled out into the crowds, "have you lived under the tyranny of a man filled with ambition of greed. For too long have you listened to the commands of a falsity.

"But I am not here to lay claim to the throne! For I am no heir, nor do I want it! I have come to place the rightful man in your lead. The direct descendant of the Good King Valdór, grandson of King Valdemar and father of the founders of your lands! For I am not here to divide a family against itself as your former leader would have, but am here to unite the Men of these lands together under the leader."

"And who is this man you speak of?" A voice called out from the crowds.

"One of your own kin!" another shouted in anger. The crowd exploded in shouts once more, angry at the thought of their kingdom being overtaken by a foreigner.

Asbjørn took a deep breath, becoming frustrated with the lack of patience and quick to angered hearts of the crowd. But he continued.

"Nay!" he shouted. "A kin to us all!" his voice boomed through the whining sounds of the angry city folk, hushing their cries immediately.

"We will begin our search from within Gammal Keep," Asbjørn announced. "You may live your lives as you have, for we mean not to intrude on your way of life. But upon the chiming of the tower bells, we will meet your King here in the center," Asbjørn ended, leaving the platform. Hundreds of his men followed him as they marched towards the Gammal Keep.

Ronan stood just on the edge of the crowd, stunned in disbelief. Luno pulled out a smoking pipe and began stuffing it with tobacco. Stelli looked over, scowling at him.

"You are having a smoke now?" Stelli asked, disapproving the timing of his needs.

Luno looked up from his pipe, slightly offended at the looks he was receiving from his brother. He simply shrugged his shoulders, stretching his face further in a slight look of surprise, then returning to his pipe. Stelli rolled his eyes.

"Well, it looks like we have found your way," Stelli said to Ronan, taking a step forward next to him and leaving Luno's side.

"Luno," Stelli began, looking back at his brother, whose head was encased in a thick cloud of smoke.

"Return to Hellen, tell them what has happened. Ronan and myself will see if we can find our way to this Asbjørn of Rhim."

Luno waved his hands around to disperse the smoke, and nodded, taking another puff.

"Come, Ronan. Let us go and find your place in the Keep," Stelli said, leading him towards the castle.

As they walked through the marketplace, they followed the natural flow of citizens of Gammal, as many were highly interested in what they would find and who these people of strange lands were. Up the road they went, winding back and forth on the cliff sides until they reached the top where, just before them, the entrance to the Keep stood open.

But in front was a solid wall of Rhim soldiers, guarding the Keep as their own. At the line, just beyond the reach of their spears and swords, dozens of men had gathered. Dozens of claims to the throne shouted out. Dozens of blackened hearts filled with greed, filled with lies. Dozens of minds ready to take advantage in a foolish hope, all wasted.

Asbjørn emerged from the Keep, the line parting so all could see him.

"So you *all* claim to be the rightful king?" he asked out loud. "You *all* would throw your *life away* at the risk of fame and glory that is not yours to take!" he shouted in anger as he ran up towards the line of men, furious with the self-proclamation that infested the steps of Gammal Keep before him.

"Tell me, my good sir," he said, suddenly calm as he approached a single man, who was quickly shifting in his mind to the thought that this may not have been a good idea. Asbjørn placed his hand on the man's cheek.

"Tell me what is your name."

"I-I—"

"But be careful of the name you give, sir," he interrupted. "For you seem to have forgotten it. But rest assured I have not forgotten the name of the greatest descendant of King Valdór."

Asbjørn stared hard into the man's eyes, who began to break. Sweat rolled down his forehead, and unable to speak through his stutters, he shook his head with no answer.

"No, I thought not," Asbjørn answered with an angry scowl.

"If any may be here to lay his claim and lets a false name leave his lips, let that man suffer such a death for so his claims be treasonous!" he shouted at the crowd. His disappointment proved to be enough warning to the crowd that the greed fell apart; men began to leave.

As the crowd thinned, Ronan stood motionless, fixed on Asbjørn who stood watching men disperse. Behind Ronan was Stelli, also watching as the shameful heads that hung low made their way down the cliffs and back to the city below.

And like the shift of the tides, as the waves of defeated men lowered, one stood among them. One stood remaining, unveiled from the sea of greed. Ronan stood, facing the armies of Rhim, facing the giant Keep behind them that taunted him with memories of torture.

But after the last false man had entered the path down, all eyes were upon Ronan. Asbjørn approached him, slowly, studying his face in disbelief. With every step he took, Asbjørn's eyes filled with tears, so that as he was upon Ronan, they were running down his cheeks.

"It really is you," Asbjørn said out loud, then fell to his knees. Behind him, waves of Rhim soldiers fell to their knees, bowing in acknowledgment of their King.

Ronan remained standing, stunned at the sudden shift in what he was expecting. But he looked down at the foreigner at his feet, who remained there, his tears falling to the soil.

"Um..." Ronan began, still trying to grasp the reality around him. "You may rise, my friend," he said to Asbjørn.

Asbjørn rose to his feet, followed by the hundreds of men behind him.

"For so long have I looked forward to seeing your face in the light of day," Asbjørn said, placing his hands on Ronan's shoulders.

"Have we met?" Ronan asked him, puzzled by how he was identified so quickly. Asbjørn smiled.

"Only in another land," he said. "Come, my King, we have much to discuss," he said, leading Ronan towards the castle.

As Asbjørn led Ronan towards the Keep, every soldier he passed by lowered his head in a bow, respectful of the rightful King and heir to the Kingdom of Nýland.

Ronan looked back at Stelli, who remained standing in place, unsure if he was part of the invitation.

"Stelli!" Ronan called back. "Come with us!"

Stelli immediately broke into a sprint to catch up, excited to have found such a happy ending to their uncertainties. As he passed the line of soldiers, he paused for a moment and leaned into one of them, whispering into his ear. The soldier nodded in agreement, and left with three fellow soldiers down the cliffs.

And for the first time, Ronan returned to the same Keep that had held him captive. Such tortures did he endure in the deepest chambers of the Keep. And strange it felt for him to return with all threats removed. Yet he had grown to hate the face of the structure that he was approaching. And he scowled at it.

But as he passed under the overly large arch, the banners of the Freeman Empire were cut from their gold-colored mounting ropes, and they tumbled down the walls of the Keep, whipping around in their descent, collapsing to the ground. And in that instance, the structure he entered into suddenly felt cleansed. And the strong feelings of despise he felt for it shifted like the tides.

As the fire crackled in the hearth, the sounds of Gracie and Eira quietly laughing and playing filled the small house. They had quickly grown in their friendship, as it was the first time Gracie had someone so close in her age to play with consistently. Though she only had a single doll that Stelli had bought her, Gracie freely shared it with Eira, who played well with her.

"Someone is coming!" Bard spoke out, startling Hellen from a quiet rest. Bard continued to look out the window.

"It is Luno!" he announced.

Bard opened the door for Luno to come in. He shook off what ash he had collected, for the falling had slowed down, and most of it only stained the bottoms of his cloak.

"What news do you bring? Who has attacked the city?" Bard said.

"Oh, goodness!" Luno answered. "Something off shores began to give birth to storm clouds, high above the waters! They looked like dragons, but were not dragons, if that makes any sort of sense," he explained.

Hellen rose to her feet and approached him, listening intensely.

"But ships arrived, just in time! Dozens and dozens of them! They first bore the flags of Brisrun, but raised a different flag upon docking on shore. The flag of Rhim," he said with a very serious look on his face.

"Of Rhim!" Hellen said in disbelief. "How can you be sure?"

"A man came off the boat, guarded by hundreds of his own soldiers. He said they were here to find the rightful King of Nýland, that they knew the one before was a farce."

Hellen sat down on the bed, her mind deep in thought.

"So, it is true then," Hellen thought out loud.

"Yes," Luno answered. "It is true. You were right Hellen," he said, getting down her level. "You were right!" he smiled.

"Where is Ronan, and your brother Stelli?" Bard asked.

"They headed to the castle in hopes of catching up with this man. If he is looking for the King, then Ronan needs to find him. Stelli asked if you may want to —"

Knock-knock-knock! The banging on the front door startled everyone inside. Luno gave Bard a look of great concern as he grasped his staff tightly. Bard stood behind the door, his sword ready for a fight should one come barging in through the door.

Bard gave Luno a nod, and Luno cracked the door open. There before him stood three soldiers of Rhim, wearing dark chain mail with the pale white face on their chests.

"We extend an invitation to Hellen, to Bard, and to the children on behalf of King Ronan to join him in his Keep," the center soldier spoke out. His accent just as thick as Asbjørn's, though not difficult to understand.

Luno opened the door all the way.

"Come on out, Bard," Luno said. "Looks like you are all invited to the castle!"

"If we come," Bard said, making a sudden appearance from behind the door, "Luno comes too."

The soldier looked at Bard with a smile, his black beard peppered with white, though cleanly kept.

"Absolutely," he answered without hesitation.

Fires were lit all along the walls of the main hall of the castle, for no light shown in through the stained glass windows. They were left cold and grey, losing all of their color and vibrant life. It was only the orange and yellow glow of large lanterns that filled the hall with light, and it felt as though night had already fallen.

Ronan was seated at the throne, an honor he still felt like he had not deserved. It was high off the ground, commanding a view of all others below him, for all who entered the hall must gaze up to see him.

He rested his arms on the sides. The throne was wide, unnecessarily wide for his size. And it was hard, and cold. A throne he felt uncomfortable to sit in for more than one reason.

"Tell me, Asbjørn," he began, trying to leave the thoughts of the throne behind and on to more serious questions. "How do you know who I am?" he asked with the most puzzled expression on his face.

"My King, this question's answer takes us far back in time. For Rhim had fallen into the Lands of Shadow during the late years of the First Era by the blood of Magnus's son, Torben. For centuries we remained in slumber, wandering the landscape without light or darkness, watching the world age with our every breath.

"But it was here we found Odin, and his son Valdór. And we watched as the lineage of Kings broke. And yet, followed the sons of Odin through the generations, for this is what was shown to us until we awoke from the nightmare we lived through."

"And so you came to find me?" Ronan asked, trying to solve the mysteries surrounding their arrival.

"First," Asbjørn added, "we had to remove the man who called himself King," he said with a serious look of intent.

"And we knew your name and your face, but only as a child," he continued. "And it must be by the guidance above that we happened upon you here at this time," he said with the look of contentment across his face.

"Certainly not by chance!" Ronan added. "But by the dedication and faith of a wonderful woman," he continued. Upon the echoes of these words, Hellen appeared at the far end of the main hall, Gracie holding her left hand. Behind them were Bard and Eira, with Luno at the back.

Ronan stood to his feet, and all turned around to see who was at the entrance. Ronan quickly walked across the room, nearly running by the time he approached her.

"Hellen!" he said as he threw his arms around her. Hellen, quite taken by what she had walked into, hugged him back with her right arm.

"This woman," Ronan told, "this is the woman who put together the plan of my escape. She openly sacrificed her own life for mine, using herself as the bait for that horrible man who called himself King."

Asbjørn approached Hellen as Ronan continued.

"If it were not for this woman and her deeds, I would not be here," he said. Hellen, overtaken with emotion, could only smile and hold back her tears.

"You have every right then to be called a friend of the city of Rhim," Asbjørn said to her, placing his hands on hers.

"And to the Kingdom," Ronan added.

"We have found him!" one of the soldiers shouted from behind, startling the group. "We have found the man responsible for the darkness carried out within these walls!"

As a group of five Rhim soldiers hurried by, they drug with them a man bound in chains. A man Hellen instantly recognized, and her heart was stung with fear in that very moment.

As they threw the man down, Edgar's face was revealed. Beaten and wet from sweat, he rolled to his side, grunting in pain. From his mouth a trail of bright red blood smeared along his cheek.

"Sire," Asbjørn asked, waiting for permission to carry out what punishment Ronan may have on him.

Pushing Gracie behind her in protection, Hellen shouted in fear and anger, "This man is pure evil! He must not be allowed to live! He should not even be here!"

Edgar grinned at the hatred Hellen had for him, for he knew he had gotten to some very dark corners of her heart.

Asbjørn remained waiting for Ronan's answer. Ronan looked at Edgar, writhing on the ground.

"This is Edgar, the snake, I presume," he said. Hellen's fury was pulsing in and out of her nostrils with forceful breaths, difficult to control.

Asbjørn looked at him closer, studying his face.

"Bring this man to his feet," Asbjørn said. The soldiers lifted him up, and Edgar stood before them seemingly broken.

Asbjørn walked up to Edgar, his face nearly touching the man in chains. A wave of goosebumps came over Asbjørn, the hairs on his arms standing up as he straightened his back. His eyes widened with concern and anger. Edgar's face turned sour with grimace.

"This is no snake, no man of the kingdom," Asbjørn said, his voice wavering as he stepped back to put space between him and Edgar.

"He is a servant of the heir of Dökkgaldur!" he yelled as he pulled out his sword. The soldiers that surrounded Edgar dropped his chains and armed themselves, keeping every tip of their blades just within striking distance of the man in chains.

"Ha-ha-ha!" Edgar chuckled loudly. "You believe me to be of some evil spirit? Have my deeds really caused that much turmoil in your lives that you cast me into such darkness?"

"And how do we know what deeds you have outstretched! How can we measure the damage done by your tongue!" Asbjørn shouted at him. "Tell me, o' servant of *svartur*, what schemes have you planted? Tell me ere I banish you from this realm!"

"And what authority do you hold to keep your threat from empty?" Edgar shouted back, doubting Asbjørn's words.

"Your master could not contain the power of Rhim forever," Asbjørn warned him. "And now, upon our return we wield the fears your master has warned you against, for we are the reason he sent you here, but upon your failure do we stand here in the presence of the true King of the Western Realms.

"Now I tell you this only once more," Asbjørn grunted with a lowered voice, getting closer again to Edgar. "Tell us what you have done, and I will not send you back to your master right here and now."

"Be done with your hollow threats," Edgar answered back. "The fate of Men is doomed, the Age of Elves has fallen, and all of this land of your precious realms will be scarred blackened and cold, robbed of life and extinct of your kin!" Edgar shouted back.

Asbjørn cried out in anger, having lost patience, and thrust his blade into Edgar's chest in defiance of the words he spoke.

But blood did not spill from his chest. For upon the touch of Asbjørn's blade, the figure that was Edgar fell apart in an explosion of chaotic black feather. The chains around his wrists and ankles fell to the ground as a dozen ravens scrambled to take flight.

"Archers!" Asbjørn commanded. As the ravens frantically flew higher into the arched ceilings high above, trying to make an escape, twelve arrows quickly released from below. One arrow for one bird, each making its mark. Like a rhythmic beat of drums, twelve arrows released at once, and twelve black birds fell hard onto the stone floor of the hall.

"Fear not, my King," Asbjørn said, turning to Ronan. "Though darkness is upon your doorstep, we are here to help."

"My many thanks," Ronan replied to him. "But what do we do now? What hope do we have?"

"This is difficult to answer," Asbjørn admitted. "For darker times have only just arrived, and I am saddened to say that the city of Rhim is without leadership, for our King has been long dead, and our Twelve Warriors never awoke from their sleep."

"What..?" Ronan said with great concern. "What do you mean they never awoke?"

"We are just as frightened without them as you are," Asbjørn said. "They fell under the same slumber, but as we awoke, they did not. They were lifeless, and remain without life still today.

"So, we built them a small catacomb, each with their own stone resting place. A round dome, beautifully constructed with a depression of death bells around the outer rim."

"Death bells..." Stelli thought for a moment, as the description Asbjørn spoke of tugged at his mind. Then it hit him.

"The twelve coffins!" Stelli shouted suddenly. Asbjørn turned and looked at him, confused but intrigued.

"I saw this in a dream! Last night it was!" he shouted in excitement.

"But, oh! Hellen! I meant to tell you of this vision!"

"Do not wait, Stelli. Tell us now!" Ronan spoke up.

"I saw a boy, Hellen. I believe it to be your Edlen!" Stelli continued. Hellen's eyes widened with hope.

"What did he look like?" Hellen asked.

"I could not see his face. But I am quite certain it was him! He was standing there, in front of —" Stelli stopped for a moment. He looked around at everyone watching him, and he became hesitant to continue.

"Well?" Hellen asked, anxious to know what Stelli had seen. "Where was he?"

"I —" Stelli paused again. "I believe what was seen was a message. A message Stelli must deliver to Edlen himself."

"A message of vision should always be respected and heard only by those who were meant to hear it," Asbjørn said in affirmation of Stelli's desire to hold onto his message.

"What, then, can you tell me of my boy?" Hellen asked, still concerned.

Stelli smiled a wide smile.

"If Stelli's visions are accurate," Stelli continued, "your boy may save us all yet."

"Although the vision is meant for this boy, what of the twelve have you seen?" Asbjørn asked, highly interested in what may be the outcome of Stelli's deliverance.

"They rose from their sleep, and this boy I saw, he is the one to raise them," Stelli explained. "I knew not who these twelve were, but after you description of their resting place, I am without doubt that what was seen in this dream of mine is the same."

"Then this message is of most importance," Ronan said. "Stelli, would you be willing to be the deliverer of this message?"

"Of course! A message having been entrusted to Stelli must mean Stelli is to be the deliverer!" Stelli answered.

"Asbjørn, may we use one of your ships to get this message to Arboran, for this is where Edlen's last known departure was from?" Ronan asked.

"My King, you need not permission to use your own fleet," Asbjørn said with a smile.

"Let us then prepare a traveling party, and we will need the best captain, for this is a message of most importance," Ronan said.

"King Ronan," Hellen began.

"Of course the mother of our hope may go, should she desire so," Ronan answered before Hellen could have a chance to ask.

"Thank you, My King. I will take Gracie with me, and Eira too if she desires so," she said, looking down at Eira. Eira smiled back at her with full acceptance.

"And Luno?" Stelli asked, inquiring what Luno's decision would be.

"*Sigh*...A chance to return to see Edlen? Though the *Elves* tend to annoy me more than I care for, I cannot let my brother venture out on his own!" Luno answered.

"Even though you have just arrived?" Ronan said. "I could use the advice of someone from Skydale in my courts. You would have a home here in the Keep should you choose to stay."

"I came to Nýland to visit my brother, not the country itself. Should my brother leave, so shall I," Luno answered. Ronan nodded in agreement.

"If I may, Your Highness," Bard inquired, being the last of the group to speak up. "This Keep is all my life has known, and it has become quite the home for myself. I would rather prefer to stay here, should I be allowed."

"You would rather stay here than to leave with us?" Eira said, her voice giving away her feelings of sadness.

"I am sorry, Eira," Bard replied. "I am not much of an adventurer, and I would rather miss my baking," he said, his head hanging low. Eira remained silent, but hurt.

"Of course you are welcome here, Bard," Ronan answered.

"Very well," Asbjørn said. "I will have my best sailors accompany you on your journey."

"You will not join us?" Hellen asked, concerned at the loss of his leadership on their mission.

"My place is here, with King Ronan," he answered.

"I do need his help and guidance," Ronan added. "I am new to this idea of being a King, and Asbjørn will prove indispensable to my stepping in as the leader of this country."

Hellen nodded in agreement.

"Let us get our rest for the night," Asbjørn concluded. "The ship will leave early tomorrow morning!"

"Please," Ronan continued, "stay here in the Keep in the guest chambers. Asbjørn's men will lead you to them."

"Thank you, King Ronan," Stelli said as they began to leave the main hall.

"I will see you all off in the morning, but get good rest tonight!" Ronan ended, his voice echoing down the stone halls as he was left with Asbjørn to further discuss the happenings of late.

High up on the top floor of the North wing, the guest chambers had their fires lit. The wood was dry, and took little time to get to a roaring orange and yellow rage. The night tables were lined with pots of hot chamomile tea and small plates of biscuits with butter and honey.

Rugs lined the stone floors that kept the warmth from seeping into the castle's structure. Hellen, Gracie, and Eira laid quiet on the oversized bed of furs and cotton-stuffed pillows, their stomachs full and their hearts warm with comfort.

"Hellen," Eira spoke up, breaking the silence before any of them had reached the edge of sleep.

"Yes, dear child?"

"I am going to miss Bard. I really wish he would come with us."

"So do I, Eira. But he is responsible for making his own decisions, and no one can make that for him," Hellen answered.

"I know, but I still would rather he came along..." Eira continued.

Knock-knock A soft knock on the wooden door came, so Hellen got out of bed and opened the door.

"Bard! What bothers you this night?" Hellen asked as Bard stood before them in the doorway.

"I have been lying in my bed, thinking about how much I would miss you all. I cannot let you leave without me to keep you company," he said rather bashful of his admission to his feelings. Hellen smiled at his kind words.

"You mean you are coming with us?!" Eira shouted, jumping out of bed.

"I figured the bakery will always be here, and you have become my new family. I could not live with myself to have you leave without me," he said. Eira ran up and threw her arms around him, and Gracie followed behind her, standing next to Hellen.

"We will love having you with us, Bard," Hellen said, still smiling with joy.

The next morning began just as the previous. Cold and dark, no breaks in the ash-grey sky above. Though the ash had ceased in its falling for the time, the six voyagers found themselves boarding the large ships of Brisrun surrounded in a constant twilight.

"May the Mother of Light guide your paths," Ronan said with his hands on Stelli's shoulders. "Your quest is honorable, and I have faith it will be completed in the right timing."

"Thank you, My King," Stelli replied. "It has been a fantastic start to our journey, to know you and see you placed on the throne. It saddens Stelli to have to leave."

"And that is what makes it honorable," Asbjørn said. The cold sea breeze blowing across their faces, and the fur that was wrapped around Ronan's neck waved violently in the cross winds.

Stelli turned and walked up the ramp to join the others already standing on deck. And with a final farewell wave, the anchor was lifted and the ship began to drift out of the harbor, chiming its large iron bells.

"Come, children," Hellen said as the spray of the sea's waters brought a nasty chill on the wind. "Let us find our warm beds. We have at least a week's journey ahead of us before we reach Arboran."

As they entered their quarters, they found much of the same comforts as the Keep. An overly sized bed lined with furs, and candles nailed down to the tables surrounding them. There were no windows save the thick glass encased in iron fittings on the double-doors that led to the lower deck, for their room rested at the rear of the ship, just above the water's surface.

And as they settled down in the warmth of the ship, they talked and told stories. The children played games that were kept on ship, and for the rest of the day, the ocean's breeze carried them with a gentle rocking eastbound, until what little light was given began to fade, and they all settled down for the night.

A few days went by as they followed the northern coast lines. Upon dawn of the third day did they pass the Western Mountains. To see their northern slopes sink deep into the waters was a beautiful sight, though the looming clouds seemed endless upon the horizon. And into the next several days did they sail, ever eastward, now deep along the shores of the Gronndelon, until the night of the fifth day on the sea.

Crash! The startling sound of a ceramic bowl falling hard to the floor boards woke Gracie up. She looked next to her and found Hellen had also startled awake.

The ship rocked violently back and forth, and all that remained in bed found it difficult to keep their balance, even while lying. Above the sounds of the rocking and battering waves, violent claps of thunder boomed through every corner of the ship.

"Stay here!" Luno spoke out, stumbling to his feet from his shared bed, Stelli pinned against the far wall the bed rested on.

Luno scrambled to the door, and upon opening it was thrown back by a violent swell of wind and water. The wave of sea rolled across the floor, racing towards the bed Hellen, Gracie, and Eira shared.

"Hold fast!" Stelli shouted as Luno held onto the foot post of his bed. The ship tilted foward again, and Luno slid across the wet floor, disappearing through the door.

"Luno!" Stelli called out, leaping out of bed and falling to the floor.

"Mama!" Gracie cried out in fear.

"Hold on, my child! Everything will be alright!" she said as she clutched Gracie and Eira close.

Bard crawled across his bed to meet the one Hellen laid on, and joined the security of the three that held onto each other. He wrapped his arms around Gracie and Eira, helping Hellen to shield them from the water. The ship creaked angrily.

As it rocked back, throwing more water into the room, Stelli had made it to the door and hung onto its frame to not roll backwards into a nearly vertical fall against the back of the room.

Suddenly, everything felt weightless. Hellen's heart floated, feeling numb, she embraced for a hard-coming impact, and held onto Bard's wrists tightly.

With a thundering break, the sounds of wood boards splitting and shattering deafened all within the ship. A rush of ice-cold water filled the room, and it stung the skin in a sudden shock.

Nothing but the sounds of rushing water surrounded them. All of the candle lights instantly vanished. Everything went dark. Everything went cold.

As though the storm itself had suddenly burst out in anger and fury to the attempt of carrying such a noble message, it commanded the sea to swallow up the large ship of Brisrun, tearing it apart in determination to prevent any such vision from being spread. And all those on board would be a costly price against the will of the storm.

The last remaining mast stood tall but askew, making one final stand against the rage that fought against it. And with one final swell, the towering sea water came collapsing down upon it, disappearing, sinking down to the bottom depths of the icy cold waters of the Northern Sea.

CHAPTER XXII

FIRES OF DRAGON RAGE

— 3rd of Winterhold, 1867 —

Silence had fallen over the entire valley. Even the harsh winter wind seemed muted and contained despite blowing furiously. Though what fell from the sky was not entirely of snow, but mixed with the ash of the same that had found its way into Nýland.

The dark ash-clouds rolled and rumbled with the furious snow storm that brewed over Festerling. The small inn at the foot of the Festning Mountain took the beating without hesitation, bathed in a mixture of ice and gray ash.

"Edlen, a word for a moment," Radholf said, continuing his stare at the Colonel's red velvet cape. He led Edlen to the side of the fireplace, and spoke softly so as to not be heard by any others.

Edlen's breathing had become labored, his face hot. He knew now that a time would soon come where he would meet the Colonel in the open, without chains, without bondage. Without anything from stopping him to plunge his sword deep into his chest, for this is what his heart was so focused on. This is what his desires burned so furiously for.

"Do not let the evil actions of one man deter you away from what is right," Radholf said to him, knowing fully what was on his mind.

"If I get so little a glimpse of that man," Edlen replied, his eyes burning with anger, "he will be dead within moments."

"No!" Radholf shouted, echoing through the main hall of the inn. This caught everyone's attention, as now all eyes were upon Edlen.

"You must not let the infectious evil spread to your heart! You are better than that, Edlen...you have the blood of a Verndari running in you."

"The blood of a Verndari!" Edlen replied back sarcastically. "What is your oath, Verndari? *To protect the realm against evil.* And what would you call that man then?" Edlen snapped back.

"I would not deem him a threat any longer!" Radholf answered. "We are protectors, *not* revenge seekers," Radholf said, leaving Edlen and returning to Kaltag.

"Let us ready," Radholf said. "I know not the reasons the Empire has for interest in finding Rhim, but I would rather find it before they do."

Pick-pick! Scrrrtch-scritch. Pick-pick-pick! The sounds of something sharp pecked and scratched at the door.

"Falk!" Camila shouted with excitement. She ran to the door and cracked it open just enough for the small falcon to waddle his way into the warmth of the inn. Tied to his back was a small rolled up letter.

"A message from my father!" she said as she lifted Falk up off the ground, cradling him with warmth and removing the paper from his little body.

Falk climbed up to her shoulder as she unravelled the parchment. As she began reading, her brows focused and her glances turned troublesome. She glanced up at Kaltag and the rest of the group.

"The King is dead," she said quietly. "There was an assassination party that arrived in Kathlon four days ago. They bore the white face of Rhim," she said, handing the letter to Kaltag.

"Assassins of Rhim have already appeared in Nýland?" Moli asked as he approached Kaltag, first looking at the letter, then back towards Camila.

"A swarm of them arrived off ships from the Gronndelon, but they were all killed," Kaltag added, reading the rest of the letter.

"A sea of pale from a land forgotten, in flown a tide to tip the balance of war," Radholf thought out-loud, deep in thought as he stared off in some distance.

Edlen stood still remaining by the fireplace, his thoughts focused on his one motive. The news of the King now dead brought relief to him, for the Colonel had no means of a higher protection from his blade. He was now king-less, and in Edlen's mind, defenseless being a foreigner in a land without governing borders.

"Lady Camila," Radholf said. "I should recommend a return letter to your father with what we have learned about the Empire sending a Colonel to also search for Rhim. I believe it is safe to assume the searching party knows not of the King's death, let alone of the assassins of Rhim appearing.

"Kaltag, did the traders or guards note how many were in their party?" Radholf asked.

"A small party, of seven, maybe ten. They had mixed stories but it is far from an entire legion. Something so large would be easier to track," Kaltag replied.

"Also note this, Lady Camila, if you may," Radholf asked, bowing his head. Camila nodded, then pulled out a small parchment from her jacket. She wrote elegantly but furiously before rolling it up and tying it onto Falk's back.

"Fly straight, fly strong," she whispered to him, giving him a small peck of a kiss on his small head. She carried him out the front door and let him loose into the wild winter winds before them.

Then Camila noticed it: the mixture of ash and snow, for the ash fell with a different trance, and fell apart into dust upon landing. The landscape was bathed in a fog.

"Kaltag! Moli! Everyone come out here!" she called back.

As they emerged, everyone's eyes gazed up at the sky. Looks of confusion and concern was written on all faces except Oatikki's. He stepped into the swirls of cold and ran his fingers along the ground.

"What is it that falls before us?" Moli shouted out towards Oatikki.

"Volcanic ash," he shouted back before returning to the porch.

"It has been too long since I have seen this before, but my memory of this stuff has only faded little."

"Volcanic —" Moli replied, thinking hard.

Oatikki sniffed the ash on his fingers.

"Dálmarki finally erupted," he said, wiping what was left of the ash on his leather pants. "A small eruption when I was little had plagued us for a season, but it reached no further than the Pillar City. Small enough to calm it for a few more centuries it seems, but I feared one day it would complete its fury," he said as he gazed into the dark morning sky.

"Let us get moving," Kaltag said, passing back through the door of the inn. "It will be much more difficult to track the Colonel's party in this weather."

The rest of the group joined him in the inn and finished packing their things. Within moments, they were all ready to continue their journey south. And after thanking the innkeeper, Radholf was the last to leave the Rolling Stone Inn, shutting the door behind him.

The journey south proved fruitless for many miles. The dense grey clouds overhead closed in around them, and the world felt very small. Lost on an endless road, unable to see the edges of the valley, Edlen's mind was trapped in a dark, colorless plane fueled by determination and anger.

He took part in no conversations, for his will was narrow and thoughts focused on one purpose. He was no longer motivated to find the lost city of Rhim. No, his heart burned with the desire for satisfaction, for the ending of the cause of all that had troubled him. He killed a giant beast that hunted him, but now he was the creature hunting. And he was filled with the same rage as the dragon.

"What troubles your mind?" Camila asked, walking up next to Edlen and reading his face well.

Edlen glanced over at her with a scowling look on his face. Camila's face dropped in sadness, as she meant not to upset him.

"What more could this world fall apart from what it has already? How can you smile, surrounded in this darkness?" Edlen growled at her.

"How can you know how bright the sun is without knowing its absence?" she responded. "There are far darker places, far darker times."

"What do you know of dark times?!" Edlen shouted, stopping his walk and looking straight at her.

Camila stood in front of him, taking the full anger he shouted out towards her. She remained silent for only a moment, carefully controlling her tone with her next words.

"I know that the days ahead will grow far darker than this," she answered softly.

Edlen stared at her, his face scrunched with anger. Her voice was so calm, and her words containing only truth, yet he did not want to give in to her. Bent on finding the Colonel, his eyes were being blinded. And with every moment that gave him nothing, with every turn of the road that led to more emptiness, his mind continued to fog. He wanted a victory over something, and it had driven him to the brink of madness.

"The world has not yet fallen into night," Oatikki said as he walked past them. "These days of dusk are but a gentle breeze of the foretelling storm that approaches," he added as he continued down the road.

Slowly, Edlen's hatred had begun to slightly shift into fear upon the realization of the seriousness about them. The rest of the party had already moved past, giving little attention to their arguments.

"Seek not the prey you hunt, my dear Edlen," Camila said to him, placing her cool hand on his cheek. Her touch, like a spell, calmed his emotions. Not from some magic she possessed, but because it was a touch out of love that she spoke this to him.

"Remain focused on what we are out here to do, for I fear the darkness that has been thrust upon you by this man you hunt will spread through your heart. And your heart I would weep over to see fall under such torture."

Camila removed her hand, breathing deep and continuing down the road. Edlen was left smoldering, not entirely robbed of his hateful fires, but certainly pulled back into a more sensible mind.

And before his growing affection could walk out of sight into the ash-grey fog, he followed behind her, catching up and continued down the road at her side.

For days they traveled south on this road winding down valleys and around the feet of mountains. Though with the constant grey cloud looming overhead, the tops of the mountains were all concealed, giving very little sight to take in.

"If it were not for the experience you have, Kaltag, I am sure we would all be lost in this haze!" Radholf spoke out. It had been four days since they left the Rolling Stone Inn, and all the landscape surrounding them looked the same.

"Even with my experience, this wickedness that hangs above us is testing even me!" he said. "But fear not, for I have not lost my way yet! But there are few paths that venture off of this one, and of those I am sure no foot has taken them this season. I am sure our paths are still straight, and if we are to continue, I should expect we will eventually find your Colonel."

As though fate had been waiting for these words to be spoken, as they rounded the next foothill on their right, the braying of ponies could be heard echoing beyond their sights.

"Hold!" Moli whispered loudly, leaning his right ear outward, trying to listen to what lay before them.

Mumbles of echoes of men in the distance came softly on the breeze. The snow had stopped all together, and the thin haze below the clouds gave them a view of nearly a quarter mile down the road, yet nothing was seen.

"They sound closer than what I can see!" Camila whispered.

"Yes! The mountains can play tricks on the ear. Echoes may be chased for miles. But the clarity may give a hint to their closeness," Kaltag said.

Oatikki and Edlen stood at the rear, watching carefully. Radholf had joined Kaltag and Moli at the front, all of them studying every horizon, every crest of each hill and rock, waiting to see something move.

"There!" Moli was the first to spot movement around the base of a foothill just at the edge of what they could see. Faint, but clear enough to see a small pony pulling a cart and several men walking around it.

"To the sides! Quick!" Radholf whispered as the group split up, finding cover behind several boulders and slumbering bushes. There they waited until the sounds of the *clop-clop* and murmurs of men were too far to hear. Oatikki was the first to stand back out in the open.

"What are we waiting for?" Edlen spoke up. "We now know where they are, let us go and capture them!"

"They would see us long before we could catch up to them. And it appears their numbers may outweigh our own. We would struggle to face them head on," Radholf said, trying to ignore Edlen's eagerness of an attack.

"Radholf is right," Oatikki said. "If we do make a hostile attempt, it should be under the cover of night."

"And why would we not try talking to them first?" Camila asked. "They are looking for the city the same as us, yes? Perhaps they know a few things we do not? And acting hostile towards them will only shut their mouths tighter."

"Lady Camila is right," Radholf replied. "It would be best to approach them with friendly intentions."

Edlen scowled at this. He was the furthest away from willing to be *friendly* towards anyone of the Freeman Empire, especially the man that killed his father.

"But we should still not trust they should do the same," Moli added. "After all, their leader should recognize two of your faces, yes? Would he not fear for his life in such vulnerability as he is out here in the wilderness?"

"Moli makes a good point," Radholf said, looking over at Oatikki. Oatikki nodded in agreement.

"So, let us wait until nightfall," Kaltag suggested. "We can easily approach them and disarm them before any violence has a chance to break out."

Everyone nodded in agreement, except Edlen. He remained silent, motionless as his thoughts turned and his plans crafted.

"Agree, Edlen?" Radholf asked, looking over at the last member of their party to cast his opinion.

"Yes, agreed," he answered.

"Good, then let us follow at some distance," Kaltag instructed. "It will be another day's walk before a fork in the road should present itself. And upon nightfall, we will have our talks with them."

Several hours passed and the grey haze that surrounded them began to lose what light the sun was able to penetrate through. Blurred shadows deepened, and the eeriness of blackness approached. With no moon or stars to light their way, the world around them fell into complete darkness.

Under the veil of night, Camila pulled out a clump of glowing mushrooms she had packed away from Arboran. Even having been a week since they left, they continued to grow in the small sack of soil each had been clumped with, and their yellow-green light shown just as bright as they would have in the wood.

With so little to shed light around them, the glow of the mushrooms vibrantly lit up their immediate surroundings, though faded fast. As Edlen held onto his clump, it felt like a small piece of relief from the daunting grey that had plagued them for days. Using these mushrooms, they continued to find their way down the road for another mile before a dull orange glow appeared before them.

"Let us wait here for some time," Radholf suggested in the most quiet of whispers. "They should be long asleep before we can approach them without giving warning."

They returned back up the road, just out of sight of the campfire's glow and around the previous hill. Here, they centered their mushrooms together and formed a circle around them. It was the only light that was at all visible, and seemed at the moment to be the center of the darkening world around them.

For several hours they sat in silence. The weariness of traveling had gotten the best of Camila, as her eyes shut and she drifted off into a light sleep.

"Edlen," Moli began in a dull whisper. Edlen opened his heavy eyes, giving Moli his attention.

"Edlen..." Moli paused for a moment, gazing upon Camila. "Has the question ever come to mind of where her mother may be?" he asked Edlen.

Edlen looked over at Camila, resting peacefully with a slight smile on her face. If she was dreaming, they were sweet dreams for sure.

"It never has until now," Edlen whispered back. He looked over at Moli for an answer.

"Just beyond a year ago, Camila, Lord Halldór, and her mother the Lady Else had boarded a great ship to travel west to Nýland as summoned by the King Gunnvald. He had a proposition to make with them, and kindly offered a stay in Gammal Keep should the family wish to visit.

"But during the voyage, a terrible storm brewed. It had awoken everyone on the ship, and the Lady and our Lord Halldór rushed on deck to help.

"But as a swell broke over the deck, one of the crew members was swept off his feet as he was attempting to tie down the sails. Seeing this, the Lady Else followed him into the raging waters in an attempt to save his life." Moli paused for a moment in silence, in remembrance of his Lady Else.

"She had misjudged her own strength, and the sea took them both. Camila witnessed her mother freely sacrificing her own life to save that of another."

Edlen continued to watch Camila rest peacefully. She was no longer the untested daughter of a high family that he had seen her as. She too had been through great loss and struggle.

"I would have never guessed something so tragic had happened to her, and so recently," Edlen replied.

Moli exhaled forcefully in disbelief of the same.

"You see, now, that she too has seen darker days," he said looking back at Edlen. "But she does not let it corrupt her heart. She mourned, yes. And I question whether she has ever stopped mourning the loss of her mother. We all took it hard. But she continues to be a light in all of our lives, a light that I have yet to see put out."

Edlen grinned peacefully at this remark, nodding his head slowly in agreement. His face fell as he took a step back in thought at the realization of Moli and Camila's relationship.

"You love her," Edlen said, looking directly at Moli with a defensive glare.

Moli looked back at Edlen, reading his face and knowing what feelings he must have been developing for her. He took a deep sigh, then returned to Camila.

"Yes, but not as you may believe. I have known her since birth, for I was very young but still remember the day she came into this world. To me, she is family. Yes I love her, but as a brother loves a younger sister."

Edlen nodded, willing to accept that as an answer, and content enough for the time being for his fondness of Camila was still young, and it was only recently that she had really touched his heart.

"Let us begin," Radholf spoke up, breaking the silence.

"Lady Camila, ready yourself," Kaltag said, laying his hand on her shoulder to quietly wake her.

Oatikki stood to his feet, stretching his legs and arms. Edlen rose, his heart beginning to pound as it struggled with the morality of his desires. He would easily be in a position to take the life that took his father's, but yet he did not know for certain if he would go through with it.

"Moli and myself will take the lead," Kaltag instructed. "No offense, but you Men are not the most silent in your approach."

"Ha-ha! You should hear Oati! Fumbling around in the dark, might as well be a boulder rolling down a mountain side!" Radholf said with a chuckle. Oatikki snorted at this.

"Camila," Kaltag continued, "You would be safest with Radholf and Oatikki."

"And Edlen," she added, looking over at him. Edlen blushed, but gave no sign of correcting her compliment, only grinned.

"Yes, and the dragon-killer," Moli said, half smiling at Edlen. Radholf glanced over at Oatikki who rolled his eyes.

"Dragon-killing may come in handy yet, but not at the moment," Kaltag spoke up.

"When we hear commotion, we will sweep in and make sure none make an escape," Oatikki said. Kaltag nodded, and he and Moli disappeared into the dark fog.

"Come," Radholf spoke softly. "Let us follow closely behind, but make not a sound!"

As the four made their way through the dark, they gave no indication of sound to their presence. Even for Oatikki, he could remain completely unheard when he really cared to.

As they approached the spot where they last knew the camp would be, they began to spread out. Their sight was limited to only a few inches at best, so any escapee would need to be caught from the sounds of their foot steps.

Edlen roamed the dark, Camila to his left and Oatikki to his right. Radholf remained on the western edges of the road, and the four created a sweeping net that sailed quietly down the valley.

"Hold!" Radholf whispered, just enough to reach Oatikki's ears. Oatikki passed the message to Edlen, and Edlen to Camila. Here, the line waited in the dark, ready to spring at any sound that came running towards them.

Silence fell over the fog. Edlen could only hear his own heart pounding. He could see nothing. Surrounded in a small world where not even his own two feet were visible. Completely shut in from the world around him, he felt lost and very alone.

Then the sounds of *clank-clank!* came from some distance ahead. Shouts were heard and Radholf took off.

"Now!" he shouted as the others joined him. As Edlen sprinted, he held out his hands, unable to know what direction he was running in. He heard footsteps to his left and right, but saw no one. He felt as though he was running blinded, and the toxic air around him choked him at his sudden need of a breath.

Before long, he noticed the orange glow to his right. He had nearly passed it but caught sight of it soon enough. The footsteps to his left continued to run.

"Camila!" he shouted, but the steps continued to trail off in the darkness. "Camila, you are going the wrong way! Come back!" he shouted at her. But they disappeared into silence.

His heart sank as flashbacks of him losing Sabrina flooded back into his mind. The difficulty to see, the bitterness surrounding him. He could not bear to lose another friend like this, and this fear nearly overtook him.

"Edlen, over here!" he heard Camila call out from his right. He turned around and followed the orange glow of the camp fire. As he approached, he found Camila, Oatikki, and Radholf standing next to the fire. Surrounding the low-glow were six men, bound in rope, their swords piled out of reach. Above them, stood Kaltag and Moli.

Edlen looked back behind himself, confused as to whose footsteps he heard.

"You nearly missed us!" Camila said to him.

"I heard someone else running! They kept running down the road and I thought —" he paused for a moment, then realized the bound man closest to him looked up at him with fear. Edlen walked up to him, and standing over him, glared at him with fury.

Remus was unable to speak with cloth filling his mouth and bound around his face. His eyes watered as he gazed up at Edlen, sweat dripping off his brow.

Edlen grasped the hilt of his sword, ready to take what he had sought for so long.

"Edlen, no!" Camila shouted, reaching out to him. Edlen paused his unsheathing, never breaking his stare at the man on the ground.

"We are not here to kill," Radholf spoke up. "But do what you must, Edlen. Follow what your heart tells you to do."

"What my heart tells me to do..." Edlen whispered to Remus. He pulled out his Dragonsbane and pointed it at the Colonel. Pressing against the soft skin at the base of his throat, Remus swallowed hard, breathing heavily and with anger. Edlen leaned in and stared straight into his eyes. This was his moment.

"Like the day you held my father captive, I too have your life in my hands," he whispered to him. "How just is it that you are now the helpless, unable to cry out for mercy despite your desperation for it. But where you gave none, how then could you receive?"

Edlen stood up straight again.

"And yet," he continued, "if not by mercy, what could possibly kill the corruption of a heart. For the blackness of yours has attempted to take over mine.

"But let it be known, Colonel, that on this night my heart stood against the test, and it did not falter. That I held your life at the tip of my sword and gave it back to you." He returned his sword to its sheath and took a step back.

"I will not forget what you have done to me and my family, *Colonel* Remus," Edlen added, mocking at the title the man had carried. "But I will not let the darkness spread through *my* actions."

Radholf remained quiet, a sole tear running down his cheek. Oatikki nodding in affirmation, and Camila in a full smile.

Radholf approached Remus. He crouched down and got close to him, looking him up and down.

"It seems you have really found yourself in quite the bind," he said, giving him a wink. "What now do you think of us splinters in your finger?" he smiled.

"But forgive me!" Radholf continued. "You see, I believe we are under the same mission, you and I. For you are also in search of the lost city of Rhim, yes?"

Remus's eyes widened and his eyebrows focused, surprised as to how Radholf could have known this.

"And now that the past is in the past," he said, looking up at Edlen. "I think we can continue, perhaps even mutually agree that there really is no need for any more turmoils?"

Remus looked around, and seeing as he was in no position to argue, nodded in agreement.

"As if you have a choice!" Oatikki added with a serious, threatening grunt.

Moli came around and removed the bindings from the Colonel, freeing his hands and voice.

"I know not how you are here," Remus first said. "Nor how you found me," he looked over at Edlen.

"But please, I beg of you to forgive me of what I have done in the past. I was blinded then, full of the richness of an empty satisfaction. The loss of others is no prize to hold onto," he said.

He took a deep breath as he watched Moli continue to free his five men.

"What reasons are you looking for Rhim?" Kaltag asked, approaching him.

"It has always held a mysterious curiosity in my heart," he said. "I have always wanted to explore these mountains in my own attempt to search for it, but I had no way to get here."

"I do not believe you," Kaltag said. "What fabrications of truth you attempt to pull over us will not work!"

"I tell the truth!" he argued in defense.

"Would the same truth remain to know that your King is now dead?" Radholf told him.

Remus stared at him in disbelief.

"Dead?" he asked. "And you accuse me of fabrications!"

"This is truth," Moli said. "We received word of the assassination of your King from Lord Halldór some days ago."

Remus slumped down, staring at the ground.

"You know of the foretellings of Rhim, yes?" Radholf asked him.

Remus looked up at him in awe. Radholf nodded in affirmation.

"You may actually see this city, for it was Rhim that took your King's life," Radholf explained.

"So, we ask you only once more, Colonel of a fallen empire," Camila suddenly joined in. Her words cut through like a vengeance and anger unheard of her voice before.

"What is your reason for wandering the ancient mountains?"

Remus took a deep breath, and looked over at his men. They were rubbing their wrists, tired, and quickly losing their will to continue. The face of a defeated man fell over him.

"I was instructed to do so," he admitted. "After we completed our campaign east to Brisrun, we were sent instructions to search for Rhim. Though the orders seemed different, as I was instructed to take a small handful of men and to keep our destination as private as possible."

"And what was your purpose? What were you meant to do once you found it?" Radholf inquired.

Remus looked again at his men, questioning whether he should give them the right answers even now. But as the King was dead and the Empire beginning to fall, he saw no reason to lie.

"It was only to report back to the city's location. They were to send relief in as soon as we had found it, but to do what, I do not know."

"And these instructions came from the King himself?" Radholf asked.

"Yes. Well, mostly yes. The writings were of his scribe this time, which first threw my suspicions as all other orders of such official business were handwritten by the King himself."

"A scribe? So, the King did not write these letters?" Moli questioned.

"No, not directly. The scribe signed it with the King's name after, so I thought nothing much of it. Here..." he said, reaching into his pocket and pulling out a rolled up letter. "You may see it yourself," he said, holding it out to Radholf.

Radholf opened the letter and held it close to the glowing embers of the fire. Mumbling the words written, he said out loud the scribe's name.

"Edgar, scribe of the High King Gunnvald," he said. "Odd that such secrecy comes from not the King himself," he added.

Screeee! The sound of a hawk overhead startled the campsite. Flying around in the dark, its sudden appearance was most unexpected.

"Falk!" Camila cried out. "Falk, we are down here!" she yelled into the sky. Out of the fog the bird came swooping down, swirls of grey mixing around at the tips of its wings before landing on her shoulder.

"You have another letter for me!" she said, cradling him in her arms and untying the note. "Though the hour is late, my friend!" she said to him, concerned. "What were you doing flying around in the darkness?"

As Camila unraveled the paper, her face fell.

"What news from your father?" Kaltag asked.

"Something is not right," she responded, then looked at Falk. "This is the letter I sent out days ago! Falk! Why did you not deliver my letter?"

The bird screeched and cried out, looking at her with his head cocked. His eyes looked frightened.

"He has never done this," she said. "It is as though he could not find my father. But even then, Falk would have at least remained in Arboran..."

"Perhaps this ashy fog proved too much for him to find his way home?" Moli suggested.

"And yet was able to find us in the darkness on this night?" Radholf commented.

Waves of fear fell over Camila, for none of this made sense in her mind.

"Something is very wrong," she added, thinking deep and trying to avoid a panic. "Something bad has happened."

Off in the distance, neighing echoed down the road, soon to be followed by the sounds of several horses galloping on the hard road. They came swiftly through the night, bright torches lighting the way.

Radholf drew his sword, Edlen too. Oatikki stood ready for what came for them with his axes in hand, but what their eyes were greeted with, they did not expect.

"Radholf! Oatikki! There you are!" a familiar voice shouted. It was Adelmar on a horse, with four other horses, riderless, being led behind. Adelmar dismounted and walked up to the group, nearly out of breath.

"I was worried I would not be able to find you!" he said as he approached.

"Adelmar! What in the green earth are you doing here?" Radholf said, returning his sword.

"Arboran has fallen under attack!" he said urgently. Camila gasped in horror. "An army of dragons appeared off shore, and before there was a moment to prepare, they began spitting fire across the lands!"

"No —" Kaltag added in disbelief. "No, you must be wrong!"

"Lord Halldór took his armies to meet them before they would reach the city, but sent me along with these horses to bring Lady Camila to safety. I am to take her to the Boreal Mountains, to the Elvish refuge underground. He asked Moli to return with her, and sent two more horses should anyone else wish to join."

"But not enough for all of us?" Edlen asked.

"Now is the most critical time for us to find our lost city," Radholf said in realization. "And it is with haste that we must find it."

Adelmar nodded.

"That is what Lord Halldór said you would understand most."

"I will continue on our quest," Radholf said. "I will leave it to the others to decide their fates."

"I will join you," Kaltag added.

"And so will I," Oatikki said.

"Edlen," Radholf spoke to him. "Do not feel any obligation either way. You must decide which front of the war you will do your battles on."

Edlen paused for a moment, thinking hard about his next path. His hand fell to his side, finding the hilt of his sword on his hip. He grasped the hilt tightly, his father's presence surrounding him.

For only a brief moment did he think silently, for his calling was now standing before him.

"This sword was meant for one purpose, and as its bearer, I am responsible to see it used for that purpose."

Edlen turned and looked towards Camila.

"I will come with you to Arboran, to save what is left of her," he ended.

"Let us return quickly, then!" Adelmar said as he mounted his horse. Camila and Moli both quickly mounted their horses, and Edlen followed.

"Adelmar," Radholf said as he approached him before bidding them off. "Of Kuoni?" he asked.

"Kuoni is safe, as far as I know. He was helping the children make their safeway to the mountains where he would remain until every one of them made it there."

Radholf nodded with a smile.

"Go quickly, my friend. And thank you!" he said as the horses took off in a fury.

Radholf turned around to the remaining party.

"Let us rest what we can for the night, for there is no use fumbling around in the dark at this hour. The sun, for what it can, may give us a bit more to see in just a few hours more. Then we will continue our hunt," he said, sitting down next to the fire as the others joined him.

Quickly the riders raced through the shadowy valley, each with a torch in their hands. The horses were pushed to their limits, though knowing their masters' urgency, gladly gave every ounce of focus and energy in a return full of haste.

Into the next day and into the night, the four riders gave little to relent. At the peak of the moon's ascent, should it have been visible through the heavy grey clouds that night, they arrived at the Rolling Stone Inn. Here, they rested for only an hour, to give the horses a chance to catch their breath and rest their achy bones.

With any signs of hunger or thirst chased away, the riders returned to the road north. Sleep was beyond them, their hearts too filled with grief, their minds too occupied with the unknown. And upon the dawn of the next day, the had passed the great dead beast along side the road. Arboran was within reach.

"We should prepare our hearts with what we may bear witness," Adelmar spoke, knowing what kind of danger he had turned his back on several days ago.

"Let us go and find what we can of our people," Moli said, "I will lay my life defending what is ours."

"Or what is left..." Adelmar said, whipping the reigns and taking off down the road.

But within moments of departing, the smell of fire and choking smoke filled the valley. A gust of wind followed them from the south, blowing a clearing surrounding them and forward into the valley.

The riders slowed their horses to a stop, and they heard not the sounds of crackling fires, but of silence of an open and void space before them. As Edlen came riding up, the last to arrive, Camila slipped off her horse, her eyes in an endless stare before them.

She walked up to the edge of the forest, her every footstep breaking char and ash as it swirled around. Tears flowed from her eyes as the clearing before them sank deep into their hearts. The nightmare they gazed upon seemingly too far from reality, a land unrecognized by any of the four.

For miles before them, trails of white smoke rolled up from the ground. A long, flat land of waste, blackened and bare, stretched on continuously until out of sight.

Nothing above flew, no light of fire. Not a single movement on the land save the ghostly white smokes of a once green and lush land. No screams, no life. All of Arboran had fallen under the spit fires of the Ashblood. These green lands were no more.

Camila fell to her knees, her mouth hung low, her tears flowing like a stream. Edlen sat on his horse in shock, paralyzed by the sights before him.

"What force could have done this?" Moli spoke under his breath, unable to keep control of his emotions as he choked on his own words. "What has such strength to have laid such havoc?" he asked as he turned to Adelmar.

Adelmar took a deep breath as he continued to make attempts to comprehend what was before them, then spoke as he turned at Moli.

"The coming of darkness," he said, fear falling over his face.

For One the darkness is prepared for, ceasing to lay his claim
ere the lands of green birth ceases to remain.

APPENDIX A

OF THE RACES

ARBORIAN

Protectors of the Forest, as they are called among other races, are beings made of earth and water. The first of these were the blessed shepherds of trees, tasked in the early days during the Age of New, before Men or Elves came to be. Their mission was to scatter all species of trees across the lands, instructing each how to grow. It is a result of their creativity that each unique species of tree exists in the West.

APPEARANCE

They stand nearly five feet tall, and have a torso, arms, legs, and a head much like an Elf or Man. Though they have no mouth for they speak not, and have no need to consume. Their entire body is made of living plant, their skin like bark. Their arms and legs split out like vines, allowing them to scale rock cliffs and easily grasp nearly anything.

Their main source of life comes from a special bee's hive in their torso. This is where their heart is. Its honey is rich, containing immense healing abilities, and giving the consumer incredible strength for a short period of time. The Arborian itself will stay alive and can quickly recover as long as the hive stays intact. Because of this, an Arborian never ages, and the ones still around today are as old as the dawn of the Age of New.

HISTORY

They began their days spreading tree seed and nut. At the end of the Age of New, after the great flames of Elderdrake swept across the lands, they gave birth to the first of Elves, thus beginning the Age of Elves. Still today, they are revered by and named "Mothers of the Elves".

It was during the dawn of this Age of Elves in which the Arborians made home the land of Arboran. This land, which lies south of the Borreal Mountains, north of the Rhim Mountains, is a vastly wide valley filled with the largest woodland in all the West. Here, the land remains as the Shepherds of Trees (as sometimes referred to in folklore) had intended the West to have been. It is here that the Elves still call home today.

In gratitude towards their ancestors, the Elves gave the vast valley to the west of their land to their Mothers. Later named the Gronndelon, this area lies between the Rhim Mountains and the Western Mountains. A lush, green valley nearly as large as their own Arboran.

Many centuries later, after the first Men arrived in the Gronndelon (during the Age of Men), it was discovered by the Men of the Gronndelon that the honey of the Arborian could be used as an enhancer to their performance in war. It took little time for Men to conjure a method of extraction that kept the creatures alive, at the same time harvesting their precious honey.

This process, though, was extremely painful to the Arborian, and was viewed as a method of torture for monetary gain by many. So in 325 E2, the Arborian War began.

In April of 327 E2, the Battle of Golden Flame took place. The Arborians had fled to what is now Bjornwood, but a large company of Men waited for them in a trap, their weapons of flame ready.

What took place on this date could only be described as a slaughter of Arborians. It was here that the infamous "Golden Flame" could be seen as their hives caught fire, emitting a powerful bright yellow flame that dotted the night-fallen landscape.

After this battle, word reached the ears of the Elves, they joined the war in June of the same year. Their superior fighting tactics proved to be too much for the Men of the Gronndelon, and by 340 E2, all Men were driven out of the Gronndelon, thus ending the Arborian War, and returning the land to its intended inhabitants.

After this point, most of the Arborians had been killed and few remained. They became extremely timid and fearful of Men, never forgetting what they had gone through. Because of this, their sightings are rare, but there still exists an unknown population dwelling among the forests of the Gronndelon and Arboran.

DWARVEN

The deep-cave dwellers, a sub-race of Men. The first Dwarven folk found their home in the Gul Mountains south of the Dalvann desert.

APPEARANCE

Much like Men, only shorter in stature. Most Dwarves reach four feet in height by maturity, and most males grow out their facial hair to help protect their faces from the most common trades of blacksmithing and mining. Because of their height, they found the caves riddled among the Gul Mountain ranges to be quite comfortable, and the numerous gold veins strung throughout gave much motivation to continue to expand their kingdom and skills.

HISTORY

The first Dwarves were actually Men that were born of low stature. Their first king, King Mossi of the eighth generation of Kings, took the throne of the Gronndelon in 300 E2. Though he was short in stature, his reputation was foremost of his short temper. He was not the bloodline of the heirs, but the previous king, King Korekur of the seventh generation, who had no sons of his own. It was Korekur's uncle, King Naddur of the sixth generation, passed on his claim to the thrown to his only granddaughter's husband, Mossi.

His short temper and greed led him to the desire of the rich honey of the Arborian race, and thus it was under his reign that the horrible tortures of these creatures took place, leading to the start of the Arborian War in 325 E2.

The result of the Arborian War led to the Elves reaching Furskarth, and having driven most of the Men from the Gronndelon, they then exiled King Mossi and sent him south of the mountains to roam the deserts in 328 E2. He took his many wives with him, as well as some devout followers.

During this journey, his party traveled from oasis to oasis throughout the desert, passing through the Pillar City, capitol of the Orkken Kingdom. Quickly they denied him, and his journey continued south until reaching the Gul Mountain range. Here, they founded their kingdom, and their capitol city Djupumelli, an underground city built into a large cave in the mountains. At this point, seeing their dwellings underground, the Orcs began calling them "Dwarves," meaning "deep-cave dwellers" in their native Orkken tongue.

Their kingdom since then has thrived in riches and prosperity, growing quickly in population as they expand their cities underground. No city is left unreachable by foot below ground, as vast roads are carved to connect all of them under the roots of the mountains.

But because of the bitterness they experienced from the Elves, and the unwelcoming attitudes of their ancestors of Men, they have never returned to the Gronndelon, nor anywhere north of the Dalvann desert.

ELVEN

Children of Arboran

APPEARANCE

Like Men, they stand six feet tall on average, though taller Elves are not rare. Their ears are pointed, a tribute to the vine-like ear cups of their ancestors. They are born of the Arborians, created as a mixture of Earth and Water.

Most are fair-skinned, with dots of freckles across their faces and upper backs, some spreading to their arms. Their hair is usually straight, a very light brown or shimmering red, especially when seen in direct sunlight.

As they are made of the earth, they rarely eat meat. Their belief of killing creatures for food is of horrible act, so most are trim and lean, with very little fat stored. Because of this, they are very light-footed, and their agility makes them a challenging foe to most warriors who have ever been unfortunate enough to find themselves pitted against one.

There exists two main classes of Elves, as defined by the color of their eyes. The blue-eyed Elves are seen as taken more after their ancestor's mothers, of water. These Elves are usually more gentle, easy to calm others, and make excellent healers.

The green-eyed Elves are seen as the higher class, as they take more after their ancestor's fathers, of the Earth. They are stronger and more lively, able to take root mentally in most intense situations, and make for the best trackers and warriors.

Because of their heritage, they do not age quickly. As Arborians never perish as long as their hives are intact, the act of aging does not affect Elves nearly as harsh as it does Men. Though they come to maturity around the same time Men do, many Elves can live centuries, and rarely die due to old age. Most whom have perished have done so through battles or physical accidents.

HISTORY

After the Age of New, the Arborians created the first of Elves, giving dawn to the Age of Elves. During this time, the Arborians gifted the Elves the land of Arboran. Thus, they are often named the Children of Arboran. It was soon after this gift that they established the only city within the Arboran realm, Sol.

Most of their history is of peace, protecting only their own land from outsiders who would rather take advantage of their natural resources. Any attempt made by Men or otherwise have always been easily thwarted, and they lived in peace for many centuries during their Age.

It was not until 327 E2, in June that they openly joined a war not initially involving themselves. The Great Arborian War between Men and their ancestors, the Arborians, forced their hand into involvement as there was little hope of the avoidance of extinction for the Arborian race.

The war ended with the Elves driving Men out of the Gronndelon, and the land being returned to what few Arborian survivors there were. This was the last time the Elves had gone to war during the Age of Men.

GIANTS

As tall as trees, and quick to anger. Little is known of these far-eastern strangers.

APPEARANCE

Because their dwellings are in the Land of Giants, what is known about this race is mostly found in folklore and fairy tales. It is said they are as tall as a fully grown maple tree, reaching fifteen to twenty feet tall in most cases.

Their diet is mostly of larger mammals, needing a large amount of animal meat to satisfy their incredible appetites. Because of their stature, they are slow to move, and can be seen walking slowly between the tree tops should one find a commanding view of the land below.

HISTORY

Very little history of these creatures is on record. The great plains and tundras East and South of where the Rhim Mountains dive deep into the earth is their home land, and there exists no map of what lies beyond their kingdom.

They have had very little interaction with Men, though we do hear rumors and stories of their lesser than typical kin finding their way into the mountains in search of a more suitable lifestyle over hunting mammoth or bison. Because of this movement some ages ago, it is not entirely unheard of to find a half-giant roaming around the Rhim mountains. Though their presence is usually unwanted by the local Men of the area, mostly due to the stereotypes of being slow in thought and short tempered (though this is rarely the case in their half-sized kin).

MEN

Made in the image of their *Creator*, Men were intended to be the solution to many of the world's challenges. With minds of accomplishing goals and being highly motivated, Men were easily corrupted and turned against each other.

Violence settled deep into their hearts, turning them black. They are the only species to have ever gone to war with their own kin.

APPEARANCE

Most men stand around six feet tall, while women stand just a few inches shorter, on average. The variations of colors in hair, skin, and eyes depends on the region, and thus in most cases, the realm they are from.

The Men of the Gronndelon hail from the lands of Gamliheim, which is connected to the Gronndelon through an unmapped span of continent that starts to the west of Gamliheim (bordered by the Dyptfjell River), expanding beyond the vast badlands, which eventually border the Land of Giants. These men (and women) have light blonde hair with very light blue eyes.

Over the centuries, the populations of Nýland have stemmed from a dense population of darker-haired men, which has led to much of the Nýland realm's population to be a lighter brown haired people, some with hazel eyes.

ORKKEN

Hot-tempered cousins of Elves

APPEARANCE

Most Orcs are as tall as Elves, only slightly taller than most Men, and are easily spotted by their paler skin tones. Shades of grey and blue, some with a hint of green, and at any stage of life, young or old, bear wrinkles in their skin. Most have black hair, and the males will have dull tusks from their bottom jaw visible through their lips.

Due to their habitat, they are notoriously tough in nature, and tend to see themselves as stronger than other races. Though this is mostly true not only to their resilience against heat and arid environments, but also to their dominance in physical size. Their hard labors also contribute to their strength, and they can live comfortably with little to drink.

It is a custom in their tribes to decorate their faces with their family's patterns in tattoos or piercings, and to let their hair grow out long. Because of this, many will braid their hair and tie the ends with rings of gold — a strong contrast to their black and often coarse hair.

HISTORY

During the first millennium of the Age of Elves, a vast migration occurred out of Arboran and into the Endeløs Mountains (later named the Rhim Mountains). Here, the migration split, and those that dwelled in the mountains became known as the Mountain Elves. Their close proximity to their Woodlen Elvish cousins kept them the appearance and title of "Elven".

However, the split-off left the remaining group to continue south, through the vast forests and around the Eastern tips of the now Orkken Mountain range. It was here they found the Dalvann Desert, and staying West (to avoid the Land of Giants), they found the northern mouths of the Höggormur River.

Just west of the Giant's Watch Hill (a large single mountain that splits the river as it flows east), they found a northern bend in the river, which had carved a vast canyon in the desert surrounding it. On the southern shores of this bend, these travelers founded the Pillar City.

Over time, the sun's heat and drastically changed diet in which the desert provided, led to the gradual physical changes into what the Orkken race is today.

Their dealings with the Men to the north were minimal until the founding of Nýland when a passage was established through the Orkken Mountains. In 422 E2, Orkken trade was officially established between the Pillar City and Nýland. At this point, their Elven cousins were seen as the enemy as a result of the Arborian War, but by the end of the fifth century, racism against the Orcs had taken over many in Nýland, and in 506 E2, the Desert War began. It quickly ended in 508 E2 with the banishment of Orcs from Nýland, and their current king, King Nyvard, was hailed as a war hero for their victories (though it was quite one-sided as not a soldier of Nýland ever stepped foot past the mountains).

By the mid-sixth century, Nýland had spread its rule beyond the Orkken mountains and into the Dalvann desert, threatening to take over the Pillar City. Feeling oppressed by the laws the Empire had placed upon them, the Orkken chiefs sought an alliance with the now thriving Dwarven people of the Gul Mountains to the south. Knowing the Empire would eventually be at their doorsteps, the Dwarven people agreed, thus starting the Orkken-Dwarven War of 655 E2. This war lasted 84 years, and slowly the Empire's strengths were weakened and eventually retreated back to their original lands north of the Orkken mountains.

APPENDIX B

TERMS AND LOCATIONS OF CULTURAL SIGNIFICANCE

BRISRUN (STRONGHOLD)

When Valmundur returns from Gamliheim (the *Motherland*) in 1100 E2, he finds much of the Gronndelon wild and uninhabited. It had been nearly 760 years since the last humans were driven out of the Gronndelon as a result of the Arborian War, in which the Arborians had left much of the land to be retaken by nature.

A year later, Valmundur officially declared his landing on the northern coast as the founding of Brisrun. This location, in the north-eastern part of the Gronndelon, sits just on the western banks of the mouth of the Vanalta River as it opens up and pours into the Great Northern Sea. Because of its early settlement during the return of Men, it is one of the oldest and longest-settled cities in the Gronndelon (without break or loss of control).

Within fifteen years, Brisrun becomes an established port on the Great Northern Sea; the only one at the time within the Gronndelon. Large ships were built quickly using the natural forested lands surrounding it, and Valmundur begins to explore the rest of the coast.

Two years later (1117 E2), the first contact with the Empire is made beyond the Western Mountains thanks to Brisrun's shipping fleet, and a new trading route is established along the coas,t bringing dawn to a trade era that continues for centuries.

Later, in 1122 E2, Valmundur plans expeditions deep into the wild Gronndelon in hopes to rediscover the ruins of the ancient city of Furskarth. Because of his anticipated leave of absence, he puts his first lieutenant in charge, a man named Thorburg.

Several decades later, after the rediscovery is a success, a direct route is established between Brisrun in the north-east, and Furskarth in the extreme south-west. This route, which cuts nearly straight through the heart of the Gronndelon, becomes known as Ravenrun.

Economically, Brisrun is one of the richest cities in all the Gronndelon thanks to being the center of the established trading route. As Brisrun became established, a large castle was built as it recognized its value and needed a proven way to defend itself: Castle Graywater.

CASTLE GRAYWATER (OF BRISRUN)

As a token of its wealth, Castle Graywater's main hall and entrance of the castle had a beautiful mosaic laid into the floor. This mosaic tells the tales of Valmundur crossing the Great Northern Sea as he battled through sea storms, giant water wisps and other vicious monsters, and eventually finding landfall at Brisrun.

The windows lining the great hall are stained glass with shades of blue and green. As the sunlight is cast through the windows and onto the mosaic, it brings the mosaic to life and fills that part of the hall with a blue-tinted light as though to take visitors back to the surface of the Great Northern Sea.

DÁLMARKI (LOCATION)

A large volcanic mountain on the southern end of the continent. For centuries it has lied dormant, but towards the end of the first era had a minor eruption. It lies deep in the Dálmar forest, a vast tropical forest fed off the constant rain from the warm tropical waters to the west.

DALVANN DESERT (LOCATION)

A large desert south of the southern mountains that stretches from the western shores to the southern turn of *the Wild* forest. It is a dry and hot location between the southern mountains and the Gull mountains with a single mighty river, the Orkkelv, flowing from out-reaches of the Land of Giants, fed by the waters of the Wild, to the Crystal Bay.

The Orkkelv River (or *Höggormur* to the Orcs) carved a deep canyon into the desert. At a bend in the river, directly south of the Western Mountains, sits the Pillar City, capitol of the Orkken race.

DESCENDING OF THE TWELVE

During the year 3426 of the First Era, the Great Warrior (an Angel in the Heavens) sends down his twelve sons to help aid the city of Rhim against their King's brother, King Magnus, as the envy of Magnus had lead him in multiple attempts of overtaking his brother's Kingdom. These twelve warriors, all brothers, are well-known in tales of folklore and song to be the bravest, most fierce warriors to have ever walked the earth. Their tales end with the disappearance of Rhim in the late first era.

THE FESTIVAL (OF FURSKARTH)

Once a year, The Festival of Furskarth occurs in mid-autumn to celebrate the life of The Good King Valdór. Over time, the festival has grown into also incorporating the bountiful harvests, and includes friendly competitions from across the realm.

At dusk on the day of the Good King's death, the gem at the top of the erected statue of the Good King Valdór shines a bright white and lights up each of his eighteen sons' pillars that surround the main platform at the base of the Misty Falls at the city's center.

FESTNING MARKET (INSIDE THE FESTNING MOUNTAIN)

A large market place carved into the base of the Festning Mountain. Its shape is unique to support the weight of the mountain above it, starting narrow and gradually opening wider as it reaches incredible heights. There are five floors, each residing along the outer rim of the market so that the walkways and shop floors are in fact the ceilings of the shops below it. Pillars along the center edges of the walkways tower up to the ceiling of the market, and the entire center of the market is a vast and open space.

In the center, out of some unseen gap in the ceiling, the Festning Waterfall crashes down the center of the market and lands on the ground floor in a large circular pool. This pool is bordered with a protective wall only a few feet high and trimmed in gold.

The entire market is beautifully carved and decorated to resemble a wooded land. Each pillar is carved to resemble a towering tree with swirling vines and leaves all around the trunks. Embedded into these pillars are beautiful gems that sparkle in the light. Lamps are placed all around the market, keeping it well-lit. Even in the darkest days of winter, the market stays warm and lively.

FURSKARTH (STRONGHOLD)

Located in the extreme south-west of the Gronndelon, Furskarth began in 61 E2, being founded by Vestmar, the eldest of the eighteen sons of King Valdór. When discovered, Vestmar began construction of High Haven Castle - the strongest and best fortified castle in all the Gronndelon. It took Vestmar and his men six years to complete the High Haven Castle.

In 101 E2, Veseti takes the throne of Furskarth, Vestmar's eldest grandson. In 120 E2, he erected a monument of the Good King Valdór, placing a beautiful crystal ball at the top. The monument branches out across a courtyard to eighteen pillars, all representing Veseti's grandfather and great-uncles.

Not much further is known about its elder history, although it proved to be a valuable place of safety during the Arborian war. However, in the end, the castle was besieged and its occupants driven out by the Elves.

Centuries later, after Valmundur returns to the Gronndelon, the remains of High Haven Castle are rediscovered. Much of the castle had crumbled, but its foundations and a few inner walls remained intact, as well as the monument of King Valdór (and his sons). At this point, a direct route between the newly redis-covered Furskarth and the new settlement in the far north-east, Brisrun, is estab-lished and named Ravenrun.

It does not take long before Furskarth is rebuilt, including High Haven Castle. Word of such a strong settlement spreads quickly, and the folks of Brisrun who despised their settlement for the harsh cold winters, found Furskarth desirable due to its warmer climate. Because of the quickly growing migrant population, in 1164 E2, Furskarth is declared the capitol of the Gronndelon with Valmundur its official Jarl.

In 1181 E2, Valmundur passes away, and Furskarth is temporarily ran as a democ-racy, much of whom the members of council were of the original finding party (ten of the men to be exact). Seven years later, it is decided that the eldest son of one of the council members (and whom traveled with the expedition party) was elected Jarl, a man named Odden. Because of this shift in political methods, each Jarl to follow could either select a successor, or leave it to the people to elect one. It was during Odden's rule in which the great city walls were constructed and Furskarth became known as a well-fortified city.

GAMLIHEIM (LOCATION)

Across the Great Northern Sea, beyond the ice caps that surround shores of Dökkgaldur, the land of Gamliheim rests where the first humans had sailed from. Upon the dawn of the First Era of the Age of Elves, the first humans arrived on the shores of the Gronndelon from Gamliheim.

In the 80th year of the Second Era, one of King Valdór's sons, Sjólfur (mean-ing "Sea Wolf"), left the Gronndelon and returned to Gamliheim.

In 1100 E2, a descendant of Sjólfur, named Valmundur, returned from Gamli-heim to the Gronndelon. At this time, the last of Men had been driven out from the Gronndelon due to the Arborian war, and had been left to the wild for 760 years. From here, Valmundur settled in what is now Brisrun and slowly repopulated the realm.

GRIEF MARCH

During the second era, the Jarl of Furskarth was known as the High Jarl. Although all major cities and holds had their own Jarl, the High Jarl had command over them. Unlike a King, however, in the sense that a Jarl could still be elected should the family heir choose to forfeit his right. Despite this, the High Jarl of Furskarth had always been a family member and ancestor to the Good King Valdór.

When a Jarl of Furksarth would pass away, their remains would be bound in a casket and carried from Furskarth to Brisrun, along the Ravenrun Road. Behind the recently deceased Jarl would follow his heir, the new Jarl of Furskarth. This was done as their way to announce to the Gronndelon realm that this tragedy had happened, as it was the fastest and most respectful method to make such an announcement.

The placing of the new Jarl within the march was extremely significant, as symbolic it was to never allow an individual of the traveling party between him and the city of Furskarth behind him. Therefore, the new Jarl was always the last member of the march in line. For it was his new duty to protect and lead the city, as well as the rest of the realm, for the coming years.

GUL MOUNTAINS

A mountain range south of the Dalvann desert, it is rich in metals and riddled with natural caves.

During the Arborian War, in the year 328 E2, King Mossi is exiled from the Gronndelon. He takes with him all of his wives and many other followers, traveling through the Dalvann desert and eventually finding refuge in the Gul Mountains.

Mossi was very short, and many of his off-spring were also short, in which these peoples found favor in the caves and caverns of the Gul Mountains. Because of this, the Orkken-folk called them "Dwarves," or "deep-cave dwellers".

GYLLENTIDES

The skirts of the Southern Mountains in the Gronndelon. On their northern edges that lead into the Gronndelon, they are covered in Aspen trees, which in the autumn, around the time of the Festival of Furskarth, cover the foothills of the mountains in golden shades of leaves.

JARL

Leaders of a town, a Jarl is often a descendant of the previous Jarl. Though it is often a descendent is not always appropriately ready (due to age or lack of children), a Jarl can be voted in by the town.

The High Jarl of Furskarth, though technically still a Jarl, holds a higher say in issues across the Gronndelon. Most laws are allowed to be handled on a town-to-town basis, but the High Jarl of Furskarth always has the right to overrule any law passed. And although the High Jarl of Furskarth could be elected, there has always been a relative descendant as far back as the Good King Valdór.

LANDS OF SHADOW

A land in between death and life, where time loses its grip and a single day in life passes by in an instant. Here, light nor darkness exists, and one is free to roam the lands of the living, seeing only their shadows and outlines. Able to hear but unable to speak, able to see but unable to be seen.

MOTHER OF LIGHT

The first Angel in which the Father creates, the Mother of Light is often the source of good will and generally seen as hope in the world. She often answers to those seeking her light, especially during trying times.

NÝLAND (EMPIRE — *THE FREEMAN EMPIRE*)

In the north-western corner of the Ardian continent rests the Nýland Empire. Its history is filled with splitting and merging of states, countless wars (which has involved every neighbor in the west), and several failed attempts of a democratic political structure. During most of its recent history, however, it had remained under the control of Kings, a lineage of Men determined to expand beyond the mountain ranges that separate them from the rest of Ardia.

It is during the late 1800s of the Second Age of Elves that King Gunnvald began to set his plan into motion, sending his armed men in a sly attempt of taking over the Gronndelon. Although he called his kingdom *The Freeman Empire*, it was mostly certainly far from it.

RIVERWOOD (HOLD)

Found just in the south-western central area of The Gronndelon, Riverwood is a larger town focused heavily on the trading of furs and crafting of all things wooden. Governed by Jarl Audun, son of the previous Jarl Sivert, Audun was young for a Jarl, but had been learning of proper governance at a young age.

The center of the town is the market where traders, hunters, and crafters come together almost daily to trade and sell. Many of the buildings remade of wood and clay, and the surrounding forest leaves the town humid and warm most of the year. It is very green with moss covering much of the lower parts of the buildings.

SKYDALE (CITY OF THE RHIM MOUNTAINS)

Ancient city founded by Kjell, nephew of King Rikk in 205 E2. The location of the city lies deep in the Rhim Mountains, and when the expedition of King Reynir made it to this location, they found a small settlement of Mountain Elves, calling this place their home.

After contact, one night in autumn, the Elves mysteriously disappeared. Many question what actually happened, with the Woodlen Elves (cousins of the Mountain Elves) placing full accusations of a slaughter during the night despite finding no evidence of bodies. The men there had recorded the oddity of such a disappearance, some claiming they retreated elsewhere into the mountains. They left behind all of their belongings, and seemed to have simply vanished.

After a time of settlement, it was discovered that perhaps the Mountain Elves were not indeed the first settlers in this valley. Dotted across the surrounding mountain range are dozens of catacombs. Most are home to ancient Men of the first era, and tales of draugr haunting their places of rest lurk throughout bedtime stories of the local children.

With stone being plentiful, much of the city is made of rock and stone from the very mountains around them. Clear streams flow of ice-cold water from the peaks surrounding, and there is an abundance of mountain life in the surrounding valleys and canyons. The surrounding caves also have proven their worth as they supply an abundance of precious metals and gems, making this location well sought after.

The city itself is the highest of any settlement known in the west. Because of this, the people there say you can feel how close you are to the heavens above. Being closer to the stars and heavens, it has become naturally attractive to those who perfect themselves in the art of magic and cosmos.

Skydale never fell under the realm of the Gronndelon as it was too far into the mountains. However, the neighboring realm of the Woodlen Elves did not want to claim it either due to its uncertain history. To them, it would have proven to be an ill omen to have accepted it. Therefore, it is one of the only settlements in which does not fall under any political boundary.

During the Wizard's War, most who wished to freely practice magic fled to Skydale as there were no laws governing the use of magic. This is what has gained Skydale its nickname, "Wizard's Refuge." Though it is not typically used locally as it brings with it negative connotations.

The city itself rests in a small bowl-shaped valley tucked between three mountain peaks. These peaks are named as follows: In the north, the peak Nordstjernen with a single point in the very north. On the west, the Festning Mountain, which casts an early shadow in the evening across most of the city (save Skydale Observatory, built on the southern edge of the city and surpasses in height both of the southern mountains). Then to the east, Mount Kaldstjerne.

STRØMMES

Three orbs carved from fiery stones that fell from the heavens during the first era. These were gifts sent from above that held the source of immense magic, flowing out in an ever-changing wisp. It took centuries of study to perfect the use of these orbs, but of them came some of the most powerful blessings.

Over time, throughout the later half of the first era, the three orbs became separated as it was believed no one kingdom should possess that much power. In a declaration of allegiance, one was gifted to the Elves while the other two remained with Men.

The one was taken to Arboran, named Forsvar to help protect the realm from any attacks of sea or land.

One was taken to Rhim, named Forandring, to aid in the conquest of the Rhim mountains and any inhabitants they may find there.

The last remained in the Gronndelon, named Angrep. Though it was fallen into the hands of King Magnus, his greed tainted the good nature of the orb, leaving it quite ineffective for his endeavors. However, it eventually passed on, through Odin, to the great-nephew of Magnus and Odin's son, Valdór. King Valdór eventually uses it to forge Dragonsbane.

During the Wizard's War of 1715 E2, the Strømmes were banished. Although only two remained (Forsvar and Angrep of the Elves and the Gronndelon, respectively, as Rhim had disappeared and their Forandring with them), it was agreed upon by both kingdoms to destroy them, as their power was abused.

At the end of the Wizard's War in 1720 E2, the Ceremony of Cleansing took place where both realms brought forth their Strømme, and with the fall of a hammer, shattered each one. Their pieces were cast into the sea beyond the shores of the Gronndelon so they may never be made whole again.

VERNDARI

After the end of the Dökkári War, at the beginning of the Second Era, King Vestmar (the Good King Valdór's eldest son), sends out a quest for any who may be true of heart. To take heed of the Good King Valdór's prophecies, they seek for twenty-five individuals who are sworn in as the Verndari. These individuals are bound to protect the realm from any evil, gifting with *Alder*, a ring which prevents aging of the wearer, so they may forever protect the realms until the return of the heir of Dökkgaldur.

The twenty-five chosen were split into five groups. One group was sent in each direction, with the fifth to remain in or around the Gronndelon.

WIZARDRY AND MAGIC

Throughout history, Men had learned to harness the natural powers surrounding them in nature. This primarily included focusing energy given from the sun and moon, and storing this power in elements that seemed capable of containing such light.

But when the Strømmes fell to Earth, they proved to be a much more powerful source of energy, enabling Men to perform incredible spells and acts. Because of this new source of power, the old ways of magic were beginning to fade.

After the Wizard's War, when the Strømmes were destroyed, the only magic left was that of the old ways, and the knowledge of many of these spells and alchemy recipes had long been lost. But over time, these were slowly recovered (through research or rediscovery), and shared among those that continued the practice.

Having it outlawed in most of the West, it is rare to find a wizard who openly practices it. Although Skydale has no such laws, many wizards have found their home in this city within the Rhim mountains.

All magic is elemental-based, and is essentially composed of two parts: an energy source (the sun, moon, or one of the Strømmes), and an item to hold and focus that energy (an enchanted item, such as a sword, gem, or special stone).

Many of the enchantments and spells of old (prior to the arrival of the Strømmes) require constant replenishment of energy from their source, another reason why these spells are seen as weaker. Whereas enchantments from a Strømme itself will never deplete, consistent in its potency and never failing.

APPENDIX C

ARDIAN CALENDAR AND DATES

Throughout Ardia and Gamliheim, Men agreed upon a calendar year of twelve months. The start of each year, the 1st of Frostfare, is defined by the winter solstice. From there, each month has thirty days, save the five summer months (two before the summer solstice, and three after), which have 31 days.

Frostfare (1)

1	2	3	4	5
6	7	8	9	10
11	12	13	14	15
16	17	18	19	20
21	22	23	24	25
26	27	28	29	30

Winterhold (2)

1	2	3	4	5
6	7	8	9	10
11	12	13	14	15
16	17	18	19	20
21	22	23	24	25
26	27	28	29	30

Starfall (3)

1	2	3	4	5
6	7	8	9	10
11	12	13	14	15
16	17	18	19	20
21	22	23	24	25
26	27	28	29	30

Rainsday (4)

1	2	3	4	5
6	7	8	9	10
11	12	13	14	15
16	17	18	19	20
21	22	23	24	25
26	27	28	29	30

Sundawn (5)

1	2	3	4	5
6	7	8	9	10
11	12	13	14	15
16	17	18	19	20
21	22	23	24	25
26	27	28	29	30
		31		

Arborden (6)

1	2	3	4	5
6	7	8	9	10
11	12	13	14	15
16	17	18	19	20
21	22	23	24	25
26	27	28	29	30
		31		

Summer Light (7)

1	2	3	4	5
6	7	8	9	10
11	12	13	14	15
16	17	18	19	20
21	22	23	24	25
26	27	28	29	30
	31			

Vamedager (8)

1	2	3	4	5
6	7	8	9	10
11	12	13	14	15
16	17	18	19	20
21	22	23	24	25
26	27	28	29	30
	31			

Gyllden (9)

1	2	3	4	5
6	7	8	9	10
11	12	13	14	15
16	17	18	19	20
21	22	23	24	25
26	27	28	29	30
	31			

Wheathall (10)

1	2	3	4	5
6	7	8	9	10
11	12	13	14	15
16	17	18	19	20
21	22	23	24	25
26	27	28	29	30

Kalddager (11)

1	2	3	4	5
6	7	8	9	10
11	12	13	14	15
16	17	18	19	20
21	22	23	24	25
26	27	28	29	30

Frostbreath (12)

1	2	3	4	5
6	7	8	9	10
11	12	13	14	15
16	17	18	19	20
21	22	23	24	25
26	27	28	29	30

CULTURALLY IMPORTANT DATES

1. 1st of Frostfall: Winter solstice; definition of a new year.

2. 1st of Summer Light: Summer solstice

3. 24th of Wheathall: Celebration in Furskarth (The Festival)

4. 31st of the summer months: Summer Rests[1]

---

[1] Having an extra day per month during the days when the sun would take longer to set, it had become a day of rest and celebration during the days of labor.

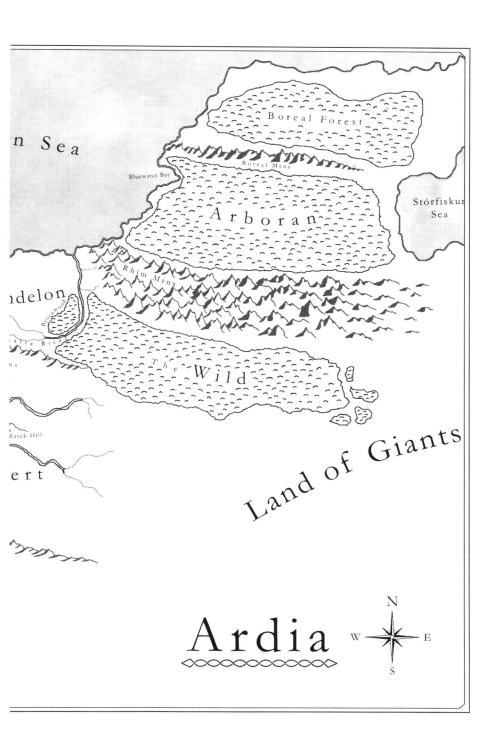

n Sea

Boreal Forest

Boreal Mtns

Bluewater Bay

Arboran

Stórfiskur Sea

Rhim Mtns

ndelon

Brownwood

alla River

The Wild

Watch Hill

ert

Land of Giants

Ardia

N
W E
S

The Gronndelon

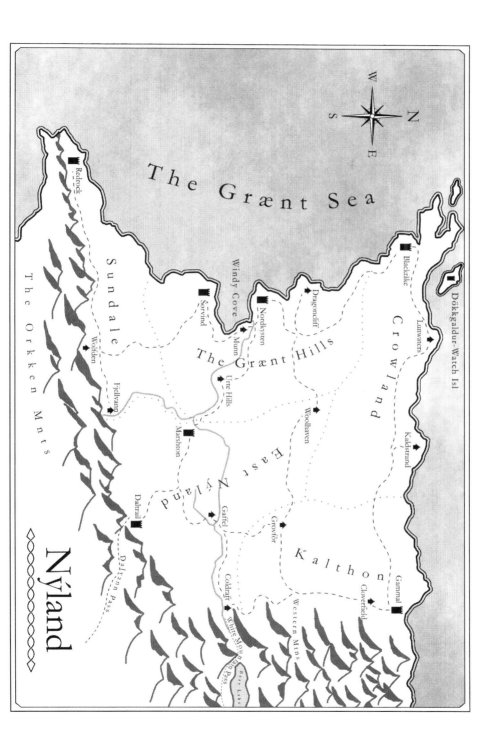

A special thanks to my wife, Tiffany, for giving unrelenting encouragement,
to my editor, Kathy, who made this book readable,
and to all of my family and friends who showed great interest
and excitement in this story.
—
Thank you all!

92477775R00256

Made in the USA
San Bernardino, CA
02 November 2018